The Forgotten King

***

Kelly Peasgood

A Kelly Peasgood Publication

Fred broke off as they noticed movement from the inner chamber.

Stefan stared in shock as a young woman, not much beyond girlhood, stepped from his bed chamber. Grime and cobwebs clung to the smock that covered her skirts, dulling a wild mane of shoulder-length auburn hair. Light grey eyes blinked rapidly from a dirty, tear-streaked face. She clutched something to her chest as she sank hurriedly to her knees.

"Your Majesty," she whispered, a sound clipped short as Fred's sword cleared its scabbard, the blade swiftly resting across her throat.

Her eyes widened even further as she took in the finely-honed weapon and the grim visage of the man holding it. She sucked in her lower lip and her chest heaved in a draught of air, but she waited on Fred and Stefan.

"How did you get in here?" Fred demanded, his voice all the more chilling by its deadly quiet.

The girl rolled her eyes back to Stefan's room.

"Passageway," she whispered. "From the library."

"What passageway?" Fred demanded, but Stefan, his attention riveted on the girl, silenced him with a quick wave of his hand. He had always suspected the existence of such tunnels, but had never found proof of them before.

"You found the secret passages?" he asked, dragging the girl's attention from Fred's sword. Her eyes sought refuge in his face.

"You're in danger, Majesty," she said instead, her voice a little stronger. "They've already surrounded these chambers."

Many thanks to Paul, John, Jen and Evy for your thoughts and insights for this book.

As always, enormous thanks and love to Mike for supporting me, believing in me, encouraging me, and allowing me the freedom to follow my dream.

Chapter 1

Emily opened her eyes to complete darkness. She raised her head from her cushioning arms and inhaled deeply, breathing in the familiar scents of parchment, old leather, and dust that clung tenaciously to several books despite her best efforts to keep them clean.

She had fallen asleep in the library. Again. This week's project—the copying of the current royal house's ascension and ancestry for the King's brother—had lasted past supper, but she had finally finished and just taken a moment to rest her eyes. Apparently that rest had lasted longer than she had intended.

The late afternoon sun had long since fled to make way for night, leaving only a smattering of stars to peer through the windows. Em reached into her smock's pocket for the stub of candle she routinely carried for just such occasions. Then she paused. She really didn't need the light; she practically lived in the library and its archives, and she knew them as well as she knew her books.

Well, not exactly *her* books, as she didn't own a single one. Rather, the books belonged to the King, and she stood as caretaker; one of six, and the only female. Forever destined to remain as Junior Assistant to the Chief Librarian, Em didn't care what title she carried, so long as she remained safely anonymous among the stacks of books she so loved.

Em remembered the day nearly a decade ago when Darien had discovered her. Now Chief Librarian, Darien had at the time held the title of Lead Assistant to the Chief Librarian, a Tutor Librarian whose duties included instructing the noble sons of the kingdom. One such noble, Gregor, son of Duke Winthrop, had tried to evade his lessons by hiding out in the kitchen of his neighbour, the Earl of Kern. Em worked in that kitchen, one of the Earl's cooks having brought her out of the orphanage the previous year. Gregor had just turned fourteen and thought he knew enough about the world that he didn't need Darien's tutelage, but Darien found him and made him sit to his lesson right there amidst the scent of baking bread and burning meat, the heat of bubbling pots and hissing pans, and the sound of people chopping vegetables, scrubbing dishes, pounding meat and mixing pastry.

Darien pushed away Gregor's pilfered plate and called the nearest scullion to wipe the table. The head cook shoved a damp cloth in Em's hand and pushed her forward. Table cleared, Darien produced a book from his wide pockets and laid it before Gregor. The boy groaned but Darien merely tapped the book with long fingers and waited. Finally, Gregor leaned forward, opened the book to a marked page, and began reading, his finger following the printed words.

Em, now with broom in hand as she busied herself in the corner, smiled as Gregor slowly started to recount one of her favourite stories from *The Travelogue of King Ludwig II*.

Her father, a minor scribe to a minor house in the east, had had a small collection of books that included *The Travelogue*, and he had taught Em to read from it, despite the fact that girls seldom had the opportunity to use that skill. He and Mama had taught Em, their only child, what they knew regardless of whether it would advance her in life or just provide a distraction of the moment. Em loved to learn and her parents had enjoyed imparting their knowledge. Until they had died in an accident when Em turned seven, and Em ended up in the orphanage. But she still remembered everything she read, an ability Papa had marvelled at, calling it Em's little piece of magic.

Even now, at the age of nine, as Gregor stumbled over King Ludwig's campaign against the Haemites, Em whispered the words to the accompaniment of her sweeping, reciting word-for-word what Gregor mispronounced or skipped over completely. It took a sentence and a half before she realised that Gregor had stopped while she continued. She paused and cautiously peered up. Darien had a hand on Gregor's arm and sat calmly watching her, his blue-green eyes calculating. Gregor looked puzzled as he stared at his teacher, then scowled at the effrontery of a kitchen servant, a small girl, so boldly daring to steal the attention away from her betters, though he clearly didn't know what had caught Darien's interest.

Em blushed furiously and quickly returned to her sweeping, hoping to escape further notice, but Darien called to her.

"Girl," he said, and Em had to stop and wait for him to continue, but she didn't look up, concentrating on her white-knuckled grip on the broom. "Girl," Darien said again. "Do you know this book?"

Gregor let out a guffaw. "Of course she doesn't know the book, Darien; she's a girl, and a kitchen wench at that!"

"Girls do not lack intellect, Gregor, only opportunity." Darien spoke so quietly, Em didn't know if Gregor even heard him.

She kept her eyes down and only knew that Darien had stood and approached when she saw the toes of his boots appear in front of her. He raised her chin with a gentle finger, forcing her to meet his gaze.

"You do know the book, don't you?"

Em nodded.

"How?"

She swallowed before answering in a small voice.

"Papa had it."

"And he read it to you?" Darien asked.

"Sometimes," Em evaded. She knew girls weren't supposed to read in this part of the kingdom, though she didn't know why. Where Papa had taught her, people frowned at girls reading, but they didn't get you in trouble. She knew, by Gregor's glare, that she would get in big trouble here if he knew she could read.

"Does he read you other books?"

"Papa died," she whispered. "We don't read anything anymore." As soon as the words left her mouth, Em knew she shouldn't have said them. Darien gave a tiny smile and a nod, then pulled her toward the book on the table. Em didn't want to go, but knew she couldn't disobey the order implicit in the firm arm Darien placed around her small shoulders. He sat her down in the chair he had used, right beside Gregor, who made to object, but kept silent at a stern look from Darien. Darien placed his finger on a sentence, drawing Em's attention.

"Right here," the tutor said. "Where Ludwig's Generals prepare to ambush the Haemite pikemen, do you remember what happens to them?"

Without meaning to, Em looked at the words, and before she thought it through, her mouth opened to answer.

"This is where the cavalry charge overcomes the wedge, not where the pikemen—" she broke off, quivering in sudden fear.

"How do you know what it says?" Gregor stammered indignantly, his voice rising in outrage as he continued. "You can read?"

But Darien gave her a reassuring smile, the edges of his eyes crinkling slightly, and moved subtly to put himself between her and Gregor. Later, she realised that he placed himself so to protect her, but at the time, she knew only that this man who so easily discovered her secret would not get her in trouble.

"You must really like the book to remember so well from a glance at a sentence."

Em shrugged. She did like the book, but her memory of the written word had nothing to do with liking or disliking King Ludwig II's Travelogue. She simply remembered everything she ever read. Whether a treasured favourite or a boring document she didn't really understand and only skimmed over once, Em never forgot a single word.

Darien thanked her and dismissed her back to her work, returning his attention to Gregor. Em grabbed her broom and made herself scarce in the farthest reaches of the kitchen, thankful to have escaped such attention and quivering in delayed reaction.

The next morning, Darien returned to the Earl of Kern's house, asking to see the young kitchen girl, and the Earl had a wide-eyed Em brought up to a small study. Darien made her sit in one of the big comfy chairs near the low flames of the hearth while he sat opposite.

"Don't be afraid, child," Darien's gentle voice soothed. "What is your name?"

"Emily Schribner," she answered, then shook her little head fiercely. "I mean, Emily." Orphans didn't have surnames.

"And your papa is dead?" When she nodded, he asked, "Where is your mother?"

"She died with Papa, two years back," Em replied.

4

"I'm very sorry to hear that. How came you here, Emily? Did you always live here?"

She shook her head.

"Cook's assistant came to the orphanage and brought me back last year. The Earl told me that I would live here now."

"And do you like it here?"

Em shrugged a shoulder. "I guess," she said. "It's better than the orphanage, but not like home. Nothing's like home without Mama and Papa." Her brow furrowed as she considered. "They're nice to me here," she decided.

Darien smiled and reached into his big pocket, producing a different book from yesterday. He held it out to her. Em took it carefully, but didn't look at it.

"Do they let you read here?"

Em shook her head again and lowered her eyes.

"I'm not supposed to read." Pale grey eyes peered up from beneath a fall of auburn hair that had escaped her clumsy ponytail, tears gathering to blur her vision. "Please don't tell them I can read, sir. I'll get in trouble. I'm already scared that Duke Winthrop's son will tell his Papa what he heard yesterday and they'll ... I don't know what they do to girls here who can read, but I know I don't want it to happen to me."

"Shh, girl." Darien took hold of her shoulders in a comforting grip. It surprised Em to see him on his knees before her. He had hair the colour of winter sunshine and eyes that put her in mind of the sea that she had seen once long ago. "Don't cry. Gregor won't tell. You're not in trouble." He paused, head tilted to the side in thought. "Do you know who I am, what I do?"

Em shook her head no.

"My name is Darien and I work in the Great Library at the Palace. We have many books there, and not enough people to keep them. In my role as one of the Tutor Librarians, when I tutor young sons like Gregor, I also look for aptitude; someone who might help us care for the books. I have found depressingly few youngsters who have what I call a natural talent."

Em blinked at him.

"You mean, you want people like Gregor to come read the books, but he doesn't get the sentences right, so he can't?"

Darien quickly smothered a smile.

"Something like that," he said. "But you get the sentences

right, don't you, Emily?" He tapped the book in her lap. "Could you read me some of those sentences?"

She stared up at him in shock.

"But I just work in the kitchen; I'm not supposed to go into the library here, let alone touch the books."

"Please, Emily. Open the book." He didn't ask; he ordered, and Em had to obey as he settled back into his seat.

She read to him flawlessly even though she had never seen this book. He asked if she could write and she told him her father had shown her how to make the letters.

"But I don't get to practice anymore," she said. "Papa was a scribe and said to practice every day and maybe I could write too, but I can't here. I haven't written since they took me to the orphanage." She carefully closed the book and held it reverently. "I haven't read since then either. Thank you, Darien, for letting me read today."

He studied her from his chair for a long moment.

"Would you like to read more, and to write too?"

Her eyes snapped up to his, excitement and yearning gleaming in their grey depths.

"You mean you could come and teach me, like you teach Gregor?" Such a concept seemed a marvel, that a great man like Darien would tutor a lowly servant like her. But he dashed that hope when he shook his head.

"No Emily, you misunderstand. I wouldn't come here to teach you." Em's shoulders sagged and she quailed at her presumption.

"Of course not," she whispered. "I'm sorry."

He leaned toward her.

"You would come to the Palace, to live. You would help tend the books." Her chin jerked up and her mouth fell open. Darien grinned at her. "You would be a Junior Assistant Librarian." He held up a cautionary finger. "I don't offer an easy job. Some of the books are very old and we must handle them carefully. Some we even have to recopy before they disintegrate. The library is very large, easily as big as this house, and we must keep every book in its proper place, and you must know where every book lies. You would have to help sweep, dust and clean. Some evenings we don't even get to our beds until long after the rest of the Palace has slept for hours, there are that many books to look after."

"And I could read any of them?" Em asked in a wondering whisper. "I mean, after I did all my work? I could read them, and I could copy them out and look after them, and I could write?"

"Yes, Emily, you could do all those things."

"Even though I'm a girl?" she asked, her voice suddenly so soft that Darien had to strain to hear her.

"Even though you're a girl." He waited a moment. "It's not all fun and games, and you might become lonely sometimes. People who seek us out don't often have time to become our friends."

"That's okay," Em said, gazing at the book in her lap, not even fully aware that she spoke aloud. Darien had that effect on people, getting them to impart information they might otherwise keep hidden. "People usually scare me. I much prefer books." She glanced up. "Thank you, Darien. I'll work hard and keep your books happy. I'll make you proud."

And she had too. No one knew the books in the King's Library better than Em, and even though she couldn't rise any higher than her current position of Junior Assistant to the Chief Librarian because of her gender, the other five librarians, from Darien, now Chief Librarian, right down to the newest lad Brand, brought in five months ago, all knew her worth. Em preferred to keep to the background and avoid any confrontations. She happily delved into research and copying old documents while the others interacted with the people who came to the library. After all, no one had to know that Em often uncovered the books people sought or copied out the information they required from tomes that could not leave the library. If a man then usually brought these items to the interested parties, all the better to avoid admitting a female held a post usually reserved for a male. And all the better for a painfully shy Em who would just as soon spend time with a book than a human. No one lied about Em's work—Darien had even had scholar's caps made for each librarian to wear, Em included, making their presence and profession clear—they simply didn't shout out the truth. With this arrangement firmly in place, everyone could keep their illusions intact.

Now, her current project finished, Em had the option of finding a late night snack, or heading off for some real sleep. A yawn cracked her jaw, deciding her. She dragged off her cap and stuffed it in a pocket, then stood, finding the carefully stacked pages of her work by feel in the dark. She had already placed the Royal Proofs—the original records of ascension and ancestry from which she had drawn her copies—back in their protective coverings, yet she still took them up with great care. Before she had closed her eyes and rested her head, she had set the scribe's area in its proper order, the ink bottles stoppered tightly, the cleaned quills back in their grooved holders at the side of the desk, and the box of sand with its blotter to prevent ink blobs and smudges carefully arranged in the corner. That left only the records themselves for filing. Em decided to wait for the light of day to do so.

The library had three special niches tucked unobtrusively away near the scribe's area, three little curtained-off rooms just large enough for a single cot and a tiny table wide enough for a book. The librarians used these rooms when their work took them long enough that they might need a rest break.

Em had taken two steps toward the nearest alcove when she heard them, two muffled voices, out of place in the library's dark silence.

As she peered into the gloom, trying to discern the owners of those voices, she saw a sliver of light approaching, a lantern opened but a slit to betray the barest flame to illumine the way. The intruders obviously didn't want anyone to see them.

Apprehension lent stealth to Em's steps as she slipped into the aisle between two massive shelves of books, her papers clutched protectively against her chest.

"And everything's set?" a man's hushed voice asked.

"Cap'n Milos has dozens of men inciting riots through the city to draw attention. King's chambers is surrounded," the second man rasped back. "Once we get the documents to the Prince, he sends word and our troops move in to take the King."

"You really think this will work?" the first wanted to know. "I mean, taking over a crown is one thing, but keeping the King and his advisors alive? Ain't good policy. Folks'll rise up to overthrow the overthrowers if they believe the real King's around somewhere."

"You didn't see what that Destiny Seat did. Powerful magic, that." The second man spat. Em shuddered when she heard the glob of saliva hit the edge of a shelf with a wet splat. The two men had nearly reached the scribe's area.

"Magic don't solve everything. Plans so often fail," scoffed the first. "We, of all people, know that."

"That's why Cap'n gets payment afore we take a job. If some big muckety-muck gets hisself killed by his own plan, we can still walk away flush, knowing we done our part."

Em peered through a small gap in the books on the shelf to her left, able to discern two bulky shapes silhouetted by the lamplight as one man opened the shutter further, placing the lamp on the desk she had so recently vacated.

"Look," the second man turned to look at the first, but Em couldn't see any features in the shadows, only the black profiles of men much larger than her. "That Destiny made somethin' that sucks out memories. Very specific memories. Like who the real King is. I saw them try it on a kitchen wench. When I asked her who the King was, she looked kinda surprised and said, 'King Whillim of course'. I says, 'What about ol' Stefan?' and she says, 'Who?' and rushes off back to the kitchens."

The first man let out a low whistle. "But she's just a serving girl," he protested. "Maybe she was scairt. Or uneducated."

"Working in the Palace and not knowing the name of the King?" the second scoffed. "But she weren't the only one. They did it to a Councillor next. Same thing. Everyone going into that room knows Stefan's the King, and when they come out again, they think it's Whillim and Stefan ain't even a thought in their minds. I tell ya, it's more 'an a little creepy."

"I still don't see why we don't just kill the King, then. I mean, if no one remembers he exists, who's gonna miss him?"

"I just follow orders. Something in the way the magic works needs the King alive. I don't understand it, but then, I don't have to, long as I get my money."

"Right," the other chuckled. Em watched his profile turn to the desk. "So we just need the Royal Proofs, and the Prince can rewrite history."

"Exactly."

"Problem is, they ain't here."

"Librarian said they was being copied. Maybe the scribe finished the task and put the original back. Prince said to check the niches and the vaults. They're here and we'll find 'em. Let's go."

He picked up the lantern and moved back toward the resting niches.

Em held her breath as the light moved off, then silently retreated along the aisle to put some distance between herself and the paid soldiers, her mind working furiously. She didn't know about magic or this Destiny Seat the man had spoken of, but she understood the danger it represented.

King Stefan ruled his kingdom fairly and wisely. His brother, Prince Whillim, luxuriated in the wealth his position afforded, preferring entertainments to policy. Em had never thought of the Prince as ambitious—quite the opposite actually—but then, she had very seldom had the opportunity to deal with him. Not until Darien had enlisted her to make the copy of the royal ascension and ancestry—the Royal Proofs—had she even seen the Prince in the library. And now he wanted to overthrow his brother? Em didn't understand that. But then, she didn't have to; the King stood in very real danger and didn't know it. She had to warn him.

But how?

Chapter 2

Dalasmar Castle had stood for centuries, undergoing many additions and changes through the years, but one thing had remained constant: the secret passageways within the walls. Em had first learned of them when exploring the dusty books in the archives when she had first come to the castle. Tucked into a little used corner of the library, the archives had the oldest records, and the fewest visitors. It had seemed a paradise to a shy young girl. Several old writings delineating each addition to the castle during its first two centuries of life had highlighted these tunnels, and Em had found their existence fascinating.

Although several years had passed, Em remembered the description of every passage, thanks to her unique memory for the written word. She had never used those tunnels, and only once taken the time to see if she could find an entrance, but she knew where to locate every hidden door, and the trick to manipulating each door's unique opening mechanism. She didn't know if any of those mechanisms still operated and she had never heard of anyone using the secret passageways, but then, she spent most of her time isolated in the library and would hardly have knowledge of the goings-on of the royals or their guards.

She did know, from these mercenary soldiers in her library, that she couldn't approach the King's chambers undetected through the halls. Even could she somehow sneak past those men, how would she gain an audience so late with the King without raising questions and possibly setting in motion the very events these men suggested?

Of course, stepping out of the wall into the King's room posed great difficulties all their own. Somehow, Em had to get in to see the King and give her warning before he or any of his guard could raise their own alarm, take her captive, or simply kill her on the spot. After all, none knew her, nor she them.

Em shook her head, trying to banish the image of her blood dripping from the King's sword. Sometimes she had far too active an imagination.

It wouldn't take the soldiers long to discover the disappearance of the Royal Proofs and to think to search the library at large. She didn't know which librarian they had spoken to, nor whether they knew she had the task of copying the Proofs, but she feared what they would do should they find her. If she tried to slip out the main entrance, they might spot her, or worse, have other soldiers waiting and guarding the way in. Leaving the library would chance encountering people, and this night, Em had reason to fear anyone she might meet along the way.

That left the secret passageway inside the library itself. Unfortunately, the tunnel started in the vault, where the mercenaries had gone looking for the Proofs. Em had to remain hidden until they came out and began searching the library, then sneak past them, unlock the vault, move a shelf of scrolls out of the way, open and close the rarely used door without losing the Royal Proofs, and hope the men didn't hear any of her progress.

She bit her lip to keep a whimper of terror from betraying her. Perhaps if she thought of herself as a heroine from one of her beloved books, or a fearless warrior from the histories, instead of a meek young woman suddenly set an important task ....

Em nodded to herself. She could do this.

She eased her way toward the vault, moving by feel in the pitch black, knowing every creak and dip in the floor, the location of each shelf and table, fervently hoping no one had left a chair pulled out too far into the aisles. She kept out of the main passages as much as possible to avoid detection, her breath held as her ears strained for any sound to indicate the return of the men. She had just gained the second-to-last shelf before the vault when she glimpsed their lantern and heard their grumbles again. She froze. Would they start searching the rows of shelves on their way back, or go right to the resting niches, hoping to find their prize there and save themselves the daunting task of hunting through the whole library? To be safe, Em drew back until she reached the end of the shelf where she could slip one way or the other, depending on the actions of these men.

And she waited.

Minutes felt like hours as she second- and even third-guessed her decision. The longer she delayed, the more danger to the King, but what else could she do? Should she have tried the main entrance? Would anyone question the movements of a Junior Assistant Librarian? How long could she wait before her resolve broke and she fled? Would the King even believe her if she found him? What if he wasn't in his rooms? Em agonized over every detail, nearly giving in to her fears, when the soldiers finally emerged from the vault.

"I ain't searching this whole bloody place," one of them groused as they stepped into the open.

"If we don't find them in those niches, we go back empty-handed," the other decided, hauling the vault door shut. "Not our fault they ain't here, and we got better things to do than hunt for them Proofs. If the Prince really needs them after he takes over, we can look again in the light of day, with more'n just us two."

"Right," his companion agreed as they turned away from Em's hiding place and moved off toward the niches.

Em didn't lose another second to hesitation or doubt. She felt her way to the door that barred the vault, discovering to her great relief that she wouldn't need her key, as the men hadn't bothered to relock it. The door opened soundlessly on well-oiled hinges. She slipped within, sliding the door closed behind her, careful not to let the latch snick.

And immediately discovered an impediment to her progress. She couldn't see anything. The soldiers had, of course, taken their lantern with them. If she lit her own little candle, they might see the light through the bars on the window of the door, but she didn't have a choice.

While she could find the correct wall with ease, she needed to see to find the secret to opening the door. If she waited until the mercenaries left the library, she could light the candle without fear, but she could very well reach the King too late to save him. She would have to take the risk of the soldiers seeing her light. But until she truly needed the use of her sight, she would work in the dark.

Em moved to the eastern wall, one hand held before her to find the table edges, the other cradling the Proofs and her copies to her chest. Once she worked her way to the correct shelf, she knelt down, placing her precious documents on the ground beside her. She needed both hands free to move the shelf and open the passageway.

She took up her copies and rolled them, slipping them into the large pocket of her smock next to her cap as she removed her candle and flint. She couldn't roll the original Proofs, but if she had to run, she wanted to make sure at least the copies came with her. She intended to bring the originals to the King, but if she had no other choice, she would leave them behind, perhaps kicked under a shelf where someone would miss seeing them.

Still crouched low, Em drew her striker across the flint, creating a spark. The little candle caught and she set it as close to the wall as she could, desperate to remain unnoticed. She took quick stock of her surroundings, relieved that she stood in the correct spot. Grabbing the edge of the bookcase, thankful it had only four shelves, Em braced her legs, lifted and pulled. Though it held only scrolls, the weight surprised her, and at the last instant, the sturdy wooden shelf thunked back down, the dull thud sounding loud in the vault. Eyes wide and breath caught in fright, Em dared not delay to see if the soldiers had heard. She found the wide block with the black smudge and traced the mortar around it counter-clockwise with a finger. Then she pressed the next stone on the left side and the one above in the centre, wondering if the entrance's mechanism would work.

To her horror, it did, the stone giving off a great groan of disuse as it ground inward, a noise the soldiers couldn't possibly miss, even through the closed vault door. She pushed at the stone, hurrying its motion as puffs of dust rose around her. The doorway, only two stones high, required her to crawl through on hands and knees. She grabbed the Proofs and her candle as the soldiers burst into the room, shoving hard through the door of the vault. Dousing her own little light might buy her some time, though she feared not enough. She did so anyway and slipped into the dark maw of the tunnel. She slapped a hand to the right and the top of the entrance. The stone started to pull back into place, but not quickly enough. One of the soldiers yelled, spotting Em as he swung his lantern her way. He rushed forward and she squealed her fear. He pushed at the rock, trying to open the door again. Although it slowed, Em could tell he needed a lot of strength to halt the stone. Before he could find something to wedge it open, or use the additional weight of his companion to force the door, Em struck out, pushing the edge of her candle at his hand, the heat from the small bit of melted wax it had accumulated surprising the man. He flinched just enough for the stone to continue its inexorable journey back into place, sealing Em into silent darkness.

Heart racing, she frantically pulled stagnant air into her lungs, trying not to cough as it dried the back of her throat. Although she had no doubt the mercenaries even now tried to reopen the door, she could hear nothing through the thick stone, and only her own harsh gasps echoed in a muted manner off the walls.

Dust and grit itched her eyes and she blinked to clear them, though she could see nothing. The neglect of ages tickled her nose and made her sneeze. Em sat in uncharted territory now. She knew the lay of the passageways, where they went and how they intersected, but she didn't know how wide or tall they stood. She would have to light her candle again, but when she tried, she found the little stub broken and useless, defeated by its encounter with the mercenary.

Em wept in frustration. She couldn't go back, which left only going forward. Forward, in the dark, in a strange tunnel, hoping she'd measure her paces correctly and find her way to the King's chambers. The whole idea seemed ludicrous, yet what choice did she have?

Steady breath, she told herself, trying to calm her trepidation and firm her resolve. She wiped the tears from her cheeks on the back of her sleeve, retrieved the Royal Proofs, and put the useless candle back into her pocket with the flint. Very carefully, she reached out to the side, trying to determine how much space she had in which to move. Her hand encountered the far wall very quickly. She could touch both walls at the same time with her elbows bent. She reached up, expecting to find the ceiling not far above, but to her surprise, found only empty space. She rose cautiously to her feet and still felt no roof. Perhaps the tunnels rose to the same height as the castle walls on the opposite side. Without a light, she couldn't tell. She wondered if one had to crawl through all the entrances or whether the one from the library vault stood apart. None of the notations from the old books had specified the design of the doors, only how to open and close them.

With no better plan in mind and no other truly viable options, Em turned to the south and started to walk, her free hand using the wall to guide her. In her mind, she pictured the layout of the passageways leading to the King's chambers, and began measuring her paces.

***

Twin points of light beckoned Em ahead. She had moved through the dark as quickly as she dared, checking her mental map of the tunnels against what her fingers found. The tunnels, though clearly not trod by human feet for decades if not centuries, did show some signs of life. Thick spiderwebs clogged some sections and Em had to push her way through the dust-covered stickiness. She heard the occasional click of small nails as rats and mice scurried out of her way, and the scent of scat from such creatures wrinkled her nose. At periodic intervals along her trek, little specks of light had drawn her eagerly forward. Sometimes only one tiny slot, sometimes two, various areas had small peek-holes, presumably disguised in some way from the opposite side. The amount of light that came through depended on whether lamps or candles flickered nearby. Em judged almost all such spy holes as corresponding to a room where an entrance to the passageways existed, although at times no light appeared where she expected, likely due to a room's lack of occupation, and therefore lack of illumination. Or simply the fact that those within slept as she had earlier longed to do. She wondered if she would have to wake the King when she arrived, then, remembering the groan of the library tunnel's entrance, hoped she had a chance to explain herself before such a noise drew guards ready to slit her throat.

In a couple of locations as she had progressed, she believed the view from the peek-holes provided a gauge as to location within the tunnels, or perhaps a way to keep track of individuals as they moved through the halls beyond. Whatever the reason, Em had looked forward to each respite from the oppressive blackness surrounding her.

If she had calculated correctly, the current respite held the King's chambers. She hurried forward. As she peered through, Em realised she had no idea what the King's rooms would look like; she had never had occasion to see them, nor would most, she supposed, save the King himself, his family (limited now to his brother), his valet, and the cleaning staff. And his guards.

The spy hole provided a limited view. She saw a door across from her and an elaborate tapestry on the far wall, as well as an ornate rug covering most of the stone floor, all lit by the hearth fire and a lantern or torch that flickered beyond her line of sight. At the very edge of her vision, she saw the corner of what looked like a green-and-gold cushioned sofa, and perhaps the end of a wooden table or desk.

Had she found the right room? If she had miscalculated and stepped out into another's room, that someone might delay her. Could she risk it? Could she not?

Em took a deep breath, trying not to cough on the dust, and fingered the covering over the Royal Proofs. She had to trust her memory and try. But where to find the opening levers? The light dispelled some of the claustrophobic darkness pressing in on her, but did nothing to show her the walls and their contours.

Find the crown and sceptre, the book had read. *Trace the one, left point down to tip and across the base, and grasp the other, middle finger and thumb, pressing to trigger.* Em thought it sounded like a carving, the shapes etched into the stone somewhere. Maybe if she ran her hands along the wall in front of her, near the spy holes, she would find the indents. She laid the Royal Proofs at her feet and set to her blind search.

Several frantic minutes proved its futility. With a growl of frustration, Em thumped her back against the wall adjoining the chamber, the minuscule light beside her. She drew in several shaky breaths, trying to calm herself. Tears traced her cheeks despite her best efforts. After a long moment, Em realised she could just make out something on the far wall, a difference in the rock barely noticeable via the muted glow beside her. She leaned forward, not daring to blink lest she lose sight of the shapes. There, chiselled onto the far wall, stood four images: a throne, a crown, a diamond, and a sceptre. She nearly laughed in sudden relief.

Em reached out a finger, tracing the crown. Her other hand came up, her fingers to the middle of the sceptre. She pressed inward. Behind her, she heard a tiny click. She spun and saw the edge of a door outlined by lamplight. She pushed and the door pivoted silently. She breathed a sigh of relief.

No time to hesitate, she thought, and stepped through.

***

"Preliminary reports suggest that, although we have the riots contained at present, tempers remain high, and I suspect the unrest will soon spread," Captain Frederick said, a large, muscled man, his hair the colour of an acorn just beginning to streak with grey pulled back into a warrior's tail. Despite the late hour, he stood calmly in his leathers as though his report held little importance. Only the angry gleam in his dark brown eyes betrayed his agitation.

"And still no idea on the source?" Stefan asked his chief bodyguard. The populace of Riverbend had shown no discontent before, and the King needed to understand why his people would suddenly rise up, what cause they had to find dissatisfaction with his rule. If he could find no cause, he could find no way to rectify the situation.

"None, Sire," Fred replied. "Although we have determined the initial outbreak centred around the taverns. It's possible a drunken brawl simply got out of hand."

"Out of hand," Stefan said flatly, shaking his head so that his dark blond hair whipped the air. Unlike Fred, Stefan had discarded his sword and belt, had released the locks of hair that reached between his shoulder blades from the confines of their leather thong. "Fred, the lower east side of Riverbend lies in flames and the street folk beat each other bloody. I need to know why, and I need it stopped."

"Of course, Sire. My men work to contain—" He broke off as both men noticed movement from the inner chamber.

Stefan stared in shock as a young woman, not much beyond girlhood, stepped from his bed chamber. Grime and cobwebs clung to the smock that covered her skirts, dulling a wild mane of shoulder-length auburn hair. Light grey eyes blinked rapidly from a dirty, tear-streaked face. She clutched something to her chest as she sank hurriedly to her knees.

"Your Majesty," she whispered, a sound clipped short as Fred's sword cleared its scabbard, the blade swiftly resting across her throat.

Her eyes widened even further as she took in the finely-honed weapon and the grim visage of the man holding it. She sucked in her lower lip and her chest heaved in a draught of air, but she waited on Fred and Stefan.

"How did you get in here?" Fred demanded, his voice all the more chilling by its deadly quiet.

The girl rolled her eyes back to Stefan's room.

"Passageway," she whispered. "From the library."

"What passageway?" Fred demanded, but Stefan, his attention riveted on the girl, silenced him with a quick wave of his hand. He had always suspected the existence of such tunnels, but had never found proof of them before.

"You found the secret passages?" he asked, dragging the girl's attention from Fred's sword. Her eyes sought refuge in his face.

"You're in danger, Majesty," she said instead, her voice a little stronger. "They've already surrounded these chambers."

"Who has? Who are you?" Fred snarled.

"Emily, Junior Assistant to the Chief Librarian. I heard them talking in the library, sir. Paid soldiers sent to retrieve these." She made as if to hand Stefan the bundle in her arms, but hesitated, staring at Fred's sword, awaiting the Captain's permission to move. Fred, recognising the gesture, grunted and pointed with his free hand at the floor. Emily carefully laid her burden down, then clasped her hands in front of her, where Fred could see them. Stefan glanced quickly down at the offering, what looked like papers protected from the elements, then did a double take when he recognised the symbol on the cover, staring hard at Emily.

"How did you get those?" He heard the harshness of his voice. Emily winced only slightly, but did not evade his blue-eyed glare. Fred tilted his head to better see the documents yet keep the girl's movements in sight.

"Are those ... what I think they are?" he asked, glancing from Emily to Stefan.

"The Royal Proofs," Stefan affirmed, his gaze locked with the young woman's.

"Chief Librarian Darien charged me with copying them at the request of your brother, Prince Whillim, Sire," she said softly. "They are not to leave the library, and I fully understand the consequences of what I have done, but to leave them to the hands of nefarious peoples who plot your overthrow seemed a worse offence, my King."

Stefan blinked in surprise, somehow charmed by her passionate response, though it made little sense.

"Do you suggest that the Prince plans to overthrow his brother somehow using the Royal Proofs and a bunch of mercenaries who presently have these rooms surrounded?" Fred questioned, doubt colouring his tone.

"That is my understanding," Emily replied, not fazed by his skepticism. "Under the direction of a Captain Milos, they started riots in the city as a distraction to thin out the King's guards, and were only waiting for confirmation of the acquisition of the Proofs to move in and take the King."

"Whillim wouldn't dare lift a hand against me," Stefan murmured. "He doesn't have the support of the Councillors nor the respect of the people. How could he hope to maintain control?"

"Through some sort of magic, Sire. Please, there's not much time to explain. You must escape. I can lead you to safety through the passageways."

"And we're to simply take your word for it?" Fred demanded, his blade never moving from her throat. "You expect me to allow the King to follow a stranger into hitherto unknown tunnels and trust that you don't lead him into further danger? Assuming this danger truly exists in the first place."

Moisture gathered in Emily's eyes as she stared up at the daunting Captain, but no further tears fell.

"Then don't take my word for it, sir, but check the halls beyond the King's chambers. Make sure you know all the soldiers guarding the area; send someone to see if there are riots in the city; see if there are two strange soldiers searching the library in the dark. But please hurry."

Stefan exchanged a telling look with his chief bodyguard, finally giving him a single nod.

"Corporal Joseph," Fred called to one of the soldiers guarding the King's door.

The outer door opened enough for a ginger-haired young

man wearing the King's livery to step into the room.

"Sir?" he queried, the slight puckering of his brow the only indication of his surprise at seeing a mysterious and dishevelled woman present and at the mercy of his Captain's sword.

"Anything unusual out there, Corporal?"

"Unusual, sir?" his green eyes flicked to Emily. "No sir. Should there be?"

"Corporal," Stefan said, drawing the guard's attention. "Do a sweep of the area. Look for any soldiers out of place." He glanced at Emily. "Look for *anyone* out of place. Keep it discreet."

"Yes Sire," Joseph saluted with a fist to his heart before slipping back out into the hall, closing the door behind him.

As they waited, Stefan plucked up the Royal Proofs, gently unwrapping their protective coverings to more closely examine the documents. Emily watched his every movement, clearly unhappy that someone else should touch the precious pages, even if that someone wore a crown. Fred kept his attention firmly rooted on the young woman, yet Stefan knew the man well enough that he could see the Captain's mind working through the consequences should the girl's story prove true, and what actions he would have to take to keep his King safe.

The Royal Seal shimmered at the top of the first page, the gilt of the golden sheaf of wheat mingling with the silvered stag head against the ruby backdrop of the rising sun, drawing Stefan's eye. The Proofs listed all his ancestors, the lines of ascension in the kingdom of Dalasham, and the lines that had failed or fallen out of favour, all the possible claimants for the throne and those banned from contention for one reason or another, each meticulously outlined. But Stefan didn't really see them; his mind searched instead for Whillim's possible motives for trying to usurp authority, and more, how his brother could think to accomplish such an incredible feat. Magic, Emily had said, but Willi had no magic. Had he encountered a wizard somewhere in his travels? A magic user with little or no scruples? Had this wizard corrupted Whillim's thinking or had his younger brother always hidden his true motives? Willi had ambitions, but they seldom extended beyond his own comfort, and Stefan had thought him content in his luxury, had even allowed a certain degree of over-excess in his brother's antics. Had such forbearance led Willi to the mistaken belief that

21

Stefan would simply roll over and hand him power? Willi did not think of the best interests of anyone beyond himself. Yet now he sought to overthrow Stefan? Dalasham under Willi's thumb would suffer greatly, and Willi wouldn't care so long as he could fulfill his own selfish desires. If this play for power proved true, Stefan would fight to protect his people, even if he had to do battle with his spoiled kin.

"Your Majesty?" Emily ventured tentatively, drawing Stefan's angry glare. "Please, your Majesty, have a care."

Stefan stared blankly at her. She cleared her throat.

"The Proofs, Sire. Please don't damage the Proofs."

Stefan glanced down, noting his white-knuckled grip on the pages, the protective covering creased with his ire. With an effort, he smoothed the wrinkled edge, trying to smooth over his emotions at the same time. He only had this Emily's word for the surprising actions of his brother. Until he had tangible proof ....

"Tell me of these passageways," Stefan said quietly, turning to a safer topic than Willi's possible treachery. "How do you know of them?"

"I found the records of their existence many years ago, Sire, in a seldom used alcove in the archives of the library's east wing." She spoke quietly, yet Stefan had no trouble hearing the soft whisper. "The parchments were very old, beneath several tomes of the castle's history thick with dust. I found them fascinating."

"Many years ago, yet now you find a convenient time for their use?" Sarcasm lay heavy in Fred's tone, then his eyes narrowed. "Or mayhap they have seen years of use? How often do you travel these tunnels?"

"Never sir," Emily protested, daring briefly to meet the man's gaze. "I had confirmed their existence when I learned of them, though never set foot within their confines."

"Yet you remember their configuration," mused Stefan.

"It is my gift, Sire," Emily whispered, eyes downcast. "To remember that which is written." She swallowed, hands clutched tightly together, in trepidation thought Stefan. "I can lead you through them to a safe place away from the castle."

"And what's to stop others from following?" Stefan asked.

The girl moved one hand slightly to indicate a dust-ridden cobweb clinging to the smock covering her tunic and skirts.

"None have walked those tunnels for a great long time, Your Majesty. It seems unlikely any would know to look for such a passageway. And without knowing the trick of each entry, for they all have a secret key, no one will have the ability to open the doors, Sire. They cannot follow you."

Before Stefan could question further, a quiet knock announced the return of Corporal Joseph.

Stefan read some truth to Emily's words in the man's grim countenance.

"Sergeant Darius and I guard your doors, Sire," he spoke quietly. "And Ambrose and Faulk stand ready at the near end of the hall with one of the pages, but beyond them, I can't say who stands guard, only that they don't feel right. They have a tense wariness that I mislike."

"A wariness that the riots can't explain?" Fred demanded.

"No Captain, more like they wait for something. I didn't approach to question them, but I don't recognise faces nor postures." Joseph glanced at Emily. "And though I saw only two too many liveried soldiers and a servant far too intent on a wall sconce, I believe by their focus that others await or approach in stealth beyond the next corridor."

"Five against an unknown number, then." Fred scowled. He glared at Emily, still poised at the end of his sword. "And a girl claiming an escape route."

Emily raised eyes shining with unshed tears to meet Stefan's gaze.

"Please, Sire," she pleaded. "I will swear to whatever oath you require that I can get you to safety, but we must go now, before it's too late and they take you."

Moved by the emotion in her voice, Stefan made his decision.

"Corporal Joseph, bring me the page, and have Darius, Ambrose and Faulk ready to join us in here as soon as the boy leaves."

"Yes, Sire." The Corporal saluted and hurried out.

"Where away from the castle?" the King asked, motioning Fred to sheath his sword and help Emily to her feet.

"One of the tunnels leads to the east wall, Sire, to an underground building designed to shield those who seek escape from the castle. I know of a cave out past the woods beyond the wall."

"The east wall," Fred shook his head. "The riots are in the

lower east side. You would lead His Majesty into a battle."

"No, it's perfect," Stefan interjected. "They will not expect me to head into danger. If, as Emily suggests, my brother has hired a mob of mercenaries, then I need my soldiers to know whom they fight. Right now, they fight the riot in the east. We go east, Captain, where you will muster the men and assess the situation."

A knock on the door announced the arrival of the page, a boy of perhaps ten.

"Kelvin," Stefan greeted him, recognising the slight blond child. "I need you to get to the barracks. Talk to only the soldiers you know by name. If you do not know them, or are unsure of their identity, pass them by. If they stand with someone you don't recognise, pass them by. This is very important. Do you understand?"

The boy paled but nodded.

"Tell them the castle has been breached and to meet me at the east wall." He looked at Emily. "What landmark?"

"The forges, Sire," she replied. "It comes out near the edge of the smithies. I cannot be more exact as the city has enlarged since the creation of the original maps."

Stefan gave a curt nod and turned back to the page.

"I take those loyal here to safety beyond the forges. Be careful, Kelvin; treachery walks these halls. Trust no soldier you do not know, and," Stefan paused, swallowing a bitter taste, "do not speak to the Prince or his followers."

Again, Kelvin nodded, his hazel eyes wide. Stefan glanced to his Captain.

"Anything more?"

"Tell them," Fred's solemn voice informed the boy, "to crow before dawn."

Kelvin blinked at him.

"Aye sir. Aught else Sire?" he asked the King.

"Make haste, Kelvin, and keep yourself safe."

"Yes, my Lord." He sketched a salute and hurried out. A moment later, Corporal Joseph re-entered, three loyal guards at his back. Stefan turned to Emily.

"Our lives are in your hands now, Junior Assistant Librarian."

"Hurry," Emily spun and suited actions to words, leading the men into the King's inner chamber and the dark passage that awaited beyond.

Chapter 3

Darkness cloaked them. Dust swirled to scratch at their noses, disturbed by the passage of booted feet, and thick, sticky cobwebs sought to impede their progress, but the six men followed the young woman none knew. Em followed the map in her mind, one hand to the wall her only guide in the black tunnel. She could see nothing, yet quickened her pace anyway, fear giving her feet reckless haste.

A gloved hand gripped her shoulder, stopping her.

"Wait," the large Captain who followed at her heels whispered, his voice a mere breath.

They had gone four dozen paces after Em had sealed the door to the King's passage, yet she could hear the quick rasp of the soldiers' breathing, anxious gasps rather than pants of exertion. Then she heard the strike of a flint and her eyes feasted on the tiny flame that appeared in one of the soldier's hands as he lit a small lantern.

"Keep it hooded," she hissed urgently as she dropped to a crouch, even though she longed to hold that bit of light herself.

Six pairs of eyes reflected back at her in that little glow, each man mimicking her crouch, bringing the light closer to the floor. She indicated the wall, though it stretched pitted and empty to their limited sight.

"There are viewports along the way. We cannot risk giving away our location."

"And if we lose each other in the darkness?" the King asked, the Royal Proofs now sheltered in his arms. "How do we find our way without light?"

"I did so from the library to your chambers, Your Majesty. It's a matter of counting our steps." Em couldn't read the King's expression well in the lantern's light, but she recognised a frown. She turned to look along the passageway they followed.

"Perhaps," she whispered, "if we keep the light hooded, we can make better time. We'll pass any viewports quickly and any who might notice the glow will discount it as imagination."

She returned her gaze to the men in time to see them exchange glances. Finally the King nodded and rose to his feet, bringing everyone up with him.

"Make the best time you can, Emily," he instructed.

Em led them on, followed by the Captain, the King, Corporal Joseph holding the hooded lantern, and finally the three soldiers from the hall. With the light behind her and mostly shielded, Em had plenty of notice before passing a lit viewport, although the ones she did not see concerned her the most. Running brought the dust to their faces faster, eliciting sneezes, so Em kept their pace to a fast walk. They heard nothing from beyond the wall, but she took no chances of being heard in return.

Ten minutes and two turns later, Em stopped, glad she had marked her progress. Darkness continued to stretch ahead, barely touched by the lantern, and had she not known to look, she would have missed the sudden descent of stairs carved into the stone.

She turned her head to those behind.

"You can uncover the light a little more," she whispered. "We've reached the castle's outer wall. These stairs will take us to tunnels beneath the city."

Now that they had more freedom to move unobserved, Em thought to run, but when she finished counting twenty stairs and reached the bottom, she discovered that the passage through the city narrowed even further, her shoulders occasionally brushing both walls. She stopped and looked back at the men, each larger than her, especially the Captain.

"Narrow," she warned, then plunged ahead. The ceiling also dropped so that she could briefly see old soot stains from the ages old passing of torches before darkness stole her sight again. The lantern light, separated from her by two bodies, gave her little comfort and she had to strain her eyes to identify one wall from the other. Yet she pressed on, trusting to her memory map.

Em heard the men struggling as they squeezed along behind her. Swords in scabbards scraped against the stone walls and muffled grunts and curses drifted through the dead air, yet they continued to follow where she led. Had she spared herself a moment to consider the outrageous situation that found a junior assistant librarian—and a woman at that—leading her King and his loyal guardsmen though old, forgotten tunnels to safety on a night of treachery and betrayal, Em might have laughed at her own audacity, but fear kept such frivolity at bay and hurried her on.

Finally, they reached another set of stairs, as narrow as the passageway they had just traversed. Em stopped again.

"Wait here," she whispered, though she knew no one would hear them from above. "I'll make sure it's clear."

"No," the King snapped. "Fred and Jo will check."

The Captain nodded and made to move past Emily, but she stood firm.

"You don't know how to open the door," she said. "I do, Sire. And there's no room to pass. I have to go first."

The King took the lantern from Corporal Joseph and held it up to regard her. A moment passed, two. Em could see his agitation and thought she understood the fierce furrow upon his brow. He had to be asking himself whether she had led him into an ambush after all, and what right had a woman to dictate to a King. A woman he didn't want to put into any more danger, for a woman's role lay under the protection of a man, not as protector. But he could also see that Em merely spoke the truth. The tunnel didn't allow space for the Captain or anyone to pass her. The King thrust the lantern forward into his Captain's hand.

"Go then. But go carefully."

"Yes Sire." Em nodded deeply, foregoing the urge to drop to her knees on the filthy stone, but giving as much deference as she could in the confined space.

She turned and climbed the steps, Captain Frederick at her heels.

***

27

Four images carved into the stone beside a sealed door confronted Em at the top of the stairs: a spiral, a tankard, an oak leaf and a cluster of grapes. Captain Frederick stared at her as she recited the pertinent script quietly.

"'Trace the spiral from out to in and lay the outer curve of your fist against the centre, then pluck the third and fifth globes of fruit with index and ring finger.'" She followed the instructions, not knowing if the actual fingers used mattered, but not daring to deviate from the directions.

A long-unused mechanism in the wall shuddered and the door began to grate open—into the tunnel. Em gasped and retreated in haste, smacking into the solid wall of Frederick's leather-clad body. He growled an oath as he shuttered the lantern, but made way as the door swung wide.

Darkness again greeted them, and very faint shouting.

Carefully, Frederick opened the lantern's shutter to allow a sliver of light through. It revealed a pile of crates blocking the way. Frederick reached an arm past Em and gave one crate an experimental shove. Nothing moved. With an irritated grunt, he pressed as close to Em as he could, holding the lantern out in front of them. Em thought to protest but realised that the large Captain merely intended to see what the crates contained. In the narrow confines, he could only do so though Em.

"Scrap metal, pitted blades, old sword hilts, bits of slag," he listed as he perused what he could see of the crates' contents. "Looks like old storage for a blacksmith."

"It seems someone found the old underground building and, not knowing its original purpose, turned it into storage," Em replied. "The passage entrances are well hidden though, so no one would know they blocked a door."

"They better not," Frederick grumbled ominously. He peered at Em with speculation glittering in his eye, then thrust the lantern at her.

"Hold this," he said. "We're switching places."

So saying, he hugged her to him tightly, ignoring her startled exclamation, and performed an awkward shifting dance until he had managed to spin Em to the rear, placing himself directly in front of the crates. Without another word, he turned back to the puzzle of the blockage. After examining the stability of the crates, he chose the right stack, crouched, braced himself and shoved at the bottom two crates. Em quickly set the lantern down and reached forward to keep the top crates from tipping. Frederick grunted his thanks and continued to push. They shifted perhaps a span then stopped. Frederick pushed again, his muscles bulging with his effort, but only managed to gain another finger width.

"Got to be other crates in front of these," he said. "You've smaller hands; can you tell?"

Em, rather than waiting for the Captain to try his shifting dance to trade places again, dropped to her knees and pushed at his leg.

"Let me through," she demanded as Frederick huffed a surprised snort, then, understanding her intent, spread his legs as much as the narrow space allowed, letting her crawl through, her arm extended to feel between the piles. She didn't allow herself any time for embarrassment or even amusement at the picture they must present as his strong limbs hugged her sides, but rather concentrated on helping to find a way out of the claustrophobic space.

Grime-coated cobwebs and rock dust clung to floor and crate, along with a hint of moisture, and the scent of mildew and disuse tickled her nose. She traced the edge of the crates Frederick had moved and scraped her knuckles on the boxes to the left but found enough room to wriggle her fingers past. More containers met her questing fingers from the right pile. The left, though, had a pocket of space. She extended her fingers to their utmost and waved them as much as she could. At the very extreme, she found the corner of another box, slightly off-set from the crate behind.

"You might be able to push the left pile along," she reported as she pulled back from between Frederick's braced legs and stood. "If you shove it at an angle, we might make an aisle between the stacks."

"Might?"

"I make no promises, Captain," she replied. "My fingers have no eyes and my arm reaches no farther than the next pile of refuse."

He grunted, acceptance or amusement.

"Fine. Keep the top from tumbling and I'll make what room I can."

Again Frederick pushed and Em steadied, shifting the other

group of crates. They made more progress, though again, the containers could only move so far.

Em dropped to her knees again, sending the lantern light into the space they had created. Darkness yawned ahead, but also the shadowy edges of the piles of storage.

"I think ..." she whispered. Rather than continue her thought, she crawled forward, wedging herself into the emptiness.

"Wait," Frederick demanded, but Em kept inching her way forward, shoving with hands and shoulders as she moved. Past the twin stacks of crates, each scraping at her shoulders, she reached an obstruction that she discerned as sturdy cloth sacks holding chain links. Pushing at them, she suddenly found herself toppling out into nothing but air. A quick look around showed three stone walls lined with boxes and sacks, the fourth leading to worn stairs directly in front of her. The middle of the room remained relatively free of detritus or other cast-offs and extras of the blacksmith profession. She saw no other evidence of a human presence, though again, muffled calls of people drifted down the stairs.

Em turned back to the crates and peered at the Captain, surprised at the tiny space she had managed to squeeze through, illuminated by the square of light provided by the lantern.

"Storage," she confirmed. "And empty of people."

As she spoke, she shoved aside as much of said storage as she could to make way for those she had led here.

When Frederick shimmied his way out, he rose, taking sword from scabbard and facing the stairs. No light came from above. With a quick flick of his wrist, he motioned Em to stand to one side of the stairway, her back to the wall and as protected as possible from anyone who might glance down. He left her the lantern and stalked up the stairs, his movements cat-quiet, his senses straining.

After a moment he rejoined Em.

"From the sounds of it, the commotion's all outside the shop, from the riots no doubt. Shadows indicate a blacksmith's workroom above, heavy wooden door partially closed to this room." He stole a look at Em. "Bring the others up, keep the King to the back, and if it's all clear above, seal the tunnel and hide the entrance. Yes?"

Em nodded and turned to do as instructed.

***

Stefan crouched next to Emily in the storage room at the bottom of the stairs, chafing at the wait while his men searched the floor above, yet understanding the need for safety. He had left the Royal Proofs in the passage, amused but gratified by Emily's precautions when he made his intentions clear. The young librarian had appropriated an unused sack from one of the shelves to wrap the Proofs in, then made sure the sack remained clear of the ground by supporting it on an empty crate, all taken to the bottom of the stairs in the tunnel. When Sergeant Darius, dark of hair and eye, his moustache failing to mask his youth, had voiced a protest at the perceived delay, Emily had scowled at him.

"You don't need to oversee the procedure, sir," she had told the lithe man. "The Captain needs you all above to secure the area, not down here babysitting us. As the King must wait until you accomplish that, as per the Captain's orders, you merely waste time here arguing over how *I* intend to keep the King safe. I suggest you do your job and allow me to do mine." Each word accompanied her efficient motions as she wrapped the Proofs, then hurried to the tunnel, feeling her way down the dark steps, for Fred had positioned the lantern at the stairs to the blacksmith shop. Dari had stared after her, speechless. When he turned his stare to Stefan, the King just shrugged.

"Go, Sergeant," he said, gesturing to the rising stairs. "The Captain will need every man if Whillim has indeed incited a revolt."

Stefan pondered that unexpected possibility while he waited. That riots had spread throughout the eastern part of Riverbend he did not dispute. But that Prince Whillim had instigated the troubles in an effort to usurp his brother's position seemed incredible to Stefan. Willi had ambition, but little in the way of perseverance or follow-through. He liked his luxuries too much and his responsibilities too little to risk upsetting his comfortable world, or so Stefan had thought. If Willi truly thought he had a chance to take Stefan's place, then the land would suffer the self-indulgence of a selfish king. The Council knew this, as did the populace of Riverbend where the castle of Dalasmar sat. Willi would need the goodwill of these people before he could

31

rule, so long as Stefan lived.

The thought made him shudder. Did Willi chafe so much at his lot that he would stoop to fratricide and regicide? Yet Emily had implied that the mercenaries outside his chambers had orders to take the King, not kill him. How then could Willi hope to maintain control?

Magic, Emily had said.

"What kind of magic?" he whispered, drawing Emily's attention. "What kind of magic could aid the Prince in taking control?"

"The soldier said it alters memory, Sire," she replied just as quietly. "It makes people think your brother rules and that you don't exist. But it needs you alive to work."

"That doesn't make sense," Stefan protested.

"I'm sorry, Your Majesty, but I didn't think it prudent to ask the man to clarify."

Stefan snorted at her humour and the audacity to use it at his expense.

Before he could question her further, a signal from Fred drew his attention.

"It's clear. Let's go."

"A moment, Sire." Emily squeezed back through the small aisle they had made of the crates to the tunnel entrance. Stefan couldn't see what exactly she did, but the secret door grated shut. She pushed at some of the crates, and when none of them moved, she hauled one from the top and shoved it into the gap. Seeing her intention, Stefan hurried over to help mask their passage. Some of the crates held quite a weight, but with Stefan helping Emily—his muscles honed from hours of weapon's practice with Fred, and she obliviously used to hefting multiple massive tomes around the library—they made quick work of their task.

They hurried up the stairs just as Fred came to see what had kept them. At Stefan's curt gesture, the Captain turned and led them to the front of the shop, no questions asked.

The orange haze of flames and chaotic shouts of panicked people in the surrounding streets drew them cautiously into the lower east side of Riverbend. Acrid smoke stung their noses and coated throat and tongue. The clash of steel on steel directed Stefan's attention down Smithy street, past another blacksmith shop, a forge and a silversmith to a group of armed combatants. He could discern no identifiable features in the fog of smoke and the twisting flares of fires dancing on nearby roofs. The handful of guards that had accompanied him through the castle's tunnels fanned out around Stefan and Emily. The King found himself in want of his sword, which presently hung uselessly in the antechamber of his room where his valet had left it hours ago, just before Stefan had dismissed the man and Fred had come with news of the riots. He cursed his lack of forethought at leaving the weapon behind.

Fred let out the call of a raven, crowing twice. One man among the fighters immediately raised a fist without pausing in his defensive parries.

"Five are ours," Fred informed the King, reading more into the soldier's gesture than Stefan saw, but he knew better than to quibble. Of the nearly dozen men battling before them, five fought for the King.

"Go," he ordered his Captain, taking the lantern from him. Fred signalled those surrounding the King, and in seconds, Stefan and Emily found themselves pushed against the blacksmith wall, Corporal Joseph serving as their shield while the others rushed to the defence of their comrades.

"I need a sword," Stefan said, his gaze drawn back to the blacksmith shop. An old pitted sword worked better than no weapon at all. He took stock of the situation before him; with Fred and his guard joining the fighting, the mercenaries wouldn't last long, but he could hear the pounding of booted feet in the next street and the calls of military men approaching. Without knowing whether friend of foe would appear, Stefan couldn't count on obtaining one of the mercenary's blades. Right now, he, Jo and Emily stood unhindered, but outnumbered in defences. He needed a weapon and hoped he had time enough to retrieve one from below.

"Thirty seconds, Jo," he called as he sprinted back into the shop and to the storage room at the bottom of the stairs.

The first sword he found barely held the blade to the hilt so he tossed it back. The next didn't have the right balance, but the blade looked sound and he didn't waste time finding another. He didn't want Jo to have to choose between guarding Emily and seeing to the safety of the King, knowing the man's attention would remain divided until Stefan returned. So he took up the unbalanced blade and hurried back to his companions.

A swirl of smoke coiled across his vision as he returned to the street and he choked back a cough. Through watering eyes, he could just make out four shadowy figures, two joined together in combat. The other two sprang at him and Stefan raised his sword in defence.

"No!" one cried out, a female voice. Emily reached him first and tried to push him back through the entrance. He faltered, the blade of the second figure missing him by a breath thanks to Emily's shove. Stefan grabbed for the librarian's arm and pulled her stumbling behind him as he dispatched the mercenary. The other soldier fell to a quick stroke from Jo and the younger guard returned grim-faced to the King.

"The Captain?" Stefan asked.

Jo nodded in the direction Stefan had last seen Fred, where now thick smoke obscured vision and flung only brief silhouettes of combatants against a flickering backdrop of intermittent flame.

"Dispatched that group as another mob joined the fray. These two slipped past."

"We have to get off this street," Stefan said. "Do we have no one to help put out these fires?"

Before the Corporal could respond, Fred pounded up the street out of the miasma, Sergeant Darius, Ambrose and a limping Faulk trailing with three other men.

"Too much fighting, Sire," the Captain said in a rush, bloodied blade held loosely at his side. "No one can spare the time to deal with the fires. Townsfolk flee and mercs swarm in after them."

"How many mercs?" he demanded.

One of the new soldiers shook his head.

"Sergeant Sim, Sire, second squad," he introduced himself. Stefan could see little detail to describe the man in the haze of the night besides the bulk of shoulders, a strong sword arm, and a slight beard softening the line of his jaw. "They keep to groups of five to ten from what we've seen, though they incite the populace in some places, creating mob rule. Any time we put down one area, another rises. My guess is there's a full company of mercenaries spread throughout the city."

Stefan cursed, his gaze roving over the destruction of his people's livelihoods. Before he could take charge of rallying his men, Fred spoke again, his focus behind Stefan.

"You have to get the King to safety. Where is this cave?"

It took Stefan a moment to realise his Captain directed his question to Emily, and the librarian replied so softly that had she not stood so close, Stefan doubted he would have heard her.

"In the cliffs to the north-east."

"More specific, girl, so we can find you later."

"We can't split up, Fred," Stefan argued.

"On the contrary, Sire," his Captain refuted. "I need to gather what men remain loyal and rally to your location. I can't do that and guard you."

Stefan growled his frustration, knowing Fred merely spoke truth. He turned to Emily, awaiting her response.

"There's a lone stand of pine trees along the east road past the gate. About a hundred paces beyond, a small trail veers north toward the cliffs. The cave lies there." She took a breath, more audible than her words. "Just before the cliff you'll find a grove of maples with a single large oak. I will wait there and lead you to the cave once the King is secure, assuming you don't take too long."

Fred grunted, a slight smile crooking his lips.

"We'll get you to the gate. If it's guarded by the Prince's men, we'll hold them off while you make a run for it; if it's still held by our men, you'll have a proper guard. Jo, Dari, you stick with the King regardless." Fred fixed his stare on Emily. "If you don't recognise whoever comes for you—"

"I'll keep myself concealed. If I don't know them, I'll stay hidden and if they head for the King, I'll lead them away. But Captain, I don't know any soldiers except those here. What if ..." she coughed. "How do I know the King's men?"

"How many know your name at the castle?"

"Just the library staff."

"No one else?"

She shook her head.

"You said the Prince had you make the copies," Stefan prompted, referring to the Royal Proofs. Emily shook her head again.

"The Prince spoke to Chief Librarian Darien, not to me. Very few people realise that a woman works in the library."

"Good enough," Fred said. "Then any who know your name

are the King's men. Code for any to continue on to the King is 'Emily's perfect memory led us here.' Clear?"

Emily nodded.

"Then let's move out. Form up around the King."

Chapter 4

The tall woman sheathed in a flowing indigo gown reminiscent of twilight glided into the throne room. Her long black hair made of itself a gentle banner in the breeze of her passage, though she kept her pace to a moderate speed, belying the anger that welled up in her breast. Not until one looked into the flinty eyes of the lady wizard, so deep a blue they gleamed nearly black, would one begin to understand the deep fury within her, and few, after that one brief glance, dared to meet her gaze at all.

The self-conceited Prince wearing a forest green cloak trimmed in purest white ermine over a sapphire silk tunic, and currently draped negligently across the throne belonging to his brother, however, prided himself on his ability to meet that fiery stare, never once realising that Destiny spared him the worst of her ire for the simple reason that she had need of him. She couldn't openly rule this land, nor did she desire to, but she could use him to change the fate of the world. But only if she could curb his impatience and incompetence.

"Is it done yet?" Whillim asked, his voice deep and surprisingly strong for all its whining.

"It is not," Destiny replied icily. "Your little soldiers have failed to procure the King."

"What?" Whillim sat up straight in the throne, his golden curls swinging to frame his face. "Where is he?"

"That, my Lord, is what you must learn." She didn't bother to keep the scorn from her voice, knowing that to have a woman question his abilities would goad him to action far quicker than a conciliatory tone. Of all her plans, manipulating Prince Whillim had proved the easiest thus far. She knew when to play to his vanity, appeal to his manhood, or threaten his life. And Whillim, in turn, knew what Destiny could do for him; how she could help secure the crown and place him firmly in the annals of the sovereigns of Dalasham. Together, they could take a throne; separately, she stood alone in a man's world, her astonishing grasp of magic notwithstanding, and he would forever stand in the shadows of greater men. Men like his brother, the King.

Whillim snarled, then shouted for his guard.

Captain Milos, the tall, broad leader of the group of mercenaries that Whillim had bought, stepped into the throne room, his dusky features betraying no emotion.

"You called?"

"Why have you not brought my brother? I issued a very simple order, and if you cannot fulfill so simple a command as 'Bring my brother to me,' then why should I retain your services?" Despite his apparent laziness and obvious love of every luxury that made him seem petty and self-absorbed, Destiny had to admire the air of command Whillim could wrap around himself when he so desired. Captain Milos reacted to that authority, his soldier's stance straightening even further and his words crisp.

"I have men scouring the city. It's only a matter of time before we bring him to heel."

"Why would you have to scour the city?" Whillim demanded. "You assured me that inciting riots would occupy Stefan and his men so that you could take him easily and unawares. I myself saw him to his rooms just before Captain Frederick appeared to inform him of your efforts. Do you suggest now that he turned around and walked past your soldiers out into the city? You do not inspire confidence in your abilities, Captain."

The Captain flicked his gaze briefly to Destiny. She could see his jaw clench as he gritted his teeth, but his rough voice didn't betray his agitation as he returned his attention to the man who wished to rule.

"The King left his chambers, though not through any means we have yet determined," Milos reported. "He dispatched a page and called guards to his room. When we entered shortly thereafter, the room stood empty."

"Impossible!" Whillim cried. "There's no other way out of those rooms."

"I tell you only what I saw, my Lord Prince. The King's chamber lies empty, and none saw him leave."

"What about this page?" Destiny asked softly. "Where did the King dispatch him?" Had she asked anything so overt of the mercenary captain a month previous when she had first approached the man, Destiny knew that her question would have met with scorn and contempt for the mere fact of her gender. But Milos had seen enough of Destiny's power—most especially the device his men had taken to calling The Destiny Seat, which she named the Focus; the tool that would ultimately win Whillim the throne and Destiny true respect, as well as the key to her real goal—that he now granted her, if not respect, than fear. Fear would do, for now.

"To the barracks, where we assume he relayed orders to deal with the riots. When we discovered the King missing, however, we couldn't find the page, nor most of the King's men. If I had to guess, I'd suggest that somehow the King learned somewhat of your plans and fled, taking his men with him."

"Stefan would never flee a fight," Whillim grated.

"Then I don't know what to suggest, save that we continue to scour the city. We'll find him."

Whillim glared at the mercenary, a hard look that Destiny recognised as a pale imitation of her own fierce scowl.

"You had better, Captain. Now get out of here."

"Sir!" Milos sketched a small salute, then strode from the throne room.

Whillim turned his glare on Destiny, but blanched at whatever he saw on her face.

"Without the King, our task grows more difficult," she said from between clenched teeth. "We will have to continue subverting those who hold any power one by one. This will take much longer than we had anticipated and introduces far too much uncertainty."

"Why can't you just ..." Whillim snapped his fingers. "What good is your magic if it takes so long?"

Destiny merely raised a single eyebrow.

"I know, I know," the Prince whined, dropping his persona of a competent leader, knowing it did not impress the wizard in the slightest. "You can't manipulate the masses without first taking their leaders. If only your Destiny Seat would hold more than one person at a time. Then we could get the whole Council in there and half our problems would go away."

Destiny snorted at the simplistic view he took. She had imbued the Focus with a Spell of Forgetfulness, the complexity of its far-reaching implications having taken years of research and long hours of toil and magic to perfect. Such a Spell, and the scope to which she wielded it, required vast amounts of concentration and energy—more than she could summon up on a regular basis and still have any strength left for herself. So she had created the Focus, the green- and rose-veined white quartz crystal that formed the Destiny Seat able to hold and concentrate her power, thus enabling repeated uses without draining her. It had the added benefit that Destiny didn't have to actually oversee the procedure, though she made a point of being in the chamber whenever it required activation. No need to let the Prince know he could also direct the spell.

Her device could alter memory, make others believe what she wished; in this case, that Whillim ruled at Dalasmar, and always had, and that Stefan had died as a child. The stronger the personality of each person seated in her device, the harder for the changed memory to remain in effect until the spell took full control, introducing the possibility that she would have to repeat the procedure. In order for this false memory to become fully accepted by the world, the one it affected most would have to sit the Seat and have his memory erased. Once the spell caused the King to forget his own identity, the best way to keep the new reality from unravelling involved the disposal of the key, and that, the Prince wished for most of all. Thus, once Stefan fell under her powers, the Prince would kill him. But without the King ... Destiny's position, and Whillim's future, lay upon the sharp edge of a knife, and she would have to work very hard indeed to prevent that position from becoming untenable.

Hence her fury when she first entered the throne room.

"Can't you help Milos find Stefan?" Whillim asked, then almost under his breath, as though he asked himself the next question, "How did he escape his room?" He waved his hand in the air, dismissing both questions.

"Never mind that. Milos will have to find Stefan on his own.

We can't keep doing this piecemeal."   Suddenly, Whillim regarded Destiny with an intensity that very nearly impressed her. "Gather those of the Council we haven't yet approached and get them to your Sanctum. I want them sitting in the Destiny Seat as fast as you can get them there. If we can convince them that Stefan is a renegade of some sort, we can use them to find my brother that much quicker. I'll make sure as many soldiers as remain are subjected to the same treatment. We will not lose this battle that easily, Destiny."

   With that, he leapt from his seat and strode purposefully from the throne room. Destiny stared after him a moment, her face set in contemplation. Just when she thought she knew all the depths—shallow though they seemed—of this would-be King, he came up with something intelligent and of use to the wizard. Destiny smiled slowly and went in search of the nearest Council member, her anger morphing into anticipation.

Chapter 5

Em grunted and sucked air in between her clenched teeth. Pain had always brought out the frightened little girl in her, and a sword slash across her abdomen had her whimpering like a child. A shallow wound, received when she had pushed the King away from the sword that sought his blood outside the blacksmith shop, but still painful. At least she had managed to keep the King and his men unaware of her distress. Now that she stood alone, the King safely tucked away in the cave with Corporal Joseph to guard him, she felt free to express her agony, if only to herself.

They had spent a harrowing half-hour getting through the east gate. The Prince's hired men had held the gate, and Captain Frederick and the troops loyal to the King had rushed into a bloody fray to keep their attention while Corporal Joseph and Sergeant Darius whisked King Stefan and Em to the safety of the road beyond. Em had led them to the cave, her every stumble explained away as lack of vision in the nearly moonless night. She had pointed out the lone oak in the maple grove as they passed so that the King's guards might know from where Em planned to watch for others of the King's men. Sergeant Darius had accompanied her from the cave back to the grove, then made his way back to the path off the east road just past the pine trees, intending to conceal himself there and wait to direct the Captain and his comrades to Em's location. He had marvelled that Em could find her way anywhere in the dark, let alone through 'uncharted wilderness', as he called it. "I can find my way to the road, trail's not too hard to follow when you see it," he had said, "but I doubt I could get back to the cave without your guidance." She thought perhaps he exaggerated to make her feel better.

She waited in the maple grove now, a handful of healing moss that had clung through the winter snows smeared across the blade mark beneath her tunic. The smock had taken some of the impact, yet the wound had still bled in a slow trickle until she bound it with a strip of cloth torn from her skirt and wound inside out where less of the grime from the tunnels had marred it. Far from a clean bandage, but all she had to hand.

She took a moment to explore her surroundings, using senses other than her eyes. She had left the small lantern with the King in the cave, and had found her way back to the maple grove through the dark, a long enough journey to ensure optimal night vision, yet the trees, with their limbs already morphing buds into spring leaves, swallowed most of the limited star- and moon-light, and she had to rely on shadowy silhouettes and the scent of the forest. The oak boasted a more massive trunk, and she could discern the difference between oak and maple bark with her hands, so she knew she waited where she had told Captain Frederick to expect her. She worried though, whether Sergeant Darius and the King's guards could find her again in the dark. Then she shook her head at her shortsightedness. *They will have their own lights, of course*, she realised. Or rather hoped.

That didn't stand as her greatest concern though. If, by some unfortunate circumstance, those in the employ of the Prince should venture here in their search for the King, Em would have to abandon her station, and that could lead to endangering the King. She needed a hiding place better than behind the massive trunk of the oak. And the best place she could think of lay above her.

Sometimes, in the warmer months and when she had brief time off from the library, Em would take her exercise by hiking through these woods, which led to her discovery of the cave. Off the beaten path for sure, she had only found it by imagining herself as an explorer from the histories, pushing her way through thick undergrowth and coming upon the hidden cave by pure happenstance. Since that early discovery at age twelve, she had made the cave her special hiding spot, often bringing a bit of food and pretending to picnic there with the animals. She didn't go often enough to lay a permanent trail, but, like her memory for the written word, she could always find her way back. Occasionally in her 're-enactment' of history or myths, she would come to this grove and climb the big oak, lying in wait with her bow and arrow for an unsuspecting brigand or scouting for the army—all make-believe of course, a shy girl playing with her invisible friends and employing her imagination to its fullest. So she knew every suitable handhold to scale the tree and find her perch above where she could wait for the King's soldiers, unseen from any who might venture below.

But the climb would aggravate her wound. She peered around again, hoping for better inspiration. Finding only darkness, she shrugged and turned to the tree. She drew in a great breath and held it, clenched her teeth, then reached for the first handhold. The pain brought tears to her eyes, but she persevered, hauling her way up to what safety she could find and settling in to await the King's men. She alone heard the muted sobs of agony and relief at the end of that climb. Well, her, and whatever ghosts clung to the edges of her imagination, gazing with sympathy at what had become of that twelve-year-old child, keeping her company as time stretched deeper into the night.

***

Fred charged along the east road, trusting to Ambrose at his side to keep watch for the stand of pine trees Emily had named as a marker, though he kept his own awareness extended to everything ahead. Sergeant Sim kept rear guard, and between them ran two dozen of the King's soldiers, five of them sporting fresh wounds hastily bound, as well as three knights and their squires, each afoot.

Sir Edvard and Sir Castel had joined the skirmish mere minutes after Jo and Dari had spirited the King and Emily out the east gate. The two knights, sons of noblemen who preferred the title Sir over Lord, served as Peacekeepers in Dalasmar, and had sought out the riots in an attempt to restore order. When they came upon Fred and his outnumbered men near the gate, they had flung themselves into the fray, surprising the mercenaries from behind. Shortly after, Sir

Pietor, a prominent merchant recently elevated to the noble ranks, had emerged with his squire from the smoke of the forges to help finish off the last of the opposition guarding access to the city. Fred took quick stock of those standing with him, then dispatched Ambrose, the two Peacekeeper squires, and Sergeant Sim's two remaining men to scout the city limits for loyal guards.

"You have five minutes," he had informed them. "Bring who you find, then we go after the King."

The five had rushed to obey.

"Go after the King where?" Sir Edvard had asked, breathing deep.

Fred realised that none of the knights truly understood the situation yet.

"Prince Whillim hired a band of mercenaries to distract us while he attempted to usurp King Stefan's position."

Edvard just stared at him mutely, but Sir Pietor snorted his disbelief.

"Whillim couldn't oust the King, even with hired thugs. How does he expect to gain any support from the nobles, let alone the commoners?"

"Why does the King flee?" Sir Castel had added, sheathing his sword after wiping it clean on a dead man's tunic. "Why do you fight in such small numbers?"

Fred shook his head. "It's somewhat more complicated than that, my Lords. Suffice it to say that Whillim has some form of magic he found somewhere that he believes can help him take over, and that we were taken unawares and nearly unprepared for such an action. A ... fortuitous warning enabled the King to escape, but gave no time for coordination. The rest I leave to the King to explain."

"Kelvin made it to the barracks with the King's message," Sergeant Sim had added, referring to the King's page. "I and my men were already on duty, and others preparing to move out as we left. I only saw two teams of third squad on our way here, both repelling attack. I lost the rest of my team before you showed up. Whatever Mercenary Company the Prince hired is good, but so are we. The Prince won't succeed, no matter what magic he's dredged up."

"I hope you're right, Sergeant," Fred had murmured. The sound of a raven caw swallowed his statement, followed by

45

Ambrose and a squad of liveried King's men. A moment later, Sergeant Sim's men had returned with another handful of soldiers, then the squires led forward another squad, plus a dozen of the Watch, all stained with sweat and soot.

Fred counted them and made a hasty plan.

"The Watch stays to hold the gate. You find any more of the Watch, put them on fire detail, but the gate remains a priority. I can't believe even Whillim is stupid enough to let the city burn if he intends to try his hand at rule. If the Watch is on fire detail with none of the King's soldiers in sight, the mercenaries should leave them be. Faulk, you stay too." Faulk, his injured leg held gingerly, didn't protest. "You recognise any more of King Stefan's men, you have them hold up in Marrick's stable until I can contact them, but no more than two days." Marrick's stood two blocks away, a stable often used to house livestock during the Spring and Fall Fairs. "If you don't hear anything by then, send them to Cranshaw Fortress." Faulk nodded his understanding. "The rest of you, come with me."

And off they ran.

"Sir," Ambrose called now, nodding ahead to the pine grove. Fred grunted, then measured his paces. He had figured on fewer than a hundred paces, given Emily's shorter height, but the girl must have estimated the Captain's gait, for nearly a hundred paces past the grove, he heard the sound of a raven's call. They slowed as Sergeant Darius stepped into the road ahead and gestured to a little path. The smudge of orange from the fires in the city behind them provided additional light to see when Dari turned and urged them to follow. Fred did so, bringing his small force with him.

When they had escaped the road far enough so that tree branches masked the path back, Dari stopped.

"Do we wait for more, Captain?" he asked.

Fred shook his head.

"This is it for now. I've left instructions with Faulk for any others."

Dari nodded. "Then I'll take you to Emily and she'll get us to the King."

"A moment, sir," Sir Castel said before Dari could move them forward. "Who is this Emily?"

"She helped us escape the Prince's notice," Fred replied.

"And you trust this woman to safeguard the King?" His

dubious tone suggested the folly of such an idea.

"I do," Fred answered shortly. Before Castel could make any more disparaging remarks, the Captain looked at Dari. "Lead on, Sergeant."

***

"Emily?" called a hesitant voice quietly.

Em, having heard the faint rustling of long-fallen leaves further back along the path, tried to see the speaker below her perch in the oak tree, alarmed that someone had crept up so close when she had thought the intruder much farther away. She could only make out a silhouette with a sword at his hip.

"It's Dari ... Sergeant Darius," the shadow said. "Emily and her perfect memory led me here." Em could hear a smile in the phrase.

"Up here, Sergeant," she replied in relief, grinning to herself as he jumped at her disembodied voice right over his head. She began the painful process of lowering herself out of the branches, hoping he would mistake her hiss of distress as the sound of her smock rubbing against the bark.

"I have the Captain and some two dozen men with me," he said, the darker blackness of his body against the trunk turning to gesture to the men in his wake. "She's here," he added as Captain Frederick's large bulk joined the slighter man, other shadows filing in behind.

Someone lit a covered lantern, its little light terribly bright to Em after an hour or so staring intently into the darkness, waiting for this moment and dreading every tiny sound of the forest and its myriad nocturnal inhabitants for fear that mercenaries should discover her before the King's men. She gained the ground, nearly bloodying her lip as she bit down in an effort to keep her groan of pain from escaping. Her wound had pulled and scraped against the tree trunk, and she thought perhaps that little trickle of moisture she felt had more blood than sweat in it.

"Captain," she acknowledged softly, then quailed as the man holding the lantern shoved it nearly in her face.

"This little mite?" he asked with scorn. "You entrusted this girl with the King's safety?"

"Sir Castel," Frederick rumbled, "This is the woman who warned the King of his brother's treachery and found a secured

47

escape route."

"So you've only *her* word for all this trouble?" The man, smaller than the Captain, nevertheless frightened Em with his imposing stature as he loomed over her. She tried to school her face into passive respect, knowing his noble status by the Captain's address, but feared she failed miserably.

"I have King Stefan's orders, Sir," Frederick stated, bringing a moment's hesitation to the knight's eyes. "If you wish to question him on our actions and Emily's presence, then I suggest you allow her to do her job and lead us to the King so that you may express your concern directly to our liege."

"Step back, Castel," another man spoke up, coming to stand in the light, a younger man matching his stride. Em guessed this second speaker also claimed knightly status, and his silent aide looked the part of a squire. "Can't you see you're frightening the lass?" Sir Castel sneered, but backed off. The second knight turned to study Em. "There, my dear, now why don't you lead on then?" His tone tried for conciliatory, though Em, quite familiar with such sentiments, knew it for amused tolerance; a nobleman playing along with a child's attempt to fit in to a grown-up world. Or a woman's attempt to find some small status in a man's eyes. She tolerated it because she had no choice; women stood as subservient to men in this kingdom, and she accepted such. But she knew from the histories, and indeed from her own childhood, that not all lands believed such, and sometimes it grated that men like these knights could find no fault in their attitudes.

She turned to the Captain.

"The way is rather narrow, sir," she began, her voice small. "Do you wish for all these men to accompany us and thereby leave a greater chance of someone finding and following our trail, or would you prefer I led but a few. Or fetch the King back here instead?"

"Fetch the King ...?" Sir Castel nearly choked on the notion of a commoner doing anything so undignified to royalty. "No one *fetches* the King for any reason. *He* summons—"

"Enough," Frederick snapped. He turned an angry gaze to Em and she struggled not to shrink back in alarm. "Would we all fit in the cave?"

"Yes, Captain, but just barely."

"Then take us there."

She turned and moved off, trusting them to follow.

After a handful of minutes, they could see the dark wall of the cliff rise up as the trees thinned. Em took them east to the edge of the cave. She paused and pointed it out to Frederick. He sent out his now familiar raven caw, which Corporal Joseph answered, stepping out into the lantern's glow, sword bare in his hand, though not threatening as he confirmed his Captain's presence.

The King followed behind, whereupon the three more richly dressed men—all knights Em realised—bowed and the soldiers saluted, a tension she had not fully noticed until that moment lifting.

"Your Majesty, it is good to see you safe," said the knight who had patronized Em.

"Edvard," the King greeted.

Em leaned against the cliff wall, letting the reunion slide past her. Now that they had gathered in the more sheltered confines of the cave's entrance, Sir Castel unhooded his lantern completely, and Em could see the men better. Some, she saw, had sustained injuries. Without really thinking about it, she scanned the ground nearby, spotting some likely spring blooms from plants she knew to have healing capabilities. She moved to gather some, gritting her teeth and clutching at her abdomen as her own wound screamed in protest.

"Emily?"

She glanced up in surprise, seeing Sergeant Darius at her side.

"The men," she whispered. "They're hurt. These can help."

"Are you well?" he asked. Em just blinked up at him. *Up?* When had she dropped to her knees? Ah, to gather the plants, of course. *Why can't I think straight?* she wondered.

"These can help." Had she already said that?

Dari took her elbow to help her to her feet. She swayed against him, then hissed in pain.

"You're hurt!" he exclaimed. She tried to brush him off.

"We need to get these ground up and mixed with water to make a poultice," she whispered, moving back toward the soldiers with the leaves clutched in her hands, Dari at her side. She rather feared that only his insistent grip on her elbow kept her upright, but she tried to hide her weakness.

As they reached the cave again, Em thought the knight had

doused the lantern, leaving them in darkness. Then realised that the light still shone; her vision had narrowed to a grey tunnel. She stopped and turned to the moustached man beside her, his face starting to blur.

"I believe I may have to sit," she managed before her knees gave way. She heard startled shouts before all faded into oblivion.

***

Stefan had waited impatiently in Emily's cave with Jo, chafing at his unexpected situation. More than once, he had forced himself to curb his desire to make his way back to Riverbend, demand answers. He indulged himself with useless pacing instead, counting off forty tense strides before turning and tracing his path again. Jo, steady as always, kept his peace, no doubt attuned to each frustrated slap of boot on stone behind him as he peered out into the night.

Stefan disliked having split up from Fred and the rest of his guards, though he understood the reason. And leaving Emily out in the dark woods alone further irritated his sense of chivalry, but he had to admit that she had a sound plan.

When the young librarian arrived with Fred, three knights, and a couple dozen soldiers, Stefan didn't know whether he should feel relieved that these people had escaped great harm or worried that so few stood in the group. Fred assured him that Faulk would see to any stragglers and that the Watch would oversee getting the fires under control. The smudge of orange haze on the horizon above the tree tops had lessened as Stefan and Jo had waited, so he assumed the Watch had managed well enough. He hoped his soldiers fared as well.

"Are you hurt, Sire?" Sir Edvard queried. Stefan gave the man a quizzical frown, to which the knight indicated a smear of drying blood on the front of Stefan's nutmeg tunic, visible now that they dared risk the full light of the lantern. Stefan shook his head as he glanced down.

"Not my blood," he said, wondering when he had picked it up. Although the heat of battle often made it difficult to keep track of everyone's location, he didn't recall anyone coming that close to him. Except when he had returned from the smithy with his borrowed sword and Emily had pushed him out of the way of a

50

mercenary's blade. That weapon had missed him thanks to her quick thinking.

He turned to look for her now, and saw her emerging from the shadows, Dari's arm supporting her as she clutched something in her hands. He blinked in astonishment as she suddenly slid from Dari's grasp to the earth, then he leapt into action as he discerned what must have happened. Whether at some point when Stefan had hurried back into the smithy looking for a weapon, or when she had pushed her King out of harm's way, Emily had sustained an injury.

"What happened?" Fred hissed, pushing Stefan back, his blade bared as he searched the darkness for whatever danger had felled the librarian.

"She's hurt," Dari explained. "Don't know how or when, but I think it's a gut wound."

Stefan shoved Fred out of the way.

"She got it defending me," the King said, dropping to his knees beside the prone woman. The two Peacekeeper knights objected, but Stefan waved off their disapproval.

"I don't know that we can get to her wound without ..." Dari paused, trying to find the right words. "Um ... revealing more of her," he finished quietly.

Stefan gently moved her arms, which had wrapped themselves around her middle, out of the way to better see the damage. He noticed the plants in her hands.

"What's this?" he asked.

"She said they'd make a poultice to help with the soldiers' injuries, Sire," Dari told him.

"She went looking for herbs to help others when she's got a great bloody gash herself?" Fred demanded.

Stefan shook his head, but somehow, even though he barely knew Emily, he could see her doing just that.

"Let's get her to the cave," Stefan said. "See if we can't get her tended to. And the other wounded too. Dari, you know how to make those plants into a poultice?"

"She said to grind them up and mix them with water."

"I've seen the like," said Sir Pietor from beside the King as he joined them. Stefan glanced up at the Merchant noble. "Back when I'd go on runs to deliver goods, some of the hired guards from the caravans showed me about making up healing ointments and such."

"Then you're our medic," Stefan declared. "We'll tend to the wounded and figure out our next move." He rose, stepping out of the way, knowing that, while his guards might allow him to get his hands dirty on seeing to the well-being of those in his care, the knights—or at least Edvard and Castel—would not understand. Right now, he needed every advantage and semblance of strength and power he could muster. He couldn't afford to show any special treatment, even to those who had undoubtedly saved his life.

Stefan moved back toward the cave, keeping out of the way yet sheltered while Fred and Dari saw to moving Emily and the men, and Sir Pietor dealt with making and applying the poultice. Edvard and Castel joined the King, along with their squires, Sergeant Sim and Ambrose. When Fred joined them, Stefan glanced at the knights, making sure to include them in the conversation.

"We need a plan of action. Somewhere to regroup that Willi won't find. I need reports from Dalasmar, find out who's loyal, who's in hiding, and most of all, what strange magic Willi has found that makes him think this usurpation will work. He's ambitious but lazy. If he hadn't thought he could get away with taking the crown, he would never have tried."

"How do you know he's using magic?" Edvard asked.

"Emily overheard some of the mercenaries in the library."

"Wait, you're basing this whole retreat on her word?" Castel demanded incredulously. "Who is this woman?"

"Junior Assistant to the Chief Librarian," Stefan replied shortly, ignoring the outraged spluttering of the two knights. "She warned me that Willi's paid soldiers had orders to take me after acquiring the Royal Proofs."

"And you believed her?" Edvard wanted to know. "How do you know she's not part of this whole plot, sent to lure you out here, away from the defences of the castle?"

"I don't," Stefan replied, startling them all into a moment of silence. Indeed, Stefan had had time to ponder that very question while he waited for Emily to bring Fred and his guards. She seemed very sincere, but that did not mean that Willi—or more likely a wizardly accomplice of the Prince—couldn't use her as an unwitting tool. He hoped she didn't act as a willing instrument of his downfall. Either way, he did not intend to take the mysterious young woman at her word alone.

"That's why I need more intel," Stefan said. "Until I really know what Willi plans, or if he plans anything—"

"That seems rather likely, given the mercenaries who torched the streets, Sire," Fred interrupted.

"But who's to say they work for Willi, Fred? Who besides Emily has corroborated that?"

Fred nodded once to accept the rebuke and acknowledge the truth of those words.

"I need information, and then I need to go where no one will expect." Stefan studied the men in front of him, giving the two knights extra attention. "And false trails," he continued. "With you two good knights in charge of a handful of men each heading out in different directions, we'll create multiple trails should any come looking for me."

"And where will you go, Sire?" Castel asked.

Stefan looked at Fred.

"That will depend on what we can learn from the castle."

"With all due respect, Your Majesty," Fred objected, "if Emily is at all correct in any of the details of tonight's troubles, we need to get you away from here quickly. If I could suggest an alteration to your thoughts?"

Stefan kept his grin to himself, knowing that, had they spoken in private, Fred wouldn't have hesitated to voice his objections far more strenuously and vocally. Instead, he maintained a stoic visage and invited Fred to share his ideas.

"We send out the false trails, and a true one. We get you to safety, as you suggest, and the information comes to you; you don't wait here for it. We find that place to regroup, but we go now. No one but those in your company will know where you have gone." He turned stony eyes on the knights. "That includes you two."

Fred held up a sword-callused hand to forestall the angry objections. "The fewer who know the King's location at this uncertain time, the safer I can keep him. Once the King establishes a rendezvous, he sends out scouts to gather those loyal to him, like you two. Because if, by some unhappy circumstance, either of you is captured as you lay a false trail, I don't want those who have you to find out anything. I don't say this to suggest either of you would willingly betray your King. But if the Prince deals in some form of magic that steals memories and can allow him to take Stefan's place, then it's not

53

beyond the realm of possibility that said magic could draw the information from you. I don't know if such a thing's possible, but I don't intend to take that chance."

After a moment, Edvard nodded slowly.

"A wise precaution, though hopefully an unnecessary one."

Castel continued to scowl, but he could find no fault with the Captain's reasoning.

Fred shifted his attention back to Stefan. "Then may I ask the King, if this strategy is to his liking, how he wishes to allocate his assets?"

"Four groups, Fred," Stefan replied instantly, having already thought through a course of action while Fred spoke. "Each knight will lead a force of ten men. Edvard will head south to the Ford, Castel north to his holding at Calsburg, and Pietor will head further east to Lord Gregor at Marlak Castle. I take five with me. If Willi's looking, he's more likely to dismiss the smaller group. He'd insist on a larger escort, and would assume the same of me. What's the likelihood, Fred, of four men re-entering the city and re-emerging with mounts?"

"Horses, Sire?"

"Not for everyone, but one or two per group." Stefan noted the slight nod from Castel, though doubted the knight truly saw the benefit. Stefan didn't ask for the comfort of the nobility.

"If we still hold the east gate, it's possible, though I don't know that I see the advantage," Fred admitted.

"It might help confuse the numbers, but more important, it will mean that, while we split up the injured, none will cast too great a burden on their companions. Here's what I want then," the King continued. "One man from each group goes to fetch mounts. If they can obtain more than eight without unnecessary risk, do so. If Faulk has any more men to aid us, bring them. I want Sergeant Sim to go back to the city for information. He and Faulk will work together to learn what we need to know. In two days time, once we have established a new base, I will send a soldier to the west gate to retrieve Sim and Faulk, two hours before noon. Based on the information they gather, we'll make a new plan. Edvard, Castel, when I know more, I'll send word to you. You will know it's from me by the phrase 'Emily's perfect memory led us here'."

Fred twisted his lips in wry amusement, though the knights merely frowned their lack of understanding.

"Until we know what's going on, if Willi really has instigated a revolt, you will not tell anyone of tonight's events. I don't want an unnecessary panic. Tell your hosts when you arrive at your destinations that you were sent on orders from the King and expect hospitality for at least three nights. Any questions?"

"How do you want the men allocated, Your Majesty?" Fred asked.

"Each knight takes their squire and eight soldiers. Castel and Pietor take two wounded each, and Edvard takes the last. I take Fred, Dari, Jo, Ambrose, and Emily with me."

"The girl?" Edvard started. "But surely, Sire—"

"I take her because, if she does work for Willi, I need to know what she knows. If she's with me, she's not with him and I can keep an eye on her. If, however, she does not work for my brother, she has valuable information on my castle that Willi does not possess and that we might need should we get a chance to quietly infiltrate Dalasmar's walls."

"What information?" Castel wanted to know, but Stefan shook his head. The knight didn't need to know about the hidden tunnels.

"Go pick your men," he ordered.

When the knights moved away, Stefan looked at his loyal guardsmen.

"Thoughts?" he asked.

"Can you trust them?" Sim queried, surprising Stefan. "If the Prince hopes to take your place, he must have some backing. How do you know it's not one of these knights?"

"I don't. That's part of why we're splitting up."

"And why you're sending me on a fact-finding mission, rather than one of your own guards?" Sim smiled slightly at the King's regard. "I am the only soldier standing here not on your personal guard, Your Majesty. With all that's going on, or might be going on, I understand that trust is a rare commodity. In your position, I would not trust any I didn't personally know, and even then .... I do not envy my liege."

Stefan coughed out a laugh.

"You're a good man, Sim. You'll do well."

Sim nodded, both men silently acknowledging that Stefan had not answered the Sergeant's question.

"You go in with our horse thieves, Sim. Find Faulk and explain the plan. Fred, have Jo go for our mounts. We'll meet

55

where the path emerges from the woods on the east road. After that, we'll see where the wind takes us."

As Sim and Fred moved out, Ambrose, silent until that moment, whispered to the King.

"I think I know a good place to the west, Sire. A farmstead my ma used to visit. She and the Goodwife were friends, though both have long since passed. The Prince would never dream you'd go rural, and it's out of the way enough that none would think to look there."

"Have you visited recently?"

"Not since I turned nine."

"Perfect."

Chapter 6

Destiny let her gaze rove over the Council Chambers from her shadowed corner. Whillim had called a session for this morning, intending to inform the leaders of Dalasmar's Council about the 'renegade' soldiers, led by an erratic person falsely claiming blood connection to the royal house; soldiers who had incited revolt and led last night's riots. Destiny herself had spent the greater portion of the dark night tracking down Council members in residence and taking them to her Sanctum to alter their memories. While she had located many, she had not found all. And of the leaders from the city, Milos' men had only brought her two. That left about a half dozen men who could upset the Prince's immediate plan, could they but speak their truth.

Destiny waited in her corner for any of these unconverted to arrive. Two of Milos' mercenaries waited for her signal at the entrance to the Council Chambers, ready to waylay those she pointed out.

Nearly three-quarters of the Council had arrived before Destiny saw her first quarry. A tall, spare man with long, elegant fingers suited to his profession, Jamison Goldsmith, second seat to the merchant class after Sir Pietor of Merchant Hill, managed three steps into the room before the mercenary guards quietly intercepted him. Destiny took quick steps to reach them, attempting to put the man enough at ease that he wouldn't create a scene.

"Master Jamison, the Prince asked that I have a word with

you," she said, her false smile aimed to distract.

The man narrowed his eyes in annoyance, but waited for her to continue.

"This way, if you please." She took his elbow, making the gesture look natural, a gentleman escorting a lady back out into the hall. "Have you seen Sir Pietor yet this morning?" she queried, for he too stood among those missing from Destiny's list. Whillim also had that list; he would point out any others who arrived before Destiny returned for the mercenaries to detain until the lady wizard could deal with them as well.

"I have not, madam," Jamison replied stiffly. "Might I inquire, Lady, as to your ... um ... position with the Prince? Why has Prince Whillim called us to session, and not King Stefan?"

"That is precisely what I wish to discuss, Master Jamison." Her grip tightened as she led him toward her Sanctum, one flight up. "I am Destiny, the Prince's wizard."

She felt Jamison tense, but they had already passed out of sight of most of the people below. She spoke a word that stilled the man's tongue and kept his feet moving. It took but a moment to reach her Sanctum.

"You will find your answers here, Goldsmith," she said, all pretense of hospitality gone as she opened her door and drew him in. He tried to resist—she could feel his will pulling at her spell—but he did not succeed. Destiny brought him to the quartz chair, facets of the stone sparkling in the morning sun streaming in through the wide window. She turned him about, and pushed him off-balance so that he fell into the Destiny Seat. She let go her binding spell and the man attempted to rise, but the Focus took hold of him.

"Just relax, Jamison Goldsmith, and you will have your answers."

Destiny walked behind the Seat, placing her hand on the crown of the chair to activate her device. A pulse of her will spread through the Focus and the quartz crystal began to glow, lit from within by her encased power.

A moment only, as the Focus flashed from gold to rose to pure white, and Jamison Goldsmith's perception of reality shifted.

Destiny pulled her hand from the Destiny Seat and moved to stand in front of Jamison once more.

"Are you well, sir?" she asked in mock sympathy.

"I dare say," he faltered, looking up at her, his eyes clearing from confusion to mere uncertainty. "My Lady, I do beg your pardon, but, if I may ask—"

"You were just telling me of the King's summons," Destiny prompted. Jamison stood from the Destiny Seat, not fully realising his actions. Indeed, all memory of the Focus would fade once he left the room, and the spell urged that none linger within this, Destiny's Sanctum. She followed him from the room, taking his arm again and leading him to the Council Chamber.

"Yes, of course," Jamison's eyes cleared fully as they headed back down the stairs. "King Whillim's summons, yes." Destiny kept her satisfied smirk to herself. "I was merely speculating on the cause of the riots last night. I supposed that to be the reason for this early session. Ah, here we are, Lady ...?" He frowned at her, trying to recall.

"Destiny, Master Jamison. Lady Destiny."

"Of course."

"Do go in, Master Goldsmith," she urged, pushing him just a little harder than necessary to rid herself of the man. She saw that Milos' men had detained another personage from her list and moved to gather her next convert.

"Good day, Lady Destiny," Jamison called after her, but she hardly noticed.

"Ah, Sir Byndorf," she said to the waiting man, taking his elbow. "The Prince asked that I have a word with you."

Jamison watched her a moment, then shrugged and moved into the Council Chambers.

***

Four still remained; three knights and a nobleman. Destiny didn't know where to find these four Council members, but they had failed to come to Whillim's meeting and did not answer at their homes. She suspected they either aided the King, or had gone into hiding, having discerned their danger. At least Whillim had recognised the problem and sought to rectify the situation.

"The renegade clearly has allies," Whillim said now to the gathered Council, pushing back the edge of his green cloak, his golden hair gleaming among the white ermine lining it, to rest a

59

fist on his hip. He stood in front of the chair set on the raised dais reserved for the King, striking his pose. "While my soldiers search him out, I must ask each and every one of you for vigilance. Should you see anyone suspicious, you must arrange for their apprehension, even should that person hold a high station. Surely some of you have taken note of conspicuous absences from among this very advisory body. It grieves me to think that some of our own may have thrown in with our enemy. I do not wish to believe so, and hope that my fears prove unfounded. But until we can account for all those loyal to us, I trust you all to keep a sharp eye and cooperate in every way possible to help us resolve the situation. I therefore ask that, those of you with men-at-arms in the city, join us in hunting down this renegade who would take my place. We must bring him to justice and make him answer for lives lost, homes and businesses burned."

Some of the more conservative members grumbled quietly to themselves, but most, Destiny noted, nodded agreement.

"I have received word," Whillim continued, "that a number of horses went missing last night, mainly from establishments near the east gate. This occurred not long after many of my gate guards died defending the city. The renegade is sorely mistaken if he thinks we will allow such violence to go unanswered. We will therefore begin our search for this man there, at the east gate. You will coordinate with Captain Milos on how best to deploy your men-at-arms. Rest assured, gentlemen, we will apprehend this fugitive and all who follow him, and restore peace to Dalasmar."

A little over the top, Destiny thought, but the Councillors seemed to hang on his every word.

Whillim soon dissolved the meeting, leaving the mercenary captain to effect the search for Stefan. Destiny doubted that the King still remained in Dalasmar, yet she had trouble believing that he would leave so obvious a trail as that suggested by the mess left at the east gate. However, he had had little time to plan anything, and a retreat that implied more haste than deception did fit with the timeline.

She wondered, not for the first time, just how the King had known to flee, and how he had achieved the task. If they could apprehend someone close to the King and get them to talk before she put them in her device, Destiny would have some answers, and she could better strategize for the future. She had made Whillim aware of the advantages of capture over slaughter, and she trusted the mercenary captain and his new command of the noblemen's men-at-arms would follow the stricture to inform the wizard immediately of any they detained. Because if they didn't, they would learn the folly of incurring Destiny's wrath.

***

"The Prince has too bloody many men out here," Faulk grumbled. Sim just nodded his agreement, his back to the wall of the building across from Marrick's Stable.

Faulk had gathered another double handful of men by the time Sim had reached him early that morning and Sim and Faulk had sent them after the knights. They had decided that Captain Frederick's alternate of Cranshaw Fortress, the King's private retreat, no longer served as a suitable rendezvous point as they couldn't guarantee the loyalty of those within, for surely the Prince would send men to search there soon. So they had sent the majority on to Sirs Edvard and Castel as the nearest safe havens.

Now, as the two coordinated another sweep of the area, the presence of yet another group of mercenaries forced them back into the shadows. When the hired thugs finally melted out of sight, Sim edged around the corner, his eyes scanning their surroundings. He kept his posture unassuming so as not to attract attention, blending in with the regular citizens of Riverbend. He and Faulk had donned crafters' garb, their livery stashed in the Stable for later retrieval.

A slight figure detached itself from the alley across the way, fleet enough, yet lacking the unobtrusive grace a street thief might possess. It drew Sim's gaze and he tracked the movement until he caught a glimpse of a pale young face, one that he recognised from the barracks.

"It's Kelvin, the King's page," he whispered, lips barely moving. Faulk grunted his acknowledgement, and even though he mostly faced away from the boy, Sim had no doubt that the guard watched Kelvin's progress as keenly as Sim did. When the furtive figure slipped into the next alley, Faulk pushed himself off the wall.

"I've got him," he told Sim, straightening his tunic as he settled into the posture of a wary citizen who had survived the previous evening's tumult with only minor injuries. Sim knew Faulk's leg pained him, but the soldier pushed the pain aside, as many shop keepers on this street had done after they fought to save their homes and livelihoods from the mobs and fires. "I suggest you continue up Crafter's Lane and see who else you can spot, sir."

Without waiting for the Sergeant to reply, Faulk sauntered toward the frightened page. Sim grinned and pushed off in the other direction.

He had not gone ten paces before he saw the men-at-arms sweeping in from the direction of the east gate. They had joined with the mercenaries patrolling the area. Sim glanced toward Faulk, but the other man had just slipped into the alley after Kelvin, and Sim couldn't see him anymore. The King's guard would have to take care of himself.

"If I might have your attention, everyone," a large voice bellowed, bringing Sim's focus back to the men-at-arms. They bore at least three different liveries that Sim could discern, but the man calling for attention wore a soldier's garb lacking any identifying house. A mercenary leading the soldiers of noble houses, Sim thought in dismay. Although most of Riverbend's citizenry would not understand the significance of such a thing, Sim recognised the Prince's hand in this chain of command; a hired man in charge of troops supposedly loyal to the royal court did not bode well.

"We need information," the man went on when he felt he had garnered enough attention. "Someone stole horses from this area last night, and we need to know who. If anyone knows anything about this, step forward now and speak your mind."

Sim looked around and saw others do the same. No doubt, most wondered if their neighbour would step forward, or if they saw any benefit to relaying gossip. It didn't seem likely that anyone actually had such information—other than Sim and Faulk—but that didn't always stop someone from making something up. Or clamming up so as not to draw the attention of authorities. Sim kept his eye on the men-at-arms as they unobtrusively moved to block off the roads leading from the district.

"These thieves have acted against the King," the mercenary

called, drawing angry grumbles from those around Sim. For his part, Sim knew others would mistake his scowl for indignation at anyone daring to harm Dalasham's leader. Few would mark it as contempt for Prince Whillim and frustration at his attempt to usurp the true King. Few even knew such a coup had taken place. But the mercenary knew the reaction his words would bring; he knew that King Stefan had the love of his people, and he purposefully used the term *King* rather than naming the person he really meant.

"You, boy!" a second mercenary called out next to the leader, a paler version of the man in charge, with a hawk stare beneath dark brows that pierced the shadows. He had his arm thrust out to indicate a youth who had emerged from a darkened alley. Before the lad or the man who moved to his side could retreat back into the darkness, yet another mercenary, short and wiry, his shock of red hair pleated in two braids, pushed forward and placed himself close to the pair. The second merc and the leader whispered for a moment before the man in charge gestured, and his crony brought Kelvin and Faulk forward.

"What's this about?" Faulk demanded. "Why single out my son? He done nothin' wrong."

Sim admired Faulk's ability to alter his demeanour and accent to that of a simple labourer, and Kelvin did his part well as he cowered at Faulk's side, a frightened child clutching at his father's tunic. Of course, Kelvin's fear was very real, a ten-year-old child confronted by large and hostile soldiers.

"Your son was in the Palace last night," the merc who had called Kelvin out said. "Sneakin' around the King's chambers."

"It's my job," Kelvin said, voice high but steady. "I'm King's page."

Sim suppressed his grimace. Now they would take him for certain. These men, or more precisely Prince Whillim, couldn't have anyone running around ready to cry out King Stefan's name. But what could Sim do? Only he and Faulk to stand against thirty or so men-at-arms and a half-dozen mercenaries?

"You ain't no page," the mercenary sneered.

"You callin' my son a liar?" Faulk demanded.

"I'm calling you both suspicious," the leader said firmly. "You are hereby taken into custody to be brought before the King."

"And which King is that?" Faulk inquired. Sim shook his head, jaw clenched tight. "You mean King Stefan, rightful ruler of Dalasham, or his traitorous brother, Prince Whillim—" Before Faulk could say any more, a man in the copper and red livery of Sir Byndorf stepped up and clouted him over the head.

"How dare you spout your lies against King Whillim," he fumed. The mercenary leader glanced around, taking note of how the people of Riverbend reacted to this display. Most seemed confused, though some appeared guarded.

"Take them in," the merc commanded. Turning to the rest of those gathered, he spoke again.

"No doubt you have heard rumours and wild stories since the troubles last night. I assure you that the King will do everything in his power to calm your fears. We will detain instigators of revolt and violence like this man and his son, and once we find those responsible for all this confusion, rest assured, we will deal with them in a suitable fashion. In the meantime, we appreciate your cooperation and assume your compliance with the King's orders."

Sim's hands ached from clenched fists, but he didn't dare voice any objections. His job was to inform the King of what transpired in his city. He couldn't do that imprisoned, or worse, ensorcelled into believing the crap this mercenary spouted.

"In the furtherance of seeking a peaceful resolution to these problems," the mercenary went on, sounding as though he quoted someone else, "we need to speak to anyone with information about the theft of those horses last night. We will begin by questioning those of you here. If you have nothing to hide, you need have no fear."

Sim barely contained his snort of disbelief, but he heard a similar grunt of derision from the man beside him, a hooded figure who had sidled closer to Sim as the merc had spoken. He turned to stare at this man now.

"I don't know what the hell's going on," he began so quietly that Sim knew he spoke for his ears alone, "but I sure as shit know Whillim is no King of mine." The man shifted just enough for Sim to see his dark eyes and recognise the angular face. "I can tell you're no more eager than I to speak to those thugs, and though you wear the clothes of a crafter, I recognise a King's soldier when I see one. King Stefan's soldier."

"And how is it, Lord Prichard, that you stand here disguised in stained traveller's garb rather than with your fellow Council members up at the castle?" Sim replied, his voice equally soft as his gaze roved over the street.

"Let's just say I saw who came hunting Council members in the confusion of the riots last night, and felt caution a better course of action than blindly following others to where I would forget things of vital importance."

Sim focused on the nobleman at his side.

"It seems, sir, that we might have something to discuss," he ventured.

"As far from here as possible," Prichard agreed.

When two men-at-arms approached a moment later, Sim and Prichard had shifted stances enough that none would know they had spoken.

"What's your business here?" one asked Sim, his voice polite, his eyes a little wide and uncertain. He barely looked old enough to shave.

"Just passing up the street, sir, on my way up Crafter's Lane to the dye-maker for some colours for the wife's wool. I'm gonna be in for it as it is, being so late back and all." He grinned at the man, drawing the tiniest smile in return.

"Do you live nearby?" the man asked and, before waiting for a response, "Do you know anything about the stolen horses?"

"Until you all stopped us, I didn't know anything about stolen beasts, sir. Wouldn't know a good horse to steal from a bad one. Had a nice looking horse once to pull my cart, turned up lame not twenty minutes out of the city, and me sitting there atop my cart with bolts of cloth and blankets and sweaters and all and no horse to get me to market. Damn pitiful day, that one. Horse I got now looks like it been through some nasty scrapes, natty thing as it is, but it hasn't left me stranded in the three years I had it."

Sim watched as the man's eyes started to glaze over and launched into another account of a crafter's woes a moment before the man-at-arms raised a hand.

"You hear anything, you let us know, right?" he asked.

"For certain, sir. I hear anything suspicious, I'll be calling. Not good for business having a city in turmoil. What's the use of crafting my goods if there's nowhere to sell 'em? Need a stable kingdom for that."

"Indeed," the man replied absently. "You can be about your business."

"My thanks, sir," Sim called even as the man hurried away to

65

speak to the next detainee.

"Nicely done," Prichard said as Sim passed him and started to walk away up Crafter's Lane. Sim knew the nobleman would follow at a more leisurely pace.

In the end, the men-at-arms took away three other people; a farrier, a saddler, and a tavern owner, although as far as Sim knew, none of them actually had any information about the horses he and the others had procured for the King. He wondered what fate Whillim had in mind for them, and he worried about Faulk and Kelvin, and whatever strange magic the Prince had that had forced King Stefan into retreat.

Chapter 7

Faulk expected the soldiers to take them to the audience chamber, or even the dungeon. Perhaps just to the barracks. Anywhere for questioning or torture or simply to get them out of the way. He had not thought that he and Kelvin, along with the three other captives, would end up waiting in one of the antechambers not far from the Council Chambers. Under guard, of course. Although he wouldn't have known what to say to his fellow detainees anyway, the mercenary guards—the men-at-arms having left them at the castle's entrance—made it clear that they'd tolerate no discourse among their prisoners.

Faulk's head hurt from where Sir Byndorf's man had hit him, but his seemed the only injury. The bandaging around the wound in his leg had held up well enough, though he hoped these men wouldn't leave them standing much longer. Already the leg had begun to throb in concert with the welt on his head. Yet his discomfort seemed of little import considering the circumstances, and the fear he could practically feel emanating from the lad counting on him for support and safety. He laid a protective hand on Kelvin's shoulder and felt the boy trembling.

"Easy, son," he whispered. Kelvin pressed himself against Faulk's side, but didn't turn his face from the soldiers. A brave lad despite his fear. "They won't harm ye."

"Quiet!" one of the mercs barked.

"He's just a boy," Faulk grumbled as he imagined a worried father might, then pressed his lips firmly together so the man knew he intended to keep further silence.

They didn't have to wait long, but rather than the Prince or some other high official or military man, a woman in indigo silks swept into the room, clearly in charge of the two mercenaries who accompanied her. She stood nearly as tall as all save one of the soldiers. A quick glance would name her attractive, but with the dangerous kind of beauty reserved for hunting cats or wolves, a sleek grace that would easily turn on you and rip you to shreds. Long dark hair framed an imposing face with the most intense eyes Faulk had ever seen, so dark a blue they appeared almost black. Those eyes examined each prisoner in turn though she did not address any of them yet.

"These men have information for me?" she asked.

"Cap'n picked them out, Lady Destiny," one of the mercs said, the hawk-faced one who had originally pointed out Kelvin. "Don't know as they know anything, but the boy's the page who went missing last night. I 'member him scurryin' past after leaving the K—" He bit off the word at the heated spark in the woman's eyes and swallowed hard. "After leavin' the renegade's chambers," he finished carefully.

Destiny—Faulk didn't recall her from the court, but then, Prince Whillim squandered his time mostly away from the presence of the King and kept his sycophants close—turned her attention to Kelvin. That focused gaze minded Faulk entirely too much of a wildcat eager to pounce upon a favoured prey.

"Is that right?" she drawled, her voice suddenly a purr of unexpected pleasure. "You spoke to Stefan before he disappeared?"

Kelvin whimpered and pressed his face into Faulk's chest.

"You leave him alone," Faulk snarled. "The boy's done no wrong."

Destiny didn't take her scrutiny off Kelvin, but she listened to the soft words of the merc.

"The boy's father, though he spoke for Stefan loud enough to cause a stir."

"Hence the blood on his head," Destiny murmured, then nodded to herself. "Bring them both to my Sanctum, and gather what information from these others that you can. I will deal with them after this pair."

She spun and strode from the room, fully expecting these men to follow her orders. Which they did with alacrity, forcing

Faulk to consider the woman carefully. Mercenaries would obey whoever paid them up to a point, but these men didn't follow Destiny because she held the purse-strings; they followed because they feared her. Faulk could see it in both eyes and stances. He remembered Captain Frederick's brief mention of the Prince using some form of magic to further his mad plans, but he knew no more than that. Perhaps this Destiny held the key to that magic? Few understood anything to do with magic, and men feared what they did not understand, so by extension, they would fear whoever wielded it. Why else would men, especially toughs with swords like this lot, fear a woman?

The soldiers led man and boy to a room a flight up from the Council Chambers, a section of the Palace that Faulk recognised as Ambassador quarters. Was Destiny some sort of Ambassador then? If so, the room gave no indication of her land. Indeed, the only feature that made the space distinctive stood in the centre of the room framed in the light from the windows; a chair formed of white quartz crystal veined with green and rose that looked neither comfortable nor inviting. Ominous sprang to mind. Faulk opened his mouth to question her, but she snapped one word to him.

"Silence!"

He found his teeth clicked together and his lips sealed as firmly as though she had glued them shut. Faulk wasted only a few seconds in struggle before understanding that she had silenced him with magic. So he ceased his efforts and stood at parade rest, waiting for an opportunity. To do what, he couldn't say, but fighting a futile battle now would avail him nothing. Wait, watch, and learn, and with any luck, he would discover what King Stefan needed to know.

Once Destiny saw he would cause no trouble, she quirked a raven-wing eyebrow and turned her regard to Kelvin.

"What did Stefan tell you, boy? What orders did he send to the barracks?"

Kelvin shook his head and leaned against Faulk, but he stared defiance at this strange woman.

"I know Stefan's troops knew to scatter and flee after you interfered, so I can guess." She moved to stand in front of the page, staring down at him with that intense gaze. She made no effort to lower herself to his level, to make the boy feel comfort or any sense of safety. Faulk wondered if she did so intentionally to suggest her superiority in this situation, or unconsciously, not caring how a frightened child saw her. Either would serve to intimidate. "Tell me now or I will slice off your father's finger."

Quick as a snake, she grabbed Faulk's arm, a flash of sunlight glinting off the blade in her hand.

Reflex kicked in and Faulk threw her off, spinning to a defensive crouch, trying not to grimace at the flare of pain from his injured leg. His hand reached unconsciously for the non-existent sword at his hip. Destiny didn't stumble, but she did back away just out of reach. The mercenaries appeared at Faulk's side, one with sword drawn, the other, his muscles bunching as he flexed and moved with deadly grace, mirroring Faulk. Destiny's nod only affirmed Faulk's mistake.

"Father indeed," she murmured. "You might disguise yourself in workmen's clothing, but I know a soldier when I see one. Perhaps one that this boy warned?"

Faulk eased himself back to parade rest, the mercenaries following suit after a moment. He met Destiny's stare, seemingly ignoring the men at his side, his lips still firmly pressed together. He knew the true threat didn't lie in steel or muscle—though, of course, one might kill him as surely as the other. No, the threat came from this calculating woman who now stood regarding him as she tapped her knife absently against her cheek.

Kelvin stared wide-eyed from Faulk to the men guarding him to the woman, then back to Faulk. The boy swallowed, then nodded firmly and tried to make his eyes go hard and certain. Faulk shook his head slightly then flicked his gaze to Destiny and back. The slightest flinch and a quick bow of Kelvin's head told Faulk that the page understood. At least, Faulk hoped he did. Telling this woman the King's orders would change nothing.

"King Stefan bid me tell his soldiers that the castle was breached and to meet him at the east wall," Kelvin said, voice strong, pulling Destiny's focus away from Faulk, though the mercenaries didn't budge. The boy said nothing more.

"What else," she demanded.

Kelvin glared at her. "To trust no one I didn't know."

"Interesting," she said. "The east wall, you say, not the east gate. This is not a small city, boy, he must have been more precise. Where along the east wall?"

Kelvin bit his lip. Destiny strode nearer and slapped him hard across the face. Faulk lurched forward, but the mercenaries held him back, iron grips digging into his arms.

"Where?" she asked again in exactly the same tone, nothing save her proximity to the page to indicate that she had even moved.

"Th-the forges," he stammered, a trickle of blood oozing from a split lip.

Destiny frowned.

"Why the forges?"

"I don't know," Kelvin sniffed, wiping the blood from his mouth. "The King said he would take those loyal to safety beyond the forges."

"But why there? Why not the stables or the gate?"

"I don't know," the boy whimpered again. "She just said it came out near the smithies, and that's where the forges are."

Destiny's attention sharpened even more; Faulk could almost see her intensity as a force, and he suppressed an urge to wince. If Destiny suspected he knew anything relevant, she would show no mercy.

"She who?" Destiny spoke in a very quiet voice, her entire being focused on the child. "And what came out near the smithies?"

"I don't know!" Kelvin shouted it this time. "That's what King Stefan said and that's what I told his soldiers."

"And you have no idea how he escaped Whillim's men?"

"When I left, King was still in his rooms. That's all I know, I swear."

Destiny studied him a moment, seeing the boy's trembling limbs, the quiver of his bloodied lips as he tried to gather bravery about him like a cloak. She turned and walked to stand behind that odd quartz chair, her hands stroking it idly. Her eyes locked onto Kelvin again.

"Come here," she demanded. By his jerky movements, Faulk suspected that Kelvin did not approach her willingly, but the mercenaries held Faulk too firmly to intercede. When Kelvin reached the chair, Destiny pointed to the seat. Kelvin shook his head violently, but still he sat.

"Do stop struggling," she said. "The Focus will not let you up

71

once you've sat in it. Not until I allow it."

Her hands moved to the crown of the chair and her gaze rose to meet Faulk's.

"Whillim's mercenaries call this The Destiny Seat. I think you will find its effects quite fascinating. Something to contemplate before I ask you questions, soldier."

Faulk could almost think she had forgotten the boy by the way her scrutiny had affixed upon himself, but her malicious smile as the quartz crystal began to glow told Faulk she enjoyed the boy's fear as much as Faulk's uncertainty. The crystal flashed from gold to rose to pure white, then faded to leave it just a chair again, with a blinking child sitting upon it, confusion writ large across his face.

"Where—?"

"King Whillim had sent you to ask whether we required any repast, boy, and you felt faint," Destiny said, her voice almost able to convey a sense of concern. "We had you sit a moment. Do you fell better now?"

Kelvin jumped up. "I—yes, thank you, my Lady." He bowed hesitantly. "Repast, yes. Did you need anything?"

"No child. Best you go back to your duties. Wouldn't want King Whillim thinking you lax, now would we?"

"No ma'am," Kelvin hastened to assure her. He glanced briefly at Faulk and the men holding him as Destiny steered him toward the door. "I wouldn't want King Whillim to think badly of me."

"Exactly, child." She held the door open for him. "On your way, then."

Kelvin slipped out of the room, leaving Faulk staring after him. Destiny shut the door and turned to meet his gaze.

"Now, soldier, shall we see what you can tell me?"

"What did you do to him?" Faulk demanded, almost surprised he could speak again.

"He's not harmed, if that's what you mean," she waved a hand dismissively.

"That's not what I mean, witch," he growled.

Her eyes flashed.

"Wizard," she snapped. "I am a wizard. And your precious King Stefan will learn that soon enough."

"While you put his simpering brother on the throne instead?" Faulk demanded. "Make yourself a puppet King to rule where no woman should stand?"

Destiny's eyes narrowed.

"I shall enjoy teaching you respect, soldier. Never under-estimate the power of a woman."

"You have no power except that which you steal." Faulk could only hope that if he angered her enough, she would use that frightening memory device on him before she could glean any important information. Or perhaps just kill him. "Big scary wizard lady just made a ten-year-old forget half his life. You couldn't even get a child to bow to your will, so you worked a spell on him. How do you expect to gain any real respect? You going to magic it out of me?"

"The Focus won't make you forget. It will change what you remember. You won't even know Stefan ever existed as a man. And as for stealing power—"

"King Stefan wouldn't let you play with his mind, so you turned to his little brother, is that it?" Faulk interrupted, hoping the flush high in her cheeks would lead to a loss of control. "Just throw your magic around and think that will gain you power and respect? Lady, you don't even know the meaning of the words."

"You might like to think that Destiny's wrath will spare you the boy's fate," a new voice spoke from behind Faulk. "Perhaps even give you a chance to escape and warn my brother." Faulk turned just his head to watch as Whillim silently closed the door behind him and strode across the room to join his wizard, his bright hair glittering in the sunlight. "But it will just bring you pain, and you will work with us regardless."

"I will do no such thing," Faulk sneered.

"Of course you will. And you won't think anything strange of it. In fact, you'll even help us hunt Stefan down and bring him here." Whillim frowned at him. "I know you," he said. "You aren't just any soldier." His frown blossomed into a terrible grin. "Oh, Destiny, it seems you have collected one of my brother's personal guards."

"Indeed," she said, her cold gaze staring back at Faulk, a careful distance kept between her and the Prince. "Then he will know what the boy did not."

She glided nearer and positioned herself directly in front of Faulk, standing so close their noses practically touched. With the heavy grips of the mercenaries on his arms, Faulk still

73

managed to lunge toward her, but she didn't flinch. He considered kicking out; the mercenaries would take his weight just long enough to get in a solid blow before realising that he intended injury rather than flight, maybe even enough to maim. As though reading his thoughts, Destiny smiled contempt at him.

"Do try," she murmured. "It will make showing you your place that much more satisfying. No?" Her smile turned malicious. The Prince came to stand at her side, golden to her darkness, and Faulk suddenly understood. Whillim would not stand as Destiny's puppet, but as her equal.

"Now, who was this woman who warned Stefan to flee, and how did you escape his rooms?"

Chapter 8

Em drifted between comforting warmth and an aching, burning pull along her abdomen, each sensation vying for her attention. She much preferred the cozy feeling of warm blankets and the sun brushing her cheeks, but the discomfort of her gut soon overwhelmed the peace. Not to mention the increasing need to empty her bladder. She cracked open an eye, startled to find not the familiar stone walls and wooden bookcases of her library with the musty smell of old books, but rather the worn planks of an oaken ceiling overhead and the feel of a straw-stuffed mattress beneath her back. Someone had pulled a rough woollen blanket to her chin. Sunlight filtered in through thin curtains on a window to the side of the room. The pungency of a farm vied with the scent of seasoned stew wafting in from the closed door she could just see past the foot of the bed.

Em blinked uncertainly a couple of times, then gingerly shifted her weight. She remembered her wound by the sword of the man attacking the King, the flight in the night, and leading the King's men through the dark to her secret cave, but she didn't recall anything after that. Where did she lie now? Had the King made good his escape, or did he sit imprisoned somewhere? This room minded her of a peasant's dwelling, not a noble's home, so it seemed unlikely that the Prince held her captive, but what of the King? Did he take shelter nearby? Would he deign to enter such a lowly dwelling? Or did Em now lodge away from the King?

The last made some sense to Em. She had warned the King and seen to his safety; he had no further obligation to her, nor she to him. Perhaps he had left her at a nearby village or farmstead, then continued to somewhere more secure. She nodded at the likelihood of that, then dismissed her speculations for more immediate concerns.

With an arm wrapped protectively across her middle, Em slowly manoeuvred herself to a sitting position and twisted until her legs hung over the side of the bed, panting with the effort. She felt a bandage tied around her abdomen beneath an unfamiliar nightshirt obviously sized for a man, but she didn't waste time wondering from whence they came, not when the pressure of her bodily needs urged her to find a privy quickly.

She gritted her teeth and forced herself to stand, stumbling and grasping at the nearby washstand as agony shot lightning bolts from her wound. Eyes squeezed shut, she breathed in ragged gasps through quivering lips and held on to the stand with a trembling grip.

"Here now," a man's voice said by her side as hands gently took her shoulders. "You shouldn't get up yet."

Em's eyes shot open and she jumped, then looked up into the youthful, moustached face of Sergeant Darius.

"Let me help you back to bed," he said.

Em shook her head, her hands transferring from the washstand to Dari's arms.

"Privy?" she whispered and might have laughed at the look of discomfort that spread across the guard's face had she not so desperately needed the facilities.

"This way," he said, guiding her toward the door he had so recently entered, left arm around her waist and the other lending support to her right elbow.

Em drew in shallow breaths as they slowly moved, then realised the import of Dari's presence. She clutched at the arm supporting her elbow, though kept shuffling forward as she glanced at the Sergeant.

"The King?" she asked. "Safe?"

"King Stefan is fine, Emily," he replied, a smile tugging at his lips. They had reached the bedroom door and he gently pulled her through. "See for yourself."

They emerged into the main room of a farmhouse, the dining table near a large stone fireplace flanked by three men, King

Stefan among them. Every eye turned to Em and Dari as they appeared. Captain Frederick, looming at the King's shoulder, straightened to regard them.

"Thought you were going to check on her bandaging, not take her for a walk, Sergeant," the huge Captain grumbled. Em knew she must have imagined the amusement she heard as those dark eyes bored into her.

"She ... ah ... needs to use ... well," Dari stammered. The Captain coughed, his hand hiding his mouth. Did the man cover a smile?

"And the chamber pot did not suffice?" Frederick spoke sternly, yet Em definitely noted the merry gleam sparkling in his eye.

"The chamber pot?" Dari said as though he had never heard of such a thing. Em knew the man had simply reacted without thought when she asked for the privy. She hadn't considered a chamber pot herself; the castle had many privies, or necessary rooms, and only the lower servants had to make do with chamber pots—certainly no one would expect to find anything other than a privy in the library where Em spent most of her time. "I didn't think—"

"Please," Em interrupted the flustered Sergeant Darius, struggling to keep the tears she could feel forming from leaking out. "Whatever is closest."

"Of course!" he replied, spinning her about. She felt the blood drain from her face as she stifled a gasp of pain, and heard muffled laughter as Dari hurried her back to the room. And they said women were flighty!

Dari pulled out the pot from beneath the bed and left her to take care of necessity, his face red with embarrassment. Em nearly cried with relief as he left.

When she had finished, she noted what Dari had originally brought into the room. A cloth draped over a bowl of water, a container of some greenish poultice, and fresh bandages lay on a chest at the foot of the bed. Em sat on the edge of the bed and pulled up the nightshirt to expose the wrapped wound on her stomach. She picked at the tied end of the bandage, holding her breath and clenching her stomach muscles, trying to find the least painful way to remove the wrappings so she could apply the poultice and change the dressing herself. She whimpered, but determination won past discomfort as she continued to work. Just when she started to peel the last bit of soiled cloth from the wound, a knock sounded at the door.

Em looked up, eyes wide. She yanked at the old bandage, feeling a slight resistance as it snagged on dried blood, but it came free and she pulled down her shirt as best she could to cover herself. Wiping the tears from her eyes, she called softly.

"Yes?"

"It's Fred. May I come in?"

"Um," she glanced around frantically, but even that pulled at her wound. No way could she move further up the bed let alone slip under the blanket without causing herself more pain. Did modesty overshadow her need for medical attention? At least the Captain should know how to dress her wound. "Yes."

The large man let himself in, staring at her a moment, at the bloodied bandage clutched in her shaking fist. He shook his head, then closed the door.

"You shouldn't even be sitting and here you are, trying to wrap a bandage around your midsection. Fool girl, don't you know how serious that wound is?"

"If it's not kept clean, it could become infected," Em recited. She knew of such wounds from a wide selection of books. "Once infection sets in, treatment becomes more difficult and the fevers could lead to blood poisoning, amputation, even death." Frederick blinked at her, his only reaction. "Which is why I'm trying to clean it."

Frederick sighed, then strode forward.

"Lie back, girl. Let me tend to it."

"I can—" she began.

"You can do as you're told," he barked, making Em flinch. "The King has questions for you and you're no good to him weak and delirious."

Em nodded hesitantly, then inched her way to lie down on the bed. She forced her fists to unclench, then tugged at the nightshirt.

"For goodness sake," Frederick growled. "I'm not going to hurt you, girl. What do you take me for?"

When she still struggled with the clothing, he finally grabbed her hands.

"Just lie still and let me do this. You'll just end up tearing open the wound again if you keep thrashing around like that. Don't you even know how to let someone help you?"

"No," Em said, which surprised Frederick enough that he just stared down at her, her hands forgotten in his grip.

"What do you mean, no?" he asked.

"I take care of myself, Captain. No one else has since ... in a very long time. I barely remember how to let someone help me. Not for something like this." She swallowed back old memories, then forced herself to relax. "But I will try." She bit her lip, then in a very small voice, said, "Thank you for helping me."

Frederick leaned back, releasing her wrists, then gave a grunt that might have meant anything. Em closed her eyes and let the man work. The feel of the damp cloth across her exposed flesh as he cleaned off old poultice and blood distracted her.

"Where are we?" she asked.

"Farmhouse," he answered, concentrating now on spreading the fresh poultice along the angry edges of her wound. "Goodman Tox has graciously allowed us to rest here."

Em snorted.

"What?" Frederick demanded.

"You make it sound as though he has a choice. No one defies their King." Then her eyes flew open as she realised what she said and their circumstances. "Well, no commoner would dare," she amended. Frederick just continued to work, avoiding her gaze.

"Why do you do this?" she asked. "Where is the farmwife? Goodman Tox's daughters? Why do they not ..." Em trailed off, sudden understanding flooding her. The Captain of the King's guards tended her because they couldn't afford to trust her. She had provided too convenient an escape in light of the Prince's betrayal. That she truly did work for the safety of the King meant little if she couldn't prove her loyalty. "I will not harm the King, Captain. I know you can't simply take my word for it, yet it is so. And I appreciate you not making me feel too much the prisoner."

Frederick grunted again.

"Goodman Tox's wife died some years ago, and he has no children. We're here because Ambrose knows the man." He didn't meet her eyes. "And yes," he said quietly. "We can't trust you entirely, though we'd like to. All of us would. See that you keep your word. Call me Fred, not Captain. Now hold this bandage in place and sit up," he ordered gruffly. "I need to finish binding your wound, and that means wrapping you all around the middle."

Em struggled to do as instructed, leaning heavily on Fred as he pulled her upright. For some reason, his bluntness and stated desire to have her prove true made her feel warm inside. Unless that was a reaction to her injury. Either way, Em found a small smile forming on her pursed lips.

***

Tox finished stacking the wood he had chopped and returned his sturdy axe to its place in the barn. He looked around and realised he couldn't put it off any longer.

He had risen early as usual despite the late-night intruders interrupting his sleep. Cows did not milk themselves; chickens did not collect their own eggs nor scatter their own feed from the grain sacks—not that they wouldn't given half a chance, bloody single-minded birds. The tough ends of the vegetables he'd used in the stew went to the pigs along with their normal grub. He had seen to the farm workers when they arrived, intercepting them before they could learn the identity of his unwanted guests, then sent them off to the fields to water and weed the crops, fresh planted now that the frosts had lifted. He had curried the plow horses along with the pair of dapple greys his visitors had brought, sharpened the scythes and his axe, then set to splitting and stacking extra logs for the fire. The farm hands would return soon for the noon meal, and Tox still had to figure out how to deal with those men in his kitchen.

With a sigh, he wiped his hands down his tunic, both to brush off bits of wood chips and to dry the sweat from his palms. Then he set his shoulders in a way his late wife would have fondly called stubborn, and went to greet the King.

Tox stomped up the two stairs to his porch, then cleared his throat loudly before pushing open his front door. His house, yes, but men with swords waited within. Nervous men with sharp weapons. One did not want to surprise such people, even if one hadn't wanted them there in the first place.

Three pairs of eyes met his as he entered. The young ginger-haired soldier had disappeared up the path to the road not long after sunrise to watch for any who might follow the

King. Tox chose to focus his attention on the only man he knew, although he had not seen Ambrose in thirteen years. He remembered his shock upon finding the young man at his door in the small hours of the night.

The pounding on the heavy oak door had woken Tox. Fearing some emergency—no one banged a fist against a neighbour's door in the darkest hours unless fire, sickness or death demanded immediate attention—Tox had slid from the comfort of his warm blanket with some alarm. He grabbed the candle from his bedside and stumbled in the dark to the banked fireside in the great room to light a taper from the coals and apply it to the candle's wick. It took a moment only, but the banging on his door came again, hastening his steps even further.

He pulled the door open, blinking in consternation at the three soldiers crowding his porch, the dark-haired one with his little moustache carrying the limp form of a woman.

"Goodman Tox?" one young man queried, ash-blond hair straggling from a warrior's tail to lie plastered to his scalp with sweat. Tox squinted at him, seeing something vaguely familiar in his pale blue eyes, though sure he didn't recognise the hard-jawed face.

"My name is Ambrose, sir. My mother and your late wife shared many an hour together, and though several years have passed, I spent a lot of my early childhood here at Havendale."

Tox had grunted and taken a firm grip on the door frame to still his shaking hand, though the quivering of the candle gave him away. He and his dear wife Amalia had named their farm Havendale for the peace and tranquility they had found there, but Tox had renamed it Haven's End after Amalia's death. He remembered the good and gentle woman who had stood second-only to Tox himself in Amalia's heart, and he remembered her son. The man who stood before him had the right age and colouring for that long-ago child. And he had the woman's eyes.

"And you thought the wee hours of the morning a fitting time for a reunion?" Tox demanded gruffly, trying to quash old memories from surfacing. Any reminder of his beloved Amalia brought sadness to Tox; seeing a young man who might have grown up with his own son had mother and child survived nearly overwhelmed the old farmer.

"We have come seeking sanctuary," Ambrose said. "We hope for hospitality and shelter for the night."

Tox glanced between the three men and their unconscious charge, then sighed.

"I guess I can find a place for four, though perhaps not much comfort. What ails the lass?" He moved to the side to offer entrance to his home.

"We have two more companions and took the liberty of stabling two horses in your barn, though we have not touched any of your fodder."

Tox narrowed his eyes, not liking the strange nature of this unlooked for visit from the past.

"Your companions may have to share in the horses' accommodations, which I'm finding more likely for the rest of you if you dredge up any more friends in uniform who suddenly turn up in the night carrying unconscious women. If not for the uniform, I might mistake you for brigands, unlikely as that seems this close to Riverbend. Another, more suspicious man, might also question why you would leave the path and come to an out-of-the-way farm rather than continue on to the comforts of an inn in Riverbend. The city lies an hour away by horse."

Tox had resumed a position to block his door. A large man to begin with, years of working his own farm had added muscles to Tox and he knew how to use his size to best advantage. The swords buckled at the men's waists gave him pause as much as their military postures, but he would not allow even the King's soldiers to bully him on his own property.

"Please forgive our intrusion, goodman," spoke a man in his early-middle years from behind the quartet on his porch, his voice cultured and polite. Tox peered into the shadows behind Ambrose and could discern two more men, one even larger than himself, waiting below. "The city has exploded into riots and the Prince seeks to usurp my position, so an inn in Riverbend would not provide the safety of your gentle farm. We will, of course, recompense any inconvenience our presence may cause."

Tox felt his jaw drop when he realised to whom he spoke. Suddenly, the little details and implications he had tried to avoid noticing came clear; the soot staining the uniforms, their colours proclaiming not just soldiers but King's guard, the scent of smoke clinging to the men, the nicks and scrapes, the tense expressions especially around the eyes. The wounded woman. Tox didn't know whether to fall to his knees in the presence of royalty or stammer out an apology and usher them with open arms and reverence into his home. What did a simple farmer do when confronted with his King's request for sanctuary?

Tox pressed his lips together and turned away, leaving the door open as he made his way to the fireplace to rekindle the flames.

The King and his entourage had entered Haven's End and made themselves comfortable.

Now Tox looked around the very room that had sheltered the King in the night and wondered what to do next. The King's chief bodyguard was not in evidence and Tox hadn't seen him in the yard. He assumed the big man had disappeared into Tox's bedroom with the woman and he frowned. He didn't know the situation with the injured woman, whether she stood as companion or captive—none of the men seemed very forthcoming with that information, though they had shared some of their incredible story regarding the Prince's actions and their own flight—but he didn't care to learn of any wrong-doing beneath his roof. Still, how did one question his King?

With a glower to the closed bedroom door, Tox made his way to the fire to stir the stew he had brewing in his largest pot there. Keeping his attention on this simple task so as not to show too much ignorance of the etiquette involved in speaking in the presence of the King, Tox spoke to the room at large.

"Lunch is nearly ready and the farmhands'll soon return looking for their meal. What kind of story you mean to tell them about yourselves? Or do you plan to hide with the Captain and that young lady?" To his surprise, Tox heard the last come out in a growl.

"We'll say you've hired us for some extra work on the property," the King said.

Tox snorted. "Looking like you all do?" He turned from the stew and met the King's gaze, finally deciding to just act himself; civil, polite, but not subservient. He had seen too many years and too much sorrow to change his nature, even for the man who could order his execution for treating the King like an equal. If this man wanted to have him killed, Tox wouldn't know how to stop him anyway, so he might as well make an infraction worth his time. "You'll excuse me for saying so, Your Majesty, but not a one of you look like a farmhand or a craftsman. Certainly not dressed like that, swords and all."

The door to the bedroom creaked open and the Captain came out, the young lady looking pale clinging to his arm, her plain features pinched in pain that she tried to hide.

"A merchant and his guards negotiating terms for trade in appreciation for the goodman's hospitality," the Captain said.

The three men at the table had risen with the woman's appearance, wrapped in Tox's blanket and decently covered, and each man shared the same bewildered expression that Tox could feel on his own face.

"Would that work, Fred?" the King asked, apparently not surprised that the man had heard their conversation.

"Not sure, Sire, but Emily thought such a thing plausible."

The stares all went to the woman and Tox sympathised when she drew back. Her eyes flew from face to face as the Captain slowly yet inexorably drew her toward the table.

"It's not unheard of, Your Majesty," she said very softly. She seemed apprehensive, but Tox couldn't figure out whether her anxiety suggested a captive or just shyness. "But I don't know the resources of this farm." She glanced at Tox. "Do you have produce or wares that might bring the interest of a merchant or a broker who might hope to solicit interest in the city or beyond on your behalf?"

He blinked at her speech, at her understanding of such matters. An advisor, perhaps? But a woman, and one so young? He wondered how much stranger the day could become.

"I do have a wide enough range of produce and perhaps a healthy enough supply, though I deal direct with Riverbend along with some of the farmhands. To suggest I might want to alter our arrangements might offend."

"We would make it clear that any benefits would extend to all, with you receiving the greatest share as owner of those goods," the King said.

"And when the lads learn of this deception and have only me to blame, where will you be?" Tox snapped.

"It is for now only a negotiation," replied the King. "But if we came to an agreement, even a fabricated one, I would make certain that the benefits remain yours. As I said before, we will recompense any inconvenience our presence causes."

Tox regarded the man with just a little more respect.

"We could probably work something out, then. But you're still too obvious in your dress. A merchant perhaps, but those guard uniforms are rather distinctive."

Ambrose and the others removed their overcoats and insignia. That left them in cream-coloured tunics that a merchant's guard might own and dark trousers, the tell-tale green-and-gold of King's men hidden.

Tox nodded, and just in time, for outside, he heard the approach of the farmhands. Time to see if he could keep the identity of his beleaguered King a secret.

***

Goodman Tox had a reasonable sized table for himself and his farmhands, but it left little room for Stefan and his men. To avoid any unnecessary grumbling, Stefan took himself outside to wait until the workers finished eating, along with Fred and Ambrose. Jo watched at the roadside for any signs of pursuit.

They left Dari inside to keep an eye on Emily, whom they had introduced as Stefan's niece. The librarian could barely walk yet and she needed food to help recover her strength. The look of panic on her face as she realised she wore a blanket and didn't have the strength to retreat to the bedroom again almost made Stefan smile as Fred closed the front door and the men made themselves comfortable on the porch.

Stefan had questions for the girl and having to wait chafed, but what else could they do? He could expect no report from Dalasmar and Riverbend for another day, and could only hope that Willi had had enough presence of mind to quell the riots his mercenaries had started, put out the fires, and see to the immediate needs of those to whom he had caused harm with his actions.

How soon would the hunt for Stefan and those loyal to him begin? Would the false trails succeed or did Willi's hired thugs even now creep toward this farm and the good man who had given them shelter? How long before Sirs Edvard, Castel and Pietor, and those he'd sent with them, found themselves under attack? And what strange madness and magic had led Willi down this road?

He needed to talk to Emily, find out exactly what she knew;

what she'd overheard, what she'd seen, whether he could make use of her knowledge of the hidden passageways. The more he knew now, the more options became available when Sim and Faulk made their reports on the morrow.

He and his men had discussed their situation earlier, what precautions to take, escape plans should Willi's men approach, staging grounds for gathering soldiers—even an army—should they need such to retake the castle. All bare-bones and supposition until Stefan had something more concrete to go on. The not knowing irked him, and the necessary delay while he had others gathering intel frustrated him, but he let none of that show.

Soon enough, the farmhands emerged from the house, nodding brief greetings as they hurried off about their work, not sure of Stefan's supposed largess but not willing to risk giving offence.

Once they had dispersed, Stefan rose and led Fred and Ambrose back into the house where Tox had just finished dishing out three additional bowls of stew and set them on the table. Emily sat in a ladder-back chair facing the fire, the blanket wrapped securely around her so that only her head showed, and the fingers of her right hand where she clutched a half-eaten chunk of bread. The flames gave a golden glow to her pale features as she chewed slowly. She looked very small sitting there, the illusion heightened by Dari's hovering frame at her side. Stefan waved the young soldier over to the table.

Tox looked as though he would prefer to flee the room, but acquiesced to Stefan's invitation to sit at the head of the table. His eyes kept roving over each man as they ate, flitting to Emily, then back again. He obviously had questions he didn't expect to receive answers to, though Stefan intended to give him as much information as he himself had now. The man had accepted them into his home; he had a right to know what danger lurked for those he sheltered.

When Fred finished his stew, scraping the last of the juices from the bowl with a heel of bread, Stefan flicked his gaze to Emily and back to the Captain. Fred nodded, then rose and moved to Emily's side. She glanced up at him, her own bread gone now, then set her jaw. Unable to conceal the wince of pain as she struggled to her feet, she kept a white-knuckled grip on her blanket. With Fred's hand on her arm, she shuffled over to join the men at the table. Dari pulled her chair over from the fireside and placed it opposite the King. By the time they got her settled, chair firmly nestled between Fred and Dari so that she couldn't move far without pushing past either man, all colour had fled from her face, leaving the girl white as fresh fallen snow, but she didn't shy from Stefan's scrutiny.

"Tell me exactly what happened last night," he said, holding her pale grey stare. "From the soldiers you claim to have overheard in the library to leaving the city. Tell me everything; leave nothing out, even if I saw it too."

Emily nodded, her eyes wide and her lips trembling. She drew in a deep breath, then began.

"I had fallen asleep after I finished copying the Royal Proofs. I only meant to close my eyes, but I woke to find that darkness had fallen. I had planned to make use of one of the sleeping alcoves rather than retreating to my room and had started toward one when I heard the voices in the dark. I know the library very well and didn't need a light, so the intruders didn't mark my presence." She spoke as though reading from a book, and Stefan found the cadence oddly peaceful despite the content.

"They carried a hooded lantern and spoke in low voices. They spoke of a Captain Milos inciting riots to distract attention, and having the King's chambers surrounded. They said—"

"Exact words, if you can remember them as well as you claim to remember the written word," Stefan interrupted.

Emily, caught with her mouth open mid-sentence, pressed her lips together, then nodded firmly. When she spoke, Stefan could actually hear her interpretation of the mercenary's tone.

"Once we get the documents to the Prince, he sends word and our troops move in to take the King."

Stefan suppressed a wince at hearing words against Whillim, but he didn't interrupt again. He listened quietly as Emily detailed the overheard conversation; the device called the Destiny Seat and its frightening ability to alter memories, the subversion of his people as this mysterious Destiny tested that device, the Prince's intention to use the Royal Proofs to rewrite history. The need to take Stefan alive.

As the girl continued to relate her story—her flight to the secret passages in the library's vault and her race against the mercenaries, her journey through the tunnels in the pitch black

87

with only her memory and a spark of hope to guide her, her resolve to do what she felt she must to warn him—Stefan marvelled at her courage, her tenacity when the odds seemed stacked against her. She didn't overplay her role in events. In fact, Stefan suspected she hid her true feelings about her ordeal in the story-like delivery of the tale. He remembered his first glimpse of her as she emerged from his inner chamber, the smudged tear tracks on her face, the trembling of her limbs as she dropped to her knees with Fred's sword at her throat. If all her words held true, this young woman had risked as much as his own sworn guards in defence of her King. It said much about her. If she spoke true.

"You went back in to the blacksmith shop to find a sword while Corporal Joseph guarded the entrance," Emily continued. "Two soldiers emerged from the smoke. Jo pushed me back to the door and moved to engage them, so I knew they didn't stand with you, Sire. One slipped past the Corporal's guard just as you reappeared. I don't know if he recognised you or just saw a man with a weapon, but he lunged at you when the smoke had you blinded. I didn't know what to do, so I pushed you out of his way. I apologise for laying hands on my King, but better his blade find me than you." She said it so matter-of-factly that it took a moment for Stefan to understand that she had just described how she had received that wound. He didn't know whether to laugh that she feared having given offence by shoving him out of the way of a potentially lethal blow, or weep that she might truly expect his anger and retribution for having touched him. Did he really have such an arrogant and ruthless reputation?

"I led Sergeant Darius, Captain Frederick, and those with them to you in the cave, Sire," she concluded, her voice worn to a soft whisper. "And when I saw the men's injuries in the lantern light, I thought to gather some local plants I'd read about that help in healing. I don't remember anything after that until I woke under Goodman Tox's gracious hospitality."

Silence stretched as they absorbed her tale.

"You leave parts out," Fred finally said gruffly, surprising both Stefan and Emily. She had lied? About what?

"For instance," Fred continued, "that you hid yourself in a tree to wait for us, guarding the way to the King as best you could with no training and no weapon. Climbed a damned tree despite having a great bloody wound in your gut that you'd tended yourself so that you could see any who tried to sneak past you and give warning if necessary.

"How the knights treated you with suspicion, derision, and condescension, yet you held steadfast, concerned only with the safety of the King.

"How you thought to help others who had taken injuries, but didn't see fit to inform us of your own need for medical attention. Damn it, girl, what if you had fallen unconscious while up in that tree? Who would have led the way to the King then?"

"Fred, that's not ..." Stefan began, but Emily spoke over him, her words strong even while sudden tears slipped down her cheeks.

"Sergeant Darius knew the way. I made sure of that before he went to guard the road. And Corporal Joseph stood with the King; he could have led him to greater safety if you had not arrived. And ... well ..." she paused, her gaze dropping as her hand clutched her abdomen. Her voice fell to a whisper once more. "I didn't know how bad the wound ... I thought it shallow enough ... I've never had to deal with anything like this before. I'm no soldier."

Tox laughed at that, startling them all.

"I don't know much about soldiering girl, but if half what you said you done really happened, and I didn't know you'd done it, I'd have thought it a soldier's story. You looked to the King's safety above your own so many times in that tale that they ought to name you a guard on bravery alone." The big farmer glanced at Fred. "Meaning no disrespect to the rest of you, of course, but this little thing fought with her brain while the rest took care of the blade work. Seems to me she deserves your thanks, not your rebukes."

"You mistake me, Tox," Fred replied. "I merely wanted to point out what Emily doesn't seem to see; that very quality you saw. She did put the King's safety before her own and may very well have saved a kingdom. What I want her to understand is that a good soldier knows when to ask for help."

"I'm not a soldier," Emily protested weakly again, gaze in her lap.

"Even more reason to ask for help then."

She smiled faintly, but it held a bitterness.

89

"Were I a man, Captain, I might have that option. However, a woman in this kingdom, and a commoner at that, loses all respect if she asks for help, for you'd see it as a sign of weakness, the frailty of a female. If any of you saw me as weak, you wouldn't have listened to me, and the Prince would have the King right now. I couldn't let you see my fear or you wouldn't have acted. If any of you knew how terrified I was the whole time .... I couldn't risk the King's safety in the hopes that you'd see my need for assistance as anything other than weakness. The kingdom couldn't afford that."

Thunderous silence. Stefan stared in wonder at this brave little librarian sitting before him now. He hadn't thought of it before, but Emily's words rang true. She had shown fear, though she'd tried very hard to hide it, and Stefan had, perhaps unconsciously, worried that she might falter because of her gender. He had even entertained the idea that she might have played to her supposed weakness to gain sympathy. He had never thought to look at it from her point of view. Did a man sit in front of him now, would they have questioned his actions? Undoubtedly, but then perhaps they would have seen his pain as an attempt to hide an injury, rather than supposing that the rigours of the night had simply overwhelmed the woman.

"Well, I do believe you've put the lie to that particular notion of ours," Stefan admitted. "And I thank you, now, for all you have done. I can wish that what you've told us proves false, but I strangely hope it holds true."

Stefan turned his gaze to Fred.

"So Whillim has a wizard called Destiny and a device that steals memories and creates falsehoods that seem real. How do we counter such a thing?"

"Seems to me if we can find another wizard to undo the damage of this Destiny Seat, we'd have a place to start."

"But where do we find such a wizard?" Ambrose spoke up. "We don't have a lot in the way of wizards hanging about Riverbend, Sire."

"Too much bad blood," Emily murmured, her eyes loosely focused on the tabletop. "Too much history and persecution."

"What?" Ambrose asked, but Stefan saw her meaning.

"History, of course," he said. "You know the histories, you've read them all, haven't you?"

Emily blinked up at him, pain in her eyes.

"Yes. And I know which kingdoms more readily embrace wizards. If we can determine where this Destiny comes from, then you'd have a better chance at finding someone who can counter his spell."

"Good. I want you to sort out your thoughts, try to match what little we know with the orders of wizards and which kingdoms they frequent. Everything you think might have some importance. You will think on this while you rest, and fill us in after supper."

"I can tell you now ..." a yawn swallowed the rest of her words.

"Go rest, Emily. I need you strong and coherent, and for that, you need sleep. Dari, will you help the young lady back to the bedroom, please?"

Emily wanted to protest more; he could see it in the set of her face, but she didn't refuse Dari's arm as he helped her stand. She thought he sent her off to coddle her. Truth, though, if Fred looked like Emily did now, Stefan would insist the man get some rest. He did feel the need to protect her—what man wouldn't?—but he would try not to let that sentiment rule him. He had learned that women needed protection, and he could see that Emily required some of that protection now, but he would try to see her as an individual, not as a member of a fragile group of people. It seemed the least he could do in light of all she had done for him.

Chapter 9

"The kingdom of Dalasham," Em recited as Ambrose and Jo helped Tox clear the table after supper while King Stefan and Fred sat across from her. Dari had relieved Jo on watch near the road while she slept. Darkness stood an hour off, and the rest had done Em some good, though she felt stiff now, and her wound pulled if she moved too quickly.

"Four provinces make up Dalasham: Nordam, Sudam, Ostam, and Westam, with the capital of Dalasmar unifying them at the core of the kingdom. The further one moves from this centre of influence, the more wild the land and its people become, though far less so than in centuries past."

"We know this girl," Fred grumbled. "We grew up here too."

Em felt her face flush at the rebuke and dropped her gaze to the clay mug of water in her hands. She couldn't know the extent of their knowledge. She herself had known so little of the world before Darien had found her and brought her to the library, but she realised these men would know so much more, and she should assume they had a much better education than her, especially the King. She studied history; he lived it.

"I'm sorry, Captain," she breathed softly. "I sometimes forget that I'm hardly unique in knowing the histories, and that you all have undoubtedly seen the places I've only read about. Usually people only ask when they don't really know. Do you know about each province's penchant or loathing for magic?" she asked. "How long since Dalasmar itself has seen true wizards compared to, say, the western province?"

"Dalasham hasn't seen wizards for two hundred years," Fred stated.

"Um," Em bit her lip, glancing at the King. She didn't want to contradict or upset the large Captain of the King's guard, but if he truly believed that, then he had missed some important facts. The King's expression didn't change, but Em had the impression that he tested her as he waited for her words. Surely he didn't believe as Fred did, did he? What if they really didn't know the histories and would think her a liar? But Em couldn't lie about something like this. She knew not everything written down proved true, but the histories all agreed on basic points, one such major point being the schism between magic users and mundanes, as the wizards named non-magic users. She would speak truth as she knew it, and let the Captain make of it what he would.

"Dalasmar and the lands immediately surrounding it have not reported wizards in one hundred eighty-six years," Em said. "Too many blamed them and feared them after Henri's rebellion. Wizards did not disappear, of course. They avoid the capital and its environs for fear of persecution, and if they do enter, they keep a very low profile. Only a few witches have openly braved Riverbend in recent years, each purportedly weak enough in magic to cause little notice. But wizards do live and practice in other parts of Dalasham. Westam has the greatest population of wizards, which, given its proximity to Bakaana, doesn't surprise me. Bakaana has several Schools of Wizardry, and information flows fairly freely across the border between the two kingdoms. Sudam also has a number of known wizards, although they most often keep to themselves. Nordam and Ostam have less tolerance for wizards; Nordam because Henri and many of his colleagues called it home, and Ostam because they saw the brunt of the damage done by the Haemite wizards and witches when they tried to invade three hundred years ago, and Ostamites have long and stubborn memories."

She heard a snort at that assessment, startled to find it came from the King.

"An apt description of many from the eastern province," he agreed before motioning Em to continue. She took some comfort in the fact that he had not contradicted her words.

"Wizards do live and practice in the kingdom of Dalasham,

but they avoid the capital. If you wish to find one, I would suggest looking in Westam. The kingdoms of Bakaana, Haemat, and Innosvar embrace wizards also, and more openly than even Westam. Kranor, Moravin, and Bash shun all magic users, from oppression of the lowest hedge witch to outright execution of suspected wizards, depending on the kingdom and the mood of the ruler on a given day. It seems very unlikely that the Prince's wizard came from those northern kingdoms, unless he fled persecution, perhaps exchanging his horrible forgetting spell for asylum. It seems to me, though, that such a spell involves great complexity, which in turn suggests higher magic. That indicates training. A wizard would find no teachers or solace in the north or east, unless they stole past the closely guarded borders of Haemat."

"Why do you think this spell is complex?" Ambrose wanted to know, joining them at the table, along with Tox and Jo.

"And how many levels of magic exist?" Jo asked. "I thought there were just two: wizards and witches."

Em shook her head.

"It's a common misapprehension to lump all magic users into only those two categories and assume that a person is one or the other. According to Wulfgang's *A Matter of Magic*, witches can only do low level magic; simple healing, growth spells for crops, weather prediction. Wizards can work these basic magics, but also higher level magic; major healing, weather alteration, multi-layer spells. The strength of a wizard determines how complex a spell they can manipulate; the more difficult, the higher they deem the quality of magic required. There are different grades of wizards, depending on which School they studied, of which I have read of five."

She turned to address Ambrose's question.

"Destiny's spell erases one memory and implants another, one strong enough that the person believes it as a truth they've known all their life. That's at least two layers of spell. More than that, it erases a specific memory—that Stefan is King. From what I understand, the more specific a spell's target, the more difficult to achieve. To attack just one memory, presumably altering it in such a way that the revised memory fits seamlessly into the victim's mind, seems very precise, and very hard."

She looked now at Fred.

"Do you respect Prince Whillim as you do the King?" she asked. Fred hesitated. "Would he make as fine a ruler?" she pressed.

"He would not," Fred answered warily.

"So imagine everything that King Stefan has achieved during his reign, only imagine that you *know* that Whillim made it all happen. If you went back to Dalasmar tomorrow, full of the knowledge that Whillim is King, and then you saw how he ruled now, wouldn't you begin to wonder what had changed? In your memories, he has ruled fairly and justly for ten years, so has he changed, or have you? How long do you wonder, how long before anyone dares act against a King they have loved? This spell must take such things into account. Can you even begin to imagine the level of complexity that requires?"

King Stefan stared at her intently and she dared meet that gaze briefly before staring into her cup again.

"This Destiny must stand among the highest levels of wizards, Sire," she said. "But all we have is a name. If you can find a wizard of sufficient strength to counter his spell, you still don't know the actual spell, nor what Destiny looks like. You will have difficulties enough trying to determine from whence this Destiny came. How can you convince a high level wizard to come to the heart of a kingdom that despises wizards in order to counter a mysterious multi-layer complex spell devised by an unknown wizard of great strength?"

She peered up through her lashes to King Stefan's eyes and saw something else, something she had allowed herself to forget until she saw the doubt reflected there.

"And how can you trust anything I might say," she whispered, "until you learn what's really going on in Dalasmar? All you have is my speculation and fires in the night."

She pushed herself gingerly to her feet as the last of the sun's light slipped below the horizon, leaving only the flames from the hearth and two candles on the table to light the room.

"Perhaps, my King, you will have sufficient information on the morrow when your men return from Riverbend. I truly hope they can prove me wrong, though I greatly fear they will not. Good night to you all."

She turned and made her way slowly to Tox's bedchamber. No one rose to help or bid her a good night, so none had the occasion to see the sheen of tears she fought to contain.

***

Stefan watched the young woman make her arduous way to the other room with a mix of emotions. He admired her passion, how her plain face lit up when she quoted from one of her beloved books. Her fierce intelligence and insights compelled him to listen to her reasoning even when spoken with such a soft voice. The way she stood up to his men when presented with misinformation or ignorance contrasted with her uncertainty in a social situation. She seemed remarkably shy, yet when her knowledge could inform decisions and actions, she overcame fear to speak her mind. And her concern for others over her own needs spoke of a nobility Stefan rarely saw among those titled with nobility.

If Emily did work for Willi and sought to lead Stefan into a trap, she did so with incredible finesse. He could not see the lie in her eyes, in her manner, yet he couldn't fully embrace this truth either. His heart went out to this girl who found the courage to step out of her arena of comfort to do what she felt right, and who tried so hard to hide her anguish when she knew that Stefan could not afford to trust her yet.

Tomorrow would bring answers. Either his own brother had violated every oath of familial bonds and loyalty, sheltering a powerful wizard to poison people against Stefan, or Emily had lied, seeking to thrust the kingdom into turmoil for her own purposes. How could he hope she spoke truth?

Chapter 10

Sim crouched in a clump of bushes a stone's throw from the road about three miles outside Riverbend's west gate, peering anxiously into the distance as he waited for the King's envoy. Lord Prichard waited silently at his side, sitting cross legged in the damp mulch of old leaves, heedless of any stains his trousers might incur. The nobleman had adopted the guise of a farmer, donning the much rougher clothing of a mean peasant rather than his usual silks and fine linen, with little fuss. After what they had seen, Sim had no problems convincing Lord Prichard to escape the city in disguise the previous evening, slipping past Whillim's mercenary gate guards with the other farmers heading home from market. Surprisingly, the man had altered his demeanour and gave evidence of the speech and mannerisms of a farmer at the gate so well that Sim wondered if he had done such things before.

Two things led Sim to hasten their departure. The first came when he had questioned one of the City Watch.

Sim had worked with Henley in past years before becoming one of King Stefan's soldiers. The two still occasionally shared a pint or two in one of the taverns, so when he saw Hen going in to The Silver Stag, joining the man for a drink had raised no suspicions. The Watch had helped hold the gate while Captain Frederick had led men to the King, and it seemed the mercenaries had mostly left them alone as the Captain had hoped, or at the least, had not hunted them as they did any in uniforms supporting King Stefan. Hen would know the temperament of the Watch.

"It's crazy, I tell you," Hen muttered, tossing his Watch cap to the table and freeing his sandy curls as he lifted a mug to his lips. "Them thugs the Prince has brought in look hard at a man, but long as he keeps his mumbling to himself and follows orders, they leave us be." He wiped a fist across the foam of ale at his thick moustache and scowled at Sim. "But keeping my mouth shut when Whillim struts about on the ramparts like he owns the place, and listening to those who speak so fervently for him as though he's the King, just makes me sick."

"How can the Prince think this will work?" Sim wanted to know. "How can anyone he's not paying take his orders?"

"You got me," Hen shrugged. "But perfectly reasonable Councillors, staunch supporters of Stefan yesterday, now demand the renegade's head to placate *King* Whillim. None as says his name, but it's clear to me the Prince has denounced the King as a usurper, and somehow made those in charge believe him."

"I heard the Prince found himself some kind of magic," Sim offered hesitantly. "Think he'd actually go for that?"

Hen shook his head, though not in negation.

"You're guess is as good as mine, Sim. It would explain the sudden change in behaviour, but why not use it on everyone, then? The Watch holds almost as many men as this mercenary band and believe me, we're close to turning on them. More than one fight between us; wouldn't take much to light the flame. We've quelled just about enough disquiet in the streets that we can turn our attention to the mercs. I know Watch Commander's sorely tempted. Wouldn't surprise me if that's his first order once he's finished with the Prince."

A shiver of dread stole down Sim's spine.

"The Watch Commander's with the Prince now?"

"Woman came from Whillim to request his presence just before I came here," Hen said. He frowned. "You know I don't frighten easy, Sim, and certainly not for no woman, but this one ... her eyes so cold and intense, the way she spoke and expected you to obey and you find, strangely, that you've done what she's asked just so you can get that frosty stare off you. I tell you, I'd rather fight a dozen hard core mercs than face that Lady Destiny again; and her attention was all for the Commander, like I didn't stand right beside him."

Hen lifted his mug again, but froze with it half-way to his lips. His eyes took on a far-off look and he didn't move a muscle.

"Hen?" Sim asked, that shiver growing to outright fear. He waved his hand in front of Henley's eyes, but the man didn't react. Hen's fingers around the mug's handle had turned white with strain.

"Hen!" Sim grabbed his arm, feeling taut muscles so tense, his friend seemed made of iron. Then Henley blinked and glanced at Sim with a frown. The mug completed it's journey and Hen took a long draught. Sim leaned back in his chair, dropping his hand from Hen's arm.

"You all right, Sim?" Sim nodded numbly. "What was we talking about?"

Sim licked his lips and chose his words carefully, not sure what had happened but certain it boded ill.

"About the Watch Commander's meeting," he said. "We were speculating on what orders you'd receive, now that the streets have grown quieter."

"Right, of course." Hen gave his mug a hard stare. "Used to hold my ale better than that," he griped. Then he glanced back at Sim. "I'm sure King Whillim will have us help search out the renegade's supporters, maybe even find the man who turned against the King hiding in some stable loft or something." He grinned. "After all, who knows the city better than the City Watch, eh? The King's paid men don't have the brains to match the City Watch. We'll find the troublemakers in no time. Why don't you join us?"

"Already have my own orders from the King," Sim forced a smile and drained the last of his ale. "And I'd better get back to it." He offered Henley his arm as he rose. "Luck, my friend."

"Here now, you all right Sim? You look a little pale."

"Must be the ale," Sim replied, though the roiling in his gut had nothing to do with drink and everything to do with magic.

He retreated as quickly as he could without causing suspicion and met up with Lord Prichard in the shadows of a tavern a couple of streets over. The nobleman wore stained traveller's garb reasonably well, but he still looked a noble to Sim.

"Nobody's talking much, but ... gods, man, you look horrible!" Prichard kept his voice low. Sim grabbed his arm and pulled him into the deeper shadows of a nearby alley.

"We've got to get out of the city with as little notice as we can.

You'll forgive me, my Lord, but even dressed like that, you're not likely to get out without questions."

Prichard narrowed his dark eyes, but did not object.

"I'm guessing you've learned more than me, then. What do you suggest?"

"Farmers," Sim answered. "We've about an hour before most at market start to head back to their farms. If we slip in with one or two of them, maybe we can escape before the Watch knows to look for us."

"The Watch?"

"And you'll have to stop looking so noble, Prichard." He intentionally left off the honourific. "Stoop or something; try to look more like you know a day's hard labour rather than the sword and a lance."

Prichard snorted at that, amusement twinkling in his eye.

"I believe I can manage that, though we'll need a change of outfits."

Which they found at a lower-end vendor. Something a few steps up from the rag bin, but still humble enough that they wouldn't present overly prosperous farmers, lacking a cart or pack mule. Before they could change into their new garb, Sim saw another familiar face and he froze. Prichard followed his gaze, cursed, then took both bundles of clothing and faded into the shadows before that face could turn and find Sim.

Faulk smiled as he approached, a dark bruise purpling his thin face from lip to right eye, all the more evident with his light brown hair pulled back in a sleek tail. Sim forced yet another pleasant expression onto his square features, not knowing what to expect, but sure from the man's lack of subterfuge that Faulk no longer hid. Given Faulk's earlier detention and apparent release, and Henley's sudden change of thoughts, Sim didn't dare trust anyone just because they had worked together in the past.

"Glad I found you, Sergeant," Faulk called. "The King wants to see all senior officers."

"I might have a rank, Faulk, but I'm hardly a senior officer," Sim objected, suppressing his desire to flee. "Besides, I already have my orders from the King."

Faulk frowned.

"And they involve you masquerading as a crafter?" Faulk asked dubiously.

"What better way to sniff out dissent than by looking like something I'm not?"

Faulk nodded uncertainly. "Guess that makes sense." He paused as though trying to remember something. "I wore clothes like that earlier," he mused, his voice so quiet, Sim had to strain to hear. "A crafter ..." he trailed off, then met Sim's gaze. "We worked this out before, didn't we? Hide in plain sight, see what we could see, looking for ..."

Sim's fingers closed into fists, wondering if he could take out Faulk before the man raised the alarm.

"Why can't I remember?" Faulk whispered, his gaze lost.

Sim leaned slightly away from the man and balanced himself, ready to bolt or fight, whichever became needful. Like with Henley, though, he took a chance.

"We were sent to watch for renegades," Sim said, drawing Faulk's attention again. "On orders from the King?"

"Right," Faulk agreed hesitantly. "King Whillim sent us to ... or was it Lady Destiny?" he asked with a shudder. "That one, I tell you ... scary wench." He shook all over like a dog emerging from the river, then seemed to draw himself together. "So King Whillim's already seen you?" He had regained his authoritative demeanour.

"Got my orders straight from the King's own mouth," Sim said.

"Excellent. Then I'll be off. Sir!" Faulk saluted then strode away, leaving Sim even paler than before.

When Prichard reappeared at his side and silently handed over the farmer's outfit, Sim didn't waste any more time.

"We have to get out of the city right now."

Prichard just nodded agreement, and they found themselves an amenable farmer just packing up his wares. The four of them—the farmer and his son, Sim and Prichard—passed the mercenaries manning the gate along side of three of the City Watch with little fuss.

Once out of sight of Riverbend's walls, they bid the farmer farewell and hurried ahead, until Sim took them off the road and into the bushes.

Sim explained all he had seen and heard.

"Like with the others," Prichard had said. "They go meet with the Prince or this strange woman, and when they come back, their memory's all scrambled. But that Watch friend of yours, you say he changed before your very eyes?"

"One minute we were talking about aiding King Stefan, and the next, he's all for Whillim. I have a theory, which is what led me to run."

"Let's hear it," Prichard said.

"Hen said the Watch Commander went to see Whillim, summoned directly by this Lady Destiny. What if they used whatever magic on him and it filtered down to those in his command?"

Prichard frowned.

"I don't know ..."

"Think about it," Sim insisted. "In the Watch, or the King's guard, for that matter, you follow orders, soldier to corporal to sergeant, all on up to captain, or Commander. You might not agree with the order, or understand it, but you trust that those above you in rank know what they're doing, so you obey. What if, in taking those in command, their altered thoughts pass down through the chain of command, just like an order?"

Prichard's features hardened, his dark eyes hooded.

"That would explain why they went after the Council last night, and why they're looking for senior officers now," the nobleman reasoned, his expression a strange mix of consideration and condemnation.

"And if they've turned Faulk," Sim added his own fears, "then they might know our plans to meet with King Stefan's envoy in the morning. If they took us, or worse, followed us to the King, imagine the consequences of changing the King's memories so that *he* thought Whillim ruled Dalasham." Prichard's face grew stony and fury erupted in his eyes. "I think that's why they hunted him last night, why he fled, leaving us to gather the strays."

"How many men does Faulk command?" Prichard asked.

"He doesn't hold rank above soldier, but he knows where we sent stragglers. If he talked before they messed with his mind, then Sirs Edvard, Castel and Pietor and the men we sent them stand in danger, but at least each knows the danger and has walls to shelter behind."

"And the King?" Prichard asked softly.

Sim smiled grimly.

"He gave a direction, nothing more. Once past the west gate, Dalasham stretches far, so Faulk could not betray his location as he doesn't know it."

"So the Prince's men might start streaming past us at any moment, hoping for a glimpse of the King or his envoy, set to arrive at the west gate some time tomorrow."

"Two hours before noon," Sim agreed. "Which is why we're here now, waiting for night to fall. I hope you don't mind sleeping rough, Prichard, because I intend to wait here until dawn, then strike out west until the road splits. With any luck, we'll catch the envoy before he gets too close to the city, regroup with the King and tell him just how desperate our situation has become. One thing for certain, we have to make sure that King Stefan doesn't go anywhere near Riverbend until we can figure out how to reverse this magic the Prince has."

They did as Sim suggested, partaking of a cold meal of berries and roots and a couple of meat pies that Prichard had obtained earlier, before taking turns trying to sleep and watching for anyone passing in the night. Dawn found them both tired and stiff, yet anxious to set off.

They used the road only while it remained unoccupied, hiding themselves in what concealment they could find when they heard anyone approach, although they saw only farmers and herders and those going to market. When the road took its first split three miles from the west gate, they settled themselves to wait in the verge.

When finally they heard the hooves of horses approaching from the west, Sim waited until he recognised the grim face of the man riding and leading a second saddled but riderless beast before calling softly like a raven. Captain Frederick pulled his mount to a halt and peered into the bushes warily, his hand dropping to the sword at his side.

Sim rose from his crouch, pulling Sir Prichard to his feet behind him.

"Captain," Sim greeted, his eyes searching the road, though it remained empty save for the Captain of the King's bodyguard. "You don't want to go any farther, and we don't want to waste any time here."

Captain Frederick studied the pair, noting their slept-in farmer's clothing and their own wary postures.

"You're it?" he asked.

"We sent others to the knights before the Prince's thugs took Faulk and ... changed his thinking. They'll have to take their chances unless we can get them word, though it might already come too late. But all we knew of the King was west. I hope I've bought us time, as they won't expect you for another couple of hours, but it's a slim hope."

The Captain glared back the way Sim and Prichard had come, then stared down at Sim.

"Take me in chains if you must, Captain," Sim said, "but the King must know what he's facing. If in doubt, demand the name of the King, and those who follow King Stefan *might* remain loyal, but for the love of all that's holy, make damned sure *you're* not one of those captured."

Fred raised an eyebrow, then motioned Prichard to the empty saddle and hauled Sim up behind him.

"Seems you have a story to tell," the Captain grunted as he turned the horses around and set them off at a brisk trot. "Start talking."

***

Something in his encounter with Sim had unnerved Faulk. He couldn't place his finger on just why the memory bothered him. Something about the clothes? A thought Faulk couldn't quite dredge up.

He continued his sweep of the area, looking for any officers from the King's men as King Whillim had instructed, but that niggling doubt refused to go away. Finally, he stopped in the shade of Marrick's Stable and gazed unseeing across the courtyard, tracing his steps back to the last time he and Sim had worked together.

Yesterday, Faulk thought, bringing the Sergeant and his crafter's disguise to the forefront of his mind, mentally placing himself next to the man in similar garb. Yes, they had stashed away their weapons and uniforms, and found men loyal to the King, sending them off to ... where? Why had they needed to send them anywhere? The riots had centred mainly in the eastern sections of the city, so why would the King want men sent anywhere else?

Faulk squeezed his eyes shut at a brief stab of pain in his temples.

Before that, he thought. We fought at the east gate. Helping someone flee. No, keeping the mob under control. No, fighting mercenaries hired by—

The wound in his leg throbbed. He tried to massage the pain away, chasing down that elusive memory. What had happened at the gate? He could almost recall a face, mostly hidden in shadows, hazy, as though masked by the smoke of the fires. Whose face? Someone he had to protect ... agony pressed against the back of his eyeballs and he slapped his hands to his face.

"How did you escape the chambers?" the wizard demanded, dark blue eyes so intense he could see nothing of her face now save those frigid orbs. "Who led the King out?" The King? Faulk remembered staring at Whillim behind Destiny. There stood the King. Or did he? What—

"Who is this woman of whom the page spoke? Give me her name."

Faulk kept his silence, though something seemed to push at his mind, fiery claws raking his brain. So long as he thought of Emily as a girl and not a woman, he could ignore that strange pull.

"The boy said 'she'. Who is she?"

"Emily," Faulk had answered, the name drawn unwillingly from his throat despite his intentions to keep silent.

"That tells me nothing," Destiny snarled. "Who is she?"

"You wanted a name," Faulk growled. "I gave you one."

Destiny's backhand slap caught him hard across the face, some sort of spiked half-glove snugged tight against her knuckles.

Faulk's hand traced the welt that had split his lip, bruised his face. That hadn't come from the skirmish at the gate, as he had thought, but from the wizard's wrath. He shook his head, trying to clear the fog pressing in on his thoughts. The Lady Destiny stood as King Whillim's right hand, and Faulk served the King loyally. What did these memories mean, then? Did they have any merit?

Again, pain lanced through his head.

"How did Stefan escape his chambers?" Whillim asked this time as Destiny's hard gaze bore into Faulk's mind. "My men saw you enter my brother's rooms, but no one came out again. So how did you escape?"

His brother? King Whillim had no brother, save an infant who had died in childhood. Faulk struggled through the pain. An infant named Stefan. Why had the King used that name? Why had the King whom Faulk served loyally subjected him to this treatment when he *knew* his King as a fair man? This Whillim from his splintered recollections would gain no honourable man's loyalty, yet Faulk clearly remembered his joy and pride at joining the King's service. How could both thoughts hold true?

"Hidden passage through the castle," Faulk's tortured half-remembrances played in his mind's eye as though watching a mummer's play, each word ground out unbidden as Faulk fought Destiny's magic demanding his surrender. *"Door in the wall. Already open. Just followed my King."*

Just followed my King. The phrase brought an explosion of agony that dropped Faulk to his knees, hands clutching the sides of his head as though pressing against his temples could keep his brain from leaking through his ears. He might have cried out. People looked his way, unease in every glance, and gave him a wide berth.

My King, he thought, trying to bring into focus that fuzzy, shadowed face, to place the name with the man. The torment blinded him, and the blackness did nothing to sharpen vision.

Whillim is King, a foreign thought intruded, spikes of conviction in this idea slashing through the darkness. Faulk tried to fight it, but the notion brought blessed relief from the pain and shreds of light to the black.

Whillim is King. He tried the thought for himself, and the pressure eased somewhat. He heard his own ragged gasps, felt the ache in his chest as laboured lungs pulled in sweet air, fastened onto these sensations as a life-line to sanity.

Whillim is King. Sight returned and the pain receded. Faulk eased himself back to his feet, leaning heavily against the stable wall, his breath evening out, returning to normal. In the back of his mind, he imagined he could see blue eyes so dark they seemed almost black. He filed them away in the recesses of his brain, knowing they had some importance, that what he had just experienced had as much truth as what he thought he knew. But he didn't dwell on it, not now, not yet.

Dangerous thoughts those, trying to remember what a wizard did not wish remembered. Whillim was King and Faulk would serve him. But he would keep the thought of this other—he didn't dare try a name or a face—safely hidden until he had need of it. Whillim and Destiny thought they had him firmly in their grip, that he would obey as blindly as all the others. *What others?* he thought, then pushed that away too. A slight pressure built up in his head again, the dull throb of a looming headache, but so long as he didn't actively attempt to recover those strange memories, it remained a distant pain. Faulk could deal with pain.

Whillim was King—*a strong and generous ruler whom Faulk had served for six years, two as his personal guard, a man who had earned respect from many, who would not back down from what he felt needful, yet would listen to wise council before taking definitive action*—and Faulk would serve the King.

He put his encounter with Sergeant Sim from his mind and continued to search for those officers loyal to the King. Whillim wanted to speak to each of them.

Chapter 11

Fatigue tried to wrap its greedy fingers around Destiny's mind, but she ruthlessly pushed it aside. She had far too much still to accomplish before she could truly rest. She had managed a couple hours of sleep late in the night (or early morning), but her constantly churning thoughts and the sense of so much yet to do kept any real rest from the wizard.

So she had risen early, before dawn even thought to kiss a blush onto the sky, and roused a sleepy mercenary to fetch the man she wanted to see from whatever slumber he might have achieved. She called for fruit and tea to break her fast while she waited, and graciously set aside a place for her guest to share the meal in her solar. A maid stirred up the fire to a soft glow and left candles to provide light before slipping off to other duties, leaving Destiny to her accustomed privacy.

When the man arrived, a charcoal cloak wrapped around his grey tunic and leggings for warmth in the pre-dawn chill, only the dishevelment of his light blond hair streaked with wings of white gave any indication that the soldier had pulled this man from sleep. His piercing blue-green eyes held no sign of any fatigue.

"My Lady," he greeted, waiting until she gave him leave to sit and join her at her repast.

"Thank you for answering my summons so quickly, Chief Librarian."

A ghost of a smile touched Chief Librarian Darien's lips.

"We grow used to rising at all hours to serve the needs of the castle, my Lady. How may I serve yours?"

"By explaining how you can misplace something as important as the Royal Proofs."

Darien leaned forward, plucked a grape from the fruit tray and took up his cup of tea before settling back in his chair to regard Destiny, meeting her narrowed gaze with his own measured look.

"I cannot say," he replied with an uncanny depth of calm. "I had them copied as per your request, under the direction of our best scribe, my Junior Assistant. As I understand it, that night saw strangers in my library with the intention of removing the Proofs, although such is forbidden without royal authorization—"

"Which they had," Destiny interrupted.

"Perhaps so," Darien allowed. "Yet I saw neither authorization nor Proofs after that night. I cannot, in fact, ascertain whether your soldiers took the Proofs upon themselves and for some reason kept them hidden, or if someone misplaced them in the confusion. I have my people scouring the library for any sign of the Royal Proofs or any indication that something else might have gone missing. Until we have completed our search and investigations, my Lady, I simply cannot say what happened to them."

Destiny speared a piece of melon from the tray, her gaze firm upon the librarian as she chewed it in half.

"You do understand that we hold you responsible for anything that happens in your little domain," she said after she swallowed. "If someone other than the King's soldiers removed those Proofs, you will share in the consequences."

"I expect nothing less, my Lady," Darien said.

"And what of this Junior Assistant? You have, of course, questioned him. What has he to say for himself?"

She saw the hesitation in his eyes, a brief flicker of unease that made her take notice as the man chose his words carefully.

"None have seen the Junior Assistant to the Chief Librarian since that afternoon. As I understand it, the copying took into the night. Often we find ourselves consumed by our work and do not notice such things as the passing of time or the call of hunger until we finish our work. So no one noticed the absence until the morning."

"So there is a great possibility that this assistant removed the

Proofs for his own reasons," Destiny pounced, ignoring the shaking of Darien's head. "Why did you leave important documents with an underling, Chief Librarian, when you should have seen to the task yourself?"

"I chose the Junior Assistant because of the efficiency the scribe would bring to the task, the speed and authenticity offered by such penmanship. My scribing is fine enough, I suppose, as is that of the rest of my staff, but the Junior Assistant has the best hand by far, and for something of this import, I assumed you wanted the best."

"Do you insist that he could not have taken the Proofs?"

"To what end?" Darien countered, spreading his arms wide in inquiry. "The Junior Assistant has worked for me for ten years, and loves the library too much to risk being parted from it. It is more home than the room that now lies vacant, none of the belongings amiss. If someone stole the Proofs from those hands that value books so highly, then they stole the Junior Assistant along with them."

Destiny found the man's devotion to his people oddly moving, and that made her pause. Rarely did another's passion touch her. If this kingdom did not shun the everyday use of magic, she might suspect that Darien tried a spell on her, urging her to trust where she should not. But she had seen no evidence of such. He might have a latent talent, though, a thought she filed away for later scrutiny; or he simply believed so much in his people. Either way, Destiny had to see past his feelings to what he did not say.

"This Junior Assistant who so loves the library, does he perhaps know the rest of the castle as well?" she asked, and smiled when the question brought a puzzled frown.

"The Junior Assistant seldom leaves the library save for walks beyond the castle walls to clear the head."

"So he would know most books in the library, and few people outside it, yes?"

"I would call that a fair assessment," Darien conceded.

"Does he have an area of special interest?"

"Everything holds that one's interest. An insatiable thirst for knowledge and the written word."

"Tell me, Chief Librarian, does your library have sketches of this castle?"

"Of course, my Lady," he said.

"Do you know them also?"

"I do."

"So you know about the secret passages within the walls," Destiny stated, receiving a startled blink where she had expected a flash of guilt.

"Secret passages?" he sat forward excitedly. "Do such exist?"

Destiny frowned.

"If they do, could your Junior Assistant have found evidence of them?"

He snorted, his lips curling into a soft smile.

"If anyone could, it would be—" he bit off his words, staring at her with chagrin. Destiny pounced.

"Tell me, Darien, why do you keep side-stepping any occurrence where you might name this Junior Assistant? Do you fear what will happen when we find him?"

"None of my librarians have done any wrong," he began.

"And yet you cannot find this one Assistant, nor the Proofs. What does he hide, and why do you protect a potential traitor?"

Darien rose to his feet and glared down at her, the heat in his eyes a fearsome thing.

"I will not sit here and have you name those in my care as traitors, nor allow your failings to bring harm to me and mine, Lady Destiny." His tone had turned cold, quite unlike the man who had sat so calmly across from her mere moments ago. Where others might quail at the sudden change, Destiny just sat back and regarded him with dispassionate eyes. "Blame me or not in the disappearance of the Proofs, but do not insinuate without evidence that any in my care are guilty of any wrongdoing. You wish to see if the Junior Assistant found any information about secret passages, I will gladly show you the likely sections of the library to search for such documentation. But if you name any of us as traitors, I'll know the reason why."

Destiny smirked as she rose to face the angry man.

"Very well, Chief Librarian. We will search your library."

Darien blinked at her conciliatory turn.

"But you will give me this librarian's name, or *I'll* know the reason why." She smiled at him, knowing the look would give no comfort. "After all, your search for the lad thus far has not proven fruitful," she reached for a strawberry. "Once you give me his name, we can work in concert to bring him in and learn what he knows of the location of the Royal Proofs. And if it does turn out that he disregarded royal commands, well ...." She popped the berry in her mouth and chewed slowly.

Darien swallowed but did not shy away from her gaze.

"Others will know his name," she murmured. "Save yourself the trouble of making me your enemy."

His eyes narrowed.

"Promise no harm will come of it," he demanded. "Promise that you will give fair hearing to what occurred and take into consideration the turmoil and fear of that night."

"Of course," Destiny said.

Darien's gaze sharpened, the intensity of his focus having its own power on her.

"Promise it in the name of the Kalima, patron to all Innosvarian wizards," he urged, taking Destiny completely by surprise. "Promise it on the source of your powers, wizard."

She gaped at him, wondering how he could possibly know her origins. She saw the flash of satisfaction in his scrutiny, though his visage had become a mask. This man would suffer no fools. She had used the Destiny Seat on him yesterday, bringing the library staff to her cause, yet clearly his mind remained his own. His loyalties lay with his people first, and his King second, and she had best remember that.

"You have my oath, librarian," she snarled. "I will listen with an open mind to what your precious Junior Assistant has to say and will not judge him foul without evidence. No harm will come to the innocent; I swear it by the name of the Kalima."

Darien nodded slowly.

"I will show you the section of library most likely to contain any records of the structure of Dalasmar Castle," he said, turning and striding for the door. As he opened it, he looked back, waiting for her to join him. When she did, he gave his answer.

"You seek Junior Assistant to the Chief Librarian Emily."

Destiny stumbled as he ushered her through the door. She knew the man grinned at her lapse, but couldn't bring herself to care as she strode thoughtfully at his side. *Emily,* the guard had named. And now *Emily,* said the Chief Librarian. They would not find her in the city, she knew. This Emily had somehow warned the King of Whillim's plot and led him to safety. Destiny would find the woman when she found the

King, and likely both with the Royal Proofs in hand. Whillim could no longer rely on forgeries to lull the other kingdoms into the belief that he ruled. So much more important now to retrieve Stefan. And with him, this mysterious Emily, a mere librarian who dared interfere in the machinations of a wizard.

Destiny could almost laugh at the irony of her plans being threatened by another woman. Almost.

***

The voices drew Em's attention first. She knew the silence of the library and had attuned herself to note any disruption, no matter how slight, which would announce visitors, and that skill served her now. The others glanced at her curiously as she rose to face the door, unconsciously keeping the table between herself and it, a paring knife clutched in her fist, leaving the carrots for the evening stew quivering forgotten on the table. Then her companions heard the newcomers also, and Jo and Dari surreptitiously placed themselves in front of the King, ready to defend should the need arise. Jo's own knife glistened with the blood of mutton and Dari's long wooden spoon dripped with broth, the pot lid fitted in his off hand as a shield. King Stefan stood close to the hearth, his hand hovering near the fire poker.

Em wondered if it boded well or ill that the Captain had returned so soon.

Ambrose, who had stood guard at the road, opened Goodman Tox's front door and ushered three men into the farmhouse. Fred led Sergeant Sim and a tall man with red-streaked auburn hair, both dressed in farmer's garb, inside, and Ambrose brought up the rear, sealing out the late morning air as he pulled the door shut.

Em felt a strange mingling of relief and terror claw at her gut to mix uncomfortably with the healing tug of her wound as Sim and this Lord Prichard recounted their findings. She finally had her story corroborated, yet that only led to fear and uncertainty. The Prince worked with an unknown wizard to erase King Stefan from history, and with each high-ranking person subjected to Destiny's device, several others fell prey to a falsehood they swore held true.

Em wondered how long before her own superior succumbed

to this folly, how long the King could trust her to remain loyal. To have her finally confirmed as behind the King only to lose her will to a magic she didn't know how to fight made her angry, and she determined to serve her rightful King by imparting whatever knowledge he might need as quickly as possible.

She had resumed meal preparations while the men told their tale, but now, with the last vegetable placed in the pot and the pot hung over the fire, she wiped her hands thoroughly on a cloth, then reached into the pocket of the smock she had donned this morning. Or rather, the lower half of the smock, having completed the slice the sword had left on the garment and discarding the useless upper portion. She had managed to save the lower section with its large pockets, tying the fabric about her waist. Only a little dried blood showed at the edges. She carefully drew out the rolled and slightly wrinkled copy of the Royal Proofs from the confines of the pocket, smoothed the pages flat, and placed them on Goodman Tox's sturdy table.

"I thought we left those behind," the King said very quietly.

"This is the copy, Sire," Em replied, her concentration on the papers before her. "They lack the Royal Seal yet, and my mark in the corner indicates this is not the original." She pointed to the tiny scroll symbol she had drawn in the lower corner, her signature used on everything she copied. Each scribe had his own mark; she had chosen the little scroll as her own. "Also, the parchment, though of finest quality, does not match the age or composition of the original Proofs."

"Why bring that out now?" Lord Prichard wanted to know.

Em kept her head down, not comfortable with the noble's attention. The man seemed decent enough, but she didn't know him. It surprised her to realise that she felt more at ease with the King and his men, despite the difference in their stations. What a strange set of circumstances to lead them to this point.

"The Prince wanted them copied for a reason," she whispered. "I don't know if determining how he planned to use them to advantage might help, but it seemed a place to start. Also, if Goodman Tox does not have paper to spare, I can use the back of one of the pages to draw a map of the tunnels for the King." Though the thought of marring any of the copies left her slightly nauseated, Em had to give the King the secret of the hidden passages, and if that meant ruining part of the Royal

Proofs copies, well ... at least they were only copies. She suppressed a slight shudder.

"Let's start with the Proofs," said the King. "How could they help Willi as they stand?"

"As they stand, they do not," replied Em. "But he could have them changed."

"And that's what your copy would do?" Lord Prichard asked. "He could alter it before affixing the Royal Seal and thereby making it the new Proof?"

"Not exactly, although you're not far off, sir," she said. "He would have to change the original, and any copies would have to reflect that."

"So why did he have you make a copy if the original still reflects the truth?" the noble wanted to know. Em found herself starting to relax with him as he asked his questions in honest curiosity and not with condescension.

"At a guess, I would surmise that the Prince did not expect anyone could make a decent copy quickly enough. He would have taken the Proofs and the unfinished copy that night in the library, then had plenty of time to make the scribe finish the copy to his designs."

"It's fortunate that you're very good at your job, then, isn't it? And that you had the good sense to pull us all to safety." King Stefan smiled at her before turning his regard to the pages on the table.

"How would Willi alter the Proofs? Could he simply remove my name and erase any sign of my existence?"

"He could not, Sire, but he could add a date of death, and a date of ascension."

The King's eyes rose to meet hers. She held his gaze briefly before returning to the parchment before them.

"If I had died in infancy or as a child ..."

"Then Whillim would have ascended to the throne," Lord Prichard finished. "And with that magic device altering memory, no one would wonder why we had missed the child's funeral or the new King's coronation." He glanced at Em. "How many other documents would the Prince have to tamper with to back up such a story?"

Em shook her head.

"More than a few to cover all traces. He would have to produce a death certificate for one, but more telling are all the decrees King Stefan has ever signed. If the true King had died as a child, to whom would all those signatures belong? How could the Prince change them?"

"With enough time, the library staff could do so," King Stefan said. "And if Willi succeeds, he will have that time. So why worry about the Royal Proofs now?"

"In case he had to convince other rulers of his right to the throne before he could change everything to his liking," Fred spoke up, expression grim. "Another sovereign doubts his place, all Whillim has to do is whip out the Royal Proofs. If any thought to look further, no doubt Whillim or his wizard would provide altered documents from Emily's boss."

Em bristled at the comment. Chief Librarian Darien would never go along with such subterfuge. Or at least, he wouldn't had he a choice. Darien guarded everything in his care with a fierce commitment, books and people. He never shied away from reality, even if it gave him pain.

Em remembered one time when Darien had found a scribe he had taken in stealing some of the histories for a nobleman's son who couldn't be bothered to sign them out himself for a class project. Darien gave the scribe every chance to confess and return the books, but the lad had continued to deny the allegations, even going so far as to blame another for his actions. Darien worked out a way to retrieve the books without the scribe's knowledge, yet in such a way that the scribe could still rectify his errors. The lad, however, refused to reform his ways, for he had taken to charging the noble for his services, and had offered said services to other nobles as well. When the Watch caught the scribe red-handed, thanks to Darien's efforts, the scribe still tried to blame someone else. Darien defended the innocent party and left the scribe to the authorities, but he had felt the betrayal, for the Chief Librarian had taken the lad in to begin with. Never had he shied away from the truth, nor tried to cover it up. Instead he had tried to make it right to the betterment of all.

Now Captain Frederick suggested that Darien would willingly alter facts to suit the Prince's needs. She couldn't blame the Captain for his words, no matter how they disturbed her, yet even under this wizard's spell, Em knew Darien could do no such thing, not without question. And that thought worried her. If Darien didn't do what Whillim and Destiny wanted, what would happen to him? And how long did she have before they used that device on Darien and changed his thinking? Would it change him enough that he would agree to forge documents, to rewrite history?

Would it change her so that she remembered reading something different?

She shook her head, forcing such uncomfortable thoughts aside. She could do nothing for Darien right now, but she could help her King.

"Using the Proofs to placate other rulers makes sense," Em acknowledged Fred's point. "Perhaps any recalcitrant Councillors as well, though it sounds like the Prince planned for them all to fall under Destiny's spell."

She paused, her thoughts spinning as she studied the copy, fingers laid gently on the paper. "Maybe to keep any questions from arising?" she murmured. Sometimes, when working through a problem, Em fell into the habit of vocalising her thoughts. Often, she didn't notice doing so unless someone pointed it out, and as most of the library staff knew of her predilections, no one had interrupted her for several years. Now, the King and his companions listened quietly as she laid out her thoughts. "Is it possible this memory spell needs reaffirmation? Proof to back up the magic? Or maybe Prince Whillim just wants an element of power in his own hands, something he can physically touch without any reliance on magic. Maybe Destiny holds the true power, and the Proofs are the Prince's way of fooling himself. Or his own proof, his way of assuring that Destiny has not used the device on him?"

She shook her head again, and as she did so, noticed the men gathered around her. Realising she had let her mouth wander with her thoughts, Em clamped her lips shut, a blush heating her face. She quickly averted her eyes and snatched her hand away from the sheets on the table.

"Those are all interesting possibilities to ponder," the King said, his tone neutral, though Em feared he suppressed mirth at her ramblings. "And it points out that we can't really know what's in Willi's mind regarding the Proofs. Keeping these and the originals out of his hands seems a wise decision, regardless of his intended purpose for them."

The others agreed.

"Then let us turn our attention to Emily's tunnels," said King

117

Stefan. "You told me you found proof of their existence in old parchments in a mostly unused section of the library, correct?"

Em nodded.

"How easily could someone else find them? Someone who might wonder how we escaped my chambers that night?"

"Not as easily as one might think," she responded promptly. "Almost all information on the structure and design of the castle traditionally resides in the vault to keep it secure from any who might want to use it for ill. Drawings and lithographs depicting non-essential information lie mostly in the south wing near the library's entrance. Anyone looking for the information would look there first. I found the parchments in the far east wing, as I said, hidden beneath several tomes of unrelated history. I thought it prudent to keep them where I found them, out of easy reach. Also," here she hesitated, then blurted out in little more than a whisper, "I had to translate them."

"Translate them?" Lord Prichard repeated. "From what language?"

"Old Dalasham, written in archaic script."

Prichard blinked.

"And of course you understand that."

"Several of the old histories use that language, and my father taught me some ancient script."

"But if the tunnels are mapped out," put in Fred, "then what does the language matter? Surely, if you can follow a map, you can understand the parchment."

"It's not drawn as a map," Em explained. "Only written instructions. It begins with drawings outlining additions to the castle in its early years, but then, when describing the passageways and each entrance's unique key, everything becomes the written word."

"And you just happened to find this information one day," Stefan said softly.

Em moved to the fire to stir the stew, keeping her focus on the contents of the pot so that she wouldn't have to look at anyone.

"No one ever went to that alcove, so no one would question the presence of a young girl exploring the stacks because no one would see me. People frighten me; books do not, so it seemed a safe haven, far from everyone. Darien told me before he brought me to the Palace that I could read anything in the library so long as I did all my work, which included keeping the books in good order. When I found that dusty alcove, it seemed a paradise to me, because I could read what others obviously hadn't for years so long as I cared for the books there. So yes, Sire, I just happened to find that information one day because no one else wanted to venture into the grime of decades to see what treasures lay hidden beneath."

She tapped the spoon against the edge of the pot and laid it aside, then finally turned to face the room, gaze lowered and hands gripping each other at her waist. Without looking up, she made her way back to her chair and sat in front of the copies of the Royal Proofs.

As the silence stretched, Em slipped her hand into the pocket of her smock and closed her fingers around a piece of charcoal. She drew it out, then reached for the top sheet of the copies, turning it over to begin outlining the layout of the tunnels with her nub of charcoal.

A warm, callused hand covered hers to halt her actions. Startled, she glanced up, her cheeks blazing hot when she saw that the hand belonged to the King.

"We'll find you something more suitable to draw upon," he said.

She shook her head, suddenly feeling the sting of tears gathering in her eyes.

"We may not have time, Sire," she whispered, pulling her hand free. "If they use that thing on Darien ... if they change him ... I don't know how long I have before I won't know to help you."

With that uncomfortable sentence hanging on the air, Em put her charcoal to paper again and began to sketch. She could always recopy the first pages of the Royal Proofs that she ruined later.

If she retained the memory to do so.

Chapter 12

Destiny growled her impatience, tempted to grab the nearest stack of books and fling them about to vent her frustration. Better than throttling the man beside her, but not by much, and equally as childish and unhelpful.

The Chief Librarian had brought her to the secure vault after their conversation yesterday. While a great deal about the structure and potential vulnerabilities of the castle—as well as how to safeguard against anyone trying to exploit them—resided under lock and key in the fortified stone chamber, nothing anywhere had indicated the existence of secret passageways within the walls.

The Royal Proofs had also once rested in the vault, Darien having pointed out the empty case that would normally cradle those important pages. Said Proofs remained as obviously absent as the information Destiny wanted, and the woman who had access to both.

Further search in the public areas of the library that housed anything pertaining to the castle proved equally as fruitless and Destiny had admitted defeat for the day, retreating to watch over Whillim and his games of power that night.

She had returned to the library just past dawn, determined to find something of use. This time, she had brought two of Milos' mercenaries, the men sent originally to retrieve the Royal Proofs. She hoped, by tracing their actions that night, that she might glean something useful, either about the location of the Proofs, the existence of hidden passageways, or the whereabouts of Junior Assistant Emily.

Chief Librarian Darien had taken his time to see to her this morning, only recently deigning to make an appearance. Had she not needed the man to grant access to the vault, she could have already finished this task and moved on to other matters. The mercenaries, already nervous by their prolonged exposure to Destiny's foul mood, seemed unsure whether to add their own grumbles to hers, or if trying to maintain some form of military discipline would get their fidgeting selves away from her faster. They clung to a shred of self-preservation and stayed out of Destiny's way as she glared at Darien.

Who stared back calmly and waited for her to set the tone of this encounter.

With a deep breath, Destiny drew a mantle of serenity and competency about her shoulders.

"Thank you for taking the time to answer to the King's needs, Librarian," she said, voice only slightly warmer than the ice she knew glittered from her gaze.

Darien, to his credit, ignored her subtle threat and nodded an acknowledgement.

"We serve the needs of the kingdom, as ever," he replied. "What more can I help you with today?"

Destiny waved a brief hand toward the mercenaries.

"The King had charged these men with obtaining the Royal Proofs. I had hoped, by retracing their movements from that night, that you and I might learn something to explain the disappearance of your Junior and those Proofs."

Because she had watched for any signs, Destiny noticed how one of the men flinched at the word 'disappearance'. Interesting.

Darien glanced at the men in question, then moved to Destiny's side.

"Then by all means, gentlemen," he said, arms open wide. "Lead on."

The mercenaries looked at each other, then the one who had flinched shrugged a shoulder and led the way.

"Went to the scribe desk first," he rasped, an old scar adorning his neck like a chain showing where a wound had damaged his voice. He suited actions to words, moving quietly despite his bulk, drawing them silently in his wake. When they reached it a moment later, he pointed unnecessarily at the tidy yet empty desk framed in the cool glow of the early sun limning one of the windows. "We found nothing here, so went on to check the vault, like the Prince—er, King," he amended with a sidelong glance to Darien. "Like the King ordered."

"We had a lantern rather than wasting time lighting the whole library," the second man spoke up. "Even so, we searched the areas King told us to and found nothing."

"You went in the vault?" Darien stopped and turned to the pair as they reached that very destination. "Unsupervised?" Destiny could almost admire the indignation Darien put into the word. "How?"

Scar, as Destiny chose to name the first merc, licked his lips nervously and looked to his equally large companion, who reminded Destiny of an Ox. She decided she liked the comparison.

"King gave us a key," Ox admitted. Darien's eyes narrowed, but he managed to hold back the snarl Destiny could see pulling at his mouth. With a sharp nod, he indicated that Scar and Ox should continue.

Scar looked at Destiny, swallowed at her expression, then turned back to the vault.

"We went in to search."

As Darien had not opened the vault yet, and seemed in no hurry to do so, Scar just stared hard at the locked door, waiting. Ox stood as though at a military review, his gaze also riveted to the barrier. Destiny suppressed the urge to sigh. While used to waiting for someone else to break the silence, she had other concerns to see to today.

"If you would, Chief Librarian," she said, her own gaze fixed on the door rather than the irate man who finally pulled out his keys. Darien said not a word as he opened the door but Destiny could feel the icy stare of his regard as she followed the mercs into the vault. Although Darien didn't pull the door closed behind them, he did stand guard at the entrance, frigid blue-green eyes fixed on the soldiers while his body served to block any others from gaining admittance.

The mercenaries didn't move far, though they kept a respectful distance from the librarian. Scar indicated the empty case for the Royal Proofs.

"We found the case empty and, seeing nothing that looked like the Proofs—"

"King told us they would bear the Royal Seal and what that looked like," added Ox. "So that we wouldn't mistake them for any other papers."

"Right," Scar agreed, flicking his gaze to the stone-faced Darien, then across to Destiny, and quickly back to stare at the vacant home of the Proofs as the safest place to rest his eyes. "Nothing here and nothing nearby."

"And nowhere did you see anything suspicious," Destiny said, keeping her tone deceptively soft. "No missing librarian lurking around, sneaking into a hidden passageway with the Royal Proofs in her hands."

And there she saw it. Ox jolted and Scar covered one hand with the other, as though hiding something, yet he kept his wide-eyed stare firmly on the case. Ox slipped his gaze slightly toward Darien before turning it to the floor.

Neither, however, made the mistake of lying to her.

With a false smile, Destiny stood beside Darien and beckoned to the mercenaries.

"If you would, gentlemen, do show me what has slipped your mind until now."

Scar shuddered and closed his eyes for a moment, but he turned and moved toward her, Ox on his heels. Both men had paled considerably. To his credit, though, Scar kept his voice even.

"We left the vault," he said, waiting for Darien to move so that they could do so. After a small hesitation, Darien stepped aside. Destiny wondered if he sought to protect the secret passages or his precious Emily, surely knowing he could do neither now.

Destiny waited for Scar and Ox to lead her to Emily's escape, but they didn't move. Scar stood staring at a bookcase on the east wall, just inside the vault.

"We headed off to check the niches King told us about, figuring if we still found nothing, we'd come back and search by light of day," Ox said, voice curiously devoid of any emotion.

"Heard a thump from back here, then a kind of grinding noise," Scar took up the tale. "We rushed back in to see a cloud of dust in a tiny circle of light. Girl doused her candle, but the lantern showed her disappear into the wall. Tried to stop her, but she burned me and the wall swallowed her up. Didn't see if she took anything with her and couldn't get the wall to

123

open again to search her out."

"If we hadn't got back here so quick, hadn't seen her disappear, we wouldn't even have known what happened. Door disappeared just like her. No trace of nothing."

Destiny tilted her head, studying the men. They clearly intended to add nothing further.

"You, of course, had a good reason not to mention this little detail earlier," she scoffed. "Outwitted by a woman, deprived of your prize, and defeated by your ignorance." Now her tone hardened and Scar, at least, had the intelligence to blanch. "You cost me three days of inconvenience, time the King could have used to search out this hidden passage and rectify your incompetence. Instead, you chose to pretend this failure didn't happen. Did you think no one would find out?"

They didn't answer, not that she had expected them to. They knew the price of such a failure. She let them suffer under her heavy regard another moment, adding just a hint of her displeasure to scald along her glare. Minor magic for her, giving the hollow reward of watching sweat bead on Ox's brow and seeing the convulsive swallow of Scar's disfigured throat. But that got her nowhere.

"Where did the wall swallow the little librarian?" she finally demanded.

Scar nodded to the shelf in front of him.

"Behind that."

Destiny glanced at the shelf, then turned with a raised eyebrow to stare at Darien. He returned her gaze placidly and she almost smiled at his temerity. Emily would have had to pull the shelf out to get behind it, so obviously someone had replaced it later. Destiny could guess who had done so, and the mercs did not stand high on the list of possibilities.

"Pull it out," she ordered. "And let's see if we can't find Emily's little secret."

***

Whillim blinked irritably at the outfit Ludwig had set out for him. Though originally Stefan's valet, Whillim had taken a certain amount of pleasure when he had Destiny place Ludwig on her Seat, turning the man into Whillim's valet with no memory of having served Stefan. Unfortunately, Ludwig's attitude and fastidious attention to protocol had not diminished a bit, and Whillim wondered how his brother had put up with the man for so long. While Whillim's own valet, Otto, knew the former Prince's proclivities, he didn't know how to serve a King, and Whillim needed people to see him as the King they had always known. So while he might grumble about Ludwig's choice of garments or find himself annoyed by the man's constant reminders of the schedule the steward had set out for the day, Whillim dared not rebuke him.

At least, not until he had fully secured his position, a task made that much more difficult with Stefan's utter disappearance. He knew Destiny worked on tracking things down (where had that woman gotten off to so early in the day, anyway?) and that Captain Milos and his men trailed those Stefan had escaped with, but in the meantime, it left Whillim with the boring task of having to deal with foreign dignitaries expecting to meet with the King. Without Destiny and her magic, he didn't know how exactly he would placate this trade delegation from Bash in the north, but with a bit of luck, he could convince them to deal with him and make no mention of his cursed brother.

He would much rather have his horse saddled and ride out to a hunt. But he had already put off this delegation for two days, and everyone kept insisting that if he didn't deal with them today, the repercussions would adversely affect the kingdom, which would in turn affect Whillim's ability to luxuriate in comfort. That didn't stop his urge to put them off again, but he knew he wouldn't. Being King had its benefits and its pitfalls; that Stefan had always clung to the responsibility side and pretty much ignored the privileges didn't mean Whillim would follow his lead, even if he did have to emulate his brother until he had firm control.

Which would happen. Soon.

And in the meantime, he would allow Ludwig to dress him in this overly-formal, uncomfortable-looking attire and endure the tedium of dealing with a trade delegation from the north. That the clothing belonged to Stefan, tailored in secret by Otto to fit Whillim, only made Whillim's scowl the more fierce. Otto, finding the whole affair a great source of amusement, had chortled enough while adjusting the shoulders of the stately doublet to fit Whillim's narrower build that the Prince had wondered about the man's sanity. But Otto merely thought the entire coup a fantastic game from which he could benefit. Whillim had threatened him with the Destiny Seat, and Otto had simply shrugged his indifference, pointing out that having him make adjustments to the King's garments—clothing so obviously tailored for a different man—would lead to unwanted questions in a servant so altered by magic, when leaving him untouched would give Whillim someone with whom to share the great joke. And truthfully, Otto had provided many an opportunity in the past to share jests with his Prince. Why should this, the greatest con of them all, provide any less amusement for his valet?

A discreet cough from the corner reminded Whillim that Ludwig waited to offer his assistance. With a last silent snarl at the offending clothing, Whillim snatched up the cream-coloured tunic and yanked it over his head. He had barely gotten it settled before Ludwig wrapped a burgundy sash of office around his liege's waist in lieu of a belt, adjusted a ceremonial sword sheath to his hip, then swung a short cloak the colour of earth across his back, fastened at his left shoulder with a ruby and diamond brooch. The colours suited Stefan more of course, as Whillim preferred blues and greens, but he supposed he cut a fine enough figure. Certainly enough to greet a trade delegation.

When Ludwig handed him the elaborate filigreed hilt of the ceremonial sword of the monarchy, the ruby and emerald gems caught the sunlight streaming in from the window, sending captive glints of light dancing on the walls. Whillim allowed himself the briefest moment to admire the flair of brilliance before slamming the blunted weapon home at his side.

"All right," he muttered to the valet as he turned to face the door. "Let's do this."

"Sire?"

Ludwig's soft voice held the hint of a question to it. Whillim turned a frown on the man, but then noted what the valet held in his long, thin fingers. Suppressing his urge to curse his own ignorance, Whillim snatched the offered item, jamming the narrow gold band on his head. Crown in place, he gestured impatiently at the door, striding out with quick steps when Ludwig pulled the oaken obstruction open.

Guards fell into step around him as he made his way to the

audience chamber. He wondered again where Destiny had disappeared to. If the woman didn't make her appearance soon, he would send one of Milos' men to fetch her. He might need her magic if these discussions went on too long.

Whillim entered the audience chamber via the King's Passage so that he needn't walk among those gathered in the room. The Passage let him out directly to the raised dais with the King's seat and the small ring of occupied Councillor chairs arced three to either side of the King's seat. He relished the expectant hush that swept through those assembled as he ambled out past Stefan's advisors and draped himself negligently over Stefan's chair. *Mine now,* he thought, running a languid hand over the armrest. *Boring and liable to take up too much time, but mine. As are these Councillors.*

He finally deigned to look up, take in those gathered kneeling before him, and then gestured to the steward to begin these proceedings.

Apparently, the steward and Councillors intended to take full advantage of Whillim's appearance to cram the previous two days worth of audiences into today's session. Whillim curbed his impatience and irritation for the first three supplicants—something about riot restitution in the smithies district, aqueduct diversion, and some farmer's cow ... or maybe bull, he hadn't really paid much attention beyond waving an assenting hand to whatever his advisors suggested—before he leaned over to whisper fiercely into the ear of Sir Byndorf, who looked about as glassy-eyed as Whillim felt.

"What nonsense is this?" he demanded. "These are not issues that need a King's attention! The Council could have dealt with all of this. Where is this foreign trade delegation I'm supposed to meet?"

The man currently kneeling and putting forth his complaint to King and Council paused a moment as the King turned his attention away, but then continued his whining to those members still listening to his spiel. Sir Byndorf glanced at Whillim and murmured his response, equally ignoring this fourth petitioner.

"Dalasmar comes first, Your Majesty. You know foreigners have to wait their turn, no matter how urgent they think their words. But I think there's only the three more to suffer before we get to the meat of the matter." The nobleman glanced sideways at Whillim, a smirk etched on his face. "What's the matter, Sire; can't wait to finally get the details of the proposal out of the way?"

"Bah," Whillim waved off the man, having no idea to what he referred, though he worried now that he should have paid more attention to the actual details, given Byndorf's lecherous grin. What kind of trade deal would elicit such sniggering?

The man prattling on below eventually ran out of breath and every eye turned to Whillim. He stared back blankly, then directed a regal nod toward Councillor Alphonse on his right, the senior most member of this little group, his long white hair and wrinkled face evidence of his long tenure in service to the crown. Whillim had seen Stefan do likewise on the rare occasions when forced to attend these sessions, and hoped it didn't just make him look a fool. By some stroke of luck, Alphonse smiled back and delivered some verdict to the sap awaiting his sentence that had the man leaving with relief in his eyes.

Whillim determined he'd better pay more attention, in case the next petition actually required the presence of the King.

By the time they finally wound around to the reason he had shown up in the first place, Whillim's stomach growled from lack of a decent meal, and his mind felt wrung out from trivialities that didn't concern him in the least.

The only bright spot he saw came just before the last petitioner when Destiny entered the back of the chamber. His wizard looked more than a little miffed—truly, a raging storm held less heat than the irritation crackling around Desi's figure—and Whillim suspected his wasted morning paled next to whatever had thwarted her.

Something they couldn't discuss until this delegation from Bash got on with their business. So, rather than call a halt to the proceedings and finding some lunch, Whillim waved Destiny to his side, then glared at the steward.

Dutifully, the man spoke the words Whillim should have first heard when taking his seat.

"The delegation from Bash, Your Majesty, to discuss the ongoing negotiations of—"

"Yes, yes," Whillim interrupted, eager to get this over with. "We have other things to see to today, steward. Do not keep us waiting longer."

Silence, and then the gentle swish of slippered feet as the Bashites came to stand before Whillim.

The man in charge of the delegation, wrapped in a stunning outfit of orange velvet trimmed in silver and gold that complemented his dusky skin and red hair, did not kneel as his three companions did, nor did he hesitate to meet Whillim's stare. He looked vaguely familiar, enough of a presence that he had clearly visited Dalasmar before, but Whillim couldn't put a name to him. The Bashite glanced briefly to Destiny, then swept his gaze over the Councillors, before bringing his regard back to Whillim.

"Does Dalasham seek to mock Bash now, first to make us wait, and now to send a Prince to speak a King's words?"

Whillim's eyes narrowed as he rose to his feet, but his heart hammered a panicked drumbeat against his ribs. *This! This is why I didn't want to meet these barbarians!* Them still recognising Stefan could unravel everything unless he could make them shut up.

"You will keep a civil tongue when addressing royalty," he said quietly. "We do not mock, but rather, we intend to honour you." He flicked his eyes toward Destiny, wondering how quickly and unobtrusively she could get these men to her Seat. "Indeed, we had intended to meet with you in a more appropriate, private setting, but protocol demanded this venue and time. I'm sure you understand."

What other venue would suit a trade delegation, Whillim didn't know, but his words seemed to placate the pompous man before him. The Bashite drew himself up with dignity, the gleam of interest sparking in his eyes.

"Sire," Alphonse spoke up. "Such a matter that will affect all of Dalasham demands the attention of all."

"Yes Councillor, and I'm certain that if we may speak with the honourable delegate over lunch, when we reconvene this afternoon to discuss the minutiae with all present, we can move matters along more smoothly with filled bellies and less temper."

"This is acceptable to us," the Bashite proclaimed before Alphonse could object again.

"Good," Whillim clapped his hands to forestall any other complaints. "Then let us retire for our meal."

Without waiting for any further ceremony, Whillim strode from

129

the chamber, taking the most direct route and trusting Destiny to usher the Bashites in his wake.

What kind of trade could Bash possibly have to share that would get everyone so worked up yet also eager to please? Had no one picked up on the titles? Or did they perhaps think the Bashite merely hoped to slight their King by calling him a Prince? Whillim could almost wish that he knew more about Bash than its location. No doubt, he would soon learn more than he wanted to know.

***

Destiny very much wanted to take her frustration out on somebody, but didn't think the Bashite envoy would serve as a good target. She had tried to ascertain the mechanism behind Emily's hidden passageway for a healthy chunk of the morning to no avail. Yes, she had seen the brick with that dark smudge, but no amount of finagling or magic spells had revealed its secret. That she couldn't simply remove that section of wall with a spell of erasure, or some other similar method, surprised her. She finally determined that, at some point in the past, someone had imbued the walls of Dalasmar Castle with strengthening magic. For a kingdom with little use for wizards, she had encountered a surprising amount of arcane power.

She would need to speak with that guard of Stefan's, have him point out exactly where in the King's chambers they had entered the tunnels, and where they had emerged, see if anything there matched the discoloured block to indicate a common entry-point to the passages, for if she couldn't get in, she could at least find where the tunnel came out.

In truth, for all Destiny knew, that blackened brick portended nothing more than an accumulation of years of grime behind those shelves, yet no other stones had evidenced even that much of a hint that might lead to a hidden entrance. Scar and Ox continued to insist that Emily had disappeared behind that section of wall and true to their description, brute strength did not aid in uncovering the door. Darien adamantly declared he had no such knowledge of the wall as anything but a wall, though he did admit to having returned the shelf to its rightful place.

"I had thought perhaps a scroll fell behind and someone

moved the shelf to retrieve it. It's happened before; why should I think anything different?" he had asked, and Destiny could find no fault with his reasoning.

Which left her with a less-than-fruitful morning and put her no closer to finding Stefan or that elusive librarian until she could speak to that guard Faulk, irritating her no end. And now Whillim expected her to employ her Focus on yet another personage, this time from outside the kingdom. Of all the things to waste her time ....

The would-be-King hadn't allowed the steward to properly introduce the Bashite nor his plea before the court, leaving Destiny with no knowledge of the man or his entourage, save that they had expected to speak with Stefan and felt their cause of enough import to affect the whole land. His dress and mannerism suggested someone of high regard, but she knew little enough of Bash beyond their aversion to magic users and their impressive supply of precious gems and metals. How far would this man's influence spread once under her spell?

She herded the four foreigners in Whillim's wake, curbing her impatience and keeping her snarl hidden behind a stoic mask. Whillim's ever present guards flanked them. Destiny suspected that Whillim didn't even see them unless one failed to open a door quickly enough, but she made note of every motion, endlessly cataloguing strengths and weaknesses. Who knew when such information would prove useful. Kalima knew such observations had helped her escape the misery of her youth.

She shook her head as they reached her sanctuary, pushing such musings aside to concentrate on the matter at hand. With a thought, she allowed Whillim to open the Sanctum's door and usher their party within. The instant she shut the doors, the envoy stopped and folded his arms across his chest.

"What game do you play, young Prince, and where is King Stefan? What is the meaning of this delay?"

"You will keep a civil tongue, Bashite," Whillim snarled as he spun to confront the man.

"I did, Dalasham, all the way from that audience hall. And now I warn you, I will suffer no more insults. Where is the King?"

In that moment, Destiny knew that Whillim had unwittingly ensnared a valuable prize. No mere merchant would take such a tone with royalty, nor achieve the affronted arrogance of this envoy and his entourage. She could see by Whillim's cold, narrowed eyes that he had yet to understand what manner of man stood before him. She took over before either could escalate the situation.

"The King will arrive momentarily," she said, sweeping in front of the Bashite and offering a bow. "Forgive my liege for his impertinence, but the King failed to explain the full import of your suit when he instructed Whillim to oversee the morning's business. Perhaps, Highness, you might condescend to placate the Prince with the bare details of your mission here so that he might better understand his error." Destiny didn't actually know the royal house of Bash, but it seemed a safe bet to assume she addressed one of them now.

The envoy did not once look at Destiny as she spoke, keeping his gaze firmly on Whillim, nor did he move when she subtly tried to herd him toward the Focus. Destiny gritted her teeth hard enough that her jaw throbbed in impotent rage at the slight, but she kept the snarl that so wanted to curl her lip locked away. One other thing she remembered about Bash: women did not have a voice without the leave of a man.

She turned to stare at Whillim, silently demanding his intention on how to proceed. If left to her own devices, Destiny would simply force the envoy into the Focus, adding a spell to instill some respect for women to the altered memories. But Whillim would rule Dalasham, not she, so Destiny would follow where the Prince chose to lead in this matter. She did not desire to rule, merely to stand in the place she had earned through years of toil and hardship. If a man wanted to rule, so be it, but let the world see the strength of the woman at his right hand, a woman who had made her own name despite the twisted contempt of those who had sought to use her.

Whillim shook his head minutely and Destiny answered with the slightest nod, standing aside from the envoy, but oh how it irked her not to have her own voice.

"Stefan did not see fit to inform me of the full import of your intentions, Hoheit," Whillim imbued more respect to his address, granting the envoy a royal title, but he didn't lose any of his arrogance. He could not afford to appear ignorant, though Destiny suspected he still did not know the actual identity of the man standing before him. "Though he did give me leave to speak with his voice."

The envoy snorted his contempt.

"If this is how Dalasham treats with our envoy, then we shudder to think how he intends to treat our niece," the Bashite said, crossing his arms in displeasure.

Whillim blinked quickly three times, an indication, Destiny noted, of rapid thinking. The Prince much preferred the luxuries of rank and leaving any work to others, but he had a keen enough mind when he chose to employ it for more than just his own gratification.

"You mistake me, Bash. I do not presume to speak to the matter of a possible royal betrothal; merely to offer the King's apologies and hospitality as we await his arrival." Whillim flicked Destiny a quick glance, and she moved to stand behind her Focus as he worked to placate the foreigner. "Please, won't you sit while we bring in refreshments."

The envoy did not move, a frown pulling his brow low. Destiny suspected he stood his ground to prove the depth of his affront rather than a refusal to continue negotiations. She wondered how far Stefan had gone in seeking an alliance through marriage, for what other reason would a foreign royal have for bringing up the treatment of a female relative. And 'niece' placed this man most probably as brother to the Bashite King—or possibly Queen, though Destiny believed that connection less likely, given Bash's attitude toward women—meaning that ensnaring him in the magic that made Whillim King would also capture a large portion of external influence.

Whillim didn't let Bash's reluctance hinder him, turning to one of his mercenary guards and instructing him to bring food and drink. To his credit, the guard didn't balk at being relegated to servant. Whillim paid Milos' Company to maintain the illusion that the Prince ruled, and if that called for fetching sustenance instead of engaging in some form of combat, then fetch food he would.

The Prince turned back to the envoy, a hardness in his expression belying the carefree tone of his voice.

"Please, Hoheit, sit while we await the arrival of the King."

The envoy glanced with disdain at the quartz chair, bare of any adornments or cushions, before glaring back at Whillim. As though to emphasize how beneath his notice he considered that suggestion, the envoy allowed one of his aides to speak, summoned by the merest flick of a finger that Destiny might have missed had she not watched for it.

"That is hardly a fit seat for a dog, let alone an ambassador," the little toad sneered, drawing himself up. "His Royal Highness has suffered your insults long enough."

"Desi," Whillim said, turning his back on the Bashite contingent, dismissing them.

Destiny gladly regained the reins of control, her own fierce stare gathering up the envoy as she snapped her fingers and pointed at the Focus. She allowed the frustration of the morning to colour the word of command she snarled at the man, forcing her will upon him more sharply than necessary. He gasped as his body began a stiff-legged walk toward the quartz chair, eyes bulging as he fought her influence.

"Witch!" he spat.

Destiny smiled without any warmth.

"Wizard," she corrected, knowing that a land that disparaged magic would not understand the difference.

Milos' mercenaries had already subdued the other Bashites, one man held against the wall at sword point, the other two flirting with the possibility of bloodshed as daggers caressed their throats. Whillim waited until he heard the grunt of the envoy as Destiny dropped him onto the Focus before he turned to regard the man again. The Bashite's dusky face had darkened even further in his impotent rage, but Destiny kept his mouth firmly closed on the fury she could sense as he silently struggled against her compulsion.

Whillim didn't say a word as he studied their captive. He raised his gaze to meet Destiny's and gave one nod. Her hand already resting on the crown of the chair, Destiny activated the Focus.

The quartz illuminated, gold to rose to blinding white. Destiny watched not the envoy, but his aides. The instant their expressions changed from panic to confusion, she waved Milos' men off with a flick of her wrist. Each had seen this magic before and they pulled back, sheathing their weapons and taking up their posts once more. Destiny dismissed them from her mind as she moved to stand just behind Whillim as the Prince regarded the seated man.

As soon as the envoy met his gaze, Whillim smiled.

"Of course, we'll have to pass everything by the Council for ratification," Whillim said, as though continuing a conversation. "But I'm confident that they will agree to all our provisions. Don't you agree, Hoheit?"

"Indeed, Majesty," the Bashite said, his confusion replaced with relief as his mind grasped to make sense of his new reality. "I am sure we can come to a satisfactory arrangement that will benefit both our lands."

"Excellent," Whillim clapped his hands together. "Shall we retire to a more comfortable room for lunch then?"

Chapter 13

The clang of clashing swords and grunts of exertion pulled Em from sleep. She jerked up with a start, trying to escape from the clinging confines of the blanket. Her injured abdomen stretched in protest but she pushed aside the discomfort as her panicked eyes swept the room. The early sun outlining the curtains provided enough light to see that no combatants had yet invaded Tox's bedchamber.

Fearing an attack on the King and his men, Em stumbled from bed. She had no idea what she could do to fend off an enemy, but she refused to cower in the shadows waiting for the Prince's men to find her.

She pressed her ear to the bedroom door. No sound from the outer room reached her straining senses. She inched the door open, peeking into the next room. A fire burned in the hearth, a covered pot warming on a nearby hook, the scent of porridge mingling with the fading aroma of baked bread. The flames provided the only movement in a chamber otherwise devoid of life. Em slipped out and hurried to the hearth, taking up the fire poker.

She crept to the front door, her impromptu weapon trembling in unsteady hands as the sounds of fighting grew louder. Heart thumping painfully in her chest, torso aching horribly, she grabbed the handle and wrenched open the door before her mind could catch up to her folly or terror could incapacitate her.

Em threw herself onto the porch in a crouch, fire poker grasped tightly in a two-fisted grip, then gaped in astonishment, her weapon sagging to the ground.

Dari and Ambrose each wielded a sword. They faced not an enemy, but the King, the three men making a dance out of sword work while Fred and Lord Prichard looked on. Sergeant Sim stood slightly apart, sword at the ready, as though looking for an opportunity to join the fray, or perhaps studying the technique to determine flaws he could exploit and so aid in the training. Although the air still held the chill of the previous night, sweat had started to mar the tunics of the combatants, yet none paused to wipe a hand across a damp brow.

Both Captain and nobleman had turned at Em's appearance, though the sword work continued unabated. Fred raised an eyebrow at her weapon, and Lord Prichard blinked his surprise. A blush heated Em's face, and she fled within, pushing the door closed and retreating to the fire. She laid the poker aside with shaking hands and stood leaning unsteadily against the mantle, waiting for her heart to slow to its normal rhythm. She pressed a hand to her stomach and tried to control her trembling.

She felt very foolish. What had possessed her to leap out like that? What had she thought to accomplish? She knew her library, not swordplay and fighting. Had the men found themselves in an actual battle, the sudden appearance of a helpless woman would likely spark their need to protect her, and that distraction could get them killed.

Em gasped in a distraught breath and squeezed her eyes shut tight, holding back tears. Drawing in a couple of deep breaths to steady herself, shaking her head at her ill-conceived actions, she slowly opened her eyes again. Movement at the periphery of her vision sent her pulse soaring.

With a yip of surprise, she spun, her back slamming against the wall beside the hearth as her hand pressed against the renewed frantic beating of her heart. Fred pursed his lips, his meaty arms crossed at his chest as he contemplated her quietly. She waited for his rebuke, but he said nothing.

"I ... I heard fighting," she managed in a choked whisper, gesturing vaguely toward the door.

Fred grunted and Em saw amusement lighten his eyes. She deserved his laughter, she thought, though the feeling turned to shame, then anger.

"Our apologies for disturbing you," he said, tone earnest. "And our thanks for your aid."

Em's eyes narrowed. Did he mock her now?

"The men have a bit of training left before we break our fast. You're welcome to come observe if you want." He pursed his lips again. "Once you've dressed, of course."

Em glanced down at her attire and saw, with some mortification, that she wore only the oversized nightshirt Tox had provided upon their arrival. Certain she blushed right down to her toes, she fled to the bedroom.

She briefly entertained the idea of crawling back under the sheets and hiding, then set her jaw and determined that she wouldn't let fear and embarrassment rule her. She'd had the best of intentions, no matter how misguided or ridiculous or unnecessary; she would not apologise for looking to the safety of others. If today proved her last day of freedom, she refused to spend it cowering.

Reaching for her tunic and skirts with a wrinkled nose, she decided she would need to find something else to wear so that she might wash her clothing. She wondered if Goodman Tox had a hip bath or if she could find a stream nearby to wash herself more thoroughly, remove some of the grime and stench of the last few days.

Only when he cleared his throat behind her did she realise that Fred had followed her in. With a squeal of fright, she held her clothes before her and nearly fell over the edge of the bed as she retreated as far across the room as she could.

Fred let out a weary sigh.

"I'm not here to hurt you, girl, but you're bleeding." Em jerked her gaze to her middle, to the slash of red wetting the nightshirt. Seeing the blood let her feel the fiery fingers of pain that she had managed to ignore until now. "I believe all your acrobatics have put too much strain on your wound."

Suddenly, all Em's energy fled, taking any semblance of courage or dignity with it. She sat heavily on the bed and couldn't stop the flood of tears that spilled onto her cheeks.

Fred, obviously taken aback by her breakdown and no doubt contemplating the foibles of foolish and weak women, appeared on the verge of fleeing the room and its distraught occupant. Then his jaw stiffened and he took up the ewer on the washstand, pouring its chilly water into the matching basin. He brought water and a cloth to the side of the bed.

"Let's see what damage you've done," he growled.

Em bit her lip hard to keep her whimpers behind her teeth. She scrubbed a hand across her eyes, frowning furiously as she tried to stem the tide of tears, then laid back and allowed the Captain to see to her wound.

Though he grumbled and groused, Fred had a gentle touch.

"Don't think you've made it much worse," he said as he sopped up a thin stream of blood. "But no more jumping around like that just yet."

Em nodded her agreement as Fred applied a salve her caretakers had left on the table beside the bed. When he had her sit so that he could bind fresh bandages around her middle, Em took a deep breath.

"I'm sorry, Captain," she breathed. He paused, looking at her with an unreadable expression. "I don't know why I ... I don't even know how ... I apologise for my rash actions."

A frown pulled at his brow before he bent to his task again, hiding his face. Once he had the binding secure, he sat back on his heels, regarding her solemnly from his crouch on the floor. He shook his head briefly and flashed her a grin, taking her totally by surprise.

"Buck up, soldier," he said, pushing to his feet. "It was bravely done."

He turned and strode to the door, the gruff Captain once more. He stopped and looked back from the threshold.

"Join us when you're ready. We have things to discuss." He pulled the the door closed behind him, leaving Em stunned as she listened to him retreat out the front door.

"But I'm no soldier," she whispered before turning her mind to the task of getting ready for the day.

***

Goodman Tox didn't know much about swordplay. He knew which end to hold, and which to point at a foe. In a pinch, he figured he could maybe swing one to some effect, but give him a scythe or an axe and he could cut a fine swath indeed. That said, he could definitely admire the skill shown by the King and his men as they turned the art of sword mastery into a dance in front of his home while Tox himself went about his daily chores. Tox spared a moment to wonder whether a merchant and his guard would engage in such a proficient display, and supposed his farmhands might wonder the same thing, but with that lethal grace unfolding across his lawn, he knew that none would question the participants their prowess. At least not openly.

Tox shook his head. They needed a better ruse if they wanted to keep rumour at bay. Not that his farmhands would purposefully endanger anyone, but it only took a slip of the tongue for word to spread and people to question, especially if more folks kept showing up, like that noble who had joined the party yesterday.

Such negotiations as their subterfuge might include wouldn't cover additional people, or this prolonged stay, even with the merchant's 'niece' still recovering from an injury—another aspect of their charade that invited speculation.

Tox shook his head as he finished mucking out the pig pen, the sows thrusting their greedy snouts into the feeding trough in the corner. That 'niece' defied description. He had seen Emily shrink from unfamiliar faces, try to hide herself in the background, never asking for extra attention while seeing to the needs of others; in general, acting as a discreet young woman from Dalasham ought while fighting a case of shyness. And then, in the next moment, asserting herself as she corrected the ignorance of others, stood up for herself and her actions though they caused her some discomfort. Even jump in to offer protection when she sensed danger to those around her, yet all done in a quiet manner, again, trying to hide in the shadows while she brought a measure of light to her situation. Tox had never seen the like and, judging by the consternation he saw on the faces of her companions, suspected that the King and his men found themselves equally baffled by the fragile package that made up Emily.

As Tox finished his task and brushed himself off, washing his hands at the pump, he watched Emily emerge once again from his house, barefoot and dressed in her rumpled skirts. She slipped unobtrusively into a corner to watch the spectacle of the King and his guards thrashing each other in their impromptu lists. She looked out of her depth as she stared wide-eyed at the proceedings. Tox sympathised.

Thinking to check on his guests' morning repast, Tox had almost made it to the porch stairs when a voice hailed him.

"A moment, if you have one, Goodman Tox." The deep rumble came from the massive chest of the King's Captain.

Tox paused, hand on the railing and foot on the first stair. He waited for Captain Frederick to join him, Lord Prichard following close behind. The Captain waved Emily closer also, and with measured slowness, she complied, hands gripping her arms in a hug as though to ward off the chill. Or possibly hold herself together.

"We need to discuss our next move," Frederick said. "We've come up with several scenarios, some of which would benefit from your aid, Tox. Will you join us for breakfast so that we can narrow down our options?"

Tox stared hard at him. Although Frederick made it sound as though Tox had a choice, the farmer doubted the man would accept any negative answer. He debated declining the offer, just to see what would happen, but hadn't he just asked himself what came next? He had to admit to a certain curiosity. So little piqued his interest these days beyond the farm, and while he might chafe to himself about the inconvenience of his unasked for guests, in truth, he felt he had needed this diversion to wake himself up from his self-imposed stupor of the last several years.

He nodded briefly, grunting an affirmative, then pushed his way into his home.

The clamour of sword against sword ceased as Tox approached the fire and the pot hanging by it. He stirred the porridge, then swung the pot-arm away from the flames. Emily appeared at his side, bowls in hand, and together, they set out the meal. Lord Prichard made himself useful by slicing the bread and setting out butter and preserves. Tox could honestly say he had never thought to see a nobleman help with food preparation in his kitchen, yet Prichard put a kettle of water to boil over the fire with no fuss.

Table set, the others filed in. Water dripped from the hair of the King and the two he had sparred with and dampened the shoulders of their tunics, as though they had dunked their heads in the horse trough. Tox had done the like many times himself, as had his farmhands, as a swift way to clean up. The thought that the King himself could act as any commoner almost brought a smile to Tox's lips.

When everyone had found a seat—Ambrose and Sim had brought in a bench from the porch—Tox said a blessing over the food, and they dug in. No one spoke at first beyond general table manners—*please pass the bread,* and the like. But once each had made decent inroads into the meal, the King broke the silence.

"We can't know how much Faulk revealed to my brother and his wizard," he stated. "Perhaps nothing, perhaps everything. We must assume this wizard learned all he knew, who we sent where, and that puts everyone allied with us in jeopardy. Haven's End here remains the only place Faulk knew nothing about." The King turned a serious expression toward Tox. "Do you know any place in the area, Goodman, where we might make camp? Somewhere few, or preferably none, would notice a company of soldiers, where we can regroup and set up a staging area? Access to water within a reasonable distance would also help. A field, a meadow, a clearing in the woods, anything out of the way, little known, yet accessible to many?"

Tox snorted out a laugh though it held little mirth. So the King planned to build an army and hide it in the depths of farmland. Not a terrible plan, if he could pull it off. Tox shook his head ruefully; he knew an ideal spot. Had briefly contemplated it just that morning, though he had pushed the idea away quickly. Now the King sought exactly what Tox could provide.

Mistaking his gesture for negation, the King pressed on.

"Would any of your neighbours —"

"Nay, Your Kingship," Tox dared to interrupt heavily. "The fewer know of your plight, the safer you'll be. No need to bother the neighbours; I've the place you need."

So saying, he pushed up from the table and moved to the hearth, taking up the handle of the kettle with a thick towel to refill the tea pot. His unasked-for companions waited quietly as he saw to the task, sitting in silence until he resumed his own seat and retrieved his spoon.

Eyes trained on the remains of his meal, Tox explained.

"I have four fields under my care. I've planted three this season, and the fourth lies fallow for the year. You could use a couple of acres of it. Field rests, conveniently enough, near the brook that supplies my well. Plenty of secluded space for a small encampment."

He dug into the last of his cooling porridge, the scrape of his spoon and the spitting crackle of the fire the only sounds. Tox peered up surreptitiously to note the significant exchange of glances between the King and his entourage, but didn't pause in his eating. Emily held her gaze to her tea cup, lost in contemplation.

"And how do we access this field unobserved?" Frederick inquired.

"It lies furthest out," Tox answered, tossing his spoon in his now-empty bowl and leaning back in his chair with a sigh, fingers intertwined across his belly. "Access from the road or by traipsing past the house. Safest to do so before the farmhands arrive just past dawn, or after they've headed home in the evening. Trick'll be to keep such uncommon traffic and signs of its passing to a minimum. Can't have a bunch of soldiers running all about my land. You keep 'em confined, and maybe no one will notice. For a bit anyway."

Captain and King exchanged another unspoken conversation in a glance.

"It's ideal," the King said finally. "And somewhere Willi won't think to look, if we can bring our people here quickly enough and in secrecy."

"How do you make sure they're with you and not working with your brother?" Sergeant Darius asked.

"Ask the name of the King," Sergeant Sim replied, drawing the attention of the other men. "Everyone I spoke with had no problems saying 'the king' in general, but when being specific, all those turned, for lack of a better word, said King Whillim."

"The men in the library implied as much also," Emily added softly, her eyes briefly flitting up before finding refuge in her tea cup again. "They don't remember a King Stefan."

"Which the Prince, or this Lady Destiny, if she's really Whillim's wizard, might consider," Darius argued. That the Prince's wizard turned out to be a woman had surprised the men and had, it seemed, hardened their hearts still further against her; a woman in command of the Prince, and thus the kingdom, didn't sit well for men of Dalasham. "We might need more than one way to make sure they've stayed loyal."

"Our first priority is to get the knights who escaped with us back," King Stefan said. "Edvard from the Ford, Castel from Calsburg, and Pietor from Marlak, hopefully with Sir Gregor. We can hope those, at least, have continued to evade Destiny and Whillim. Ambrose will ride north to Calsburg; Dari east to Marlak. I'll send Jo south to the Ford, but he'll have to go afoot unless he can find a horse." The King addressed Ambrose and Darius alone. "Demand details of their escape; if the knights remember without hesitation or prodding, they may remain uncompromised, judging by Sim's experience with Faulk and his friend on the Watch. If you feel, for any reason, they pose more danger than aid, get away."

The two guards nodded their understanding.

"Next," King Stefan continued, drawing them all into the plans again. "We need supplies. Food for certain, as we cannot continue to abuse Goodman Tox's hospitality." Tox started as the King regarded him directly.

"We have already placed you in some difficulty and, I fear, the danger will only increase if we take you up on your generous offer of your field. I won't continue to take food from your table without recompense."

Tox marvelled at how this man took charge, yet made everyone around him feel included, valued even. As King, he could have simply taken what he wanted as his right, as the Prince—so rumour spoke—always had. Yet instead, Stefan continued to ask and show his gratitude, making the duty to serve this King an honour rather than a burden.

"We need to obtain food for a fair sized host without raising suspicions and we need to bring it here unobserved," said the King.

"We'll also need tents, clothing, and weapons," Frederick added. "Most of that, the knights can provide. It'll raise less suspicion coming from outside the city. But they're a couple days away, with no guarantee they're not being watched, so safer to assume a week before they can arrive with any relief."

"Smaller numbers on the roads will attract less attention," Sim put in. "Might work better if they stagger their arrival, though it'll cause further delay."

"The longer we wait, the more time Willi has to use that wretched device," King Stefan said. "But I agree. We need help here soon, but not at the risk of exposure."

"We'll stress the need to the knights, Sire," Ambrose assured him.

"Good. Then we just need food while we wait, and less notable clothing. We need to prepare a camp and, should any note our presence, we need to look as unobtrusive as possible. Which means, we need to get into the city for supplies."

"No," Frederick interjected. "*We* don't go into the city, Sire. You stay here."

"As do you," Sim declared, drawing a warning glare from the Captain. "I said it before, Captain, and I meant it," the Sergeant continued undaunted. "If you're captured, all the King's guards fall under Destiny's influence. We can't risk that."

Frederick growled, but nodded his acquiescence.

"Which leaves me and Sim as food envoys," Lord Prichard spoke up, slowly spinning his tea cup on the table.

Tox snorted a laugh, drawing the startled gaze of the noble.

"Begging your pardon, my Lord," said Tox. "But how many folks under your governance? Seems to me that no one of any influence ought walk into the Prince's clutches, and a Lord and Council member like yourself'd be right at the top of the list of those this Destiny wants."

"You did say they came looking for you the night of the riots," Sim agreed. "Which, I guess, just leaves me to slip into the city."

"You'll need a cart," Tox suggested. "One man buying enough food for ten trying to carry it out the gates on just his shoulders?" Tox shook his head. "And who's to say your friend Faulk don't see you again. Then what?"

"You've a better suggestion, Goodman?" Sim asked.

Tox heaved a sigh, having already decided his next action. He spared a brief thought as to why he bothered, then pushed ahead before he changed his mind.

"You hide your features better, disguise more than just your clothing, and I come with you. I've gone to the city often enough this time of year, it won't seem out of the ordinary. I got a cart'll go faster with two pulling than one. You let me do all the talking. I got a better idea at what'll raise questions and what won't in the amounts we'll need."

"How do they pay for it?" piped up a small voice. Tox looked at Emily. He wondered, by the startled expressions on some of the men's faces, who else had forgotten the presence of the quiet librarian. The calm speculation of the King suggested he, at least, hadn't. Emily glanced up, almost meeting the regard of that King. "They don't have access to your treasury, Your Majesty, nor could they barter in your name. How can they get all that you require without money or trade goods?"

King Stefan slid a ring off his finger and laid it on the table.

145

An emerald flashed between two rubies in a band of pure gold.

"This should fetch an appropriate amount, I should think," he murmured.

Lord Prichard gasped, Captain Frederick frowned fiercely, and Tox gaped. But Emily just shook her head sadly.

"It's too obvious, Your Majesty," she said. "Your brother will recognise it should he bother to look, and then he'll know you're nearby, as well as obtain a description of our dear Tox. Any broker worth his salt will know the worth of the ring—which is far more than you'd need for those supplies, if the broker has any honesty—and will have made note of who sold it to him. If questioned by the Prince or his wizard, the broker would quickly divulge all he knows of that individual. Better a smaller, less notable token." She pulled something from the pocket of her skirt. "Something more like this," she murmured, gazing at her closed fist a moment before opening her hand to reveal a delicate pendant on a gold chain.

This time, she met the King's gaze. "People will have lost their homes and businesses in the fire and riots. A young couple down on their luck with a family heirloom to sell to get back on their feet will raise less questions than a kingly ring."

"Emily, you can't sell—"

"A young couple?" Frederick interrupted the King. "You can't mean to go with them."

"Why not?" she retorted. "No one's looking for me."

"Faulk knows you," Darius said, eyes worried. "He could recognise you as easily as Sim."

"I can disguise myself as easily as Sim," she retorted. "And I'm used to hiding in the shadows."

"This isn't like your library, girl," Frederick growled. "You're found out here and it's not a night sweeping as penalty."

"I'm well aware, Captain," she shot back, the sudden fire in her voice taking them all aback. "Just as I know this isn't a story in any of my books, or whatever other such rot you'll drag up next."

Frederick blinked in surprise and sat back in his chair as Emily went on.

"But I do know that we need a reasonable story to get us into and out of Riverbend with the supplies you require without suspicion. A farmer who came to bring his daughter and son-in-law home after they lost their home in the riots would not be unreasonable."

"How do we make your story work if the gate guards see us arrive together?" Sim asked.

"We fled the trouble that night and took refuge with my father," she gestured to Tox and he surprised her with a wink. He liked her spunk when she chose to bring it out. He received a ghost of a smile in response. "Before we can eat him out of house and home, he's brought us to the city for supplies. I'm too nervous to try to reestablish ourselves in the city until things quieten down, so to placate your flighty wife, you've agreed to help out father on the farm this season until you can earn enough to hopefully return to Riverbend in the fall. If we added a couple bolts of base fabric to the supplies, well, I had to replace our ruined clothes with something, didn't I?"

She glanced around the table, then quickly lowered her gaze, knuckles going white as she gripped her tea cup, as though only now realising to whom she spoke and in what tone. Tox's heart went out to her. The poor little mite, so out of her element and so unsure how to fit in. She reminded him a bit of his Amalia as she brought forth her ideas and questions. Amalia had often known her mind and wouldn't shy from speaking it, at least to Tox. Emily would speak up when she feared to do otherwise would endanger those in her company, though she clearly felt uncomfortable under any scrutiny. He wondered if she could pull off the part of flighty farmer's daughter without trying to fade into the background. But then, that just described any woman's role in Dalasham, didn't it?

Excepting Lady Destiny.

Tox shook off a shiver.

"Emily's plan might work best," he voiced, pulling the attention away from her. "And if it's something we want to see to today, then we'd better get started. Daylight's wasting, and that's something no farmer wastes."

"Right," the King clapped his hands together once, then rose from the table. "Ambrose, Dari, you'll need to set out today too. Fred, get a list together of what we need from the city. Tox," here, Stefan paused. "You put yourself at great risk—"

Tox raised a hand in protest as he stood. "I do what I feel's right, Your Kingness," he said with a grin, then headed for the door. "Cart's in the shed behind the house," he called over his shoulder to Sim. "Best we get a move on *son*."

147

He pushed out the door and down his porch, heading to the back. Let the others sort themselves out; he had a fake family to see to. Long time since he'd worried about such things as family.

Chapter 14

Em didn't have to pretend her nervousness. Whenever she had left the safe confines of the library for the bustling streets of Riverbend, she had done her business quickly and with little fuss—and with as little interaction with the myriad strangers of the city as possible. More often, she had simply hurried along the thoroughfares to one of the gates and out into the quiet comfort of the surrounding countryside, avoiding any prolonged contact with people. She found, if she simply looked to have a purpose and firm destination in mind, the townsfolk ignored her as much as she shied away from them. Simple clothing and a plain face kept most lewd advances at bay, and her mien of purposefulness provided safe passage. Re-admittance only required her to show her librarian's badge, so any speech with gate guards usually amounted to a grunt and a wave of the hand.

But now she had to rely on Tox and Sim talking their way past rough-looking guards who stared at her with a frightening intensity that left her wanting to bathe. Surely some of the mercenaries that the Prince had hired, for King Stefan's men had never displayed such disdain for visitors to the capital of Dalasham.

She huddled under the protective arm of Sim as these guards stared suspiciously at the trio and their cart. Em had disguised herself with extra padding so that she appeared pregnant—which also helped in keeping her wound well cushioned—and Sim wore additional layers of clothing to simulate a man of larger girth, but they, along with Tox, had made sure that nothing of what they wore would suggest any sort of wealth. Even still, Em had little doubt that, had they actually possessed anything of value, these thugs would try to profit from it, and she worried how they would retrieve what they needed from the city without incident.

"What with the trouble them nights ago," Tox said now to the gate guards, exaggerating a rustic accent, "m'girl and 'er man 'ere didn' bring much and we gots ta find some stuff as'll help fill the larder some til the crops're ready."

Tox leaned in toward the guards as though taking them into his confidence, although he spoke in a loud enough whisper that the next folks in line waiting to get into the city had no trouble hearing him.

"My little Amalia, here, love 'er ta bits ya understands, but she's got it into 'er wee head that tisn't safe to git back home to stay jus' yet. So we needs the cart ta git enough provides for two plus a wee littl'un to lasts until me an' Ranolf can bring in the harvest, or until she feels safe agin, whichever comes first. You know how women worry so."

One of the guards smirked at Emily as she cowered beside Sim. The other yawned, exposing a mouth full of rotting teeth.

"If she didn't have a brat in her belly already," the smirker leered, "we could point out a way to pay for extra supplies, though I know some wouldn't mind the extra weight."

Tox stared at him, mouth agape, and Em felt Sim's entire body go rigid. She clutched the front of his tunic in her fists and turned as though to hide her face against his chest, when she in truth pushed back against his desire to lunge for the throat of the offending guard. Even those waiting in line stared in shocked silence that turned into affronted murmurs.

The merc's companion gave the smirker a hard elbow to the ribs, eliciting an annoyed grunt and a glare even as Tox drew himself up to voice his indignation.

"Apologies, Farmer. His mouth works faster than his brain sometimes."

"Why you—" the first man started, but the other gave him a negligent cuff across the back of his head.

"Knock it off, you ass," he snarled, no longer seeming so bored. "That's not how we treat the citizens of Riverbend." He turned back to Tox, his expression almost pleasant, though no kindness reached his eyes.

"Again, apologies. Go about your business and best of luck to you."

Then he moved his attention on to the next people.

Tox blinked and shook himself, glanced very briefly at the offensive mercenary who had murder in his eyes, then hurriedly grabbed a handle of the cart. Sim missed Tox's imploring look, his own gaze fixed on the mercenary. Em grabbed Sim's arm hard, jerking his attention away from the man who so obviously wanted a fight. She put her anxiety, her utter desire to quit this place, and her trust in Sim to keep them safe into her expression. He set his jaw and gave her a grim nod, then took the other handle, and together, he and Tox got the cart moving, keeping Em on the far side, as far from the other men as possible. Em didn't envy those next in line the ire of the uncouth guard, but she certainly didn't want to wait around to see what would transpire.

Did the Prince have so little control over his hired thugs that they felt they could get away with such behaviour, or did he have so little concern about the common folks? She feared both possibilities.

Tox led them to a farmer's market in the west quarter.

"I've done some business here," he murmured to Em and Sim, regaining his equilibrium. "So I'm not a complete stranger. I've also brought a farmhand or two to assist, so *Ranolf* here won't raise any questions. I'm also enough of an outsider that folks don't know my family much and shouldn't think overmuch about *Amalia* being my daughter instead of my departed wife, but even so, we ought to keep our story to ourselves unless someone else brings it up."

Em and Sim agreed quietly while the group paused on the outskirts of the market.

"This place will have all we need, and will raise the fewest questions."

"I know somewhere next street over where we can trade Em—ah, Amalia's—pendant," Sim said, remembering belatedly to use their aliases. Em bit her lip to keep in her moan of distress, not at Sim's near-slip, but at the thought of actually going through with having to sell her mother's pendant. She had so little of her parents left—a book from her father, a scrap of leather from her mother to mark her place in that book, a

151

small signet ring they had made for her on her sixth naming day, and this necklace—that to part with any reminder of that happy past would near break her heart. But what else could they use? The King's fine jewels would raise too many questions, and Goodman Tox had already given more than he should spare. What did a small gold pendant amount to in the face of what Whillim would do to the land if he destroyed the King?

It didn't ease Em's heart any, but she couldn't let her sentimentality get in the way of doing the right thing.

So while Tox secured the cart and began his search of what they would purchase, she followed Sim to the next street, taking little note of her surroundings, though she knew her memory would allow her to retrace her steps with or without the King's man at her side.

When Sim ushered her into a little shop nestled between a tavern and a silversmith's, it only took Em a moment to register all the lost memories displayed in the subdued lighting. Knick knacks and trinkets, jewellery and mementos of more affluent days, the desperation of disparate people fallen on hard times, all commingling in cases and on shelves, awaiting previous owners who could muster up funds to buy them back, or new owners who would purchase these heirlooms for their own households. Em swallowed her pang of sorrow at the sense of shattered dreams surrounding her, and moved with Sim to the proprietor awaiting them behind his counter to add her own little dream to the collection.

As Sim recounted their devised tale of escaping Riverbend on the night of riots and losing everything to the fires, Em gazed unseeing at the floor beneath her feet, her fist clenched tightly around her pendant. It took Sim's touch on her elbow for her to glance up, startled, to find the proprietor's empty hand waiting to examine their offering. Em couldn't tell whether the look of sympathy on the shop owner's face held any truth or just hid his antipathy over another sad story.

She opened her fist and gently laid the gold links onto the stranger's palm. With a surprising reverence, the man examined the prize, his scrutiny changing from mild interest to evident intensity in an instant. His gaze flashed briefly to Em's face before returning to the necklace, as though to determine if she knew the true value of the piece. Em made sure he could read that she knew exactly what she intended to part with; pure Haemat gold worked into the symbol of the Weaver's Guild of Dalasham.

While her father had worked as a minor scribe to a minor noble, her mother had carded and woven the finest threads into the most sought-after cloth on the continent at Ostam's most easterly Weaver's Guild, counting herself among the best in the business. In a profession where women could actually find some sort of standing and even renown, Em's mother had excelled and won the pendant as a sign of her prowess. The Guild had kindly passed it on to Em after her parent's death as a sign of respect, and a memory of her mother in recognition of her service. And now, Em would relinquish it as part of her own service to the crown.

"It's a fine piece," the man remarked. "Of course, with so much happening recently, I've had a lot of folks trying to sell stuff, and not as many buying." He pretended to study the pendent more, but Em could already tell that he planned to try to cheat them.

She leaned toward Sim, keeping her whisper subservient yet certainly audible, and her gaze downcast.

"Are you sure we shouldn't try the goldsmith your friend on the Watch told us about? He'd jump at the chance to get his hands on something as rare as pure Haemat gold."

Sim patted her hand on his arm in an absent fashion. She thought she detected a hint of mirth in his eyes, though he kept his expression neutral, gladly playing along.

"It's alright, Amalia," he murmured back with a slightly impatient sigh. "I already told you we know the appraised worth. I'm sure this fine broker here knows quality when he sees it and will give fair value." He looked back to the proprietor and spoke louder, as though the man could not have heard their exchange. "You were saying, good sir?"

"Ah, I would be happy to buy this piece from you for—"

"Nay, you misunderstand," Sim interrupted with a raised hand, surprising Em. Hadn't they come for just this purpose? What game did the Sergeant play? "We don't wish to sell. We came to you to borrow against that. I'll want a promissory note with the option of buying back extending to one year."

Em's eyes filled with tears at the possibility of retrieving the necklace sometime in the future should they succeed. The broker's eyes, however, filled with something more akin to greed.

"Ten percent interest on five gold marks," he said.

"Three percent on twelve," Sim countered immediately.

The other man's lip quirked in a near smile as they set to haggling. Em left the bargaining to Sim, her gaze lingering on the gold chain the broker absently fondled. She hadn't dared hope to see it again once she had offered it, and indeed might not given the odds against them, yet Sim worked to keep the possibility open. How she would afford to buy it back, she didn't know, but just having the opportunity to regain that small piece of her mother lightened her heart a bit.

"Deal!" the broker exclaimed, thrusting his arm across the counter to shake Sim's hand and seal the bargain. He briefly disappeared into a back room to gather whatever coins Sim had agreed to, then, money and promissory note exchanged, bid them a good day. Sim secured the fortune in an inner pocket, tucked Em's arm into the crook of his elbow, and led her unresisting from the shop.

It took until they had nearly returned to the cart before Em found her voice.

"Thank you," she whispered, swallowing the slight lump in her throat.

Sim smiled down at her, then paused with a surprised blink when he noted the dampness of her eyes, the tears glistening on her cheeks. He glanced around quickly, then headed to the side of a building out of the way of any people.

"Emily, what's wrong?" he asked in a low voice.

"Nothing," she swiped the back of her hand across her eyes. "I just ... I didn't think I'd see Mamma's pendant again, but you ... I don't know how I'll ... thank you for the possibility to get it back."

Sim leaned over her, a hand to each side of her shoulders, trying to read her expression. She kept her gaze downcast.

"Emily," he spoke very gently. "You didn't think the King would let you just sell that for him without recourse, did you?"

Shocked, she glanced up.

"Why wouldn't he?" she demanded. "He's the King, and he has every right to demand that we sacrifice to keep him as such. I'm just a junior assistant librarian, yet why would I assume my duty any less than yours? I had the means to aid the King and I did so."

"And he intends to thank you by seeing to it that you get that necklace back."

She closed her eyes, trying to hold back more tears. With a deep, shaking breath, she opened them again and looked at the man hovering over her.

"Thank you," she said simply.

A frown rippled across his brow and he opened his mouth to say something, then thought better of it. With a shake of his head, he pushed off from the wall and took her arm again.

"Come on, we need to find Tox, pay for our supplies, and get back."

She just nodded and accompanied him to find their friend.

Chapter 15

He had signed on as a sell-sword before his eighteenth birthday, seen employment in three mercenary companies by age twenty-eight, and had captained his own group for the last ten years. In that time, Milos had seen his share of warfare and waiting, power plays and politics, strong leaders and weak, and he could honestly say he'd rather the intensity of planning followed by the heat of battle than the boredom of sitting on his arse in the hopes that something might happen soon.

Captain Milos had accepted this assignment in Dalasham in the hopes of an easy payday. Hang around for a while, insinuate themselves within the King's forces, help the Prince make a grab at the throne, then head back to headquarters once Whillim had secured his position, flush and able to relax until another opportunity arose to their benefit. Like many a noble's plan, that scheme had gone to shite. Unlike most patrons, his employer had written the possibility of an extended campaign into their contract, meaning Milos and his mercenary company had to stick around and help create a more promising outcome to a situation becoming more complex by the day. Breaking the contract did not cross Milos' mind; a Company lived or died by its reputation, and Milos had never backed out of a commitment.

No matter how uncomfortable his employer made him.

The Company ostensibly worked for Prince Whillim (although Milos ought to accustom himself to calling the man King Whillim, he couldn't help but think the title ill suited the conceited Prince), but in truth, Lady Destiny had hired them.

Milos had worked with wizards before, even had a few women in his ranks who gave him pause, but the combination of a woman and a wizard had seemed so foreign when he had first met Lady Destiny, and he had at first thought her just the pretty mouthpiece for the Prince. It had taken less than five minutes for Milos to revise his opinion, to realise that the wizard would drive the attack rather than the royal, and that this woman stood as one of the most terrifying people Milos had ever had the misfortune to encounter. Yet by then, he had somehow already agreed to her terms, signing over the use of his Company's swords in Whillim's bid for power.

With payment in advance, of course.

So now, almost two months after Lady Destiny and Prince Whillim had first acquired their services, four days after Milos' failed attempt to grab the King, losing more than a score of good fighters in the process, he sat with a handful of his men in a sheltered copse of trees just within sight of the road that led between the little town and Calsburg Manor, watching, waiting, hoping for a fruitful outcome to the boredom of not having any action to take. Victor, Milos' best scout, had discovered a cave not too distant from Riverbend where he found traces of Stefan's flight, and of four trails leading away. While each trail had led to a section of the main road and thence into obscurity, they had all taken slightly different approaches, and Victor had extrapolated possible directions from each trodden path, later corroborated by the information Destiny had extracted from Stefan's captured guard. Given that one of the knights who had escaped Lady Destiny's clutches had a holding along one of those routes, Milos had started his search there. However, without the influence of the Destiny Seat, Milos knew that no one within those walls would bow to the demands of the Prince, not if Sir Castel had indeed fled with Stefan and the knowledge of the identity of the true monarch.

Leaving Milos and his men to wait and watch for signs that might lead them to Stefan.

"Why don't we just demand entrance and proof that Castel harbours no traitors?" Kristoff, a captain of Sir Byndorf's men-at-arms, wanted to know. Milos didn't bother to hide his scowl, and he didn't take his attention away from the manor. The Prince had ordered Milos to take some of the soldiers from his nobles' ranks along on the hunt for Stefan, both to flesh out Milos' numbers and to keep those troops occupied. While it gave Milos more men to cover more ground, it also saddled him with people who didn't truly understand the situation. He couldn't very well inform Kristoff that the people in Calsburg Manor had yet to fall under Destiny's influence and therefore wouldn't consider Stefan a traitor.

"We gather information, study the lay of the land and the routines of those within," Drummund answered, saving Milos from having to acknowledge the three soldiers not of his Company. He imagined his second-in-command rolled his eyes at the ignorance of their unwanted comrades. "We observe before we act."

"For how long? My arse is going numb."

"For as long as it takes," Drummund replied, using his hawk-like glare to its best advantage. "And if you're beat already, maybe you should crawl back to Riverbend and your cushy Lord's manor, leave the real work to us."

"Quiet," Milos snapped before Kristoff could bluster a response to that, his voice rough from years of bellowing commands. Although an altercation might provide a bit of entertainment, he thought he saw something approaching on the distant road. Nearly four decades had not dulled Milos' sharp sight, and soon, the others in his little group also marked a figure riding closer. No colours identified either rider or horse, but Milos recognised the easy gait of an experienced soldier. Whom he served, Milos couldn't say, but he thought it highly unlikely the man would raise a cheer for Prince Whillim.

"Do we take him?" Drummund asked quietly, voice pitched for Milos' ears alone.

"We wait," Milos replied in kind. "We don't want those entering unless it's ..." He paused, eyes barely flicking to those not of his Company. "Unless it's the renegade. Keep an eye out for those leaving, and mark that rider. If he comes back, follow him."

The rider—scout, messenger, spy, man returning from leave—continued on to the manor, seemingly unaware of the eyes marking his progress.

Captain Milos wondered if other riders approached other manors or castles along the watched routes Victor had projected from scouting Stefan's flight, and if any would actually lead to the missing King. It looked like they would have to sit around on their arses for a bit longer, but at least boredom had morphed into anticipation.

***

Ambrose kept his gaze firmly focused on the looming entrance to Calsburg Manor as he rode with the rosy glow of sunset just beginning to blush shyly over his left shoulder, but the taut muscles in his neck screamed at him to turn and look back at the shelter provided by that copse of trees he had just passed. Had he set up a post to watch for riders approaching Sir Castel's abode, he may have chosen such a site, and Ambrose felt certain that he had spotted a flash of colour and movement that didn't belong. His imagination, perhaps, given a hard day of riding behind him, but he wouldn't take the chance that an enemy lay in wait, guarding the approach to those loyal to King Stefan, nor alert such soldiers to his awareness of their presence. He felt the itch of watching eyes on his back right up to the closed gate.

"What's your business?" asked the sharp-eyed guard manning the palisade. Ambrose dismounted and met the man face to face through a grill in the gate.

"A message for Sir Castel," he said.

"What message?"

"Emily's perfect memory led me here," replied Ambrose.

The guard's eyes widened briefly and he glanced over his shoulder. Ambrose heard the sound of quickly retreating footsteps beyond the wall. Giving a firm nod, the guard turned back to Ambrose and indicated the nearby sally port with the thrust of his chin. Ambrose wasted no time leading his horse through the door to the safety within Castel's walls.

He waited under guard there for word of his arrival to reach Sir Castel, the deepening shades of sunset painting the three-storey manor with its turret tower red and orange. Ambrose didn't begrudge their caution, and indeed, the soldiers manning the gate made him welcome enough, though they made no bones about his restricted access to anything beyond this outer courtyard.

After a short time, a young man approached from the manor proper in the company of two other soldiers. Ambrose recognised him as Sir Castel's squire.

"I remember you," the youth said as he stood before Ambrose. "From the cave with the King."

Ambrose nodded but didn't fill in any details. He needed to hear the knight's remembrance of that night; to supply the squire with Ambrose's own recollection could only bias what Ambrose most needed to know. Did Calsburg Manor remain under King Stefan's influence, or had the Prince sunk his claws into Castel's mind?

The squire waited a handful of breaths for Ambrose to speak. When it became clear that Ambrose intended to keep his tongue, the squire only frowned minutely before turning on his heel and leading Ambrose, still under guard, toward the manor and the squire's master.

Ambrose soon found himself escorted into a small study, the door open to the full view of the two guards in the hall, and the squire busy in the corner filling a goblet from a waiting flagon. Before Ambrose could sink into one of the chairs, Sir Castel strode in. Ambrose bowed slightly. The knight studied him a moment, then accepted the goblet from his squire.

"You rode with King Stefan," Castel stated after taking a swallow. He moved to a chair and sat, indicating that Ambrose should join him while the squire slumped against the wall beyond Ambrose's shoulder. "Where is he?" the knight demanded.

"Safe," replied Ambrose. Castel's eyes narrowed in a frown. "Before I can tell you aught else, Sir Castel, I must ascertain where your loyalties lie."

"You mean, has the Prince convinced me he's the King?" Castel asked, a wry twist to his lips. He waved off his squire before the youth could take umbrage at such an implication. "No, Rastov, the man has to make sure of our allegiance." The knight turned hard eyes on Ambrose. "So, King's man, what proof do you require?"

"Details of the escape would help," Ambrose said.

"Which part?" Castel scoffed. "The part where Edvard and myself saved your sorry arse, along with Captain Frederick, near the east gate, or where we followed you blindly into the night to meet with some slip of a commoner—a wee girl who serves in the library at that—with delusions of knowing the minds of Prince and King alike? Or mayhap how Edvard, Pietor and myself acted as bait to lay false trails, forced to walk the whole damned way here with wounded atop a couple of sorry nags, and no knowledge of where King Stefan intended to secret himself away from Whillim's covetous hands. So tell me, did that child have the right of it before she fell on her face? Did Whillim use some form of vile magic to take Stefan's place? Or have we sat cowering in this manor while bandits watch from the woods for no good reason?"

"You've seen them then?" Ambrose leaned forward, hands clasped together tightly between his knees.

"Not with any ease, but enough to identify King's colours alongside those of Sir Byndorf. Seems to me, though, King's men wouldn't sit concealed among the trees when I've a whole manor able to offer shelter. Which sadly only lends credence to your Emily's fanciful tale." The knight heaved a sigh. "Tell me King Stefan has a plan and that it doesn't include me continuing to sit as bait while the Prince tries to steal his kingdom."

"He does," affirmed Ambrose. "It requires men, supplies, and stealth. Haste would also not go amiss, but we need those mercs waiting around the bend to remain ignorant of any move you make. How easily can we slip around them?"

Castel presented a wolf's grin.

"Young man, my ancestors made a fine art of paranoia through architecture. Those petty thugs won't even know we've left the manor."

Ambrose had the distinct impression that Dalasmar Castle did not boast the only secret tunnels in the kingdom, and that he would soon find himself tramping through yet more dark halls in an effort to keep his King safe. He wondered if the horses would like the confined space any better than he did.

Chapter 16

They didn't make a big fuss over their departure, but Stefan and his little group did make sure to pass by the small cluster of homes occupied by Tox's farmhands as the merchant, his niece, and their guard (currently down to three men, though hopefully, if any watched, they wouldn't note that those three differed from the original party) took their leave of their generous host early that morning. Once beyond the houses, Sim led them back, out of sight of the road, to the field Tox had designated for their use.

Upon their return from the market the previous evening, Tox and Sim had hauled their cart of goods to the minimal shelter provided by the threshing shed at the edge of the field, and Emily had helped secure a tarp over everything. Now, this morning, Emily set about sorting their supplies while Prichard and Sim devised canvas walls for the open-air parts of the structure. The shed—basically a roof over a section of flagstones—had two sections; one with low walls to store excess hay, and one used for separating chaff come harvest time, mostly open to allow the wind free access to the threshing floor. Stefan planned to use this area as a temporary barracks until they could obtain and erect enough tents, and as a kitchen and storage area once more troops arrived. If they arrived.

Stefan reflected on the disparity of his position today compared to last week. Even walking in solitude in the gardens to clear his mind, the King had always had an awareness that he didn't walk alone. He knew guards stood at every entrance, servants roamed through the halls. Nobles and visitors peopled the castle and the town ringing it, high born and low, knights and dignitaries, Councillors and scribes and stewards, kitchen staff and cleaning staff, City Watch, urchins and thieves, artisans and scholars and librarians; always he knew hundreds of folk surrounded him wherever he went. Now he stood nearly alone in a field, hoping for the arrival of others. Four individuals only attended him. *Captain, soldier, nobleman and librarian,* he thought with a wry twist to his lips. No schedules, audiences or appointments, no one clamouring for his attention or judgement, leaving a strange sensation of ... not freedom exactly, but ... disjointedness, perhaps? Definitely dislocation and an unsettling lack of structure to his day. He couldn't decide if so much true solitude and uncertainty provided a kind of thrill or whether it simply terrified him. If the reason for so much potential chaos hadn't stemmed from the horrifying truth of Willi's treachery and bloodshed, then maybe he might find more enjoyment in this unlooked for change to his normally safe existence.

Better if he didn't dwell on his lack of support and stability and instead concentrated on how to regain a modicum of control.

Stefan and Fred moved to examine the field beyond their makeshift barracks.

"Here for latrines, I think," Fred swept his hand across a slight rise in the fallow ground. "Far enough from the stream and shed, yet near enough to the encampment."

"Picket lines for the horses there?" Stefan pointed out a likely spot as they walked. Fred grunted in reply.

"Least we'll leave Goodman Tox with some fertilizer for his field," the Captain said, kicking idly at a stone churned up by last season's plow.

"I can't believe we're doing this," Stefan said softly, his gaze distant as he stopped moving. "That it will come to civil war and half the people involved won't even realise it."

"Half if we're lucky," mumbled Fred. "If the Prince and his wizard get their hands on enough of your subjects—"

"I know," Stefan replied, his eyes now tracking a flight of birds as they soared overhead. "This could turn into a race. Willi with his mercenary Company and all the nobles in Riverbend against a handful of us, combing the countryside looking for allies. At least we don't have to convince those nobles and knights about who I am, while Willi will need to get them to Riverbend and this Wizard Destiny to consolidate his supposed legitimacy. Or so we can hope. We're somewhat outnumbered now and without any means of transportation while my brother has every horse in the city at his disposal."

"The men will reach the knights, bring back reinforcements."

"Still, only a drop in the bucket to what Willi can call up now. I worry about his head start, Fred." Stefan shook his head, his gaze returning to the field. "I worry about damn near everything Willi might do while I sit on my hands here."

Fred didn't bother trying to placate him. Both men knew they stood in a tenuous situation and that time did not serve as their friend.

"If we could just get into the castle," Fred said after a moment of silence. "Find whatever magic Destiny uses and destroy it."

"I wish it were that simple," Stefan replied, resuming their walk. "But we can't get into the city without notice, and even if we could, we don't know what to look for or how to destroy it once we find it."

"So we prepare to fight."

"We prepare for the possibility," Stefan amended, his thoughts dancing. "But if we can find someone who knows what Destiny's done, maybe we won't have to fight."

"You mean to do it, then?" asked Fred in a low voice, though no one would overhear their words. "Head west, look for a wizard who might help us heathens from Riverbend?"

Stefan chuckled.

"Yes, basically. Once the knights arrive and we have a better idea of what numbers to expect, we'll set out, gathering those still loyal to me along the way."

"Whillim sees a notable swath of soldiers marching along, it won't take him long to figure out you're behind it," Fred said. "He'll send his mercs after you."

"You have another idea?" Stefan wanted to know.

"We head west unobserved, let the knights reach out to your subjects. Give Whillim more paths to follow, hopefully keep him chasing his own tail, while we find an answer."

"More false trails and us on the least-trampled path again. This dance will grow old quickly, Fred."

"It'll keep us alive."

"We can but hope," Stefan sighed. He shook his head. "If we can find a way to break Destiny's hold over Willi, someone who can counter her magic, we may not need an army."

"And while we can pray for this miracle, we dare not count on it, Sire. Better over prepared than defeated by wishing."

Stefan snorted his amusement.

"Have no fear, Fred. I don't plan to give up. We'll make sure to build up troops even while we search for a less lethal solution."

They explored Tox's field further, making plans for assembling, training, and outfitting their army with what resources they might hope to accrue given Whillim's control of the castle, city, and treasury. By the time they had circled back to the threshing shed, Prichard, Sim and Emily had devised a fairly decent shelter, given the limited materials to hand.

"Emily," Stefan called, drawing the young woman's attention. She looked up, placed a last basket of hardy vegetables on a make-shift shelf of sturdy tree branches they had scavenged, then came to stand before the King. She dusted off her hands and folded them at her waist, head bent in a sort of bow.

"You told us before that Destiny's spell has many complex layers," Stefan said. "Based on what you know, how well could you describe each layer and how many might exist?"

"It's impossible to say, Sire," she answered. "It erases one very specific memory and supplants it with another, yet leaves the underlying emotions intact. That is, it transfers the beliefs and feelings of the original memory onto the replacement, causing people to mistake their obligations to you, as their King, as obligations to the Prince, ascribing him your attributes. It also filters down onto people who have a loyalty, a duty, to someone so spelled, thereby capturing those of lesser ranks by ... corrupting the thought processes of their superiors. That's a minimum of four levels that we can describe. If it needs reaffirmation at any point, that's another level."

"Does the fact that she uses an actual, physical device, this Destiny Seat, add to or detract from the complexity of the spell?"

"Hard to say, Sire. I would imagine that imbuing the spell into an object that she can use at will rather than risk depleting her personal reserves would add some complexity, but I don't know if that adds a layer to the spell or if it simply acts as a focus to absorb her power."

"Do you suggest," Prichard wanted to know, he and Sim having moved to join the conversation, "that she could cast this spell without the Seat?"

"Given an incredible amount of concentration, reserves, time and total lack of distractions or interruptions, maybe, but the likelihood of all those factors working to her favour seems remote."

"And you understand all this based on a book?" Fred asked.

Emily shifted, shrugged a shoulder. "A few books," she admitted. "I've never met a wizard of any high order, so I can only hypothesize based on what I've read."

"Have you met wizards of low order?" asked Sim.

"None as openly admitted such, given their shunning in the capital," she hedged. "But perhaps I suspected one or two whom I helped in the library over the years."

"What?" Fred blurted.

"Scholars looking for innocuous tidbits, history and architecture primarily, but with applications that an observant librarian might link with minor magics." She glanced up just enough that Stefan saw the steel in her eye as she challenged the Captain. "Magics that could perhaps benefit a village by securing a water supply, improve crop health, avoid bandits. Nothing that would cause harm or threaten a kingdom." She dropped her gaze again.

"Then you know enough about some forms of magic to distinguish between helpful and harmful," Stefan said. "Making you the closest thing we have to an expert on the subject. Tell me, Emily," he continued, turning the course of the conversation. "Can you ride a horse?"

The question surprised her enough that she looked up at him, a brief flicker of confusion clouding her features.

"I rode accompanied when but a child, Your Majesty, but have not ridden in years. Why?"

"How well do you know the languages of Westam and its neighbours, the different dialects of the region?" he asked instead.

"I can read them well enough, Sire, though I've had little occasion to speak them."

"I can get by speaking some of them," Stefan said. "But having more than one of us versant in their tongues can only help us."

"Help us what?" Prichard asked, though Stefan suspected he knew what lay in the King's mind.

"You mean to try to find a wizard in Westam who can help counter what Destiny has done, don't you, Sire?" Emily said quietly.

"We can describe how complex a spell she's built," Stefan counted off the points on his fingers. "We know her name, and we know she's a woman. Surely that gives us enough of a place to start."

"What about this encampment we're planning here?" Prichard argued, his arm sweeping behind him to indicate the newly canvassed threshing shed. "A ruse or a backup?"

"A precaution," Fred told him. "If we learn nothing from this little venture, the King will need loyal soldiers to take back his throne by force. If we somehow discover something to counter Destiny's magic, we still need a way back to the capital through the Prince's mercenaries, and that likely means manpower."

"Your Majesty," Emily said with just enough force that Stefan wondered if she had called for his attention before and they had all missed it. All four men turned to regard her, but she kept her attention focused on Stefan. "You cannot possibly mean to include me on such a mission."

He blinked, feeling a frown crease his brow.

"Why not?"

A sheen of moisture glistened in her pale grey eyes and she bit her lip before answering.

"Because you can't know how long until she takes Darien's mind. Once Destiny has control of the Chief Librarian—"

"What makes you think she doesn't already?" Fred interrupted, snapping her gaze away. "We have to assume that when the Prince didn't get the Royal Proofs, he had the library searched and the librarians questioned. They have to plan to alter documentation at some level, so again, those charged with safeguarding such documents would become prime targets of the Destiny Seat. Either way, she likely took control of Darien the morning after we escaped."

Emily shook her head.

"That doesn't make sense," she whispered, a hand rising unconsciously to her throat. "If Chief Librarian Darien fell under her spell that long ago, then ... then ..." Stefan knew she

167

couldn't bring herself to admit the fear that shone so readily upon her face.

"Then why do you still know the truth?" he filled in for her in a gentle voice.

She stared at him with wide eyes, looking lost and vulnerable. *She's barely more than a child,* he thought, not for the first time.

"When you figured out the danger that night in the library, what was your first thought?" asked Fred.

"To warn the King," she replied promptly.

"You didn't spare a thought for Darien, think to maybe take the problem to him?"

Emily gave a barely perceptible shake to her head.

"What could he do?" she murmured. "Even if I could have escaped the library entrance without notice, if I found him in time, Darien couldn't get to the King before Milos' soldiers did."

"But *you* could," pressed Fred. "You put the King's safety ahead of your own, time and again. You sat bleeding in a tree to make sure no one found him, guarding the King with your life. Hellfire, girl, you jumped out of a sickbed with a fire poker to defend him. I'd say that puts your loyalty with Stefan first and foremost, far beyond any loyalty Darien might command. Destiny will have used her device on Darien by now, but you remain free from her influence."

"You put too much faith in me," Emily breathed, tears tracing a gentle track down her cheeks as she shook her head.

"No more than you can handle, I'll warrant," Sim said. Neither he nor Stefan mentioned that Sim had kept a close eye on Emily the previous day in the city to note any aberrant behaviour, nor that he continued under the same orders for the foreseeable future. Stefan and Fred both believed she somehow remained protected from the trickle-down effect of the Destiny Seat; even so, neither would chance that trust proving incorrect. And none of them saw the point in distressing the young librarian further.

Sim turned to look at the King. "How do you plan on getting to Westam, and under what guise?"

"When the knights arrive, they'll have horses," Stefan replied. "We ride under assumed names and avoid drawing attention to ourselves, which means some of the meaner inns, or roadside camps. Myself, Fred, Emily, Sim, and my guards. Prichard has some estates in the west and his skills will give us another advantage. That's eight of us. We leave the camp under the care of Sir Edvard."

"And those aliases?" Sim pressed. "We're not merchants or peddlers, lacking goods to trade. Mercenaries seems a bit of a stretch. A patrol might explain our appearance, so long as the Prince doesn't think to question any reports, though our numbers don't add up to a normal patrol. So who will we pretend to be?"

"Scholars," Emily whispered, her gaze distant, as though drawn into the plot against her will. But she focused her gaze on Sim, then, briefly, on Stefan, before staring into nothingness again. "A scholar and his research assistant, Your Majesty, escorted by guards, seeking information for his dissertation or an essay. It will give you access to the universities, and from there, an easily explained expansion to the Schools of Wizardry. So long as we come up with a plausible enough topic."

Stefan considered that notion a moment, then nodded his approval of the idea.

"Brilliant," he decided. "And something Willi would never guess."

"Now all we need are able bodies to fill our camp and sturdy horses for our journey," declared Fred. "And some arcane subject for you to study up on that only the wizards of Westam could help you with. Easy."

Stefan snorted his amusement and they turned to the task of readying the camp for the King's loyal soldiers. He pushed aside the fear that their preparations would come to naught if even one knight fell into Willi's hands first. The trepidation he saw in Emily's eyes as she no doubt considered Darien's plight he could work on eradicating, but his own worries would take far more to alleviate. In the meantime, he pushed it to the back of his mind as he busied himself with plans for their near future.

A week ago, that future had involved trade treaties, the possibility of a marriage alliance, and governing a kingdom. Now it revolved around suppressing an unthinkable revolt by setting up the probability of a civil war and learning of things magical while trying to keep three steps ahead of a surprisingly ambitious brother and his inventive wizard. He longed for the quiet days of state dinners where he kept nobles and dignitaries to a semblance of civility with well-chosen words and subtle actions. Yet a small, dark part of his mind quietly thrilled at this prospect of action that contained more than a mere element of danger and the threat of real struggle where he could truly stretch his mind and battle skills. What that said of him, Stefan didn't dare dwell on overmuch, at least not today.

Chapter 17

Em stared at the fabric in her hands in dismay. It had sounded like a good idea at the time: purchase some bolts of cloth, thread and needle, and fashion new outfits, mayhap give them all a second set of clothing. She hadn't thought ahead to who would put together those garments. Funny how she could consider who would pay for the material without a treasury to hand, yet completely fail to contemplate who might assemble that cloth into clothes without a seamstress.

It took until Fred dumped the fabric into her arms with a gruff "This ought to make good tunics," before Em realised every one of her companions assumed she could handle that assignment. While she had sewn the bindings of books—leather bound or cloth—she didn't know the first thing about making tunics. Or leggings, or boots, or gloves, or scarves, or any other article of clothing. She worked in a library, and while she had access to any book therein, she had never had the slightest interest in clothing or how to fashion or assemble it, so hadn't even had an inclination to read anything on the subject. Yet these men thought she knew how to make an outfit. After all, what woman didn't know how to sew?

A librarian spoiled by castle life, Em thought as she blinked owlishly at the dun coloured linen bolts trying to slither out of her trembling arms. *One who never had to sew her own clothes or cook her own food.* But now she would have to learn.

She glanced down at her own shabby tunic. Despite her

attempt to clean it, she could only do so much given the blood-stained gash and stubborn grime from several days of sweat and hard wear, and even so, didn't think trying to make a copy of her own attire would suffice for the men. She'd have to study someone else's clothing, then, and hope some insight helped her figure out how to measure, cut, and join fabric into tunics.

Raising her eyes, she searched out her companions. She only saw three. Lord Prichard, she knew, worked within the confines of the make-shift barracks behind her, assembling straw pallets for sleeping from the remnants of Goodman Tox's winter supply of the stalks. Out here in the growing warmth of late morning where her breath no longer plumed the air, she watched as Fred joined the King and Sergeant Sim at their task in the near distance. The Captain likewise took up a shovel and set to attacking the ground as the trio worked to dig out a pit latrine. That the King bent his back to such menial labour surprised Em, but she supposed with only the five of them in this little encampment, they needed every hand to prepare for the hoped for arrival of more soldiers and supplies. Especially if those clouds on the horizon indeed turned to rain, as she thought they might before the end of the afternoon. No one wanted to dig about in mud, and more hands made less work.

The King and Sim had shucked off their tunics as they worked despite the cool spring weather. No doubt Fred's would soon join the small pile. Perhaps she could retrieve one to use as a template for her new job. With that thought in mind, Em approached the men, her eyes fastened on the rumpled clothing.

As she neared, she heard the thud of Sim's pick axe striking earth to loosen the winter-hardened soil, the thunk of the King's shovel head sinking into the dirt, the whoosh of the removed detritus landing in a growing pile beyond them, but as she dropped to her knees next to the tunics and reached for the top one, all sound ceased.

"What are you doing?"

The Captain's voice froze Em's hand and she felt the bolt of fabric awkwardly cradled in her other arm sliding free to sprawl half in her lap and half on the ground. Her face heated as she hastily clawed the stray cloth more fully onto her lap, then, clutching the material, raised her gaze to Fred's baffled stare.

"I needed an example," she whispered. Silence met her

confession.

"An example of what?" the King finally asked in mild consternation.

"Of how to—"

She lost the power of speech as she turned to regard him. She couldn't help it. He and Sim stood staring at her; Sim with the pick axe resting on his shoulder, the King leaning on his shovel, giving a quick scratch to the beard he had started to grow out. Their steady regard didn't still her tongue, but their physique did. Both men glistened with sweat, finely-toned muscles flexing, the epitome of masculine strength. Em swallowed hard. She had never seen an unclad man before, and no one she worked with in the library could boast such fitness as these two specimens. Heart suddenly thundering in her chest, feeling flushed from head to toe, Em ripped her eyes away from the startling spectacle before her. She took refuge in the bundle of linen in her lap, trying furiously to remember what the King had just asked her.

"Emily?" the King called as he took a step closer, crouching to see her face, making muscles in his abdomen and chest bunch in an alarming yet fascinating manner. "Are you well?"

"Um ..." she managed faintly, trying not to see anything in her mortification. *Tunics,* she thought frantically and snatched one. "I need to borrow this."

Again silence. And then Fred's voice from overhead as his boots stomped into view.

"Why?"

"To see how it's made?" She didn't mean to make that a question, but that's how it came out.

"What do you mean, how it's made? Speak up, girl."

Em blinked quickly, caught now between a fierce desire to run away, bury herself in the pit they dug, or break down crying. She squeezed her eyes shut. For some reason, Fred's words from a few days ago bubbled to mind: *A good soldier knows when to ask for help.* She took a steadying breath.

"I need to see how this tunic's made so that I can duplicate it," she managed to say.

"You don't know how to make a tunic?" Sim blurted out.

"I don't know how to make any clothes," she admitted, her eyes slitting open slowly and choosing Fred's gaze as the easiest to meet, given that he still wore his shirt. He towered over her, forcing her to crane her neck, but she dare not look elsewhere. "But if I can study some, I hope to figure it out."

"Why didn't you say so?" Fred demanded.

"I just did," Em replied with a frown.

"I mean before," the Captain exploded. "When I gave you that cloth."

"Because it's rude to speak to a retreating back," she said. "And that's all you presented me."

The King snorted a laugh when Fred growled at her answer.

"Have any of us made clothing before?" King Stefan asked.

"Repairs only," Sim admitted.

"Women's work," grunted Fred.

"Seamstress' work," corrected Em. "I'm a librarian, re-member? Not a seamstress."

"Still a woman," Fred said. "Thought you all learned sewing."

"Know how to plow a field, Captain?" she shot at him. "How to plant crops and harvest them? How to treat blight on the corn or keep livestock healthy?"

"'Course not, girl. That's farmer's work."

"It's men's work," she retorted.

Fred opened his mouth to reply, paused, sealed his lips. She watched as the heat left his eyes, leaving wry amusement in its wake.

"A fair point," he admitted. "And I apologise for my assumption."

Em stared at him, her own mouth dropping open in astonishment.

"Well," the King said, mirth colouring his tone as he rose and stepped back to join Sim again, "now that we're all more aware of our limitations, I think it's time to get back to our work. It's too cold out here to stop moving for long, and Emily needs the use of my tunic more than I do right now."

Em didn't think she could blush any brighter, but she didn't let their laughter drive her away. As they turned back to digging their pit, she spread the King's tunic out before her and studied its design, doing her utmost to ignore the flashes of bare flesh she could see from the corner of her eye.

*****

It felt good to finally *do* something, even if that something

174

involved slinging around piles of dirt as they dug a latrine. Not that they had sat idle, Fred acknowledged. You couldn't plan any sort of campaign without reconnaissance and strategising, but Fred had always found more satisfaction in action. He could *see* progress through action, whereas words meant little without follow through. And the knot of anticipation that sometimes lodged in his stomach before plans became action had finally subsided to a more manageable weight of accomplishing something as he worked a shovel beside his King.

"We're going to have a problem with Emily," Sim said quietly, drawing Fred's attention. The little librarian had retreated to the shelter of the threshing shed a few moments earlier with the bundle of cloth clutched to her like a shield, having studied the King's shirt to her satisfaction.

"What kind of problem?" Stefan asked, his shovel dragging across the floor of the pit as they levelled out the bottom.

"The kind that any lone woman in a camp full of men might have, compounded by the fact that *that* young woman has no idea how to truly interact with men."

"She's done a remarkable job so far," Fred countered, tamping down a section of dirt.

Sim thudded his pick into the lip of the latrine, resting his weight on it as he turned to meet Fred's stare.

"That's because we're honourable men who had survival on our minds. What happens when tedium, the strain of uncertainty, and the possibility of warfare overcomes honour? A handful of us can put aside her sex, but a small army?"

"We won't stay long once the knights arrive," Stefan affirmed. "That will get her out of any unseemly sights."

"And once we're on the road, Sire? She's inexperienced and, judging by her reaction to us just now, innocent. What if she decides to explore that innocence? What do we do if *she* instigates something?"

"Hellfires, man, she just a child!" Fred blurted out.

"She's not, Fred," Stefan said quietly, leaning on his shovel now. "She's a very young woman who has led a sheltered life and whose main knowledge of the workings of the world comes from books. And while our intentions may remain honourable, we're taking her out into that world full of people who won't see her as we do. They'll see that young woman as no more than

175

an opportunity to slake an urge. And she may not know how to refuse."

Fred narrowed his eyes, his grip almost painful on the handle of the shovel. They spoke nothing more than the truth, but the acidic burn in his gut and the haze of anger that crossed his vision surprised him with their intensity. Emily might not have a face to ensnare on first glance, but that wouldn't stop someone who felt it his right to try to possess her body, and that thought awoke a protectiveness the little librarian had kindled in Fred every time she did something foolishly brave. An affection that had nothing to do with lust. He wondered if this was how it felt to have a child.

"Then we teach her, and we guard her," he said. The expression on both Sim's and Stefan's face made Fred pause, then shake his head in quick denial as he realised how that had sounded. "We teach her how to defend herself," he explained. "We all know she has the spirit for it, but clearly lacks the skills. Hellfire, I thought she'd stab herself with that fire iron when she thought she had to rescue you, Sire." Both men grinned ruefully at that memory. "If we can teach her to harness that spirit," Fred went on, "actually know how to hold a blade or throw a punch, then folks would have a much harder time trying to force her against her will. And we keep a guard on her when we're not in camp. Any young woman journeying as we propose to would have one."

"If she instigates?" Sim pressed. "She's never had an opportunity to explore what it means to be a woman; what if she uses that thirst for knowledge to search beyond books?"

"You want to have that conversation with her, Sim?" Stefan asked. The Sergeant blanched and Stefan chuckled. "Nor do I. If it happens, we'll deal with it then. In the meantime, Fred, I'm charging you with her training. Get her competent enough that her good intentions don't cause damage.

"And now, gentlemen, we'd better get the benches set on this pit before those clouds wash away our efforts."

The three men clambered out of the completed hole under a darkening sky, hastening to finish the job before the first drops of cold rain could dampen their achievement.

Chapter 18

Ambrose led Sir Castel, the knight's squire Rostov, and three men-at-arms off the road and into Goodman Tox's field. Four days previously, when he had left to fetch Castel, he remembered noting a threshing shed near the stream, and he headed in that direction now as the likely location Captain Frederick would have chosen to establish an encampment. The rest of Castel's 30 men—including those who had taken refuge with him after the riots—and the supplies the knight had arranged would follow after dark to keep their presence as unobtrusive as possible should anyone chance to look.

Evading the mercenary group spying upon Calsburg Manor had proved remarkably simple. Sir Castel's ancestors had indeed built hidden tunnels, and to Ambrose's surprise and relief, they had designed their escape routes large enough to accommodate not only the height of a man on horseback, but also wide enough to allow the passage of an unsprung cart, ideal for carrying goods. Calsburg may have had more than one series of tunnels scattered throughout its foundations, but the one they had made use of to evade the mercenaries originated at the back of the stables. Ambrose rather suspected escape did not feature solely in the design of the well-shored up tunnels; smuggling supplies *into* the manor grounds would work as well as getting people out should a need arise. As both Ambrose and supplies for the King had found their way through those underground passages, Ambrose felt no cause for complaint.

They had emerged from a hillock some distance from the manor around mid-day with the mercenaries none the wiser. In fact, Castel had sent out a small patrol early that next morning to distract Whillim's men, leaving the King's true support a safe window in which to slip away. The rest of that day, they had travelled at the speed of the supply cart. This morning, Ambrose and Castel had left the main group with instructions to follow while they rode ahead.

Leading to this small party who now walked their horses through Tox's fallow field to rejoin their King.

Ambrose had not expected to find the Captain in training, or at least he hadn't anticipated with whom he trained.

Emily hadn't spotted them yet, though Captain Frederick kept careful track of their progress. Emily stood with her back to them, facing the stream, the Captain quietly standing to her right. She wore her own stained and tattered tunic over a pair of trews rolled at the ankles and tied at the waist with a frayed rope, trousers obviously borrowed and adjusted to her stature as best she could. One hand held a thin tree branch about as long as her arm, and the other alternately served as counterbalance and guide as she flowed through a series of exercise forms Ambrose well remembered from his own early days of weapons defence training. Simple forms to build strength and muscle memory, and well suited to one favouring an injury. She performed the forms surprisingly well, given she couldn't have known them more than a couple of days. Unless she somehow had prior experience? *Probably read about them in one of her books,* Ambrose thought. *I certainly couldn't execute those forms well for at least a month.* She did them near flawlessly.

Until she turned and saw the five of them staring at her. She froze for an instant, then quickly lowered her arms to her sides, face red from more than exertion as she studied her feet, trembling slightly as though caught doing something wrong. From the mortified, gaping stare of Sir Castel, the knight clearly thought she had. While Ambrose may have found her actions startling—he had seen few women take up arms, and every one of them a mercenary—if the Captain himself deigned to set Emily some training, Ambrose would not question it.

"What goes on here?" Castel demanded.

"Training," the Captain replied gruffly.

"Training?" Castel's word choked off with incredulity. "Her?"

"Yes, her. Sir." Ambrose had seen that look on the Captain's face before, the scowl that strongly suggested you change the subject before the man decided to thrash you. Sir Castel obviously had no experience with it.

"Why would you waste your time trying to get a girl to understand what only a man can do? And why is she even here?"

Emily went from red-faced to pale as snow and she ducked her head even further, her auburn hair falling forward to hide her expression.

"This woman likely knows as much about warfare as you do, Castel, and she's here because I value her advice," another voice said from behind them.

The five of them turned and bowed to varying degrees as the King, Lord Prichard, and Sergeant Sim approached.

"Fred's training her because I believe everyone who risks what we do should have every advantage possible," King Stefan added.

Stuck now between offending the King and adhering to his own bias, Castel bowed again with a quiet "As you say, Sire," that he obviously didn't believe. Ambrose could sympathise. Had he not spent time with Emily, had he not heard her point out just how ingrained their belief that women were no more than frail creatures needing protection with little ability to think on their own, he might have had similar reservations.

But he had seen her drop from a tree in the middle of the night as she guarded the King, heard her recite history without flaw, watched her take up a fire iron when she thought them in danger, listened as she helped engineer a plan for obtaining supplies without raising suspicion, going so far as to offer up her own possessions as payment so that the Prince couldn't trace their whereabouts from the sale of the King's ring. However, without that acquaintance, Ambrose knew that most would think like Castel and, judging from Emily's meek looking acceptance of that treatment, he understood that she expected that behaviour and likely wouldn't challenge it. He didn't know whether to call the sour feeling in his gut anger or resignation at that thought.

"You arrived in good time," the King smoothly changed the subject. "I had not dared hope any would arrive so soon."

179

Castel puffed up his chest a bit at the compliment and Ambrose suppressed the urge to roll his eyes, but he had learned even in his short acquaintance with the knight that flattering his ego would spur the man to his best efforts. A vain man, but an efficient one.

"Sir Castel had anticipated most of your needs, Sire," Ambrose spoke diffidently. "He stood ready to bring aid near as soon as I rode through his gates."

"Excellent," the King replied, his gaze sweeping over them and clearly not seeing any supplies.

"Your man made it clear that we cannot draw too much attention to this encampment," Castel said. "So the rest of my men and some supplies will wait until nightfall to approach. I have food, shelter, a handful of extra mounts, and some clothing." The tone with which the knight said this last had Ambrose take more notice of the King's attire. He, Prichard and Sim wore tunics of base material, but closer examination showed the stitches as rough, though adequate. From Emily's suddenly flaming face, though still mostly concealed behind a short curtain of hair, Ambrose suspected he knew the source of those stitches.

The King glanced down at his tunic with an odd smile before meeting Castel's gaze.

"All most welcome. For five people with limited resources and more military knowledge than domestic experience, I feel we did rather well preparing for the arrival of our loyal subjects, but a few extra comforts won't go amiss now that you've arrived." Ambrose wondered if Castel heard the soft rebuke in the King's words, even as he wondered if such a rebuke had indeed existed, or if Ambrose had only imagined the slight edge to the tone. "Come Sir Castel," King Stefan continued, his arm sweeping forward in invitation as he turned the knight toward the canvassed threshing shed and away from Emily. "Let us find you a suitable place to pitch your tent."

After a couple of steps, the King paused and threw back over his shoulder, "Stay and finish the lesson, Fred. You too, Ambrose. I know you could use a break after completing your task so quickly, but I fear you'll have to wait to find any rest if you hope to keep up with the trainee." Then he led the others away.

Captain Frederick grunted before looking at his two charges.

Ambrose knew the King expected him to make a report to the Captain about his trip, but Frederick shook his head minutely, then pointed to the spot beside Emily.

"Into line, soldier," the big man ordered. "And draw your sword."

Ambrose did so without hesitation, raising his weapon into first position and waiting for the Captain to call the start. Emily stared at him, then at the Captain, the uncertainty and timidness suddenly vanishing from her expression as resolve took over. She stepped up beside Ambrose, drew her own thin branch up into position, mirroring Ambrose's sword, and gave a firm nod. The Captain smiled thinly, a whisper of pride flashing through his eyes before he wiped it away with determination.

"Begin," he barked, and Ambrose soon found himself grinning even as he concentrated on keeping his motions fluid and steady. Emily matched every move, her gaze flicking between him and the Captain as they danced through the forms, adjusting her posture on those rare occasions when she misstepped.

On the second iteration of the forms, his body moving by rote through the exercise, Ambrose gave his report to the Captain. Neither he nor Emily faltered, and Ambrose marvelled that the distraction of his voice didn't throw Emily at all. Perhaps her memory extended to more than just the written word.

This woman likely knows as much about warfare as you do, Castel, the King had said, and Ambrose could believe it.

***

Milos ran the curry comb along his horse's left flank one final time before laying the tool aside and giving a last stroke down Blaze's chestnut and white neck. Hefting his saddlebags over his shoulder, the mercenary leader left the stables and headed toward Dalasmar Castle. He had a wizard to find despite his misgivings at actually having to speak with that formidable and frightening woman. But after the debacle at Calsburg Manor, Milos knew they had to change their strategy.

Unless by some wondrous trick of fate someone else had located Stefan by now. Or, even more unlikely, Whillim had grown a pair of balls and simply made public his usurpation. Until one of those two events came to pass, Milos would just have to make the best of the situation, bringing him to Lady Destiny with a request.

He had no idea whether the wizard could adapt her spell in the way he had envisioned, but he intended to find out. Anything that helped them move forward rather than chase their tails.

He stopped only long enough to toss his saddlebags onto his cot in the barracks and pull on a fresh tunic before he went in search of Destiny. At this time in the afternoon, he hoped to find her either in the audience chamber, the King's solar, or her own quarters. He started with the audience chamber and finally tracked her down in the hall outside the solar. Thankfully, she had just taken leave of Whillim, so Milos didn't have to bother with acknowledging the man and thereby putting him off his task. Of course, that also meant Milos had no reason to delay actually speaking with the wizard.

One look into her flinty eyes confirmed the truth of his suppositions: Stefan remained out of Destiny's grip.

Shite, he thought to himself. He suspected she had the same thought as she took in his countenance with an irate frown. He steeled his resolve.

"We need to talk," he said quietly, avoiding her dark gaze as his own swept the hall for anyone who might seek to overhear them, although he couldn't imagine who would so foolishly risk incurring the wrath of Lady Destiny. Other than Prince Whillim, who had since disappeared around the far corner.

Destiny didn't reply, but she led him to an empty receiving room and shut the door behind them. A grouping of chairs encircled a small table set before an unlit hearth opposite a moderate window which let in just enough light from the overcast afternoon to avoid the need for a lantern. Milos sank into one of the chairs and waited for Destiny to choose her own seat across from him. Then he spoke before she could prompt him.

"I'm certain that Sir Castel aids Stefan, but he didn't shelter him. I have men still searching for the others who escaped that night, but we're hampered by both Whillim's insistence that his converted men-at-arms accompany us and by the fact that we can't simply demand admittance to a keep in the King's name and then go on and demand information on Stefan's whereabouts. We need a better plan, Lady."

For a moment she didn't move, just stared at him with her intense blue eyes, nearly swallowed to black in the dim light. Then she spoke, one word with enough frost in it that Milos fought off a shiver.

"Explain."

Milos took a breath, reminded himself that he had fought for nearly as many years as this woman had seen life, and that, while she paid for his sword, she had no claim to his soul. He would always remain wary of her, but he refused to let his fear overwhelm him. With his composure firmly in hand, he gave his report, outwardly unaffected by her icy stare.

"Castel sent out a decoy force while he escaped with aid for Stefan. While my crew figured out quickly enough that this decoy force merely toyed with us, Byndorf's men kept up the pursuit, so fervent in their desire to avenge the slight against their *dear King Whillim*,"—Milos made sure she heard the sneer in that term—"that they refused to take orders from any but their own overly zealous captain. Instead of risking Whillim's anger if we let those fools get themselves injured or killed by soldiers openly taunting them, I had my men accompany them while I circled back to find Castel long gone. My man Drummund detained one of the decoys and learned of the ruse, though no one save the messenger from Stefan knew where Castel headed."

Milos felt no need to expound on Drummund's techniques, and the slight gleam in Destiny's eyes informed the mercenary leader that this wizard well understood the art of torture.

"These Dalasham soldiers slow us down," he continued. "Add to that having to tip-toe around who sits as King, and our ability to question outside, uninfluenced, nobles and knights becomes seriously hampered."

Destiny's eyes narrowed.

"Do you seek to lay the blame for your failures at my feet, Captain?" she murmured, voice conversational but tone deadly. He returned the mien.

"Not at all, Lady. But I do seek an alternate vessel for your magic."

She sat back, fingers laced on her stomach as she regarded him.

"Do you now. And what sort of vessel do you imagine?"

"Something portable, tuned to someone besides yourself. I

ask you to consider, my Lady, if it's possible to create a smaller Focus, something I can present to one as yet outside your influence and trigger to bring them into our delusion. A trinket or amulet or some-such that looks innocuous. I imagine a smaller device would have less range, but I would only need something to work long enough to enforce cooperation. If I can't demand Stefan's whereabouts without starting a riot, then I can't move forward with any speed. So I ask: is such a use of your magic possible?"

She didn't move, but Milos read calculations flitting across her face, and he knew she considered his proposal. He waited, making sure he didn't fidget or otherwise belie his air of nonchalance. Finally, she gave a little hum.

"Perhaps," she said. "I will consider this. In the meantime," she sat up straight, "I have something to help in your unfruitful search for the King." She took a piece of folded parchment from a pouch at her belt and handed it to him. Milos opened it to see a sketch. A girl with plain features looked back at him. He glanced at Destiny, brow raised in question.

"Her name is Emily and she helped Stefan escape. Look for her and you may find the King."

Milos nodded and refolded the page, sliding it into his pocket.

"I have another task for those you can spare," Destiny added, regaining his attention. *Yes, because we don't have enough to do,* he thought bitterly, then scrambled to his feet when she rose and headed for the door. He followed.

She led him to King Stefan's chamber, ignoring everyone they passed, though for the most part, anyone they encountered in the halls quickly changed their own direction before having to encounter the determined wizard. When they entered, she moved to the inner room and stopped to stare at the wall beside a massive wardrobe. Milos looked at the wall, back to the wizard, then at the wall again. He frowned, wondering what claimed her attention. Finally, Destiny raised a hand and allowed it to hover in front of a brick with a slight notch in its upper right corner.

"According to the bodyguard your men detained, Emily led Stefan through a tunnel that started here."

Milos nodded slowly to show he understood. At that, Destiny turned and left, an impatient grunt from the door prompting Milos to again follow. *Or perhaps I don't understand,* he allowed as she swept through the halls toward the library. Once there, she gathered up an indignant librarian and demanded entrance to the vault.

"I don't see what you hope to accomplish, my Lady," the man had the nerve to say as he took his time leading them past rows of books. "You haven't found anything new in days of studying it."

"Just open the vault, Darien," Destiny grated. Milos wondered whether the man truly did not fear Destiny or if he simply didn't care about inciting her wrath with his frank words. But he also didn't disobey, at last granting them passage into the vault.

"Here," Destiny said, pointing to a section of wall behind an askew shelf. This time, she indicated a wide block with a black smudge on it. "Where Emily first entered the tunnels."

"Okay," said Milos slowly, sensing she wanted some kind of reaction besides bafflement. "So, you're saying there's secret passages beyond slightly marred stones and this girl," he pulled the drawing of Emily from his pocket, "used them to—" He stopped, staring hard at the librarian still standing beside them. Darien's lips had pinched in what looked like anger when he saw the sketch. Milos quickly put it away again and cleared his throat. "That she used them to help the renegade escape?" he finished, shifting to put his back to the librarian and face the wizard.

"Yes, Captain, that's exactly what I'm saying. And I need your men to search out any other indications of hidden tunnels."

Darien choked out a laugh. Destiny's right eye twitched, but she gave no other acknowledgement of the man, keeping her gaze locked on Milos. Milos took a moment to rein in his own incredulity. When he felt sure he could speak without snapping at her, he did.

"You do understand the enormity of such an undertaking, of course. This castle has stood for generations—"

"Centuries," Darien interjected. Milos gritted his teeth, forcing his shoulders to loosen even as they fought to reach his ears.

"It must have a staggering number of stones with defects, but you want us to locate them all and see if they lead to any secret passage?"

"Not at all Captain," she said, voice falsely sweet, so that Milos knew he'd better tread carefully. "I merely want them

185

pointed out, not searched." She turned, ignoring Darien as she swept from the vault. "There's a third you need to see in the city, near the forges," she spoke over her shoulder, again expecting him to follow. Which he did, leaving Darien to lock up the vault behind them. "That's where she led them out and your men failed to capture them."

Milos nearly stumbled as he processed this new bit of information.

"So, you also want us to search in the city for defective bricks?" he demanded, fighting to keep his voice from screaming the absurdity of that.

"No Captain, I have someone else for that. I need to know where in the castle we should watch for their return because unless you know where to guard, how can you possibly keep the King safe? To do that, I must know the likeliest locations of those tunnels." She turned her head to glance at him as she continued walking. He caught up to stride at her side. "And think, Captain, you have a large selection of men-at-arms peripherally at your command. I need the castle searched; you have an excess of overly ambitious and less-than-useful soldiers. No reason why your Company cannot continue to hunt for Stefan and Emily while the men of Dalasham secure their home." She looked ahead again, her attention turning to other things.

"It seems that would solve one of your problems without disobeying Whillim's whims."

And with that, she departed the library. Milos shook his head, marvelling at her solution. A terrifying woman, but clever as well as dangerous. He would do well to remember that.

Chapter 19

Em sought refuge in the kitchen—formerly the threshing shed, and briefly their sleeping quarters until Castel's men had arrived with tents—not because she particularly enjoyed the work, but because she felt even more of a coward when she hid in her little tent. Her year in the Earl of Kern's kitchen had seen her sweeping and scrubbing pots rather than doing any of the actual cooking, but she knew the basics. Luckily, for both her and the men who would partake of the evening meal, both Castel's cook and Sir Edvard's cook only allowed Em to wash, peel and cut the vegetables they had selected, taking on the chore of preparing the food themselves, each man placing himself in charge of alternating meals.

Jo had returned from the Ford with Sir Edvard and his contingent of soldiers early yesterday, bolstering King Stefan's little army by another 35 men. Another 35 people milling around, adjusting to the lay of the land, the interplay between soldiers, the fact of Em's presence—one woman among 60 men. While no one made her feel as uncomfortable as that mercenary at the gate to Riverbend, some few did slide looks her way that made Em want to scurry away and hide. Others thought her a servant to do their bidding, and nearly all of them sneered in derision whenever Fred insisted she practice the weapon forms he and the King wanted her to learn.

While she had enjoyed the solitude and peaceful state she could sometimes achieve in working those forms, once she became a spectacle rather than a training partner, she lost what little confidence she had started to gain. And so she retreated out of sight as best she could while they waited for Dari to return, hopefully with Sir Pietor and Lord Gregor. Assuming Dari did return, and that the Prince hadn't found him or converted those he had gone to fetch.

Em shook her head, trying to banish such dark thoughts as she laid aside a peeled potato and reached for another to divest of its skin. She tried to put her mind instead to what would happen once Dari arrived, the journey she and seven men would take to Westam to find a wizard who might help them. Seven men, not 60, not 75 or 100, or however many would make up the camp by the time they could finally leave. Seven men who didn't treat Em like a servant or an object or something to endure if they couldn't ignore it. She had found a place for herself among the books in the library where her co-workers found value in her skills and didn't shy away from her company. She had never expected to find similar acceptance anywhere else, let alone with the King and his closest guards, and while she longed for a return to the anonymity of Junior Assistant to the Chief Librarian, she found herself strangely open to the possibilities this voyage would present.

She would travel lands she had only ever read about, perhaps find books not in the King's library to peruse, hopefully expand her knowledge of things magical should any wizards actually deign to speak with them. She could continue to make progress in exercise that engaged both body and mind in a dance she had thus far found soothing, if Fred kept his word and expanded her training once away from malevolent eyes. All this in the company of men who, for the most part, accepted her, if not as an equal, than at least as someone not to shunt aside based solely on a preconceived notion. Em found that concept both startling and exhilarating.

"Stop lollygagging and keep yer mind on yer work," Castel's cook interrupted her thoughts. She blinked to clear her gaze, realising that she must have stared blankly at nothing for the past few minutes. But her hands had not remained idle, as the growing pile of peeled vegetables beside her attested. She wanted to tell the man that the mindless task of peeling didn't require her full attention, but instead just bowed her head and reached for another tuber. The cook grunted and turned away.

A shadow darkened the entrance briefly before retreating, but not far enough that Em couldn't hear the ensuing conversation.

"Don't see what all the fuss is about," one man said. "She ain't much to look at."

"Yeah, but she's the only one we're likely to see for a while," a second man replied, his voice somehow marrying disdain and lasciviousness. Em suppressed a shudder and continued to peel, trying to block her ears.

"Ease off lads, she ain't for us," a third soldier added his input. "Captain's orders."

"He ain't *my* Captain," the second grumbled.

"He's King's Captain," the third said. "I'd mind what he says, 'n I was you."

"Man just wants ta keep the action to hisself," muttered the first, to which his companions laughed.

"Thought you said she weren't much to look at, Wilf," said the second.

"Don't need to look at her, Markel," Wilf answered, and Em couldn't help but imagine the horrible wolfish leer that went with that statement. She finished peeling and turned to cutting the vegetables, knife held firmly in a hand she refused to allow to shake.

"You're insufferable, Wilf," the third man said. "Been here only a day and already you just want to whip it out, to hell with what Captain says."

"Just don't see why the man should keep all the fun, Johann. Man gets to bring himself a toy and we're forbidden the same luxury."

"Way I hear it," Johann said, "she ain't here for that anyway."

Silence met that, and Em desperately hoped they had moved off, tiring of their sport. But a moment later, the second man, Markel, put the lie to that.

"What else she here for?" he asked in consternation. "She might cook for us, clean our clothes, but when night comes, what else gonna keep her busy?"

A snigger she figured came from Wilf.

"She ain't here for none of that, way I hear it," Johann insisted. "Word is, she got the King out of the castle then led Sir Edvard an' t'others to him. King trusts her."

"To do what?" Wilf demanded. Markel's lewd suggestion to that had Em biting her lip and fighting off tears of rage and humiliation.

189

"Don't matter," Johann scoffed at his companions. "Point is, leave her alone if you wanna avoid trouble."

"An' if I don't wanna?" Wilf challenged.

"Your funeral, man," Johann replied. "You wanna risk the anger of both Captain and King, you do whatever you want, but don' say we didn't warn ya."

"Ah, little runt ain't worth it anyway," Markel said. "Be like diddlin' the stable boy."

The three let out great guffaws at that.

"Come on lads," Wilf's still amused voice floated in. "I ain't gonna waste my time with that anyway. Jus' wanted ta see what the fuss was about." His words started to fade as they moved away. "Let's get to the training field afore they notice us missin'."

Em managed three more precise cuts to the potato under her blade before her hand started to shake. She bowed her head and took a deep breath, knife clutched firmly in her hand as she willed herself back to calm.

Only a few more days, she told herself. *Ignore them all a little longer, and you'll get through this.*

"I told you to stop lollygagging and keep yer mind on yer work, gel," the cook's voice intruded. "What good are ya if ye cain't—"

Em's head snapped up and his voice froze when he met her glare, fisted hands on his hips going slack. She stood up and laid down her knife, facing the stunned man.

"I have quite finished, sir, if you would even bother to notice," she said, voice soft yet firm as she pointed to the pile of sliced vegetables. "And this is not my work, it's yours. I merely offered to help."

She turned and left the kitchen, needing to get away, yet not knowing where to go.

The cook watched with the distinct impression that anyone getting in her way right now would regret it, though he had no idea what had set the girl off.

Em had taken less than a dozen paces before a familiar voice hailed her. She turned as the young moustached man hurried to catch up. Her hand flew to her heart, the feeling of relief that washed over her so intense she almost couldn't keep her feet.

"King Stefan sent me to find you," Dari said with a grin.

"Wanted to let you know that, now that Sir Pietor and Lord Gregor have arrived, he's eager to set the plan in motion."

Em stared at him a moment, then felt her own grin stretch her mouth wide. Dari studied her reaction with a raised eyebrow and a bemused half-smile.

"Do I want to know the nature of this plan?" he asked.

"It means you'd better get some rest while you can, Sergeant, because we're not going to stay here much longer."

With a bounce to her step and a lightening of her heart, Em took Dari's arm and spun him back in the direction he had come from and went to find her King and his Captain. Finally, they would escape this oppressive encampment. If she couldn't retreat to the comfort of her library where no one would think to treat her like those abrasive soldiers, then at least she could return to a certain obscurity among people who valued her for more than her sex.

Chapter 20

They had left the camp and recruitment efforts under the care of Sir Edvard, informing those remaining behind—Sirs Castel and Pietor, and Lord Gregor, each tasked with aiding Edvard—only that they intended to seek help against Destiny's spell. Fred had made it clear that he would not risk revealing Stefan's destination in case Willi's men found the camp and put everyone to the question. Ensuring Stefan's safety outweighed their need to know the King's whereabouts, although Stefan made it clear that he expected to return within two months, and hopefully much sooner. Edvard hadn't liked not knowing, but couldn't argue the point either.

With horses and enough supplies to get them started, Stefan's group had headed out, quietly and unobserved, before dawn the day following Dari's return with Sir Pietor, Lord Gregor and their near 40 men.

As part of his training to wear the crown, Stefan had spent time among the border patrols as Prince. Every heir did, in part to practice the art of war, but also to understand how to command, not as a leader but as a foot soldier. *You must know how to follow before you can learn how to lead.* One of his father's favourite phrases, and one Stefan took to heart. How could you lead an army if you didn't understand its structure, the trials faced by the men in the field? How could you rule a country if you didn't understand at least in part how it worked at every level?

Stefan knew well how to ride light, what it meant to make

camp and subsist on the bare necessities, no stranger to squatting in the bush, sleeping in a tent, eating food perhaps overly charred. He could almost think of the first few nights after setting out from Tox's field as a reminder of those patrol days as the eight of them rode more or less cross country, avoiding the main roads as much as possible.

But now, on this third evening as the weather threatened to turn from light drizzle to heavy downpour, they had decided to stop at a somewhat crude inn, and Stefan keenly felt the truth of his situation sink in. For the first time in his life, Stefan started to realise just how much his position had defined him, how much he had unconsciously relied on his stature, and how little he truly knew about living as an ordinary, untitled man. His training may have taught what it meant to follow orders as well as give them, but it had never truly taken him out of the role of royal. One could play at common soldier, but at the end of the day, apparently no one but himself had ever seen Stefan as less than his title.

Until the innkeeper and patrons of this mean place.

"Ye've got the choice of finding yerselves a mite o' space on the floor 'ere, or fittin' yerselves in the loft out in stable," the innkeeper informed Fred when he inquired about accommodations for the night. "Ain't got no other space, party your size, but both is dry enough."

"What about food?" Stefan asked, stepping up next to Fred. "Supplies for the morning—"

"Ain't got extra," the innkeeper interrupted, sucking through his teeth. "Bowl o' soup and mug o' beer with the floor space, bit o' bread for 'nother copper. You want more 'n that, might be some'at left at bakers."

As King, Stefan could have commandeered one of the rooms, demanded extra supplies, insisted on better food, special privileges, but as a commoner, none of those options existed. He and his party could expect no different treatment from anyone else in the inn.

Stefan almost asked about special accommodation for Emily anyway, until he remembered the girl's quiet subterfuge. She had pilfered a set of trews from one of the squires—far closer to her size than Sim's trousers that she had used for training—and donned a simple scholar's cap rescued from her now discarded smock to contain and conceal her mop of hair. While not specifically disguising herself as a lad, Emily had explained how it might raise fewer questions if their party travelled without the obvious presence of a female. It also raised less eyebrows if any saw the long dagger at her belt. While the rest of them, as guards, would cause suspicion had they not worn swords, women simply did not bear weapons. So Emily kept herself quiet and in the background, eyes often downcast and shoulders drawn in to call as little attention to herself as possible, and for the most part, people ignored her.

In fact, they paid more attention to Prichard, acting as the scholar among them for this first part of their journey. Stefan would take on that role as they neared the border, but for now, Prichard assumed the role, insisting they call him Malcolm, his little-known given name. This left Stefan free to watch the reactions of those around them as they tried to ascertain how far Willi's reach had spread. Scholars didn't often go armed, so Prichard's practical weapon elicited a few comments. Until he drew it, clumsily flourishing it without any skill, and people would laugh at the scholar who fancied himself a soldier. The man's acting ability amused his companions, each of whom had seen his proficiency when they practised each morning, a regimen Fred insisted they maintain when no eyes could watch, even as they had at Tox's farm. Stefan wondered how much longer they might go before he and Prichard had to reveal just how far the nobleman's acting skills stretched.

Fred paid the innkeeper from the funds the knights and Lord Gregor had provided, and the two turned to join their group as they found places to squeeze in among the three long tables in the common room, already decently occupied by previous patrons. Emily sat between Prichard and Ambrose, Sim opposite them. Jo and Dari had managed to spread enough on either side at the next table over to save room for Fred and Stefan, so they made their way over as a serving wench brought them each a frothing mug of thick beer, eventually followed by bowls of thin soup.

Most of those sharing the tables looked like locals, but six of the men bore the mien of mercenaries. Given recent events, Stefan and his people tried their best to avoid drawing the attention of those men, not easy in such close confines.

"Where you in from?" a labourer to Fred's left asked, the man's thick-muscled frame turned away from the mercs on his other side as though to dismiss the paid soldiers. Stefan wondered whether he did so in ignorance, or in order to display his displeasure at these sell-swords for taking the best rooms and food. Stefan spared a brief consideration for the man's feelings had the King done the same.

"Westrose," Fred replied with a grunt.

"Heard anything out of Riverbend?" the labourer wanted to know. With a small thrust of his head, he indicated the mercs behind him. "This lot 'ere says there's trouble. Some kind of riot?"

"That so?" Fred widened his eyes as he took a swig of his beer.

"They claim they's lookin' fer *instigators*," the man mock whispered, his careful pronunciation of the last word making it clear what he thought of using fancy words when simple ones would do just as well, or so Stefan supposed.

"Well, then it's a good thing we ain't headin' that way," Jo said from beside Fred. Dari and Stefan grunted their agreement from across the table.

"Where is ya headin'?" the wiry man next to Dari wanted to know, the pattern of scars on his hands naming him an artisan of some sort rather than a mercenary, like the weathered man next to him.

"Back to boss' patron," Stefan said, jerking his chin in Prichard's direction. "Man wanted some rusty ol' trinket peddler sold the cooper back in Westrose, sent us an' the scholar to fetch it. Like as not, man don' even know what it's fer, but he do like to collect odd knick knacks."

"Waste of time, you ask me," Fred grumbled, pushing aside his empty bowl. "But it makes 'em feel important, and keeps us fed."

"I hear that," one of the mercenaries mumbled into his ale, earning an elbow to the ribs from his companion. "What?" he snapped, glaring at the other man. "Not like we're like to find anything useful here either."

"Take it up with Milos," the ginger merc beside the labourer said, and Stefan's heart tripped a little faster. He'd suspected these men worked for Willi, and now, with the naming of the mercenary Captain, had his confirmation. He thanked any powers listening that he had opted to grow out his beard, and prayed it would prove disguise enough when these paid soldiers turned their attention to him.

As they did now. The ginger man pushed past the labourer, earning a scowl before the local grabbed up his beer and swung away from the table with a muttered oath.

"How long you been travelling?" the merc demanded, ignoring the locals.

"Couple a days," Fred said, putting a little more distance between himself and the merc. "Why?"

"You come across anyone like this?" he asked, pulling out a cheap piece of parchment from a satchel at his belt and unfolding it. Stefan felt his blood run cold and forced himself to study the picture, allowing nothing other than feigned boredom to cross his features, hoping his men maintained an equal indifference. A difficult proposition when staring at a decent likeness of the face of the Junior Assistant to the Chief Librarian. He had expected to see his own clean-shaven features depicted, not Emily's visage.

How had they connected her to him? Then he sighed inwardly. Faulk, of course. Sim had told them how Faulk had fallen to Destiny's magic; Stefan just hadn't properly considered the ramifications. Destiny and Willi would know about Emily and the secret tunnels, and now Willi had sent mercenaries to search for her in order to find him.

"Ain't seen 'er," Fred said after a moment's study, sitting back and regarding the ginger mercenary. "Who's she supposed to be and what she done?"

"She helped a man trying to take the throne from the King," a second merc said, the one who had complained about wasting time.

Dari burst out laughing, startling them all.

"Ye gots ta be kiddin'," he snorted, his rural accent better than both Stefan's and Fred's. "Ye sayin' some woman gots herself a plan ta usurp a King? An' someun went along with it? How she manage tha'? Ain't got the looks to sweep 'im off 'is feet, so mebbe she rich-like? Promise 'im lots a gold? Or was she supposed ta seduce the King? How else a woman think ta take a throne?"

The locals chortled along with Dari at the thought, and Stefan and Jo managed a semblance of mirth to help Dari in his subterfuge. Fred just grunted, his eyes dark with anger.

The mercenaries, however, kept their silence. From what

Stefan had heard about Destiny, he could imagine these men well knew a third option to promising a crown, one involving magic. And from the disquiet he saw in their eyes, they didn't take the threat of the wizard's powers lightly.

"Ain't always what they seem," the complaining merc said, again earning an elbow to his gut, but this time, he kept his peace as the laughter died away.

The ginger refolded the sheet and tucked it back into the satchel.

"Well, you come across her, be sure and let a King's man know it," he said, pushing back from the table. As though the motion signalled a command, the other five mercenaries rose to join him, heading for the rickety stairs that led to the private rooms above.

The locals seemed to breathe in a sigh of relief at their departure, then turned to each other in various conversations.

Stefan caught Dari's eye and nodded his thanks for the lad's quick thinking, then met Fred's stare across the table.

"I'm thinking the loft over the stable for tonight," Stefan said quietly, all trace of accent gone. "And an early departure in the morning."

Fred gave one sharp nod. Stefan's gaze rose to meet Prichard's at the next table. The Lord would have heard everything and, while he hadn't seen the picture, he couldn't help but know what it showed. Prichard gave a barely discernible nod, even as he continued to regale his table companions with some ridiculous story he had concocted on the way to play up his role as pompous scholar who'd rather be a guard.

Emily had her gaze firmly fastened on the nearly empty bowl in front of her, keeping herself as small and unobtrusive as possible.

Chapter 21

The constant dull throb behind his eyes sharpened to a spike of agony as the slight blond boy passed him. Faulk leaned his weight as surreptitiously as possible against the wall to steady his balance. Every time he saw the page Kelvin since right after the riots, this spat of pain would assault Faulk, as though his brain had sent a mental slap to jar his thoughts. Bad enough the ever-present ache that followed him through the day, that suggestion he had tried to lock away that something stood amiss, but to have that reminder reinforced by Kelvin at every encounter had grown beyond irritating days ago.

I bloody know something's wrong, he chided himself, pushing off from the wall and resuming his post standing guard at the door to the King's audience chamber. *I'm not helping myself figure out the truth if I fall into a faint when my brain nudges me.*

He shook it off, drawing himself up straight and ignoring his fellow guard, one of Captain Milos' men. None of the King's personal guard would stand watch with Faulk, calling him traitor and worse for his part in allowing the renegade to escape. Which left him with men he himself didn't trust, every one loyal to money—and maybe their Captain—but not to the King.

As for why Faulk didn't trust Milos ... *he's not my Captain.*

Where Captain Frederick had gone, Faulk didn't know, other than that he had disappeared at the same time as the renegade. The would-be-usurper who, for some reason, no one ever named. Frederick had served the King longer than

Faulk had and would die to protect his monarch, yet no one had found any trace of the Captain. King Whillim seemed undisturbed by this lack, turning to Milos for might of arms, and any time Faulk tried to pursue the matter too deeply, he just caused himself more pain.

So he filed this away, like so many other discrepancies, easing the pain with his meaningless mantra: *Whillim is King*. Meaningless because it felt wrong, even though it brought a modicum of relief from his discomfort. With each passing day, Faulk saw more and more how wrong his world had become. He saw the frustration of King and wizard at every report citing failure to find or capture the renegade and those with him; witnessed the mercurial moods of King Whillim; watched from the background as Whillim and Destiny took angry or bewildered or recalcitrant people into Destiny's Sanctum—people who then re-emerged with a changed view, affable, amiable, sometimes even relieved—and he *knew* that his memories of proudly serving under this King didn't fit the man sitting on the throne behind him, impatient to get through the morning's audiences.

Whenever King Whillim saw Faulk, the golden man either smirked or sneered, as though both gloating at Faulk's presence and seeing a reminder of failure. At first, Faulk had assumed the King felt the obvious lack of loyalty displayed by one of his personal guards (for hadn't Faulk betrayed him by aiding the other?), but as time went by, and Faulk learned to endure more pain as his mind fought to remember a suppressed truth, he recognised that Whillim sneered at his *own* failure in finding the man Faulk had helped. Faulk's presence reminded the King that, while he had captured Faulk, he had lost the other. Knowing that, Faulk endured the smirks and revelled in the sneers.

A commotion from the entrance to the audience chamber drew Faulk's attention. The broad form of Captain Milos strode in, drawing a far more slender man in his wake, a man in decent though slightly threadbare clothing. Likely a shopkeeper, and not the kind of person usually brought before the King during his weekly audience—the King having deemed once a week sufficient to hear the plight of those he ruled.

The man currently kneeling before Whillim finished speaking and noted the King's diverted attention. With a negligent wave of his hand, Whillim left any response to Councillor Alphonse, his gaze sharp on Milos. A kind of hunger filled the King's eyes when Milos merely nodded a greeting then took up a stance to await formal acknowledgement. Almost before the petitioner had risen to his feet to bow his way out of the presence of the King, Whillim beckoned Milos and his charge forward.

"Sire, we have protocols for petitioners," Alphonse began, his voice growing as wizened as his face with each passing day.

"And I have orders to bring such matters before the King immediately," Milos interrupted.

"Audiences are done for today," Whillim declared, and before Alphonse or any other Councillor could say anything, he ordered the room cleared. No one openly complained, though Faulk suspected that had more to do with the swords around the King and the icy glare of Lady Destiny than with the notion that no one objected.

Once only the King, Destiny, the shopkeeper and Whillim's guards remained, Whillim leaned forward, impatience replaced with intensity.

"Speak," he said.

"Watch found this man once someone bright enough finally thought to re-question shopkeepers with sketch in hand." Milos took out his copy of said sketch, the picture of the girl who had helped the renegade. Though Faulk vaguely recalled Destiny demanding details, he had only betrayed her name and a general description, claiming darkness stole most of Emily's features. *Betrayed her name?* Faulk wondered at his own choice of words, and the extra sense of pressure in his head confirmed that he needed to push this idea into that part of his mind where he locked away all incongruities from that night. Unfortunately, others had known her face better than he, and the library staff had filled in the details now clutched in Milos' hand.

"Tell 'em," the Captain said, slanting his eyes toward the shopkeeper.

The man hastily dropped to his knees, bowing his head. *Probably so he doesn't have to meet Destiny's stare,* Faulk thought, somewhat alarmed at her sharp interest, even more pointed than Whillim's.

"Man and woman came into my shop a few days after the riots, Your Majesty," he began, gaze focused on the stone

200

beneath his knees. "Looking to borrow money against a pendant. Many came to me around that time, the fires having damaged many homes, so they just seemed another couple down on their luck."

"You're certain this is the woman?" Destiny wanted to know.

"I believe so, my Lady, though if not for her condition, I don't know that I'd remember that face."

"Her condition?"

"Pregnant, my Lady, near as far along as my daughter, who's due early summer. Their plight put me in mind of her, so I paid more attention."

Silence met that. Both Whillim and Destiny glanced briefly down to Faulk, but they must have seen his amazement. Emily had certainly shown no signs of pregnancy, so whoever this man had encountered ... *knew enough to disguise herself,* thought Faulk, trying to keep his expression bewildered rather than impressed.

"And the man with her," Whillim spoke. "Describe him."

"Dark hair and beard, tan complexion, had a bit of girth though somewhat lean in the face with a square jaw," the shopkeeper paused, considering. "Well enough spoken for a farmer and knew how to haggle."

"Farmer?" Whillim said, voice losing interest as he sat back, disappointment filling his face and the beginnings of anger glimmering in his eyes.

"It's what he claimed, Sire, but that doesn't make it the truth," the man spoke diffidently. "Many come into my shop with tales that don't always reflect reality, but who am I to argue? The piece they borrowed against had value enough to make a deal."

"Do you have this piece?" demanded Destiny.

"I do, my Lady." He reached into a pouch at his side. "Haemat gold commissioned by the Weaver's Guild. And the promissory note with it."

"Did she leave a name?" Destiny edged closer as Milos took the pendant from the man, examining it before advancing to lay it in the wizard's palm, and then retreating to resume his post near the shopkeeper.

"He called her Amalia."

"You mean Emily."

"Nay, my Lady, definitely Amalia. I wrote it down on the chit."

Destiny swept down from the dais and crouched next to the

201

man, snatching the drawing from Milos' hand.

"Yet this is she?" she snarled, thrusting the image in front of his face. "You have no doubt?"

Faulk heard the man swallow hard and saw his arms tremble, but he gathered up his courage and answered.

"I can only say what I believe I saw, my Lady, and the woman in my shop matched this picture, of that I have no doubt."

"Did she say where she was going after?" Whillim asked. "Or who else she was with?"

"Nay, Your Majesty."

"You will describe her companion in greater detail," Destiny ordered, "so that we may get a picture of him as well." She glanced down at the pendant still in her hand. "I'll keep this," she decided, rising to her feet and returning to the King's side. The shopkeeper looked as though he wanted to object to Destiny claiming his property, but knew better than to voice any complaint.

They called in the Court Artist, who listened to the man's description. While they worked, Whillim and Destiny spoke in hushed tones that didn't reach to Faulk. He wondered if the image the Artist came up with would better illuminate the hazy face that brought Faulk pain if he concentrated on it—the face of the renegade—but from the King's dismissal of the initial description, he rather doubted it.

The picture that finally emerged didn't evoke unbidden memories from Faulk, but when coupled with the idea of someone in disguise, he could put a name to the face. *Sergeant Sim,* he told himself, keeping the name firmly behind closed lips, even when asked if he recognised the man.

"Got my orders straight from the King's own mouth," Sim had told him the morning after the riots, when the ever-present headache had first started, along with Faulk's questions. And Faulk knew the lie in his mantra, even as he clung to it to keep the agony at bay. *Whillim is King.* He stared at the woman preoccupied with Emily's pendant. *But only through some trick of that wizard.* Faulk quickly averted his gaze before Destiny could see it, working through his pain.

"Take these sketches to your men," Whillim commanded, speaking to Captain Milos. "Especially those on the gates in the days following my—the traitor's—escape. See if any remember a pregnant woman with this man. If they came back to the city, they might not have fled as far as we thought."

"Yes, sir," Milos nodded, then turned to leave, gathering up the shopkeeper with him.

"He might be closer than we thought," Whillim murmured to Destiny, just loud enough to reach Faulk.

"Perhaps," she answered, lost in thought. "And if not, perhaps I can find a way to locate her with this." She fondled the gold, eyes distant, and without another word, swept from the room, not even waiting for the King's permission.

Why bother with pretenses when only guards made loyal to Whillim remain? Faulk managed that thought without any accompanying agony. Or perhaps he had just grown used to shunting it all away.

Keep him safe, Emily, he thought, following on Whillim's heels as the man left the audience chamber.

***

One wouldn't think establishing a link when one held a personal item would cause much difficulty to someone who had perfected a multi-layer memory spell, yet Destiny had troubles tracking Emily using the gold pendant currently clenched in her cramped fingers.

She had faced similar difficulties in trying to track Stefan, if for a different reason. Under normal conditions, a wizard might create a link to another through a personal item and thereby open a connection to follow or spy upon someone without their knowledge, although the closer to the wizard that quarry stood, the stronger the connection. The spell required a certain level of finesse, needing both patience and a strong will, and not all wizards could claim proficiency with that degree of concentration and power. Those limitations didn't greatly affect Destiny. However, a magical loophole to hunting the King existed in the form of one spell obfuscating another. Destiny hadn't expected to have to compensate for Milos' men not bringing Stefan to her quickly, so hadn't considered the ramifications of her grand memory spell interfering with being able to identify the King. Most of the anchor objects Destiny might use to track Stefan revolved around the trappings of the monarchy, so when she set the spell to look for the King, it weakly pointed out Whillim. The uncertainty created by her incomplete spell (and until Stefan sat in her Focus, that multi-layer spell would remain incomplete) vied with anything she could find to link to the King, and any truly personal items of Stefan's had become imbued with Whillim's essence, at least in the eyes of spell-casting. Which left Destiny with no reliable means of tracking him using magic.

That loophole didn't affect Emily's pendant. Had the librarian stood anywhere within a day's journey of the city, Destiny knew her tracking spell would point her out, but the wizard felt nothing beyond the faintest tug that could just as easily come from her own imagination and fierce wish to capture the girl. Through much cajoling and hard-won effort, Destiny had managed to learn a little of Emily's past from Chief Librarian Darien, but beyond her having come from an orphanage before a brief stint in a minor Lord's kitchen, Darien couldn't (or wouldn't) provide any details. This tug Destiny fancied she felt now might point to that orphanage, or to Emily's original home; or it might give an indication as to Emily's current location. Too tenuous a link to guarantee any certainty. Destiny refused to credit any doubts that the piece belonged to that elusive little librarian; had a local farm girl relinquished the memento, Destiny knew she would have no problems establishing a link to someone so close. That she could find no resonance to anyone nearby lent credence to her gut's insistence that she held a tangible part of Emily's past, not some trinket *Amalia* had sold.

Emily had likely returned with one of Stefan's guards to arrange supplies for those who had escaped, believing no one would recognise her. Smart of Stefan to send an unknown, yet surprising that he would entrust such a task to a woman. But who else would he sacrifice? He must see Emily as expendable, the one member of his party who couldn't bear arms but who could obtain food.

Bold, remaining so close to Riverbend three days after Whillim made his move, but then, a wise man would take stock of his situation, learn all he could of his enemy, do reconnaissance. Had the King sent others back into Riverbend with the girl besides the one guard? Could he truly still hide somewhere nearby?

If so, he didn't hide with Emily. Destiny would have to wait, see if the direction changed, or grew stronger.

She rose from her cross-legged seat on the floor of her

receiving room, shoving the pendant into a pocket of her gown as she smoothed her skirts. For the first time since bringing her proposition to Whillim, Destiny contemplated removing the perimeter spell she had erected when she chose Dalasmar as her refuge. Without that shield—again, one spell disrupting the efficacy of another—she might extend her reach and have a better chance of finding Emily and thus Stefan.

Without that shield, her enemies had a better chance of finding Destiny.

She tried not to dwell on why she had originally erected such a ward, forcibly attempted to suppress the tiny voice of a frightened little girl, but the memories swept over her.

Five years old and already well accustomed to a hard life in the kitchens. My head and upper body deep in the large cooking pot, knobby knees firmly planted on the cold stone floor as my thin arms scrubbed and scrubbed, fingers wrinkled from being immersed in dirty water. Far better here, mostly hidden, than under his *disdainful glare in the highest room, hand clamped over the blood from yet another shallow cut in arm or leg. Experimenting, always the experiments, trying to take from me what no one can take. I still didn't understand what the wizard hoped to gain, couldn't yet comprehend Mama's fears, but I knew about the hate. Mama hated* him *even while she went to his rooms most nights. I hated him too, though many moons had passed since I had learned to hide my emotions. Instead, I showed nothing, no matter what* he *did, and that lack of reaction puzzled him. He believed he had broken me, turned me into some mindless slave. He had not.*

And that oversight allowed me watch him, listen to his muttered words and study his exaggerated gestures, begin to learn what he had not intended to teach.

Mama hadn't told me anything about my father, but I listened to the others talk, no longer even hiding their scorn and envy in front of a child who seemed simple. So I knew why he *had sired me, why* he *kept summoning Mama to his chambers, why my little brother, not even a full year younger, would never have to scour a pot beside me. I just didn't know why the wizard wanted my blood.*

He wanted my power, and young as I was, I felt quite certain he would never steal my magic through my blood.

When he first took Mama, planted a baby in her stomach, he had hoped to sire a wizard like himself. As Mama came due, he had rejoiced, for he felt great power from the child. But then I came into the world, a tiny, squalling girl child, and his elation turned to disgust. Females didn't make great wizards. Mama had saved me, promising to do better. While he believed I couldn't possibly master magic, he couldn't deny my potential, so he had tried again, as soon as Mama could physically bear his touch.

Her second babe, my brother Nathan, also bore the mark of magic, and for this, the wizard granted Mama permission to keep me. Before Nathan, he used me as a means to control Mama; after, I only became a source for experiments, for now he had what he wanted. He still used Mama as a brood mare, hoping for yet another source of power, but he didn't put as much urgency into the endeavour. Twice more Mama had conceived, though both times, the child had died before birth.

The second time, I had seen why, and Mama swore me to secrecy.

"I won't give that foul wretch anything more," she had said. "My body is the only weapon I have, and I swear by all that's holy I will use it to keep you safe, Girl." No one ever called me anything but Girl. People overlook someone without a name, and Mama taught me how to use that anonymity to our advantage. "As long as he thinks I might give him another son, he'll keep me alive. But you have other weapons, Girl. Here," she touched my forehead, then my heart, "and here. You have power beyond what's between your legs, even if he won't acknowledge it. More even than your brother. Learn it, harness it, use it. Show them a woman's more than just a vessel to spawn vain men's ambitions."

Nearly a year later, though I didn't know it as I knelt half-submerged in that huge pot scouring away the remnants of breakfast, my Mama's weapon ceased to provide me any protection.

Even as she lay bleeding on the floor, a lesson to a four-year-old boy that he shouldn't rely on the flesh of a woman, Mama gave me what strength she had left. Two simple sentences.

"Write your own destiny, Girl. Don't let him win."

Those words crystallised the path my life would take ...

Nine years old, my bent neck might appear a sign of

submission, of meekness, but I only kept my expression masked behind a dark fall of hair. I could pretend indifference, but I couldn't always hide my hatred, my contempt. Or my desire to learn, even from the man who broke my world.

The wizard had made me Nathan's personal slave, to wait on my brother and to take any punishment for minor infractions. At first, this had kept Nathan in line, but as the years passed and the wizard continually enforced his belief that I was some sort of defect, my sweet, shy little brother grew more and more into a little terror, a frightening copy of our father.

Gone the nights when I would console him, sing him to sleep in an off-key voice, comfort him when he woke whimpering from nightmares. Forgotten the sister who tried to shelter her sibling from the fickle wrath of the wizard. Now a haughty boy thought himself my superior in all things, though only his height surpassed me. That and the treatment he received from the wizard's other servants, at least to his face. Behind his back, they knew him for the spoiled son, deserving respect only because to show otherwise would bring pain.

But I kept my mouth shut and my eyes and ears open. I became a fixture, the quiet Girl who shadowed Nathan. And in so doing, I learned everything he did, with no one the wiser.

Reading and history, spells and potions, levels of magic, all absorbed into a mind starved of all desire and purpose save two: revenge, and the need to prove myself the equal to any man. To write my own destiny.

So I endured Nathan's scorn, cleaned up after him, avoided drawing attention, and accepted his punishments in silence.

The wizard eventually ceased his bloody experiments on me, and contented himself to ignore me as I sat in my corner, by all appearances cowed as I waited for Nathan's lessons to finish ....

At thirteen, I had my first moon blood, and in a panic, I had hidden it. I knew this visible sign of growing maturity would renew the wizard's interest in me. Nathan's lessons had reached a kind of repetitive stage, a barrier broken only through puberty, when a wizard's power would swell to a new level. I had far surpassed Nathan's abilities even through second-hand learning, and this new phase of my life would, according to all that the wizard had taught, jump up my magical prowess even more. I already had enough difficulties hiding my skills; with my moon flow, would the wizard notice a new energy about me and renew his experiments? Would he try to take my power for himself even though he now insisted such spells unreliable and nigh on impossible?

I hadn't considered he might try to create another child. After all, although I despised him and he barely acknowledged my presence, let alone my ability, he had sired me. Any union to harness my magic through breeding with him would scream abomination, anathema. He didn't see it that way when he discovered, thanks to a sycophantic servant, that my flows had progressed for the last six months ...

By fifteen, I had perfected many spells, but two stuck out. A disguise spell for those horrible nights when he had to find an outlet, and I would weave my face onto one of the other servants; and a memory spell for when he caught me off-guard and alone, which convinced the wizard he had sated his lust even as he wondered whether I would ever conceive or if some flaw had made me barren.

But by now, Nathan had also undergone puberty, raising his magic level to something rivalling the wizard's, and at this point, if he remembered me as his sister and not his slave, he had taken his father's disregard for that kinship to heart and started to look at me in a new light.

And that last slap to Mama's memory I would not allow.

I had absorbed all the spells this wizard could impart, either through Nathan's lessons, or through the many stolen hours in his library in the deepest darkness of the long cold nights. If I ever wanted to truly take Mama's words to heart, I had to do so now.

Write your own destiny. Don't let him win.

Time to unleash some new spells, show the world the real wizard created when he first planted his seed in Mama's belly ....

I wiped blood and grey matter from my eyes, wincing as my hand encountered the long gash over my left brow. Hand cradling broken ribs and favouring my right leg as I limped as fast as I could from that tower room, I made my way to the stables. The wizard would never bother me again, but I didn't have the strength to withstand both him and Nathan, and I only had minutes before my brother broke free and came after me.

I stole his horse and set the others free, then sent the stables *up in flames with the simplest fire spell I knew, drawing on a reserve of strength lent me by desperation as I hauled myself into the hastily cinched saddle, feebly kicking the horse into a bone-jarring canter. Gritting my teeth against the pain, I fled that house of torment, relying on my memory of the maps I had studied in the library, the ones that had shown where to find the school of magic. If I could reach that, learn more spells, gather more strength, then even Nathan could never hurt me again ....*

He tracked me to the heart of Innosvar at seventeen, but by some stroke of luck, I saw him first, surrounded by his guards and two lesser wizards, and I wove a disguise an instant before he saw me, eyes passing over a young man instead of his sister. He may have recognised the signature of my magic as his gaze swung back around, but by that time, I had already turned the corner of the nearest building, then ran as fast as my feet would take me. Not ready to face him, I returned to the room I had rented and cleared it out, stuffing the grimoires I had yet to study in my sack with what little clothing I owned, then I fled before he could follow my trail.

That night, I cast the perimeter spell for the first time, set in a circle spanning a dozen paces around me. Then I moved on to find my next teacher, a step ahead of Nathan.

Though loath to teach a female, most wizards did not deny my abilities and would reluctantly part with a spell or two in exchange for something I had learned through my travels.

And so my magic and reputation grew. While Nathan followed in the wake of his sister, he failed to make the connection between the Girl he had grown up with and had sworn his own vengeance upon, and the wizard who made her own Destiny.

Still, by the time I devised the plan that brought me to Whillim of Dalasham, I maintained and expanded that perimeter spell, never daring to let down my guard.

Destiny blinked, rousing herself from those memories.

How great a risk did she truly face now, if she stopped hiding? She had escaped Nathan and Innosvar five years ago, dispatched the third assassin sent after her two years later, and hadn't felt anyone push at the edges of any perimeter spell she had put in place for over a year. No one would have envisioned that she might choose Dalasham as a place to seek refuge and refine her powers. Wizards, though tolerated in some of the outlying districts of the kingdom, shunned the more urban areas, and certainly avoided the capital. Destiny didn't worry that anyone would notice her perimeter spell or recognise it should someone prove sensitive, yet she confined it to a day's ride from the castle. Once, she had used herself as the focal point, but she ran no longer. Now, her Sanctum worked well to anchor the spell.

But it also prevented her search for Emily from extending any further through magical means. Besides having the ability to warn of the approach of anyone with significant magical prowess, the spell kept her presence hidden from scrying eyes and prevented her magics from calling to outsiders. Unfortunately, it also kept any spells she wanted to cast from passing beyond the boundary of her ward. While this wouldn't prevent the power of her memory spell from holding sway should those affected leave her area of influence (those currently returning to Bash, for instance, would remain under the belief that Whillim stood as King of Dalasham), it did hinder any tracking spells.

If Destiny could guarantee that a tracking spell centred around this gold pendant would work, she would have deconstructed the perimeter spell, even knowing that to reactivate it, she would have to travel to one of its outer edges. She had hoped, by the faint trace of Emily's emotions that Destiny could feel imbued upon the pendant, that the librarian's obvious attachment to the trinket would heighten any connection that would form a link. A false hope, she knew now.

If she knew where they headed, she could scry for them, send out her senses to watch from afar, though again, only after deactivating her perimeter spell. Without knowing where they had gone, though, she would only waste her time searching the land, and Dalasham did not cover an insignificant area. Better to leave that kind of search to Milos and his mercenaries. Time to put her efforts into something closer.

Besides, how did she know Emily still accompanied Stefan? Unless it became unquestionably necessary to dissolve the perimeter spell, Destiny would leave it alone. For now.

Somewhere in the back of her mind, a little girl heaved a sigh of relief.

Absently patting the pocket with Emily's pendant, Destiny turned her attention elsewhere. She had done what she could with a tracking spell, creating a link that would sense when Emily crossed her ward. If the girl returned to the city, Destiny would know.

Chapter 22

"Okay, let's go over the plan again," Fred ordered as they approached the gate to Augsden, leading the horses at a slow walk.

Although Stefan had planned to make use of one or more of Prichard's holdings here in Westam, the presence of those mercenaries two nights ago had changed his mind. The paid soldiers hadn't headed west solely in the hopes of finding Emily, but also because Prichard remained at large. Willi didn't know the full importance of Prichard's role in gathering information vital to Dalasham, but he understood enough to realise that any Councillor not under Destiny's influence stood firmly behind Stefan, and that, the Prince couldn't have. Even if Willi thought that Lord just a minor inconvenience. So Stefan's group had proceeded under the assumption that all of Prichard's known holdings would currently have one of Milos' men watching in case the Lord appeared, hopefully with King in tow.

Leaving them currently nearing the low-walled entrance to Augsden, one of the larger border towns with Bakaana. Augsden boasted a decent University and had a good relationship with wizards, standing only a half-day's ride from Bakaana's easternmost School of Wizardry. If they didn't find anyone who could help them in Augsden, then they would slip over the border, and hope that Willi hadn't yet considered the possibility that Stefan would seek outside help. If he had, or if Destiny had foreseen that possibility, then crossing the border, even disguised as scholars, might prove problematic.

One concern at a time, he thought, turning his attention back to Fred.

"Jo, Dari and I, under my given name Malcolm, will take the mounts and secure an inn," Prichard recited in answer to Fred's request. "You, Sim and Ambrose will accompany Scholar Gerald and his young half-brother Emmett,"—he indicated Stefan and Emily, still dressed as a boy—"as they make their way to the University. Once we have secured lodging, I will explore the town to find the best venues for my master during his tenure here, as any good assistant would. As I gradually make my own way to the University, I will keep my eyes and ears open for any sign of the Prince's influence in Augsden, including any indication that Milos' Company has ventured this far west."

"Jo and I will learn the layout of Augsden," Dari took up the recitation. "If we need to leave in a hurry, we'll know the best routes."

Fred nodded, then turned his gaze on Stefan.

"Emmett and I," Stefan quirked a small smile in Emily's direction, "will request access to the University's library and to anyone who can help us expound upon my thesis of multi-layer spell-casting and its effects on the natural world." Stefan hoped anyone they *did* find who could speak to that topic would have a penchant to talk rather than listen to his own supposed theories. They had decided that, while *Emmett* had joined his brother's research team to get him out from underfoot of their latest step-mother, he also had the research skills and knowledge of languages to benefit *Gerald*. Mostly true and thus easy to recall, so long as each remembered to answer to their aliases. If another scholar asked questions Stefan couldn't answer, Emmett could just as easily respond as Gerald, making the doting older brother proud of the interest his half-sibling had shown for his work. Or so they hoped.

"And we're there to watch their backs or cart around books, whichever seems most needful at the time," Sim finished, a wry twist to his lips.

Again, Fred nodded, accompanied by a satisfied grunt. They hadn't really needed any reminder of the plan, but Stefan knew Fred chafed at the delay as they ambled toward the gate, and sought to distract himself with the reassurance of his companions' competence.

It didn't take long to pass through into Augsden where they split up. As Prichard moved away, Stefan noted Emily's lingering gaze on the Lord. Her eyes had narrowed just a bit in speculation, then she glanced up at Stefan as they walked side by side, as any brothers might, Ambrose leading the way, Sim and Fred trailing behind. He waited for her to speak.

"Have you noticed that, even with the same teacher, people develop their own quirks in fighting that complements their abilities and might give them an advantage?"

Stefan blinked at her question, tried to reconcile it with what he had expected, and gave up.

"Pardon?" he said instead, having no idea where she would go with this.

"For example," she continued, gaze forward again. "Ambrose has an uncanny ability to anticipate an opponent's moves by taking note of his stance and the flick of an eyelid." A soft snort from ahead as Ambrose shook his head. "Fred uses his size and strength to fool an enemy into thinking him slow in both reflex and mind, thereby taking great satisfaction when he can prove them wrong." A snicker, quickly covered, from Sim behind them and silence from the Captain. "Sim has incredible control of balance and a good awareness of his own centre of gravity, enabling him to wait longer than the average soldier before shifting his weight, thus drawing others in and off balance. Dari's fast, Jo's flexible. All received similar training, yet each has adapted to take advantage of their strengths."

"And?" Stefan asked when she stopped.

"And you borrow from all of them, able to spot that strength and turn it against them, adapt your own style to suit any opponent."

"I—" he paused, flattered by the assessment, yet completely off-balance by the observations.

"And Prichard makes you look an amateur."

"He is a master swordsman," Fred said. "Trained with the best."

"I believe he's more than that," countered Emily in a whisper, this time meeting Stefan's gaze directly and speaking to him alone. "I think he can adapt to *any* situation, on the field or off. Blend in where he needs to, stand out if someone requires a distraction, learn a great deal from a glance or a word, and

214

bring back information others don't yet recognise as important. And I think *that's* why he's with us, more than the convenience of his holdings in Westam."

When Stefan neither confirmed nor denied her speculation, she smiled slightly, the expression lighting up her pale eyes.

"But that's just what I think," she said loud enough for the others to hear now and turning her sight back to the road in front of them.

Stefan fought to keep his grin to himself. He wondered what his master spy would say when Stefan informed him that Emily had guessed his secret. Somehow, Stefan doubted it would surprise Prichard in the least.

***

Em rubbed at her eyes, blinking a few times to clear them before focusing on the book in front of her again. Although nowhere near as large or impressive as Dalasmar's Library, Augsden's University boasted an impressive array of titles not available back at the castle, most having to do with magic. She had already gone through *Witches and Wizards* by Adrac, Lovnik's *Deviations of First Order Spells*, and Teasdale's supremely boring recitation in *A Matter of Layers: Building Upon Power*. While the latter had sounded promising, Em had learned more from the first two books, yet not a great deal that she hadn't already known or speculated upon. The current volume on the desk before her now, *How Language Affects Thought*, written by the Haemat philosopher-wizard Honodar, finally hinted at something potentially helpful.

She would have to thank the librarian who had surreptitiously pointed out the tome to her, as the title alone would not have garnered her initial attention in their search.

When they had arrived early in the day, Stefan (or rather, Gerald) had put forth his needs for his 'scholarly' research. The head librarian, who reminded Em of the Chief Librarian at Dalasmar before Darien had taken that role, had led them to this section housing books of reference relating to magic. Before the man could do more than point out some general titles pertaining to magic and the natural world—Lovnik's and Teasdale's works among them—Stefan had declared a challenge to his younger brother.

215

"Lad needs to earn his keep on this trip," he had said in a good-natured tone with a flawless Westam accent. "Lets see if he can't suss out some other gems on his own, prove he's our father's son and can do research with the best of us."

While Em hadn't expected this ploy, she took full advantage, not even hesitating before scanning other titles and selecting a pile that now lay in front of the King. The librarian had finally nodded grudging acceptance after noting the books she had chosen and the care with which she pulled them off the shelf.

"If you require further assistance, Scholar Gerald, don't hesitate to call," the man informed them before returning to other duties.

After a few more minutes examining the section and making other selections, including a couple of books in foreign languages, Em found herself standing next to a young man wearing a typical librarian smock. He smiled shyly at her before reaching in front of her with an apology to refile a book. As he moved off, she saw that he had pulled out another title part way. She glanced at him quickly. He smiled again, put a finger to his lips and nodded before hurrying away. When she looked down, she saw *How Language Affects Thought*. Recalling a time or two when she had helped out a hapless academic assistant to 'discover' a useful manuscript that would impress his mentor, she plucked the book off the shelf and brought it to her pile on the table.

"Find anything interesting?" Stefan asked now as he leaned back in his chair, hands reaching up to stretch cramped muscles. Fred, sitting nearby and looking like he wanted nothing so much as to close his eyes and fall asleep, roused himself enough to sweep the area with a gaze before settling back into his chair. Em suspected he merely acted, and in truth kept a very close watch on his surroundings. Sim and Ambrose prowled the area, keeping to the shadows and out of everyone's way as they patrolled the library without making it obvious that they guarded Stefan. Had any danger actually followed them into this building, Em felt confident that these three overseers would stop it before it ever came near this quiet corner.

"I think," she began, drawing out the sentence as she put her thoughts in order, "that magic might have its own language."

"Do you mean as in, knowing how to put the right words

together for a spell, or literally, like Dalsh or Innosvar?" Stefan leaned forward now, providing Em his absolute attention, which both flattered and terrified her. But he spoke as a scholar, not as a king, and that helped her regain her footing, librarian to researcher.

"Its own actual language, dialects and all," she confirmed. "I'm still trying to determine if it's a widespread, universal concept, or if it's reserved only for higher level spells. Or only certain spell forms or Schools of Wizardry. Certainly not all spells require this separate language, and some magic doesn't even use words of any sort. Witches, for example, wouldn't use this language at all as they rely more on an earth connection, borrowing and manipulating the essence of nature, a power outside of themselves. Only some wizards would have the skill and inner aura or strength to interpret the nuances, and even then, I don't know how many will have learned this language.

"Based on what we know, or believe we know, of the Destiny Seat, the complexity would suggest a knowledge of this language of magic. If we knew Destiny's actual spell, we might determine where she came from based on the dialect. Or at least where she studied." She shook her head, gazing back down to the pages of the book on the table. "It doesn't help us right now, but you asked if I'd found anything interesting, not anything pertinent."

Stefan laughed, keeping it muted so as not to draw attention from the other patrons in the library.

"So I did." He leaned back, tilting his chair a bit on its back legs. "The best I've managed thus far gives us some names of prominent wizard families, but nothing so obvious as 'Wizard Destiny did this and here's how to stop her.'"

Em smiled at that.

"I do find it interesting, however, that every family draws its lineage solely from the male line," Stefan went on, frowning back at his own research. "The book only mentions women to establish nobility or bloodlines. For example, Baroness so-and-so, daughter of the Wizard such-and-such, birthed Wizard whoever. Like infusing new blood into a dying family, or pointing out that a skip in a generation could still produce a wizard. Not one of them shows a female wizard."

"I wonder if it truly skips the female line, or if a patriarchal house simply refuses to acknowledge a woman with power,"

Em mused, leaning over to see Stefan's book.

"And if a woman with the potential to become a wizard does not receive the proper training, what happens? Women can do magic, as I know hedge witches lean more heavily female." He grinned at her startled blink as she met his eyes. "We don't have wizards in Dalasmar, but I'm not totally ignorant of their existence." He lowered his already quiet voice to a fake whisper and leaned his head close to hers, all four legs of his chair settling back to the ground. "Scholars looking for innocuous tidbits possibly linked to minor magics didn't stumble into your library merely by chance, Emily. I may not have known who helped them find those tidbits, but I know the information exists, and I trusted Darien to choose his staff wisely."

Em felt her face heat in a blush and quickly tore her gaze away, almost wishing she didn't wear the scholar cap that confined her hair. She had nothing to hide behind without that fall of hair. Stefan chuckled before returning to his point.

"I find it hard to believe that a woman couldn't learn to become a wizard, unless witch and wizard magic differs far more than I'd thought."

"Not that I've read," Em whispered, indicating *Witches and Wizards*. "It's a matter of having the ability to manipulate the natural world using external versus internal forces. A witch can only exert external control, altering what already exists, whereas a wizard can supplement that with internal prowess, a strength born within. For example, I could use a lever or some form of pulley system to help me lift heavy objects, but Fred could just pick them up." An amused grunt indicated that the Captain did indeed pay attention, despite appearances. "In a similar vein, you could read a paragraph several times, committing it to memory through repetition or training, whereas I have this ability to just remember the words. Some manipulation of external forces versus an innate ability, witch and wizard. It has nothing to do with gender so far as I can tell."

"Perhaps not in terms of ability," Stefan said slowly, his gaze losing focus as he pondered. "But if you're right in terms of patriarchal training, then perhaps women are simply not taught. Which might make our search for Destiny's identity a great deal more difficult."

"Her identity, yes, but her spell clearly exists. We need to counter that." Em pursed her lips. "Or maybe it does help, for surely, if a woman did become a wizard against the expectations of the wizard families, someone will have noted it somewhere.

"Does your book cover every wizard house, or just those in a specific region?"

Stefan closed the cover to see the title, keeping a finger in to mark his page.

"*Wizard Houses of the West*," he read. "But I suspect you're correct; these may just cover Bakaana, and Bakaana does make much of the male line." He glanced around at the many shelves surrounding them, full of books. "Perhaps lineages from Innosvar or Haemat will provide more illumination."

"We'll see if we can find you something along those lines," Ambrose said, appearing at their side. Em jumped, then saw the smug smile from Fred as the Captain, who had obviously subtly called Ambrose and Sim over, stood to stretch, turning to lean against the table and so planting himself where he could conveniently watch anyone who might approach while his subordinates searched the shelves.

Stefan shook his head with a rueful grin.

"We'll see what else we can learn while we wait." With that, he opened his book again. Em pulled back in her own seat and gathered Honodar's *How Language Affects Thought* to her, mind working with what they'd discussed while looking for new information.

She suspected, though, that what they needed didn't lie in books, but rather in the mind of a wizard. She just hoped they could learn enough here to know how best to question a wizard who would have nothing invested in providing any answers.

***

Malcolm Prichard didn't often get out to his estates in Westam, preferring to leave the day-to-day running of affairs to his more than capable steward, but when he did find occasion to visit the area, he more often than not used his alias Pendar Reece. As Reece, he had a basic routine established that he could alter to fit circumstances, and now, with the uncertainty of the political landscape, he chose a very circumspect protocol to follow.

The very aptly if unimaginatively named Tavern sat nestled between a herbalist's shop and a decent clothier. The Tavern catered to commoners with a bit of means, yet had an atmosphere that would discourage any affluent nobles from taking advantage of its customers, thanks mostly to the larger-than-life presence of the proprietor, who simply went by the moniker of Tasha, and her well-muscled assistant Andos. Tasha could get away with her less-than-reverent criticisms of any who thought to disparage her because of her gender by the fact that you wouldn't find better food anywhere in Augsden.

"Keep their stomachs full and you keep 'em happy," she'd say, cheerfully pointing to the door if any called into question a woman owning and operating so successful a business without the watchful eye of a male overseeing her every action. Andos didn't count, as his simple world view began and ended with the perfection of Tasha, who had saved him from the streets. Andos would agree with anything Tasha said.

As anyone with Prichard's status would avoid such an establishment, on principle if nothing else, he could easily get away with sending Pendar Reece in his stead and not having to worry about recognition. He still took precautions, of course, but the Tavern provided a solid base from which to organise his inquiries while the King and that most intriguing little librarian followed what leads they could at the library.

Prichard ensconced himself at a small table off to the side that both afforded a modicum of privacy and allowed a good view of the door and most of the floor space. He ordered a meal, then gestured over one of the two lads sitting on a bench by the entrance. One other advantage to the Tavern for those who knew to look; it offered a runner's service. Small, fast boys who knew the streets of Augsden and would deliver messages for a fee. Prichard hadn't visited the Tavern recently and didn't recognise either boy, but a subtle nod from Tasha told him that both knew their trade.

"I need you to find a man named Heinrich," he told the boy when the youngster approached the table. "Let him know his friend Pendar Reece is in town, if he has a mind to catch up."

The boy nodded, his eyes straying to Prichard's hand curled lightly on the tabletop as the Lord revealed a glimpse of copper in his fist. Once he gave the tow-headed lad further instructions and sent him off with a suitable handful of small change to ensure fleet feet, Prichard sat back to watch and wait.

Prichard's meal had come and gone, and he leaned back in his chair nursing an ale when the wiry man with dark hair and deceptively soft features strode into the Tavern. With barely a glance around, Heinrich headed straight to Prichard's table, took the spare seat and spun it around to straddle it, elbows leaning on the short chair back. He called for his own ale and sat silent, eyeing Prichard, until the drink arrived, which he acknowledged with a grunt. The server moved off and Heinrich took a long pull of the frothy victual before nodding with an appreciative sigh and pushing the mug aside, turning his suddenly piercing gaze on Prichard.

"Imagine my surprise at finding you in town Reece, just a day after folks came looking for the Lord of the estate, concerned for his safety." Heinrich stood as one of the few people who knew him as both Lord Prichard and Pendar Reece, among other aliases.

"Did these kind folks give any reason for their concern?" Prichard wanted to know. Whillim's men, no doubt, but by all accounts, no one in Augsden knew anything remotely significant about recent events in Riverbend. He needed to know how the Prince's mercenaries hoped to find him, let alone expect him to surrender himself. Or if, like those they had encountered at the roadside inn earlier in the week, they merely sought to cover their arses, making motions to find those not yet subverted by Destiny's device while not truly expecting any results.

"They had concerns you may have inadvertently fallen in with rebels to the crown and now wanted a means to escape," Heinrich replied, "or that you had, instead, fallen into the hands of those who would seek to profit from your return. Either way, unwitting traitor or kidnappee, these soldiers sporting the green and gold of the King strongly suggested that any news of the whereabouts of Lord Prichard, and any who might travel with him, would meet with suitable appreciation."

Prichard said nothing as he contemplated that.

"Now, anyone who didn't know better might worry about the well-being of that foppish, slightly foolish Lord," Heinrich continued, referring to the persona Prichard affected to lead people into the belief that he had more interest in fashion and

221

other frivolities than in politics and the well-being of the kingdom. "But those of us with more sense know you'd sooner put out your eyes than betray the King to some rebel. And the notion that you'd fall victim to ransom demands without some ulterior motive ..." Heinrich snorted at the thought. "Anyone who dared kidnap Lord Prichard would soon find themselves in want of a more honest living."

"I don't suppose these concerned soldiers wanted any news one might have of Lord Prichard's whereabouts taken to the border barracks?" Prichard asked.

"Funny you should mention that," Heinrich said without a trace of humour in his voice. "To save those at the estate from having to travel so far should the wayward noble appear in their midst requiring desperate attention, they would station a man at the nearest inn, for our convenience. They didn't, of course, mention the other three soldiers set to watch the comings and goings of those under your governing hand."

"And can I assume one of those now wallows in his cups, having lost the Master of Coin as he answered the summons of a tow-headed lad?"

Heinrich grinned, reaching again for his ale.

"If he's smart, he's availing himself of the pleasures of Tersar's House. If he's dumb, he's still waiting for me to emerge from the loving embrace of one of Tersar's fine ladies."

Prichard nodded his satisfaction of Heinrich's skillful evasion of a tail.

"Though that lad you sent—" Heinrich said, wiping his mouth with the back of his hand after another draught. Prichard waved away the concern.

"He's off running superfluous errands before returning to a less-than-reputable establishment across town. He'll have anyone following him so lost into the maze of back alleys that it wouldn't surprise me to learn someone relieved him of his clothes along with his purse."

"Then you expected something of the sort," confirmed Heinrich, unsurprised. Prichard didn't employ stupid people, and he only trusted the most astute. Heinrich had stood in Prichard's employ long before being raised to the position of Master of Coin for his Westam holdings.

He briefly explained Whillim's elaborate plans to take Stefan's place as King of Dalasham, outlining what he knew of Lady

Destiny and her abilities in the process.

"What I need to know," Prichard added, "is how far this influence has spread. From what I can gather, no one this far west has yet taken to naming Whillim King, but I can only ask in so many places as Pendar Reece." Heinrich nodded his understanding. "More than that though, I need to know everything you can find about this lady wizard. Unusual enough for a woman of such obvious power to go unnoticed before this, I find it more than distressing that she has worked so close to the capital—right under my nose no less!—for long enough to nearly pull off Whillim's coup. I imagine we'll find better answers across the border. If I knew whom to speak to and what questions to ask, it would save us a great deal of time."

Heinrich went still, staring hard at Prichard. Prichard stared back, not flinching, and in that steady gaze confirmed the other man's surmise. He had just revealed that he did not travel alone, and Heinrich had played the game long enough to understand the vital piece of information that Prichard had just shared; King Stefan travelled with Prichard in search of an answer to his brother's treachery.

"I'll see what I can find out," Westam's most capable agent informed the master spy with a nod as he finished off his drink, and rose from the table. He hesitated a moment before whispering without moving his lips. "Keep him safe."

Then he moved to the door and escaped into the afternoon.

Prichard paid his tab with a generous tip, then went his own way, the research assistant to the Scholar Gerald hurrying to reassure his mentor that all amenities would fit his standards while he enjoyed his tenure in Augsden.

Chapter 23

"We're looking for Wizard Castillo," Prichard reminded them under his breath as he, Stefan, Emily, and Fred approached the administration office of Bakaana's easternmost School of Wizardry, charmingly nicknamed the Frontier School. Dari, Jo and Sim, currently sporting the garb of day labourers, milled around outside the walls of the school, keeping watch from the shadows, while Ambrose scouted out the nearby market, both for supplies and for any hint that Willi's mercenaries had pushed past the borders of Dalasham in their search for Stefan. Stefan highly doubted his brother lacked the wisdom to recognise that sending any armed troops into a neighbouring kingdom would prove problematical at best, but he had no desire for Willi to prove him wrong again. He had already suffered for his faulty knowledge of Willi's mind; no need to compound that by underestimating the Prince's ambition.

After spending nearly two days searching the University library in Augsden, they had crossed the border themselves into Bakaana the previous evening with little fuss, using documents provided by Prichard and sticking to their cover of scholars in search of research information.

Now, as per Prichard's informant back in Augsden, they sought out the senior wizard of the Frontier School for his vast knowledge of layered spells and those he knew capable of casting them, both in and around Bakaana, and throughout the wider wizarding community. If anyone knew something of Destiny's past and how to counter her spell, surely Castillo did.

224

Prichard led the way, followed by Stefan and Emily, both wearing scholar caps now in keeping with their researching personas, and Fred brought up the rear, his size and fierce expression more than making up for his lack of a sword. They didn't permit bladed weapons in the Frontier, though Stefan wondered at the prohibition given that most of the people striding through the halls wore wizard robes and would likely have no need of weapons of any kind to inflict damage, each having the use of magic at his command. He understood on an intellectual level that they also forbade offensive magic outside certain practice rooms, yet the ability still rested within these men of power. He supposed removing the visual temptation of violence such as a sword swinging at a hip might ameliorate those with a short temper, though he still nursed some discomfort at their vulnerability, and knew Fred did as well. If going unarmed bothered Prichard, the Lord didn't show it, and Emily had spent most of her life unburdened by an ingrained need to show the face of a warrior.

Perhaps Stefan should try to emulate her unconcerned strides instead. After all to her, this excursion must feel more like walking into a new library rather than into a potential pit of danger. She revelled in adding new knowledge to her repertoire, whether through books or spirited discussion (at least among those she felt comfortable enough to engage with in such debates), as he had witnessed in Augsden's library. There, he had seen just how capable a resource he had to hand in the young librarian. If she could hold her shyness at bay when they spoke to Wizard Castillo and employ that remarkable mind of hers to fully describe what they knew of the Destiny Seat as filtered through her understanding of magic, then he felt certain they would finally have a tool to use against Willi and his pet wizard.

The door to the administration office stood open, and Prichard ushered Stefan and Emily inside, following quickly as any good assistant might. Fred stayed just outside, leaving the three of them to face the stick-like man perched at a desk that took up half the space. Stefan saw another door to the right, this one closed, and recognised that they stood in an outer office.

Prichard bent his neck in a slight bow to the man who peered up at them through narrowed eyes.

"Greetings again, Administrator," Prichard began, having already spoken with this man earlier in the day. "May I present Scholars Gerald and Emmett, requesting an audience with Wizard Castillo. I hope I have remembered the appointment correctly?"

The administrator blinked a couple of times, and Stefan realised that his squinting expression indicated a case of short-sightedness, not disfavour. A theory soon confirmed when he suddenly smiled pleasantly.

"Of course, Master Malcolm." The reedy voice matched the man as he pushed back from his stool. Standing, he reached only a little taller than Emily. "Wizard Castillo is expecting you."

He moved to the inner door, knocked twice, then pushed the door open.

"The Scholars have arrived, Wizard Castillo," he announced. At an unseen signal, the administrator nodded and stepped back, waving the three in and closing the door behind them.

Stefan didn't know what he had expected Castillo to look like, but he had to admit that the large man with his salt-and-pepper hair covering his ears, silver beard trimmed close to a square jaw, and weathered, wrinkled face the colour of thick ale and the texture of old leather, didn't fit his image of a wizard, despite the dark robes the man wore. A seasoned soldier perhaps, even a scholar, but a powerful wielder of arcane forces?

Stefan berated himself for his folly; he ought to know better than to judge a person based solely on appearances. Had he ruled his mind with the foolishness shown only by his vision, he would never have followed Emily through the tunnels of his castle and Willi would have won long since. He glanced at her briefly. Dressed as a man, her scholar's cap struggling to contain that mop of auburn hair, she held herself with more confidence than she had when they first met—a girl covered in cobwebs and the dust of ages, tears trembling in her grey eyes and staining her cheeks, desperately trying not to show her fear while simultaneously attempting to save his life—but had he not known her, he still might underestimate her value if he allowed his eyes to rule his reason.

He brought his attention back to the wizard who now sent his hand toward Stefan in greeting following Prichard's introductions, vowing not to judge the man before he even opened his mouth.

"Welcome to the Frontier School of Wizardry, Scholar Gerald," the large man said as he shook Stefan's hand, his voice a deep rumble, the rounded vowels of the Bakaana language giving his speech a pleasant roll. "We don't often have travellers from Dalasham express such an interest in our art, so I will endeavour to provide as much assistance as possible in the hopes that you may become the first of many." He said this with a smile, but Stefan detected an underlying wariness. No doubt the wizard feared the ignorance of Dalasham would colour any questions Stefan would have. Luckily, he had Emily to keep his lack of knowledge from wasting the older man's time. Or so he hoped.

Castillo turned to shake Emily's hand next, but paused mid-way through, his expression growing more guarded. He pulled his hand away more quickly than Stefan thought polite and knew the wizard had seen through Emily's disguise. While she had passed as a lad not old enough to shave at a distance, close up that illusion fell apart. Expecting that, they had determined she should speak her mind quickly upon discovery and pray Castillo would recognise her intellect.

"Wizard Castillo, you will pardon our subterfuge I hope, but events in Dalasham have necessitated our discretion," Emily said, her Bakaana slightly stilted, but confident. "I have, in the past, had occasion to assist some of your wizards in their scholarly research, which led my liege to hope I might converse upon such arcane natures as we seek to understand in a more fluent manner than he might achieve alone."

Castillo glanced at Stefan with a frown, which Stefan returned with as much regal grace as he could muster under the circumstances. Something got through to the man, as he raised just his right eyebrow in speculation before passing his regard briefly over the now taciturn Prichard, and then back to Emily.

"And what manner of the arcane brings you to my door under false pretenses?" asked Castillo guardedly.

"False personas," Emily disagreed, "but not false necessity. We have a wizard within our realm who has employed a multi-layer spell using a focus and we need to know how to counter it."

Castillo jerked back, blinking hard, his brow creating a series of hillocks between dark eyes. His expression softened slightly

227

as he nodded toward a couple of chairs pushed against the far wall, retreating back to his desk as he did so.

"Sit, young lady," he said gruffly, settling himself. "I'll need more details than that, but perhaps even so uneducated a Dalash lass as yourself can provide enough for me to go on."

Stefan opened his mouth to rebuke the older man, but a glance at Emily showed she took no offence at the insult. Indeed, she looked relieved and gave Stefan an encouraging nudge toward one of the chairs as Prichard pulled them into place before the desk.

"I thank you for your courtesy, noble wizard of Bakaana, and can only desire that my paltry efforts to describe what so clearly lies beyond my understanding might spark some recognition from within your vast stores of great wisdom, enabling you to inspire our awe and profound gratitude." She said this in an earnest tone, eyes wide with feigned innocence, not once cracking a smile to show whether she mocked or kowtowed. She even offered a small curtsey before perching on the edge of her chair, never taking her gaze from the wizard.

Castillo let out a hearty guffaw and relaxed at her overly sweet tone, leaning back in his seat with hands folded lightly across his stomach. Stefan shared a look with Prichard and saw the master spy shrug minutely. Perhaps not the avenue Prichard would have taken, but, it seemed, one Castillo enjoyed.

"Yes, you've definitely dealt with my brethren before," Castillo smiled. "I could even hazard a guess as to which of my esteemed colleagues taught you how to deliver such insults and rebukes masked in subservient flattery, but that would spoil the game, wouldn't it? A pompous group of fools, the lot of us, overly impressed with our own stations. But enough of this verbal foreplay, young scholar. I can see by the expressions on your companions' faces that they do not appreciate our banter."

"Time does not sit as our friend, Wizard Castillo," Emily said. "The spell Wizard Destiny has wrought continues to spread its insidious influence with every moment we delay searching for answers."

"Wizard Destiny," Castillo repeated, eyes distant in thought, one finger idly tapping against its opposite's knuckle. After a moment, he shook his head, gaze sharpening again. "I don't recognise the name, but he may have adopted it to hide his identity and make it harder to trace his origin and school of learning."

Emily hesitated, and Stefan could guess her thoughts. Did they tell Castillo that they dealt with a female wizard, or should they concentrate on how to unravel her spell first? They had discussed the merits of either approach before coming here, and now he had to trust that Emily could read this wizard well enough to choose the more profitable road. He knew which line he would follow.

"Destiny has created a spell with at least four layers, perhaps as many as six, although it's entirely possible it contains aspects we have not yet ascertained," Emily explained. Stefan watched her fingers turning pale as she squeezed them tightly together in her lap, hiding their slight trembling from Castillo's sight behind the desk, but had he not seen this sign of her anxiety, he would never guess her discomfort at so openly facing, and discoursing with, so powerful a figure as this wizard. Her voice remained calm and professional as she went on. "The spell utilises a Focus some have named the Destiny Seat. We have not seen it with our own eyes, so can only surmise it employs a chair of some sort. To our knowledge, only that one device exists to augment the spell, although my bare understanding of magic suggests that, with enough strength and concentration, Destiny could cast the spell unaided."

Castillo said nothing, waiting for her to continue.

"This spell affects the mind by erasing one very specific memory and supplanting it with another. The underlying emotions related to the initial memory remain intact, transferring the beliefs and feelings of said memory onto the replacement. The spell further filters down onto others who have a loyalty to someone so spelled, thereby ensnaring those of lesser ranks with the altered memory by contaminating the thought processes of their superiors. It is possible that the spell needs reaffirmation after a space of time to prevent attrition, but we have only hypothesised that, not witnessed it."

"And what is this memory's target?" Castillo demanded, leaning forward, hands clasped on the desk in front of him. "What specific memory has you so worried?"

Emily flickered her eyes toward Stefan, as though seeking permission or forgiveness for her next words.

"The identity of a man," she said. "The knowledge of his very

229

existence."

A raised eyebrow met that statement, but Castillo betrayed no other response.

"An elaborate way to eliminate someone," he grunted. Although the wizard kept his regard focused on Emily, Stefan had the distinct impression that the man studied both him and Prichard anew. "One would think capturing or killing said man would prove less taxing."

"They have tried to capture him and failed," said Emily. "As to killing him, I overheard an unlearned soldier state that something in the way the magic works needs the ... man ... alive. I do not presume to understand why."

"But you have a theory," Castillo insisted with a firm nod.

To Stefan's surprise, Emily broke eye contact with the wizard, ducking her head.

"Out with it, girl," Castillo snapped in a tone Stefan imagined had his students jumping to obey. Instead of jerking her awareness back up, as Castillo no doubt expected, Emily cringed. She hesitated a moment longer, then took a steadying breath and sat up straight, though her gaze didn't reach past the wizard's chin.

"They need him alive," she whispered, "to use the spell on him. To affect everyone at once, in our kingdom and beyond. Only then, at the moment that everyone believes the altered memory is true, will they kill him, ensuring none can break the spell."

Prichard exploded with a foul oath before checking himself, fists clenched at his sides. Stefan couldn't seem to stop shaking his head in denial. Bad enough that Willi tried to steal the throne, but fratricide and regicide? Surely not even his brother would stoop to that. Yet evidence of the past weeks continued to show that Stefan didn't truly know his brother at all.

For his part, Wizard Castillo merely nodded sadly, regarding Emily with a soft compassion that she couldn't see as she closed her eyes against Prichard and Stefan's reactions.

"For someone who purports to have little understanding of the magical arts, you have a surprising grasp of its possibilities," Castillo said gently.

"I know only what I've read," Emily disagreed, her soft voice finally shaking in time to her trembling hands. "The rest I can only guess, and conjecture does not even come close to understanding."

"Nevertheless—" Castillo pushed back from his desk, rising to his feet and drawing their attention.

"*They* suggests your wizard does not act alone, and few people can affect an entire kingdom, let alone the wider world." The large man stared hard at Stefan for a moment, and Stefan let all pretense fall from his expression, the King returning the Wizard's gaze. Castillo's lips twisted in the briefest smile before returning to stoicism.

"The spell you describe, and the likely repercussions, takes great skill given the human factor involved, and I know few who might have mastered such. Come," he headed for the door. "We have an archive that records the achievements and potentiality of the higher-level wizards. Let us start there to learn the identity of this Wizard Destiny, and I shall ponder possible solutions to a counter-spell."

He opened the door as Stefan and his companions rose to follow, which drew the attention of the administrator. The wiry man stood, ready to offer assistance to the Frontier's senior wizard. Castillo paused on the threshold and looked at Stefan.

"With your permission, Scholar Gerald, I should like to outline the basics of this troublesome spell to some of my more accomplished colleagues in order to effect a more speedy discovery of said solutions."

Stefan nodded, understanding that Castillo intended to keep their secrets. He and Emily would play scholar siblings for a while longer. Taking a page from the librarian's example, Stefan offered the wizard a bow.

"We would be most grateful for any assistance you and your most knowledgeable brethren could render, noble wizard of Bakaana."

Castillo's snort of amusement seemed to startle the administrator. Stefan chose to take it as a sign that they might find answers at last.

***

Wizard Castillo led them to a room three doors down from the administration office. The administrator—Em didn't know his name—had offered to take them instead, but Castillo insisted he didn't require aid. Em recognised the resigned look on the administrator's face, having seen a similar expression on Darien in the year leading up to the previous Chief Librarian's retirement. The look said, *You're doing my job, which is far beneath you, and please don't mess up my system.* Em bit her tongue to keep from chuckling in sympathy.

The archive room had shelves lining three walls, and a long narrow desk populated with two stacks of blank parchment, quills and stoppered inkwells sat next to the door on the fourth. The shelves to the left and straight ahead held what looked like ledgers with brown, black, and dark blue covers, each colour grouped in some manner indicating a sorting system. Scrolls rolled tightly and tied with coloured ribbons took prominence on the upper two shelves of the right wall, while the remainder of the space boasted a dozen thick tomes in burgundy, identical in size and shape but clearly differing in age, along with a staggering collection of dissimilar books and loose paper jammed in to overflowing. Em shuddered at the disparity of organisation, and hoped that whatever records Castillo searched for would reside in the more readily accessible sections. If he had to rifle through the tightly packed mish-mash, they might miss their next three meals.

Stefan followed the wizard into the room, Prichard behind him—Em still felt uncomfortable referring to these men by name rather than title, but the King had insisted. After stepping in long enough to take a look around, Em elected to return to the hall and wait with Fred. She loved books, but something about the brown, black, and navy ledgers had her shying away, and the scrolls made her skin itch. Castillo noticed her reticence, and with a frown, waved his right hand through an intricate gesture, muttering under his breath. The sensation of unease dissipated and Em sighed in relief, but she didn't return within. Whatever ward or protection guarded those tomes, Em decided she didn't need to understand. Her forte lay in history, not magic, and she saw no reason to alter that now.

The wizard shook his head and moved to the burgundy books on the right. He pulled the one nearest the door out and flipped briefly through it, his arms trembling slightly from the weight of the book. Then he returned it with a grumble and reached for the next.

"Norbert!" he called suddenly, startling them all. Fred

reached for his absent sword before checking himself, but Castillo didn't even notice as he skimmed more pages.

The administrator popped out of his office so quickly that Em suspected he had waited for such a call. When the wiry man brushed past Em and Fred and saw Castillo about to shove the book back on the shelf, he winced slightly before donning a long-suffering expression. Before he could open his mouth to complain or offer assistance—frankly, Em could see either possibility written across Norbert's face—Castillo spoke again, his gaze narrow as he glared at the remaining burgundy books.

"Higher-level wizards," the weathered man said. "Their specialties and potential."

"Eighth volume, Wizard Castillo," Norbert replied promptly. "Section three. Assuming you want those still living. Otherwise—"

"No, no," Castillo said, reaching for the indicated book. "This wizard is very much alive, according to our foreign friends here."

A dark haired, moustached and lightly bearded man in wizard robes rounded the corner, head down and gaze distant as he walked. Em moved out of his way before he even noticed others stood in the hall. The man appeared deeply absorbed in thought as he continued past the archive room without any acknowledgement of his surroundings, then turned the far corner, still oblivious. Em smiled slightly. A lot of visitors to the library had worn similar distracted expressions as they pondered some obscure bit of trivia.

"Can you share a description?" Norbert asked, drawing her attention back to the topic at hand. His fingers twitched as though fighting a desire to take the book from Castillo and find the information for the senior wizard all the quicker. "Perhaps I could help narrow the search?"

"Master of multi-layer spells, the ability to alter specific memories of identity on a mass scale and filter it though others, the ability to create, or at least manipulate, a focus to aid in seemingly flawless assimilation." Castillo paused, fingers tapping on the as-yet closed cover of the tome in his hands. "Let's see, what else? Ah yes, the capability to hide such an output of power from outsiders while yet effecting a far-reaching range, and the wit to hide in a kingdom that has not embraced magic for nearly two centuries."

One hundred eighty-six years, thought Em, *but close enough.* She wondered what he meant by hiding the output of power.

"And a woman," Stefan added quietly.

That met with silence and incredulous stares from both Castillo and Norbert. Castillo slid his gaze out to Em. She nodded solemnly.

"By all reports sir, Wizard Destiny is a woman," she confirmed. Slight movement in the hall caught her attention, and Em turned this time to watch a cleaning woman stride past, bucket in hand, cloth tossed over her shoulder, and gaze downcast. Until she stood even with Em, then she glanced up, a strange expression on her face. Em wondered at that, trying to decipher some meaning to that look as she noted tendrils of dark hair escaping the kerchief on the woman's head, the heavy cream apron wrapped around her bark brown dress, and the piercing amber eyes in a lined face a few shades darker than Castillo's. But the woman continued up the hall and around the corner without another glance, and Em decided the maid had simply reacted to hearing Em speak; a woman in Bakaana openly addressing a wizard as though his near peer no doubt stood as a rarity.

"We have had few females study with us," Castillo said, his tone sounding a little cooler to Em's ears. "And while some have shown surprising talent, none come close to the level you've described."

"Do your records include wizards from other realms?" Stefan asked. "Wizards from, say, Haemat or Innosvar, or even the lands beyond our shores?"

"Wizards from beyond do not travel to our shores," Norbert replied stiffly. "Our magics are not compatible."

"But the southern kingdoms may have seen more women looking to learn the mystic arts," conceded Castillo. "And Haemat holds many secrets beyond what little information comes from trade. Norbert, where do we find the lists of foreign wizards?"

"Eleventh tome," the administrator said, reaching for said book before Castillo could exchange it for the one already in his hands. "If this Destiny is registered, she'll appear in section forty."

He took the volume to the desk and began flipping pages.

"Could we discover who trained her?" Prichard asked. He hadn't spoken since introducing Stefan and Em to Castillo, and from the startled glance from both wizard and his aide, Em suspected they had dismissed the Lord's presence. "If we don't find her in any records, perhaps knowing who taught her will lead us to someone who will understand her spell and can undo it. Her master or another student perhaps."

Castillo grunted, but Norbert turned thoughtful.

"An interesting avenue," the smaller man mused as his fingers flew over the pages of the book in front of him now. "It will widen the search, but the level of complexity you've described still can only lead to a small number of wizards. Relatively speaking, of course."

And with that, they set to work, both Castillo and Norbert jotting down details as they perused their burgundy bounty.

Em heard the whisper of cloth and glanced to the end of the hall. The maid she had seen earlier popped her head back out of sight, and Em frowned. She showed herself again and beckoned to Em.

"I'll be right back," Em whispered to Fred.

"Stay in sight," he whispered back, and she knew he had noticed the woman's behaviour as well. "Whatever she has to say, make sure she doesn't lure you away."

Em nodded and hurried to the corner. When the maid started to edge away, Em shook her head, then sank to sit on the ground, hugging her knees to her chest. The maid grinned, showing three missing teeth, then lowered herself to her knees. Taking the cloth from her shoulder, she thrust it into her bucket, pulled it out to wring soapy water from it, and proceeded to scrub the floor.

"You're a smart one," she murmured in an accent Em couldn't place. "But you're not like to find what you need in them books." She said nothing more for a while, and Em began to wonder if the woman had just wanted some company. Finally she spoke again.

"Grew up far from here," she said quietly. "Li'l village far to th' south, across th' border in Innosvar. Lord of th' manor thar was a wizard who liked us to call him Master. Don't know his right name. Cruel bastid wanted more magic than th' gods given him, and found a way to strengthen his seed, hoping to take power from his offspring. Found he couldn't do tha' from his first kid, so moved on to train the second, make a devoted copy of hisself he could control.

"His mistake was ignoring th' first 'cause she came to this world a girl, and he had no use for women save as vessels for his seed."

Em caught and held her breath, waiting for the maid to continue, daring to hope she held the secret to Destiny's past.

"I served in th' kitchen when Girl came into th' world, saw Master's disappointment. Wouldn't let no one call her nothing but Girl, as though to point out how li'l he thought of her. But Girl had a quick mind. You could see her thinking, watching, listening. Every experiment Master did on her, Girl would learn from. She and her mama tried to shelter th' brother when he came along to replace her, but Master wouldn't have tha'. Broke th' bond when he took Nathan away for good, killed th' mama, and turned Girl into his personal slave, all before Girl's sixth year.

"But tha' just put her where she could learn, and hate, and plot." The maid paused, shaking her head. "I watched Girl grow, saw her practice spells beyond her years when she didn't know I watched, heard her vow to escape and learn enough to never fear and slave again. And after ten years of this, I saw Girl take revenge on Master when he had nothing left to teach her. And I heard Nathan swear his own vengeance as Girl fled."

Again, Em waited, but it seemed the woman had finished her tale. She realised that the look the maid had given her in the hall when she passed them at the archive room didn't indicate surprise at Em speaking to Castillo, but had come as a reaction to Em naming Wizard Destiny as a woman. She chose her words carefully.

"You think Girl became Wizard Destiny. Why?"

The maid sat back, damp cloth held loosely in her wrinkled hands. She regarded Em with a steady gaze.

"Girl went through hell growing up, and the only love she ever knew died with her mama at the tender age of five. Master made sure none could replace her mama and punished those tha' tried." She held up her left hand, palm facing in, to show her missing pinkie finger. "Tha' kind of torment for so many years, bound to turn a child into a monster, one tha' don't know much difference 'tween right and wrong. But it also forged a weapon under its own control, an' tha's what her mama told her. 'Write your own destiny, Girl. Don't let him win.' Them's th' last words her mama spoke to her as she bled out on th' kitchen floor, and the words Girl cried herself to sleep with when she thought no one listened."

Em gaped at the old woman, who merely nodded sadly back.

"Seems to me, someone trying to escape tha' kind of pain and torment would reinvent herself in unexpected ways. Tha' she'd seek to choose her own destiny."

"Or become it," Em breathed. "From a girl with no name to Wizard Destiny, spitting in the face of those who dismissed her out of hand."

"Exactly," the maid agreed, finger touching her nose. Then she threw her cloth back into the bucket and rose from creaky knees to steady feet. "'Course, I don't know if Girl is your Wizard Destiny, child, but if so, you won't find her in any registry. Master would never have admitted her existence, and she's too clever to leave any trace for Nathan to follow."

Em blinked, rising to her feet also.

"Her brother still hunts her?"

"Don't know for certain," admitted the maid. "But far as I know, he never found th' woman who once tried to shelter him with her own tiny body, and Master warped him bad enough tha' only death would end his search for vengeance."

She turned to retreat further along the hall, but paused and spoke without looking back at Em.

"If Girl's your problem, remember tha' he unwittingly trained her to become a monster despite her mama's desires. She's forgotten anything else."

With strong strides, the maid escaped the hall and hurried around the next corner. Only then did Em wonder how the woman had come to work in the Schools of Wizardry. Dismissing the question as irrelevant and wondering if any part of her story indeed related to Wizard Destiny, Em rejoined Fred and retold the maid's tale in a quiet voice so as not to disturb those within the archive room. Then they waited in silence for names Em no longer felt confident would help them in any way.

Her assumption proved not entirely correct.

***

Wizard Marcus had made his home at the Frontier School of Wizardry for the last two years, not for any particular desire to study within its vaunted walls, but rather to keep his ears open for any sign of the murderess who had fled from his master's wrath five years ago. Two years of fruitless spying, never even catching a whisper of the slave's whereabouts, or even a suggestion of her existence.

Until now.

Marcus had noted the arrival of the foreign scholars—as he noted every visitor since he had accepted this posting—and contrived to wander the halls near the administration office with his habitual 'lost-in-thought' expression firmly in place. Amazing what one could overhear and get away with if others feared to interrupt a wizard deep in thought. People simply moved out of his way and went about their own business.

Luck walked with Marcus as he found the foreigners congregating in the archive room with Wizard Castillo and that fastidious little Norbert aiding them in whatever search they wanted done. A simple matter to wander by, shift out of the way of a passing maid at the next juncture, then pause, senses extended beneath a very minor ward that both heightened his hearing and bent the eye away from his presence.

Allowing him to hear something he had waited two long years to discover.

A female claiming the powers of a wizard had hidden her vile self in a kingdom with very little use for magic. Coupled with their accented Bakaanish, Marcus extrapolated that these foreigners most likely came from Dalasham, possibly from the capital city itself.

If this female had truly mastered some layered spell form as these scholars described, then she certainly would have had the power to kill a brilliant wizard caught unawares. And in all honesty, how many women would have the gall to steal a wizard's title and the necessary strength that went with it, let alone the twisted need to take on a name like Destiny?

Nathan had searched long for the Girl who had betrayed them all, and now, Marcus believed he had found her. He pushed off from the wall and hurried back to his room. He had a message to send to a very angry wizard.

Chapter 24

"If what Emily learned has any bearing on truth," Stefan said that evening as they gathered in the courtyard outside their inn, "then the Wizard Shelton listed in the archives before his death matches the rather pompous title of Master. If so, then the apprentice Nathan trained with Destiny. And if that's the case, Wizard Nathan might know how to counter her spell."

"Or eliminate her altogether," Fred added.

"Is that our goal?" asked a soft voice.

Stefan glanced at Emily, but the haunted gaze of the librarian didn't touch on any of them, seeming instead to focus on a point beyond the inn. He had feared the maid's tale had garnered Emily's sympathy, even wondered if the woman had intended that outcome with her story for some reason.

"What's your ultimate goal here, Stefan? Your ideal ending?" Emily asked, dragging her pale gaze closer to Stefan.

"To end Destiny's spell and take back the throne," he replied, trying to hold his exasperation in check, wondering why she suddenly felt the need to spell it out.

"Yes, of course," she shot back, her own exasperation showing in that sharp tone. "But after that?" She bit her lower lip and swung her gaze away again, her tone losing its bite. "Fred's intent on removing the threat of Destiny, as he should, given he's your chief protection. But what do *you* intend? To imprison her or to kill her?"

"I intend to do what's right for my kingdom," Stefan said. "If we can find a way to stop her without her death, I will of course consider it." Yet that small, dark part of himself questioned whether he really meant that. He ruthlessly silenced it and went on. "Though I don't know how to stop a magic user, I certainly don't intend to return with only her death on my mind." *Don't you?* He snarled at his brain to keep silent. "But I can't rule out the possibility that the only way to stop her is to kill her."

"And the others?" she asked. "What will you do with them?"

For a moment, Stefan stared at her in confusion. *What others?*

"We'll likely have to fight the mercenaries to get to her," he acknowledged. "They're paid soldiers, they understand how this works. If they surrender and leave Dalasham, all to the good, but I can't spare them if they choose to fight."

"I don't mean Milos and his men," Emily said with an irritated huff.

"We can't hold the nobles and knights under Destiny's influence accountable," Fred joined the argument. "They think they're defending the kingdom."

Emily turned a sour glare on the Captain, and Stefan's patience began to wear thin.

"Look, Emily," he said, trying to placate what looked like the beginning of hysterics. "I don't want bloodshed, but I have to eliminate the threat, even if you've found some sympathy with her."

"I'm not talking about Destiny," growled Emily. "Can't you see that? I'm asking about the Prince!"

Stefan frowned.

"Of course Willi will be held to task for his part in this—"

"Will he?" she demanded in a strangely quiet voice. Usually, when she turned quiet, it indicated some uncertainty, but this time, Stefan couldn't place the emotion in her tone.

"Yes," Stefan said firmly, seeing her eyes start to shimmer. *She better not start to cry,* he thought. *Women don't hold high positions for this very reason.* He took a deep breath, forcing calm to his voice. "I won't allow my brother to think he can try to overthrow me with impunity. He will receive a just punishment."

"Punishment," she replied, as though never having heard the word before. "And what if he refuses to accept your punishment? What will you do then?"

"What are you asking?" Now Stefan heard his own voice drop dangerously low. "You want to know if I'd kill my own brother?"

"You speak of killing Destiny, but only punishing the Prince. Do you not see the dichotomy?"

"She used magic to corrupt the Prince," Ambrose said from his place beside Fred.

"Did she?" Emily asked. "Do we know this? How do we know the Prince didn't find her first? How do we know he didn't ask for this spell? Will you condemn her without a trial while assuming the Prince's innocence?"

"How can we trust she won't use her magic to escape anyway?" Dari wanted to know. "She's made people forget our King. What else can she do?"

"The Sergeant makes a good point," conceded Fred. "If we try to put her on trial, what's to stop her from using magic to change our thoughts again? Or to simply escape?"

Emily looked at each of them, and Stefan began to hope she finally saw the dangers of Destiny rather than the supposed frailty as intimated by that maid. Then she shook her head slightly and dropped her gaze.

"Forgive me, Your Majesty," she whispered. "I forgot my place. Perhaps all this intrigue has upset my delicate sensibilities. Please excuse me." She bobbed a very slight curtsey before retreating back into the inn.

After a long moment of silence, Fred spoke.

"What the hell was that?"

Stefan shook his head.

"I think that drivel about Girl's childhood touched on her love for a good story," Stefan said. "She can't understand that sometimes violence is the best answer to prevent greater turmoil."

"No, Sire, I don't think that's what's troubling her at all," Prichard said, breaking the silence he had held since returning from the Frontier School.

"Then what, Prich?"

"I'm not certain, but I'll go find out." So saying, the master spy walked away.

"Fine," Stefan sighed before turning back to his guards. "So how do we stop Destiny?"

"If this Nathan really trained with her, he'll know how to

counter her magic," Fred said. "We neutralise her powers, we make her vulnerable, and then we can strike."

"So how do we find Nathan?"

***

Prichard caught up to Emily before she could slam her door in his face. Her expression didn't betray someone on the edge of breaking down, but rather a woman furious with her situation. Tears of anger and frustration hazed her pale eyes, though he suspected Stefan hadn't seen past the presence of tears to their source. Emily stared hard at Prichard as he caught her door, then turned to sit on the edge of the bed as the only piece of furniture besides a rickety-looking stool perched beside a worn desk barely large enough for a sheaf of parchment.

"Are you here to console the damsel in distress?" she asked acerbically, swiping at her eyes.

Prichard snorted, then hooked his foot around the stool and dragged it close. It wobbled, but he managed to sit without breaking it.

"I'm here to find out what's really bothering you, because it's not Destiny's fate."

"They don't see it, not a one of them," she said in a raw voice. "I wonder if you see it, master spy?"

Prichard blinked, and only years of experience at hiding when something caught him unawares kept him from nearly falling off the stool. Did she know or did she merely guess? He managed a bland expression as she stared at him.

"I have no idea what you're talking about, young lady," he said breezily.

Emily smiled briefly, but it looked bitter.

"The King has such nobility in him, but he's also a stubborn fool sometimes," she said, then shot to her feet, hands waving as though to erase her words. "Forget I said that; I didn't mean it."

"But it's true," Prichard agreed, still trying to reconcile the fact that she knew his secret. His statement halted her nervous pacing. "Now sit back down and tell me which bit of foolishness has you so agitated."

He surprised a laugh out of her and that seemed to deflate some of her ire as she sank back onto the bed.

242

"I'm afraid the King's so focused on Destiny that he'll ignore the role anyone else has played in this saga. I'm afraid his prejudice will fail to prevent something much worse because he can't see past this one event and the one person he believes perpetrated it. He'll take the quick and easy solution, eliminate the threat as he sees it, without understanding the whole. I'm afraid he'll get himself and others killed because he doesn't want to see what's right in front of his face."

"And what is that?" Prichard asked mildly.

"Destiny doesn't have the Prince under any sort of magical control. He knows full well the consequences of his actions and continues to push for Stefan's capture. Destiny may have ulterior motives, but right now, her spell works to the Prince's benefit, not her own. The King doesn't want to see that, so he concentrates on destroying the wrong source of power."

"So you do think he should kill his brother."

"I don't think he should kill anyone!" She threw up her hands in emphasis. "But in his current state of mind, I don't think he'd consider a fair trial for anybody but the Prince, and even that wouldn't come through as fair because he refuses to see the full extent of Whillim's sins. I fully believe the Prince acts of his own free will, and that Destiny is as much his tool as he is hers."

"And if Stefan rushes headlong toward eliminating the threat that Destiny poses, he might fall into the Prince's hands, is that it?"

"If he heads blindly for Destiny," Emily qualified, shaking her head, "he won't even see the knife in Whillim's hand."

"That's a bold accusation, young lady," Prichard said, leaning back as far as the stool would allow.

"Do you think I'm wrong?" she challenged, her regard steady on his face.

Sadly, he didn't, and she could read that in his eyes.

"Right now, they're all scared of Destiny's magic, thinking up ways she can use it against us," Emily continued. "Without truly knowing what magic can do, they can only come up with terrifying scenarios, and that makes thoughts of killing her justifiable. They'll try to guard against magic and forget to guard against the physical. And killing Destiny won't solve the problem."

"No?"

"I'm no wizard, but it seems to me that a Focus will act like any constructed talisman."

Prichard frowned his incomprehension. She saw it, then took a breath to explain. He wondered if she knew she dropped into a tutor's cadence when she tried to describe something she thought others should have seen for themselves.

"A wizard constructs a talisman for a specific purpose, imbues it with power that will flow when triggered, but that same wizard doesn't have to operate it. In fact, many talismans have long outlived their creators, and many don't require magic or the touch of a magic user to operate. If the Destiny Seat works anything like a talisman, what's to stop the Prince from using it whether the King kills Destiny or not? Killing Destiny won't stop her device, but the King won't listen to me now that he thinks he has an answer."

"He's listened to you before. Why wouldn't he now?"

She gave him such a look of bitter sorrow and pity that Prichard momentarily felt like an unlettered schoolboy.

"I'm not useful to him anymore, Malcolm." She had never used his given name and that told him, more than her haunted expression and acerbic tone, how vulnerable she felt. "He doesn't want my memory or research skills, sees no need of a history lesson, doesn't require my knowledge of his hidden tunnels. I certainly have no use in any battle he may encounter and in fact, would only get in the way if it comes to bloodshed. I've gone from companion to fragile female in need of protection, the hysterical little librarian overly susceptible to a sad tale that might have come from one of her books, who only sees another downtrodden woman instead of a mortal enemy. My feminine frailties won't allow me to contemplate the hard necessity of taking a life to save others because women have no capacity to think along those lines. I've gone back to the false stereotype they all grew up with, and everything I've helped them achieve thus far, I could only have done due to extenuating circumstances.

"All that makes anything I might say tainted by the shadow of my sex. The King doesn't want to hear anything against his brother, and he has settled on Destiny as the main hurdle between him and regaining his crown. Putting me back in the box of girl needing protection allows him, allows all of them, to ignore anything I might say."

Prichard opened his mouth to deny her harsh critique, but she held up a hand, and he waited for her to continue.

"You don't believe me, I can see that," she said. "So I suggest *you* deliver my concerns to the King as though your own, and see whether he gives you his ear. He still might not agree, but I can almost guarantee that he'll at least listen. And that's more than I'll ever get so long as they so keenly feel the threat of Destiny."

"You have to agree, though, that Destiny does present a fairly large threat," Prichard felt impelled to point out.

"And you have to agree that, were Destiny a man, the King and Captain would not so easily forget the equally large threat posed by those helping her."

Now she had lost Prichard, and he raised an eyebrow in invitation for her to explain that cryptic remark.

"This is what you all fail to see," Emily's voice grew softer, an odd sort of compassion filling it. "Yes, you're all threatened by Wizard Destiny and her unfathomable skills with magic, but that alone doesn't blind you to everything else. What does bother you all, what none of you truly understand, is the very thing the King now uses against me."

She paused to draw in a deep breath.

"Destiny has taken a position you all feel reserved for a man. You would have no conflict if Wizard Nathan stood in Destiny's place, because you feel it the place of a man to try to take and maintain power. But you put a woman in that role, and you don't know how to handle it. That makes her something outside of your experience, something you never thought possible, and what you think should not exist, you must eradicate to restore the world to something that makes sense to you. We live in a world that believes a woman doesn't have the strength or capacity to achieve what Destiny has done, therefore you must remove the anomaly, return women to their rightful place. Destroy Destiny, slot me back into overwrought woman, regain control in a manly fashion, following the plans of men. Because a woman can't know what she's talking about, according to the universal untruth that you've allowed yourselves to believe. She lacks experience and is physically incapable of aiding herself.

"Destiny frightens you because she's a woman, not because she's a wizard."

"That's unfair, Emily."

"Yes, it is," she murmured. Prichard shook his head.

"We knew Destiny's sex before we came here," he pressed. "Her *powers* frighten us, what she and the Prince have done to Dalasham, not her gender."

"And yet, once Wizard Castillo put forth his doubts that a woman could have the wherewithal or mental capacity to piece together a layered spell, what happened?" she demanded. "Destiny became more of an abomination instead of just a gifted magic user, because Castillo reinforced the concept that women cannot do what men can. That list you compiled, how many women does it contain? Not one. You found instead a man, someone who might be her brother, someone who might help us counter what Destiny has done. But if any part of the maid's story is true, he might pose a larger threat. But the King doesn't see that; he sees a man who can undo what a woman unnaturally wrought, a man who can restore the proper balance to your worldview."

"So what would you suggest, Emily?" Prichard enjoined, anger leaking into his voice. "That we forgive her because she's a woman who's had a hard lot in life? That we stand in awe that a woman has accomplished more than a man?"

"That you acknowledge Destiny as a *person*, that you treat her the same as the Prince, that you don't allow fear to guide your actions when that fear causes you to overlook the dangers presented by *all* parties. Don't blindly hope that simply finding a way to kill what frightens you will solve all your problems. That you don't let your bias against what a woman *should* do interfere with your capacity to plan how to solve the real problem."

"The real problem being?" asked Prichard.

Emily let out an incredulous sound somewhere between a groan and a laugh, pressing the palms of her hands to her eyes.

"That the Prince has stolen the crown with the intent to kill the King!"

Prichard couldn't help his startled reaction this time, and the stool toppled as he leapt to his feet and stared down at her with wide eyes. She nodded frantically, pushing up from the bed.

"We're so concerned with what *Destiny's* done, how to counter her magic, that we keep glossing over the fact that it's

Prince Whillim who holds the power. Yes, she has helped him, made possible what should never have occurred through the use of magic, but ultimately, it's the Prince's ruthless ambition that started this. You're all so concerned about Destiny's role that you forget the Prince's intentions. Ignore the fact of Destiny's sex and treat her as any enemy in collusion with the true perpetrator.

"And that means that the King must recognise his brother's very real and immediate involvement in this whole plot. If he keeps thinking of him as just the younger brother led astray by occult forces, a boy needing protection instead of the monster he's become—"

She suddenly stopped speaking, mouth still open as though ready to continue, but her eyes lost focus. Prichard had seen how Emily would sometimes grow distant when a thought had occurred to her, how she would speak those thoughts absently out loud as she worked through a problem. She did that now.

"The younger brother needing protection," she muttered. "Could it be as simple as that? It might help explain her intentions." She shook her head. "But then why kill him? If she wants him to remember who he used to be, then why death to seal the spell? Are we wrong? Could we keep the King alive?"

At that, Prichard took a step toward her, gripping her shoulders.

"Out with it girl," he whispered, hoping to hear the full course of her thoughts. "How do we keep Stefan alive? What are you thinking?"

Emily blinked up at him.

"What if the Destiny Seat is an experiment?" came her quiet reply as her eyes grew steady on his. "What if Destiny wants to perfect a memory spell to turn Nathan back into the younger brother she helped care for and love? Somehow, she and the Prince come together with a similar purpose; alter how the world sees their brother. In the Prince's case, erase that brother from history, but in Destiny's, remind the brother that he wasn't always a monster, that their Master stole a sister's love and moulded a power-mad wizard in the place of a strong man. If she wanted to get her brother back, she must have a way to seal the spell without killing the subject of the spell."

Prichard's thoughts tumbled along with hers, new possibilities flashing through his mind.

"Unless she hoped to erase the memory of the Master," he countered. "How might the spell work if the subject already lies dead? Could she instead force Nathan to see the Master as she did? The monster who stole and warped her brother while turning the sister into a slave?"

Emily's lower lip trembled.

"But then, that wouldn't help us. They'd still need to destroy the source of the memory, kill the King."

"It gives us something else to consider. We don't actually know how this spell works. Even Castillo could only give us conjecture based on our observations. It seems to me," Prichard said, stepping back from Emily as his thoughts raced, "that we need to take Destiny alive if we want any answers. Which puts us back to finding a way to counter her spell, not killing her. We need to find a wizard who can help us capture both her and the Prince."

"Do we?" Emily asked, drawing his attention back to the young woman. She gave a hoarse laugh. "Or have we wasted our time trying to find the wrong answer? Destiny knows how to counter her own spell; we need a way to make her use it."

"So how do we make that happen? How do we subdue a wizard?"

"I imagine a good blow to the head ought to do the trick," Emily said. Prichard stared at her a moment, then burst into laughter.

"She's as human as the Prince and everyone around them," she went on when Prichard paused to catch his breath. "If we can incapacitate Destiny, make sure she can't speak or use her hands, then she can't use her magic against us. I think. Though we might want to confirm with Wizard Castillo whether a wizard can conjure harmful magic in any other fashion. Perhaps he would consider sending someone back with us who could help keep her subdued, someone he trusts, freeing us from even having to consider the unstable likes of someone like Nathan. The trick, then, is how to make Destiny undo her spell once we unbind her rather than seek to harm us. She has no reason to help, and every reason to suspect we have her death on our mind. And we'd still have to get to her and the Prince, take them unawares before they strap the King to the Destiny Seat."

"We need to discuss this with Stefan and Fred," Prichard decided. Emily's expression shuttered and she dropped her gaze to the floor.

"Tell the King our concerns," she whispered, "but please, Lord Prichard, make him believe you thought of them. Until he sees a need for me, if he ever sees a need for me again, the King will only hear the fears of a young girl trying desperately to find her way in a frightening world, and that won't lend any credence to our theories."

"That's not fair, Emily." He remembered saying that before.

"But it's true," she said, so quiet now that he had to lean forward to hear her. "And he's not wrong." She turned away and sank down to sit on the bed. "That's what makes it so hard to counter their instincts. The King sees through my false bravado; he just can't see past it to acknowledge that I might have a point regardless."

Prichard studied her a moment as she tried to rub at her eyes without making it obvious that she wiped away tears.

"Why do you do that?" he asked softly. She glanced up, a hint of heat igniting in her grey eyes. "Why do you keep calling him the King? King, Captain, Lord. We put away titles as we journeyed here, but now you've reverted. Why?"

She sniffled and wiped her damp hands on the legs of her trews, then met his stare, though it looked like it cost her some effort.

"Because, master spy," she finally answered. "Names are for friends, those who support you even if they don't agree with you. Titles are for those who have power over you. Scholar Emmett could afford those friends; Junior Assistant Emily doesn't dare, and the sooner she remembers her place, the less painful it will feel when I'm back in the library, just another nameless face."

She rose and moved to the door, breaking eye contact. She opened the door and held it for him, her gaze on the hallway beyond.

"The King needs to know our concerns before he commits to doing something we may all regret," she said to the empty hall. "I think you'd all best be served if I stay here and rest while you come up with a firm plan."

She's holding on to her dignity by a finger, Prichard saw. *So desperate to overcome the stereotype of overwrought woman that she'll fight beyond what's reasonable to appear strong.*

But this, he could give her. As he passed, he lowered his head in a small bow.

"I shall present our concerns so as not to upset the King, and I shall inform you of the outcome." Then he looked right at her and spoke in a mock stern tone. "But don't think you get to laze around while I do all the work, young lady." He winked, then strode away to the sound of her surprised laugh, muffled behind her hand.

Now he just had to find a way to confront Stefan with some of the harsh truths that Emily had revealed without making her sound unreasonable to a man facing an enemy he didn't know how to fight.

Just another day in the life of a spy.

Chapter 25

Faulk had spent less time guarding the King lately and more time patrolling the streets. He didn't know if Whillim had finally gotten tired of whatever Faulk's presence reminded him of, or if he honestly hoped Faulk might discover something on his rounds that no one else had yet. Whatever his motives, Whillim had Faulk patrolling the city like any man of the Watch, only draped in the livery of King's guard.

At least it removed him from the cold gaze of Wizard Destiny and the erratic tempers of the King. It also gave him time to think and learn new ways to cope with the pain of weeding out false memories. He still couldn't remember the hazy face of the man he believed he truly served, or call to mind a name—either brought blinding agony—but he had put together an outline of the events that had led him to his current situation. So long as he kept his suspicions firmly locked behind his subconscious, he could function past the pain.

He glanced at his surroundings, noting that today's rounds had brought him to one of Riverbend's market squares that he remembered frequenting on his time off. Across from him stood Swallow's Flight, a tavern he and Ambrose sometimes visited, occasionally accompanied by some of the others who had disappeared that night with the renegade, nearly three weeks past. The Swallow had decent ale with good prices, and like every other drinking establishment he recalled from before the riots, Faulk avoided it. Far too easy to try to drown his pain instead of embrace it.

Besides, he had found a better way to deal with the effects of whatever Destiny and Whillim had done to him that didn't include losing more memories to alcohol. He rubbed absently at a healing cut across the back of his left hand with his right thumb. Many guards and men-at-arms—*and mercenaries*, added that part of his mind keeping track of such anomalies—sported fresh cuts and scrapes daily, whether due to regular training, brawls, or altercations. That Faulk's injuries came from his own blade, drawn across arms or thighs to provide a different outlet for his pain, didn't register in most who saw him. But Faulk had found he could redirect the fire of Destiny's spell by causing a separate pain, use the physical wound to distract from the mental one. It let him think through what he should not remember and better piece together Whillim's scheme, so long as he coupled it with his revised mantra: *Whillim is King, with Destiny's help.* The addition of the wizard's name in that thought no longer brought added pain, and since he barely remembered a time when his head didn't pound like someone played a drum against his temples, he found he could more easily bear the constant pressure.

Pulling his gaze away from Swallow's Flight, Faulk moved to continue his rounds, but something snagged his attention. Each square throughout Riverbend had a notice board, with the intention that any pertinent news and information would spread to the whole city on the tongues of the literate who would read such messages to their neighbours. Those boards would sometimes also hold pictures to draw in citizens, literate or not, with descriptions and ideas that required no words. For instance, a tailor wanting to hire a day labourer might draw a pair of shears, or a needle and thread, and couple it with a diagram to their place of business. Or a farmer needing help with planting might draw a figure dropping seeds into the ground, and include an image of the sun three times, suggesting he wanted someone for three days' work. A missing pet or object, or even a suspected criminal, would often end up pictured on a notice board, though often so far from reality that finding said thing or person ultimately proved unlikely. Not so the picture that stole Faulk's attention now. Emily's face, next to Sim's, sat pinned on many notice boards, and as like to reality that no one could mistake her for someone else.

He remembered following the man with the blank face as he followed Emily into a secret tunnel, recalled how precisely Emily had described where she would wait for them while the man found safety in a cave, heard again the Captain link a safety phrase to Emily's name—marvelled that somehow he had managed to keep those last two memories his own, safe from the clutches of King and wizard. In short, he remembered well the girl in that drawing, and knew her picture alone had not turned his attention to that board.

The man standing in front of that picture trying not to stare, however, redirected Faulk's feet and he approached almost against his will. He didn't patrol these streets alone, though none actively partnered him, and he didn't want to point out his own trepidation at this man's interest in Emily's picture.

The stranger had a face that had seen many hours in the sun and calloused hands that had held many tools. His clothing, worn but serviceable, named him a labourer, probably farmhand or builder's assistant or some other profession that kept him outdoors for hours on end, and his sturdy build spoke to years of such experience. When he felt Faulk move up next to him, he peered over from lined eyes hooded beneath thick brows. Recognising the King's colours named him local, but his discomfort suggested he didn't frequent the city often enough to know how to address a King's guard. Likely from one of the outlying settlements, then.

The man took a breath, as though to steady himself for an unpleasant task, then spoke without looking at Faulk.

"She an outlaw?" The gentle tenor voice didn't match what Faulk had expected from the stubbled face.

"Not at all," he replied quietly. "Just someone of interest we're trying to find."

The man grunted, still staring at Emily's picture. Then his gaze slid to the image posted beside it.

"And him?" he asked, jerking his chin toward Sim's picture.

"Someone helping her," came Faulk's strangled response, and he cleared his throat of his anxiety.

The man shot him a look from the corner of his eye, judging, assessing.

"Is it her uncle looking?" he asked, and that made Faulk pause, his heart speeding up.

"Her uncle?" Faulk queried back.

253

"Mmm," the man made a sound in his throat, his narrowed eyes belying his unease. "The merchant. Or maybe his guards? They all looked after her while she got better." He turned to look directly at Faulk. "She in trouble?"

Faulk tried not to gape at the man. He may have even succeeded, but then the man's gaze slid past Faulk and his expression shut down as he swung back to the notice board.

"My mistake, no doubt," he whispered hoarsely. "Forgive my interruption, sir."

With a tug at his forelock, the worker started to move away, but then Faulk saw what had distressed the man. Faulk cursed under his breath, but he couldn't move fast enough to guard the man's escape from Drummund, Milos' hawk-faced lieutenant.

Drummund sauntered up, thumbs hooked behind his belt, as he purposefully blocked the man's way.

"What've we got here, Faulk?" asked Drummund, his voice oily.

"Just a labourer looking for work," Faulk replied, holding the merc's stare without flinching. "Wanted to know about any new notices."

"That right?" Drummund turned his dark glare on the unnamed man, who kept his gaze firmly focused on his boot-tops.

"Yessir," the man murmured, his rural accent turning thick under Drummund's close scrutiny. "Lookin' fer werk over summer, sir."

Drummund stared at the man for a long moment, but he could only see the man's bowed head as his calloused fingers slowly kneaded his hat in a circle. The man never took his gaze from his feet.

"What kind of work?" Drummund finally demanded.

"I'm farmer, mostly," they heard, that tenor voice still aimed at the ground. "But I ain't 'fraid of other werk."

"And these pictures you studied for so long?" Drummund asked in a tone dripping honeyed sarcasm. He casually leaned up against the board. It gave the farmer room to flee if he chose, but Faulk could see the mercenary's taut muscles flex, ready to intercept if the other man bolted. "Nothing tickled a memory? No one you may have encountered somewhere?"

The farmer flicked a brief glance at Faulk before seeking sanctuary in his hat again, shaking his head with a mumbled 'no.' Faulk tried not to close his own eyes in sympathy, but he knew this farmer had no chance to escape Drummund now. Even had he known nothing, Drummund had evidently decided to take the poor man in for questioning.

Faulk couldn't let that happen.

They all looked after her while she got better, the farmer had said. Not just Sim, but also this 'uncle' and his guards, keeping Emily safe. Faulk might not remember a face or a name, but he felt pretty damned certain this farmer knew the location of the man Whillim hunted, the man Faulk truly served.

Faulk stepped in front of Drummund. The two stood of equal size, though Drummund had the greater weight.

"You heard him, Drummund," Faulk snarled, trying to wave unseen behind his back to the farmer, urging him to flee. "He's looking for work, not our runaways. Let him be."

Drummund snorted, a dangerous gleam in his eyes. He didn't make a move, nor speak, but then Faulk realised his mistake. Drummund had not approached them alone.

"Whadya think, Drum?" a voice drawled, and Faulk moved just enough to keep an eye on Drummund while searching for the newcomer. He cursed when he recognised the wiry form of Victor, another of Drummund's men, his twin braids swaying as he nodded toward Faulk. Victor had the farmer by the arm. "Watching this traitor finally paying off?"

"Possibly," Drummund grinned, sending icy fingers of dread down Faulk's spine. While he had occasionally felt eyes on him since the night of the riots, he hadn't thought Milos had assigned a permanent spy; Faulk didn't hold a position of any great importance, so why watch him? "Why don't we take them both to Wizard Destiny, see what she thinks."

Faulk imagined cold eyes the colour of twilight ripping into his soul, and it took every ounce of self control to keep from fighting a return to Destiny's impartial stare as Drummund and Victor closed in. But if Faulk fought, Destiny would certainly throw him back into that room that stole memories, if not worse. After fighting so hard to separate false memories from true, even if he had to hide that truth deep in his own mind, he couldn't fall victim to that magic again. Fighting would guarantee that; submitting to Drummund's shoves might at least buy him time. For what, he didn't know, but this farmer held part of the key Faulk needed to break free of Whillim's lies.

He knew about Emily and those with her. If Faulk couldn't keep that information from Destiny, then he needed to find a way to use it to his own advantage.

He just didn't know how yet, and that meant playing along with the usurper and his mercenaries.

A cloud of pain washed over Faulk at naming Whillim a usurper, but he tore it away with the slash of a sharpened nail across his palm, the red haze of torment helping to clear his vision as Milos' men escorted him and the farmer to the castle and the false rulers waiting within.

Chapter 26

Tox heard the banging on his door mingling with a commotion in his yard as he emerged from the pig pen, mud and crap caking his boots. When he saw what manner of men milled about his yard, he seriously considered returning to the sty and rolling around in the excrement, if only so that he could drive away his unwelcome guests with his filth and stench. But a couple of the hard-eyed soldiers saw him, so he continued as far as the barn, then leaned his large, muscled frame against it, arms crossed, waiting to see which of the eight men would address him first. A ninth face in the crowd caught his attention, and Tox sucked at his teeth before spitting. He gave no other reaction to Jacob's bruised face or cowed presence. Whatever had brought his battered farmhand in the company of these men boded ill for Tox.

"You're farmer Tox?" One of the men strode forward, the reins of his horse tossed negligently to a companion, suggesting the broad shouldered man with his dusky complexion expected the other to care for the beast as a matter of course. *The man in charge, then,* Tox decided, noting the others giving way. He seemed to command a certain respect, not unlike Captain Frederick, though Tox doubted that respect came entirely from the man's benevolence, given the raptor glare he fixed on Tox. The soldier tried to hide that sharp ruthlessness behind a grim smile. Tox didn't buy it for a moment.

Tox nodded warily.

257

"That I am," he answered the hail. "Who are you?"

"Captain Milos, head of the King's guard," came the answer. Tox refrained from groaning aloud. Not just any hard-faced soldier, but the very man that Emily said headed the Prince's mercenaries. Fantastic.

"What would any King's guard want at my farm, let alone the head of said guard?" Tox demanded. "Unless one of you's the King, shouldn't you be elsewhere?"

Milos' eyes narrowed in displeasure, though he couldn't fault Tox's logic.

"We're here on a matter addressing the King's safety," the mercenary said. Before Tox could think up any other way to stall him further, Milos went on. "It has come to our attention that you harboured a fugitive recently."

"Did I?" Tox made sure the man heard surprise and alarm, not admission. He even went so far as to straighten from his slouch. "If I did so, were against my knowledge."

Milos paused as though to assess his veracity. Then, without taking his gaze from Tox, he signalled to one of his men, who hauled Jacob forward.

"You know this man?"

"Of course," answered Tox promptly. "Jacob's one of my farmhands when I need extra help. Though he's not usually given to brawling, so I'm grateful if you rescued him from a beating."

Milos barely managed to bite back a frustrated sneer. Either that, or the man had a sour stomach.

"Your Jacob has told us of the men you gave shelter to a fortnight and a half past. A group of men accompanied by this young woman." Milos unfolded a scrap of paper and brandished it as though waving a victory flag.

"I did," Tox confirmed, adding a touch of consternation to his voice. "A merchant and his guard, Schmidt by name. That girl's his niece, Amalia, and I let them stay 'til she recovered from her fever. We worked out a trade for my inconvenience. They left a little over a fortnight ago." He met Milos' eyes, saw the simmering rage there, and hoped he hadn't overdone it. "You're saying one of them's a fugitive?"

Milos' lip curled in a snarl.

"And you're saying some merchant and his sick niece just happened upon your farm? Forgive my suspicion, but I find that hard to believe. You're not exactly on a main road here."

Tox snorted, surprising a blink from Milos.

"Shocked the hell outta me too, when they banged on my door," Tox agreed. Together with Captain Frederick and Emily, they had concocted a story for how anyone might have come across Tox's farm for this very eventuality. Now he just had to sell that tale to a hardened mercenary. "Seems something spooked the girl's horse and Schmidt, more concerned for his already feverish sister-daughter's safety than his cart of wares, went tearing off after her, leaving his guard little choice but to follow. By the time they caught the beast, it had made it most of the way here, and Schmidt decided to seek shelter, as night had fallen. I tell ya, when they brought that girl to my door, she looked white as snow and limp as grass in the rain." It helped that on this, he spoke true. "Ain't no one with any semblance of mercy gonna turn away their fellows in such need. And when dawn came, I could hardly turn them out until the child recovered some strength."

Milos stared at him through narrowed eyes for a long moment. Then he turned his glare on Jacob.

"This true?" he demanded.

Jacob shrugged awkwardly, as though something in his right shoulder didn't work quite right, then nodded.

"She were pale the morning we met her, and movin' slow like when yer sick. An' she slept a lot." Tox didn't know whether Jacob intended to sound less intelligent so that Milos would underestimate him, or if he couldn't speak any clearer given the swelling in his jaw. "An' like I tol' you afore, the man named hisself a merchant."

"Meaning you think he wasn't?" Tox asked, fists to hips in mock outrage. "You think they lied? 'Cause I can guarantee, that girl wasn't well."

"But you can't guarantee the man was a merchant," one of the other soldiers stepped up beside Milos, glaring from beneath a dark brow. "You said they abandoned their cart to chase the girl. Did they ever retrieve it?"

"He sent one of his guards back for it in the morning," Tox replied, giving a small shake of his head. "But he never found it."

"So you only have their word on their identity."

"Seems so," Tox agreed. "That, and the chit he provided

when he left, promising me recompense when next in Riverbend."

At that, Milos' gaze sharpened, as did his glower.

"He left you a promissory note?"

"Suppose that's what you call it," Tox shrugged.

"And I suppose you've already used it," the other mercenary sneered. "So that we can't trace it."

"No, sir," Tox countered, trying not to sneer in turn at the man's surprise. "Have it safe in the house."

The chit and seal came from Emily's pen, but they had all gambled that no one would actually try to trace it, and even if they did, so many merchants did business in Riverbend that trying to track down this one—had he truly existed—would still take time, Schmidt and the goods of smiths in general being a common enough name and occupation. The existence of such a document should lend weight to Tox's story, and remove him from any burden if someone did detect the lie. How could they expect a mere farmer to suspect the identity of a merchant when he provided so much proof?

"Did you want to see it, see if you know this merchant's seal?" asked Tox.

"If you would be so kind," Milos growled.

Tox nodded and pushed away from the barn, heading to his house.

"Drummund, go with him." The scowling soldier beside Milos followed Tox inside.

"How many guards did this merchant have?" Drummund wanted to know once Tox got his door open.

"Man came with four," he said.

"And how many did he leave with?"

Tox turned his head to give the man a flat stare. "Three. He sent the fourth ahead to arrange a comfortable inn in Riverbend. As you can see," he swept his arm around the main room. "I don't have a lot of space for extra bodies wanting to stay in any comfort."

"So they went back to Riverbend when they left?"

Tox shrugged again.

"That's what they said. Headed that way when they left, but then, as your Captain said, I'm not on the road to anywhere save other farms, so I only have their word for it." He eyed the man cautiously before putting forth his next words in worried tones. "Your Captain really believes I harboured fugitives?" He shook his head as he reached for a box on the mantle. "They seemed so sincere."

Drummund snorted as Tox pulled out the document Emily had fashioned.

"Here, let me light a taper so you can see it better," Tox offered, managing to bend toward his banked fire before Drummund snatched the document from Tox's hand.

"Never mind that. I'll take it out for Milos to see."

Tox would have liked to linger, at least long enough to light a candle—those in the King's encampment might not see the signal in the daylight, but if any watched as instructed, they might at least have some warning of Milos' presence—but Drummund didn't give him the opportunity.

It occurred to Tox, as the soldier passed Emily's chit up to his Captain, that Drummund couldn't read. However Milos, frowning down at Emily's carefully penned words, obviously could.

"This merchant Schmidt left a fortnight ago, you say?" the Captain asked.

"A little more than that," Tox said. "Early in the morning to reach the city quick-like. Only stayed here three full nights."

"You didn't accompany Emily to town, say with this man?" Milos jerked his chin at another man who pulled out another image. Tox frowned at the picture, as though trying to place the man shown. But this drawing had him shaking inside, for it showed Sergeant Sim in his disguise when he and Tox and Emily had gone for supplies. *Careful,* he told himself.

"I didn't bring anyone to town," he said slowly. Walked with, yes, but bringing implied they required some kind of assistance, and he, Sim, and Emily had walked under their own power. A very subtle difference, but Tox would take what he could get. *The key to a good lie,* Captain Frederick had told him, *is to stick as close to the truth as possible.*

"Don't know no Emily," he continued. "Unless you're saying the girl who called herself Amalia changed her name. But that man looks a bit like one of Schmidt's guards called hisself Ranolf. Not exact, mind," he shook his head, "but close enough." He brought his attention back to Milos and waited. Offering any other information might make him seem desperate for these men to believe him, and while Tox deeply wanted

261

them to trust his story, he dare not oversell it now, not with that unnerving speculation edging Milos' keen regard.

Finally, after what felt like an eternity, Milos handed the chit back to Tox.

"If you ever see this merchant Schmidt again, farmer, you'd do well to find a way to inform the King and his guards."

Tox took the sheet and gently folded it up again.

"I most certainly will endeavour to do so, Captain," he assured the mercenary. Milos frowned, as though wondering whether Tox mocked him. But Tox spoke the words with absolute sincerity, no lie in his eyes. If he saw the 'merchant' again, he would certainly inform the King about Milos' inquiries.

Milos grumbled as he swung himself back into his saddle and he and his troop made ready to leave. Tox wondered if they intended to take Jacob back with them or if they would release his farmhand now that Tox had told them about merchant Schmidt. He wondered what he could do if they tried to take him.

The question quickly became moot as another mercenary soldier rode into the yard, red braids flying behind him as he halted Milos' departure. Something about the predatory gleam in the man's face sent claws of dread down Tox's spine.

"What is it Victor?" Milos called as the newcomer pulled his horse to a stop.

"Think you might have reason to try out Destiny's new toy," the man said, a wolf's grin twisting his features. "A few folks up the way need a reminder of who they should serve."

The direction Victor indicated confirmed Tox's fears. The man had found King Stefan's encampment.

Milos glared down at Tox.

"Guard them," he snarled to one of his men, then rode out after Victor in a cloud of dust.

Tox stared at the broad-shouldered young man left behind, who promptly drew his sword and advanced with a grim expression.

Shoulda kept my door shut that night, he grumbled to himself as he raised his hands and followed Jacob to his knees.

***

Milos had watched so many times what should have spelled

the end of this miserable contract turn into some sort of disaster that he hadn't allowed himself the luxury of hoping this newest lead would evolve into any kind of victory. While it seemed that this farmer Tox had unknowingly sheltered Stefan and his group immediately following Whillim's take-over, he fully believed that the King had long since left. Tox might not espouse the full truth in his dealings with Stefan, but Milos read no lie when he claimed this *merchant Schmidt* had stayed only long enough to regroup while he came up with some plan as yet a mystery to Milos.

None of his gate guards from the days following the riots had convincingly recalled seeing Emily or this Ranolf, although three separate instances suggested maybe someone similar may have passed their posts, but in truth, the girl just didn't have that memorable a face. One such report *had* included a tale with a farmer. A long shot, to put this Tox together with Emily and her companion at the lender's shop, but the farmer had named Emily as Amalia, same as that shopkeeper. Milos wondered, if any had more fully recalled the trio, which of Stefan's guard would match the description of the farmer.

Tox's true role didn't even occur to Milos, until Victor rode into the yard as they made ready to depart. He had sent Victor to scout the area without any real hope of finding anything. It had rained enough in the past fortnight that even so skilled a man as Victor would have difficulty resurrecting a hint as to Stefan's whereabouts. But he had found something that animated the man like Milos hadn't seen in months.

A quick glance at the farmer failed to discern surprise, relief, fear, anxiety—any reaction—and that screamed suspicion to Milos. Instinct may have abandoned him in recent days, but he chose to trust his now.

"Guard them," he snarled to Petrov, a young man who had joined his Company last fall and who eagerly sought to prove his mettle. Milos felt confident he could handle two farmers. He turned back to Victor and guided his horse next to the scout's.

"Talk to me," he said in a low voice as Victor led them away.

"No surprise that the road eventually turns into more of a path out beyond the third farm, I'd guess used near exclusively by farmers and those who trade with farmers. So when I see evidence of more traffic than reasonable at the start of growing season, given the likely population hereabouts, I take note. Especially when someone's gone to the trouble to try 'n hide that traffic."

He had Milos' full attention now.

"How much traffic, and where does it lead?"

"Leads to a fallow field currently sprouting about ninety tents," said Victor. "Also around sixty horses, and more than a hundred soldiers, most sporting the colours of men Destiny would really like to add to her collection, including Sir Castel's russet hues."

Milos felt adrenaline infuse his body at the implication. Castel had eluded him once, played him for a fool. Not this time.

"Any sign of Stefan or his group?" he demanded, almost daring to believe that they could at last quit this region. Victor shook his head, quickly quashing that false hope.

"But whoever established this camp definitely has a military eye," the scout went on. "If I had to guess, I'd say Stefan's using it as a recruitment base. At the very least, it's full of men loyal to Stefan, and not Whillim. Brilliant, actually, to stake it this close to Riverbend, yet so far off the oft-travelled roads. If that farmhand hadn't tipped us to that girl's picture, we'd have never found this place."

"Not brilliant enough to properly cover their tracks, though," Milos said.

Surprisingly, Victor shook his head again.

"In truth, Cap, if I weren't so frustrated with chasing so many false leads, I might have missed the signs. It's a fallow field, but it looks tilled 'cause someone had the idea to exercise their mounts to create what resemble furrows. Also helps hide the horse shite. Took me a bit to notice no green had started to sprout in those furrows, though. That little fact chased me well past the last farm before it penetrated my brain. Even then, I might not have noticed anything overly peculiar about the deadfall cunningly spread to disguise the entry point they're using for the field, if I hadn't seen the shadow pissing against one of the windbreak trees lining the field."

"And you figured this shadow didn't belong to a farmer because ...?" Milos invited.

Now Victor grinned as he spat over the far side of his horse.

"Because farmers don't prop swords beside said tree as they

water it before returning to their sentry post."

Milos let out a small guffaw.

"The sentries are well placed," Victor continued, more serious now. "I slipped past to take stock of the situation, but chances of repeating the process with more bodies ain't great. Nothing's visible from the road, and once the sentry ducked back out of sight, he's hard to spot too."

"But you saw enough to know who's in the camp," Milos pressed. Victor nodded.

"The three knights who escaped our net, and a handful of other minor players."

"Can you lure one or all of the knights out?"

"Not with a hundred or so soldiers milling about, but if that trinket Destiny gave you works like it should, a sentry with his thoughts scrambled gone to fetch a knight would cause little stir."

Milos considered that strategy. Destiny had fashioned an amulet that she claimed worked like her Seat, just as Milos had requested. While it didn't have the scope of the Destiny Seat, it might work enough to give them these knights. Worth a shot, anyway.

"Then let's net us a sentry," Milos said. "We turn him, he brings us a knight, and with luck, the amulet's magic will work long enough for us to get that knight back to the city. Destiny works her full magic on him, and that gives us the camp. Whether they're here with Stefan's knowledge and blessing, or just hoping to find and aid their wayward King, it'll diminish his power and strengthen Whillim's claim. Either way, it's gotta help us finish this contract the sooner."

"I'm all for that," Victor agreed with a growl. "This whole trying to take over with magic gives me the creeps."

Milos couldn't agree more.

Chapter 27

Em swung her weighted willow branch through a sword form viciously enough to produce an audible *whoosh*. She scowled at it, but continued her motions.

Such a stuck up, pompous ass, she growled to herself, trying and failing to put the arrogant wizard whom Castillo had enlisted to join them on their return to Riverbend out of her mind.

Whoosh went the bough again, only heightening Em's frustration. Difficult enough to move through these new forms silently, the addition of the heavy makeshift weapon added another layer she had yet to master, especially if her concentration kept shifting.

After the third whistling whirl of the branch, Fred called a halt. Beside her, Ambrose and Dari lowered their real swords so that the points gently kissed the ground. Em resisted the urge to slam her piece of wood down next to her, and instead just let it droop in her hand.

Fred stomped over and glared down at her. She glared right back, shoving a strand of hair that had escaped her unruly braid off her face. The Captain shook his head, then barked,

"Again."

Ambrose and Dari moved in silent unison into the first move. Em followed suit, but Fred grabbed the willow branch, immobilizing it. He leaned in close, looming over her as he glowered down. The other two didn't falter.

"I don't care what has you in a snit," Fred grated out. "I do care that it makes you sloppy." He backed up a step, shoving at her weapon as he did so, unbalancing her. Em stumbled, but quickly regained her footing. "A good soldier will do what with their emotions?" he asked louder.

"Use them before they use him," both Ambrose and Dari called, again in unison, neither breaking form. Em strove to match their fluid motions once more.

"That's right," Fred said, hands behind his back as he watched, shadows stretching long as the sun continued its descent beyond the edge of the forest. "If you're angry, focus it into your weapon. If you're sad, focus it into your weapon. If you're anxious, focus it into your weapon. If you're happy, focus it into your weapon. If you're horny ..."

He trailed off and Em tried to keep the form despite her surprise at Fred's words. She felt her cheeks redden from more than exertion. But beside her, Ambrose and Dari finished the sentence anyway, flowing unerringly from one form to the next.

"Focus it into your weapon."

Em's eyes flicked briefly between the two, but she managed not to stumble again.

"If you're embarrassed ..." Fred stared straight at Em this time, and she dredged up the merest hint of a wry smile.

"Focus it into your weapon," she replied.

"An enemy will use every advantage he can; don't give him another because you can't master your emotions."

Em heard someone snort across the clearing, and immediately knew who had emitted such derision. But this Wizard Marcus had already made known his opinion on Em's presence and abilities, and she decided then and there that she had to take Fred's lesson to heart.

Focus the anger into a weapon. *Don't let him rile you,* she admonished herself, slowly melting into the forms instead of slashing through them. *His opinion doesn't matter, even if he does think you should act as his personal servant. Let his insults roll off you. Don't let him dictate your actions.*

Lord Prichard had talked the King out of a dangerous mission to search out Wizard Nathan, and instead, the two had met with Wizard Castillo again. Castillo confirmed Em's belief that all but the most advanced forms of magic—usually those already harnessed into a talisman or other enhancing agent—required some outer stimulus to come into existence. Words or gestures

267

moulded most magic spells. If they could incapacitate Destiny before she could bring her powers to bear, they had a chance of subduing her. He surmised, however, that the Destiny Seat might work with a thought rather than a word or action and, if Destiny truly had mastered such a feat, she might have other objects she could trigger even while bound. Unless they could bind her with magic as well as chains, as Em and Prichard had discussed.

After some deliberation, Castillo had agreed to find a wizard to travel with them back to the castle who might offer such assistance. Unfortunately, the only wizard who seemed willing to take on the onerous mission—not only would he face Destiny, whom many didn't feel posed a true threat anyway, but he also ventured into a land that had no love of magic users—had many less-than-desirable traits, to Em's thinking.

"He probably won't have much luck deciphering any layered spells," Castillo had admitted when acquainting the two parties, "but in the two years he's lodged here, Wizard Marcus has proven very adept at wards. He should have no difficulties binding a wizard."

He *did* seem to have some difficulties understanding Em's place among the party, and even keeping to the fiction of her as a relation to Stefan—they had gone back to niece, seeing as brother no longer worked, though she still wore men's clothing for convenience on the road—did not diminish Marcus' firm belief that, as the only female, she must act as servant to all (and him especially). Why else would they have brought her?

It didn't help that they hadn't disclosed their true identities. No one felt safe revealing that they travelled with the King of Dalasham and his close guard, nor that Prichard held a noble rank. In fact, Prichard acted like the scholar's aide to the point where he had slid himself into the role of camp cook. This left the wizard with the false notion that he stood as the most important person on this journey, and he clearly felt entitled to their respect as well as Em's servitude. Being a 'scholar's' niece didn't afford her much respite, and Marcus looked on these training sessions with Fred as a useless endeavour, unsuitable for a woman. Surprisingly, Fred's silent stare a couple of days ago had finally convinced Marcus that the Captain wouldn't tolerate Em skipping these lessons, but it didn't stop the wizard from showing his contempt through eyerolls or snorts of derision.

Marcus sat now, as the sun set two evenings later, propped up on his saddle blanket and leaning with an air of discontent against a fallen tree trunk, a soft ball of magic light at his shoulder as he scribbled something in a little book he kept at his belt. Perhaps a journal to document how put upon he felt on this less-than-comfortable trip? How these backward people who didn't know anything about magic refused to travel the main roads or take advantage of the luxuries afforded by an inn?

But they had decided, before Marcus joined them, that they didn't dare ride the most direct route back to Riverbend, not with Milos' mercenaries stretched so far in their search for Stefan. Now that they had a more concrete plan—even if that plan in part relied on a truculent wizard—they had even more reason to shield the King from his brother's greedy hands. Marcus didn't understand—couldn't understand—their reasons for such subterfuge and he didn't hide his disgust for cross-country travel, especially travel on horseback when he'd far prefer a carriage. He'd had to settle for an extra pack horse for his paraphernalia—Em suspected clothing made up most of the excess rather than an abundance of magical accessories, but she had no real desire to confirm that by examining his saddlebags—and he made no effort to disguise how barbaric he considered such treatment to one of his obvious stature. Em would have laughed at his over inflated ego if she hadn't feared the reprisals. He had just enough immaturity that she couldn't guarantee that he wouldn't return to Bakaana in a huff if he felt pushed too far, and magic enough without restraint that he could cause damage if in a pique.

That first night out, once Marcus fully comprehended that they didn't intend to search out any accommodations beyond their tents, he had used his magic to bind and asphyxiate a partridge.

"For supper," he had grunted at the time, but Em had watched how he carelessly flung his spell at the bird when he didn't get his way, and the sensation of seeing that had left her feeling unsettled. He had immobilised and killed the avian because of anger, not for any altruistic reasons. Only once he realised that Em had stood nearby with Fred at her side did Marcus offer the fowl as food.

Em had absolutely no desire to become the wizard's next prey, so she suffered his insults and condescension in silence. Other than the swoosh of her make-shift sword.

Focus the ire into the weapon, she intoned to herself now, and by the second iteration of the sword forms, Em had mastered the moves without misstep, her mind translating the movements as though recalling text on a page. She slowly came back to herself, only then realising that she had fallen into a sort of trance as her body obeyed her memory of Fred's instructions. A strange frown marred Wizard Marcus' expression when she happened to glance his way, the angles of his face distorted even further by his little ball of light, but she turned from his scrutiny to bow to Fred in unison with Ambrose and Dari, students acknowledging their teacher.

"Good," the large Captain allowed a brief smile to flit across his face before dismissing them with a wave. "Get cleaned up. Malcolm's waiting to serve supper."

The sun had vanished, leaving a darkening stretch of navy just beginning to sparkle with starlight above the treetops ringing the clearing that Jo had found for their little camp. The fire Sim and Prichard had built provided enough illumination, along with Marcus' blob of light, that they had no trouble finding their way to the bucket of water someone had thoughtfully left for the trainees.

Em, Ambrose, and Dari quickly cleaned up, taking turns with the water, then they all settled around the fire. Prichard had steaming bowls of soup, hard bread, and a slice of cheese each waiting for them. Marcus had ceased complaining about the simple fare after Fred informed him on the third night that he could eat what they served, or find and prepare his own meals. On this, the fifth night out from the Frontier School, the wizard let his scowl speak his displeasure at camp food, but his voice remained silent as he slurped Prichard's offering.

They met tonight to determine the best approach back to Tox's fallow field. Marcus, of course, didn't know their final destination; he only knew they hoped to confront Destiny at the end of the journey, and that seemed to satisfy him even as he chafed at their mode and method of travel. But tonight, they had to decide whether to rejoin the main road near Haven's End, or if circling around the back-country would prove the more prudent course. Tomorrow would see the fork in the path

270

they currently followed that would force the decision. Heading for the route that led eventually to the road would take less time, but expose them to greater danger as the Prince's men still surely patrolled, searching for Stefan. The safer route would have them cross through various woods and fields, trespassing on others' lands with no real road to follow, only Stefan's knowledge of the area—based a great deal on maps rather than first-hand experience. Em's knowledge too, for she also knew those maps. Less chance of exposure to Whillim's mercenaries on this uncharted path, but more chance an angry landowner might try to intercept them. Also more days with less stable footing for the horses, days where they'd have to forage for extra food to supplement what remained of their rations. On another man's property, where they couldn't risk naming the King to forgive their presence. Safer from mercenaries, but far from safe.

Em listened with half an ear as the others propounded the pros and cons of either route. She knew the maps, yes, but had little else she could contribute to the conversation that the men wouldn't already know. So she sat studying those around her as she ate. Most specifically, she watched Wizard Marcus, her mind drawn back to something Castillo had said that had bothered her. She chased down the memory, then, setting aside her bowl, moved to sit closer to the moustached man. He liked the intrusion even less than she, but before his contemptuous sneer translated into words, she spoke, keeping her voice low so as not to disrupt the others.

"How much residual magic would typically follow from the use of a multi-layered spell?" she asked. Marcus blinked several times, his mouth a thin line as he stared past her at the fire, but he didn't say anything, as though she didn't exist. Em suppressed a sigh (mostly) and tried again. "Wizard Castillo called it 'the capability to hide such an output of power from outsiders while yet effecting a far-reaching range.' What did he mean?"

Em saw Prichard lean slightly toward them from the other side of the wizard even as he kept his gaze on Stefan and Fred as those two debated. She knew she had the spy's attention now too, though he cleverly disguised it as merely putting down his own bowl, freeing his hands to wrap around his bent knee.

Marcus didn't hide his own long-suffering sigh, but he still

271

didn't answer, even going so far as to turn his head slightly away, looking toward Dari and Sim where they sat between Prichard and Fred. Em narrowed her eyes and fought the way her lip wanted to twist in frustration. Then she thought of a way to turn this snubbing into a weapon.

"Or perhaps," she said softly, making her voice sound meek and submissive, "that's a level of magic you don't understand. I apologise for my presumption and misunderstanding of the extent of your education, sir wizard."

She curled her own knees to her chest and hugged them, shifting her attention away from the wizard. Ambrose, on her other side, had a hand to his mouth when she glanced over, and she realised he hid a laugh, having also heard the exchange. She couldn't help sending him a little grin in reply when she heard the growl from deep in Marcus' throat as the man fought, and lost, a battle against pride. The wizard could pretend that Em lacked the wit do more than serve and clean, but to not answer a detailed question about his area of expertise would suggest his own ignorance in the matter. That Em, and not one of the men, had posed the question would irritate him, but to not show off his knowledge would hurt his pride. And Marcus had displayed a fair amount of pride. So, suffer the indignity of answering a woman's question, or accept the insult to his intellect?

Marcus answered the question, though he addressed his words to the fire.

"Multi-layered spells do not necessarily leave a residual, but the nature of this spell causes a ripple effect. Your wizard alters a memory, which of necessity changes reality. Other wizards will sense that change as it spreads outward from its source. That no one in Bakaana felt any such ripple suggests your wizard set up a ward to keep that effect undetected. Yet to remain effective, one assumes the spell must last beyond that ward, requiring the altered reality shift to exist where we should sense it. As we have not, Wizard Castillo correctly theorises that the spell includes an element of self-contained shielding. A ward masks the initial use of the spell, while the embedded protection maintains its efficacy beyond that barrier."

"Self-contained shielding," Em repeated slowly. "Does that suggest that the initial ward, the one that contains the output of power, perhaps exists external to her memory spell rather than as an additional layer? Two spells that exist independent of each other, the first complementing the second?"

"It is a valid hypothesis, especially given our lack of awareness of a wizard working so far within Dalasham," Marcus grudgingly agreed.

"Do you usually know where wizards work, what spells they perform?" Prichard asked quietly. "It would seem to me some wizards might appreciate a certain anonymity." Marcus took his gaze from the fire to meet that of the spy as he would not meet Em's. She rolled her eyes at the churlishness of it but kept her peace.

"It is a courtesy to inform the Wizard Schools where you intend to practice, but not a necessity," Marcus explained. "Those who travel may wish to confer with their brethren; students might seek teachers; both would require knowledge of a wizard's whereabouts. On rare occasions, one spell might adversely affect another, so ensuring no other wizards can inadvertently damage your intent becomes vital. However, the use of most spells will go unnoticed in the wider world because they affect so little. Your wizard has employed magic that should leave a mark, given the range you claim."

"So she hides it behind a ward so as not to draw attention," stated Em. "A ward that might just as easily hide other spells of which we have no knowledge."

Marcus' snort practically screamed *obviously,* but Em didn't care. Too busy chasing a related thought.

"Would such a ward also detect outside magic?" she asked. "Or even serve as a warning should that outside magic seek to enter her domain?"

The question surprised Marcus enough that he turned to look at her with a frown. Prichard also gazed at her, but with a speculation that indicated the nobleman had reached a similar conclusion.

"A ward that also shields?" Marcus asked, curious despite himself. "Able to rebound or even absorb an attack?"

Em shrugged. She didn't know if a wizard could create such a thing, but Marcus seemed to find the notion intriguing rather than frightening.

"I was actually wondering if Destiny would sense your presence if you cross her ward. Does a wizard have to use magic for another to recognise him? Or might your presence alone alert her of your proximity before we can even approach her?"

Marcus' countenance seemed to darken in the play of shadows from the fire, but he considered her question with an air of concern. *Perhaps I've finally given him something to think about besides my inherent frailty,* she thought, though she found no satisfaction at having potentially breached that barrier.

"Can you discern the location of her ward without giving yourself away?" asked Stefan from across the fire, and Em only now realised that everyone had followed their discussion. She wondered how long since the King and his Captain had shifted their attention from deciding routes to this matter of magic. "Our plans come to naught if they know where we are."

Marcus stared across the blaze for a moment in silence, his posture rigid. He finally heaved a sigh that seemed to deflate him, his shoulders rounding slightly as his head bowed forward.

"I can search for your wizard's ward, but I cannot guarantee that that search will not trigger a warning, not without knowing the exact nature of the ward. It is unlikely a mere search will trigger anything, but your wizard has apparently accomplished some surprising things."

"Why do you keep calling her 'our wizard'?" Dari asked suddenly. "Why don't you ever call her Destiny, or even acknowledge that she's a woman?"

Em looked at the young guard in surprise as she realised the truth of his words. Had she not noticed the wizard's careful phrasing whenever he spoke of Destiny because she had allowed herself to become so wrapped up in his condescension? She wondered if Marcus himself had even noticed the distinction, but a quick glance at his angry scowl suggested he had chosen his words consciously.

"Women do not become wizards," Marcus sneered. "They lack the capacity. But you obviously have a problem with someone claiming a wizard's power. This presents a dilemma for me, one I have difficulty reconciling. So I will call this problem *your wizard.*

"And I will not name the Girl Destiny, a title she has so obviously contrived to give herself more importance. Names have power only if they have meaning, and I will not allow hers to have meaning."

Em shot a disturbed glance toward Prichard, saw her own

274

worry reflected in the look he returned. So, she had not imagined the stress Marcus had put upon the word Girl. Or if she had, then Prichard had imagined it too. Could Marcus *know* Destiny? And if so, what ramifications would follow?

Suddenly, the man's aversion to Em took on a new and more disturbing meaning for the librarian. Did he disdain her sex because of the actions of a young Girl against a powerful wizard many years ago?

Or did Em read too much into this?

They would need to keep a closer eye on Wizard Marcus until they knew more.

In the meantime, she again allowed herself to fade into the background as the men around her discussed first how Marcus might avoid triggering Destiny's ward, and then went back to deciding which road to follow on the morrow. She had enough to occupy her mind, and not much to add to the conversation. If they wanted her opinion on anything, she trusted Prichard to call her attention back from the depths of her thoughts.

Chapter 28

Ambrose rode hard, knowing time rode against him. A plan had emerged late that evening five nights ago as the fire built by Sim and Malcolm—Ambrose had reconciled himself to using the nobleman's given name, though he still found himself uneasy when referring to the King as anything other than Sire or Majesty—burned itself to ashes. After some pointed questions, Wizard Marcus had stalked off to his tent, the rest of them gradually retiring to their own rest. Ambrose had stood first watch, so he had witnessed the shadow he knew as Malcolm move to sit next to Stefan's tent, the larger bulk of Fred joining him. Ambrose didn't hear the words, nor see any gestures—he watched outside the camp, trusting his Captain to watch within—but he knew these three worked on a more concrete plan for the days to follow, and that the morning would bring a new course of action.

It in fact brought three.

Ambrose rode now, the last to have left camp. He knew only that the other two groups needed more time to get into place; he didn't know where, nor what activity would occur in those places. Malcolm had made that very clear when Ambrose discovered the man waiting for him at the end of his watch. Dari had relieved him, and Ambrose had just crawled into the tent the two shared to find the nobleman already waiting within. Ambrose briefly wondered if Dari had received his own instructions before taking his watch.

"We split up in the morning," Malcolm told him in the black

confines of the small shelter, a disembodied voice in the dark. "One group rides with the King, another with me. Neither company will know the route of the other." Ambrose remembered nodding, even though the other man couldn't possibly have seen. "You, however, have your own path to take, and you'll take it alone."

"And will I know my own destination?" he had asked quietly, eliciting a low chuckle in return.

"Yours is the only destination we all know," Malcolm had replied. "You ride for Tox's farm, and the camp we left behind."

He did so now, fully a day behind the other two groups. Malcolm had only told him that the others needed the opportunity to get into position, but that Ambrose would nevertheless require time to marshal their forces.

"You must have Sir Edvard and those loyal to Stefan in place and ready for the King's signal. If you move too soon, the Prince's mercenaries along with those mind-altered to follow Whillim will more easily and quickly discover you, but if you wait too long, you leave the King exposed. So ride with care."

The sun followed behind his shoulder now as Ambrose urged his mount along the road that would take him back to the farm where he had spent time as a child. *Travelling a circle,* he thought to himself, having no one else to share the thought with save the horse.

At least until he neared the cut-off that would take him to the fallow field and the King's meagre army. He reined in when the soldier dressed as a farmer carrying a staff hailed him from beside the road, and regarded the other man with trepidation. If the Prince had subverted anyone in the encampment, Ambrose's mission would end quickly.

"Where you heading?" the sentry posing as a farmer asked.

"To meet some friends," Ambrose replied cautiously. He watched the man closely when he added, "Emily's perfect memory led me here."

The man's posture relaxed minutely.

"'Bout fucking time," he grumbled, the staff leaning casually now against his shoulder. He jerked his chin in the direction of the entrance Ambrose had used when leading Sir Castel's men here ... he thought back; more than three weeks ago now? Not so long, and yet an eternity. "Knights're anxious for word. You know the way?"

Ambrose felt a frown flicker across his face. Then he followed the soldier's no-so-subtle glance to the nearest windbreak tree protecting the field and saw a second soldier, arrow nocked and aimed at Ambrose.

"We're tired of waiting, but we're not stupid," the man with the staff said, a small smile quirking his lips. "If you've come to betray us, you won't make it out alive."

Ambrose nodded.

"Fair enough," he said and squeezed his thighs to nudge the horse forward. The sentry on the road let out a redwing's trill, a call quickly answered from somewhere in the depths of the fallow field, alerting the camp to the new arrival. Ambrose passed between two archers, knew others must also guard the way in, though they remained hidden. Soon enough, another man approached, though Ambrose knew no one would see this soldier from the road. Sir Edvard knew how to establish a hidden base. Still, tension sang along Ambrose's spine, tightening his neck and shoulders. Wizard Destiny only had to enspell one man to put them all at risk.

The soldier hailed him, bidding him to dismount. Ambrose thought he recognised him from Castel's garrison, but couldn't recall a name. He swung down off his horse and led the mount in the soldier's wake as they made their way over churned earth toward the cluster of tents Ambrose now saw. Perhaps two dozen more than when he had left with the King, though others might stretch closer to the stream.

A young man trotted out from one of these tents, offering to take his horse. Ambrose recognised him as Rastov, Castel's squire. Ambrose reluctantly surrendered the reins as the knight himself pushed back the tent flap. Ambrose read relief in Castel's eyes, mixed with anticipation. This man and those in the camp had waited three weeks for tidings. Although the King had allowed for a longer absence, Ambrose well understood how soldiers anticipating battle might chafe at any delay, even an expected one.

Castel's gaze flitted briefly past Ambrose to the empty space behind him, then came back to rest on his face.

"Scouting ahead?" he asked.

Ambrose grunted something non-committal in replay. Castel laughed.

"Still cautious, I see," noted the knight. "A good trait. Come,

278

we'll take your tidings to Sir Edvard."

So saying, he led Ambrose further into the encampment. Sir Edvard stood waiting outside another tent, only slightly larger than Castel's. A pole held open the entrance, allowing the afternoon light access. The older knight acknowledged Castel and met Ambrose's stare. With a curt nod, he gestured behind him.

"Let's take this inside, gentlemen," Edvard said. "There's room enough." To his own squire, he said, "Bring some ale. I have a feeling our guest might have a bit of a thirst." Then he turned to make his way into the confines of his tent, expecting the others to follow. At a gesture from Castel, Ambrose went first. The tent had a cot pushed against one side, leaving room for a small folding table and two collapsible stools.

"What news?" Edvard demanded once the three men had settled, Castel electing to perch on the edge of the cot while Edvard and Ambrose took the stools.

"I think reassurances first," Castel said. "As I recall, Ambrose will stay quite taciturn until we can assure him that we consider King Stefan's safety and the security of the realm to be of tantamount importance. And rightly so, too."

"Indeed," Edvard nodded his approval. "What assurances will you accept? A reminder of our fealty? Details of our escape and recruitment? Platitudes to our noble King?"

Ambrose's tension spiked at that last. Did the knight offer mockery or trust? He couldn't read him, and that uncertainty set him on edge.

"Ale first, then," Castel said at a motion from the entrance, the words almost enough to distract Ambrose. But he sensed a larger presence than that of Edvard's squire. Ambrose leapt to his feet, the stool tumbling in his wake. He spun, hand to sword hilt, blade already partly drawn. He felt the slap of a slight weight against his chest.

Ambrose completed his turn, weapon drawn, and glared at the craggy soldier who had entered behind him, but the man made no move against him. Instead, he uttered something guttural, and Ambrose found himself lowering his sword as he fought off a wave of dizziness. He glanced down, noted what had struck his chest. An amulet of some sort, off-bronze in colour, the chain suspending it around his neck of middling quality. He brushed his fingers across it lightly, then glanced up, waiting to see what sort of attack this newcomer represented. The man stared at him impassively, then spoke, his voice rough, as though used to shouting orders.

"Where is the renegade?"

Ambrose shook his head, fighting an impulse to answer. He didn't know this man, couldn't afford any mistakes that would harm—

Who would they harm?

He had come to make a report, something the King needed done. Yet the details had become strangely hazy. Why couldn't he bring his mission to mind?

"Who are you?" he asked instead, trying to concentrate, to put his fractured mind back together. He knew something terrible had just happened, but he didn't know what.

"Milos, of the King's guard," the man replied. "You know me."

"King's guard," Ambrose murmured. He should know this man, then; they both served the same King. Yet for a horrifying moment, Ambrose didn't remember the name of the King. *Whillim is King.* A stray thought that helped solidify his scattered memories. "King Whillim," he said softly.

Interestingly, Milos' hooded gaze showed the slightest hint of relief before the man masked his emotions again.

"Of course," Milos confirmed. "Now, where is the renegade? What did he instruct?"

What renegade? Ambrose wanted to ask. Without conscious direction, his mouth started to answer the question, as though it knew what Milos wanted, even as his mind struggled against an invisible barrier.

"Assemble the troops and wait to the north for the signal."

"When?"

"Tomorrow, at nightfall," Ambrose heard himself reply. He put a hand to his temple as a shaft of pain shot through his head, sending red and purple lightning bolts jagging across his vision. His sword tumbled to the floor of the tent as his hands fought to keep his head from splitting apart in agony.

The face of his King kept wavering in his mind's eye as a foreign voice thundered *Whillim is King* again and again. Ambrose clamped his teeth shut on a scream, but a moan escaped his throat anyway.

"What's wrong with him?" he heard one of the knights ask, the fact that he couldn't tell which a distant concern.

"He's fighting the truth," Milos said, a hard bite to his voice. "I need to get him to the castle quickly. Destiny will set him right and we'll learn what he knows."

Destiny, Ambrose thought. The wizard they had gone to Bakaana to defeat. *They who? Who came with me to Bakaana?* He tried to think past the pain.

He remembered Emily describing the Destiny Seat, the little librarian so earnestly trying to help them find a way to counter the wizard's spell. A spell that altered memory. The memory of a king. Ambrose gasped as he fought against the memory trying to intrude. He knew in that moment, with absolute clarity, that he must do everything in his power to keep out of the clutches of Wizard Destiny.

Milos took that choice away from him with a swift punch to the side of the head. The blinding pain ironically faded with that punch as Ambrose slid into unconsciousness.

He didn't notice when the mercenary captain removed the lesser Focus of Destiny's memory-altering amulet from around his neck.

***

No plan ever worked perfectly—Prichard well knew that from experience—but this one hadn't yet gone even remotely as expected. At least not after the second day. And that greatly vexed Dalasham's master spy. It worried him too, though he kept both thoughts from crossing his face.

It had seemed a viable course of action, splitting up their resources as they had. Ambrose would bring the King's army into position even as Prichard used Wizard Marcus' presence to draw out Destiny, allowing Stefan an opportunity to take back his throne as their enemies stood distracted.

Following his third of the plan, Prichard had ridden due east with the wizard, Sergeant Sim and Corporal Joseph accompanying them. They would ride until Marcus sensed Destiny's ward, and then they would blaze through it, Marcus making sure that, however this particular ward worked, the Prince's wizard would know exactly where a rival had crossed her boundary. He would ensure he had Destiny's attention and thereby draw her out. If they could distract Destiny's notice from other incursions heading toward Riverbend, they had a chance. She would either send out men to find this interloper, or, if luck truly favoured them, would come investigate herself, diverting her resources out of the city and far from Stefan.

Dangerous for Prichard's party, a wizard and three warriors against whatever arsenal Destiny and Whillim sent against them, but essential to divert attention from the real infiltration, buying Stefan time to slip into the tunnels. He didn't think Whillim would have them killed; the Prince preferred subverting minds to permanently eliminating them, as far as Prichard had seen. But bought soldiers—especially frustrated ones—weren't always careful and 'accidents' happened. The price a loyal man sometimes paid.

The plan did rely a great deal on Marcus' skill, but Prichard understood that the man had some sort of vendetta against Destiny, though the wizard would no doubt deny it. For whatever reason (and the spy felt confident that at least part of that reason resided with Destiny's brother Nathan, and Destiny's actions when she escaped her enslavement all those years ago), Marcus had made it his goal to bring Destiny down. To do so, he had to draw her out, bring her within his sphere of influence. Using that thirst for domination, Prichard knew Marcus would act out his part of the plan to the best of his ability.

Destiny could not fail to notice Marcus' presence; they had but to wait for her response.

Prichard had not expected silence to stand as her answer.

"You're certain she knows you're here?" Jo asked, the same question, in one form or another, each of them had asked over the last three days as they circled the southern edge of Riverbend.

Marcus scowled. He had already evinced uncertainty, fear, anger, confusion, and disgust at Destiny's lack of reaction, and at the questioning of his companions. Now the wizard had sunk into a sullen resignation.

"You're certain she has any real power at all?" Marcus snapped back. "Any wizard could see me standing here, emitting random bursts of magic, potentially casting debilitating spells, yet this one shows no reaction."

"The ward existed," Sim countered. "You damn near fell off your horse when you smashed through it."

"That doesn't make it *her* ward."

"Someone cast it, and someone has altered memories," Sim insisted. "That I can personally attest to."

"Perhaps she doesn't see you as a threat," Prichard murmured, using Emily's tactic against this prickly wizard. Prey on his pride, his ego, and Marcus would push himself to prove his prowess.

"Or she fears to face me," Marcus replied, his chest puffed out. "Some wizards only have one or two spells that they do well, making a name based on a novelty without any real strength to back them up. Perhaps your wizard has only mastered this trick, worked through a Focus, and has nothing in reserve to face one such as I."

Ego, or truth, Prichard wondered, eyes narrowed in thought. He suspected the former, recalling Emily's words. *Destiny has taken a position you all feel reserved for a man. We live in a world that believes a woman doesn't have the strength or capacity to achieve what Destiny has.* Granted, none of them (with the possible exception of Marcus) had ever met or even seen Destiny, but by all reports, people feared her. Sim had reported at least two seasoned soldiers admitting their fear of the woman, as had the mercenaries Emily had overheard in the library. A wizard with only one or two spells under her belt didn't elicit such a reaction, suggesting that Destiny did not lack for strength.

Prichard didn't believe a lack of reserve kept Destiny from seeking out an intruding wizard, nor did he think a reluctance to counter a like ability stayed her hand.

Stefan rules Dalasham. He formed the thought in his mind, as he had every morning since they parted forces, reassuring himself that, whatever else had happened, Destiny had not yet found and eliminated the King. That possibility terrified him more than encountering a wizard who thought so little of their incursion.

"We have little choice," Prichard said, turning his mount to face the distant castle. The others ranged around him. "If we can't get Destiny to come to us, then we must go to her. For whatever reason, she has chosen to ignore Marcus' display of opposition. So we'll force her to acknowledge our presence." He glanced to the wizard. Did they ride so openly still, screaming their presence through Marcus' magic, or should they try subterfuge now? What would aid the King more?

He wished desperately that he knew how Stefan's group fared. Lacking that knowledge, he could only proceed as he thought best.

"Let's ride for Dalasmar with what secrecy we can, gentlemen. Once we reach the castle's gates, Marcus will unleash his wrath. We'll see if Destiny dares ignore us then."

Marcus grinned, a startling intensity firing his eyes. Jo and Sim simply nodded, checking their swords, and waited for Prichard to lead the way. Prichard pushed his horse forward, fear lying heavy upon him though he hid it behind a shroud of confidence.

He hoped Stefan's part of the plan had unfolded with more clarity.

***

"They're watching him, and he's not happy about it," Dari reported after slipping back into the secure cellar they had discovered. Fred had led him, the King, and Em here late last night after a harrowing but ultimately uneventful journey through a rather narrow and fully functional sewer tunnel that left the quartet covered in pungent slime and filth. They had gambled that the guard rotations had not altered significantly at either outlet of the sanitary system since the Prince had taken control. That chance had paid off, allowing the four of them to steal through the dark streets of the north-western quarter of Riverbend to this unoccupied storefront with its attached cellar. Avoiding patrols, Dari had brought water from a nearby fountain so that they could wash off the worst of the foul-smelling sludge before morning and the next part of their plan.

They had ridden out at the same time as Prichard, but soon parted ways as the nobleman continued straight east while the King's party turned more northerly. With luck, the wizard would divert attention, giving them time to infiltrate the castle while hopefully avoiding Destiny's gaze. Once in, they would either try to take the Prince, the wizard, or the wizard's Focus. To attempt the latter, they had to know where to find the Destiny Seat, and for that, they needed someone who had seen it.

Which led to Dari's excursion this morning. Anyone who had sat in the Seat could likely lead them to it, but they would need someone who might help them without raising an alarm. With

284

that in mind, they took an even larger gamble, sending Dari, as the most expendable and unknown member of their little group, to search for one specific man.

"Any way of confronting him without notice?" Fred asked. "Or of determining if Sim's conjecture is right?"

When Sim had first rejoined them at Tox's farm, he had described Faulk's behaviour as hesitant, as though not entirely sure about his memory. Speaking with Sim again before they parted, the Sergeant had confirmed his initial reaction.

"He seemed less sure of his new memory than Hen did, or any of the men-at-arms that took him," Sim had said. "It's anyone's guess whether that means he really was fighting the magic, or that something hasn't happened in the meantime to solidify him to the Prince's cause."

Dari shook his head in reply to his Captain's query.

"The watchers suggest they don't trust him, and I doubt they're going to let him out of their sight, but I don't know if that speaks to Faulk breaking from Destiny's control or just to general suspicion."

"How many watch him?" the King wanted to know.

"One makes himself obvious, and another keeps to the shadows."

Em watched the King as he considered this new information. Then he exchanged a glance with Fred, and the Captain nodded, his hand brushing the hilt of his sword.

"Lead him here," Fred ordered. "Lose his tails if you can, but we'll be ready if you can't."

Dari gave a crisp salute, looking very much the soldier despite his labourer's garb, then slipped back out into the streets of Riverbend.

Fred had surprised Em, and likely Dari as well, when he explained their portion of the plan the night after they had left Lord Prichard. She had thought the Captain took the King to safety, away from any possibility of either capture or danger from Prince or wizard, while Prichard and Marcus would attempt to bind that wizard. She hadn't imagined they intended to steal into the city, and then to the castle itself—she distinctly recalled Stefan believing that too dangerous, if not impossible—especially not alone when a small army awaited their arrival to the west in Goodman Tox's field. That Ambrose would bring that army to reinforce them hardly mattered if the enemy took the King in the midst of his clandestine mission and thereby changed loyalties irrevocably. She didn't understand their reasoning for this undertaking now, or rather, she didn't understand why the King would risk himself to see it done, nor why Fred would allow, even encourage, this course of action. But then, she didn't have to understand the reasons; she just had to get them to and then through the hidden passages of Dalasmar Castle. King and Captain kept their reasons close to their chests. The fewer who knew the full plan, the less risk to the realm, and if either Stefan or Fred (or even Lord Prichard, whom Em suspected knew at least as much of the intention behind this folly) fell prey to Destiny's device, no reasons would matter anyway, for the Prince would have won.

Or so it seemed to Em, as they waited for Dari to return with a man who would either aid them or betray them. She supposed time would tell whether they embarked on brilliance or disaster.

***

Faulk didn't know what kept drawing him to the vicinity of the Swallow's Flight on his routine rounds, but when he found himself glancing into the alley next to the tavern on this chilly and overcast day in mid-morning, he saw something unexpected, and briefly wondered whether he had waited for this moment.

Distinctly aware of Drummund's shadowing presence, made the more obvious since that day when the farmer had recognised Emily's picture, Faulk kept his expression neutral, his gait even, betraying no sign that he had seen a familiar face staring from the darkened alley. Sergeant Darius knew Faulk had seen him though, and gave a brisk hand signal known only to the King's guards before the young man drew back. Faulk maintained his measured pace even as his heart sped up. No one had used that language of hand signing with Faulk for nigh on a month; no one trusted him enough since the day the false King had appeared on the throne.

A barely noticed raking of fingernails across a raw scab on the back of his left hand sent a tingle of fire to his brain and a small smear of blood to his fingers, quickly rubbed away, allowing even that thought against Whillim to stand today as he changed course.

Faulk might find himself constantly drawn near the Swallow, but once in the neighbourhood, he seldom followed the same route, making this alteration unsurprising to those who followed. Unlike every other day however, Faulk now had an actual destination, or at least someone he hoped would provide a clear path. He passed the alley and walked to the next street, to where Dari had indicated he would wait.

Rounding the corner of the market square, Faulk caught the next signal before Dari faded into the milling crowd, vanishing before Drummund could clear the line of the building. Even as Faulk continued to follow the silent instructions, he wondered at his easy acceptance of the Sergeant's directions, but for the first time since the night of fire, he felt right, unconflicted, as though duty no longer warred with conscience. If he walked blindly into a trap because of this sense of liberation, then he did so with an open heart.

He hoped to finally learn the truth, perhaps even put a face and name with the hazy image that brought him pain. Otherwise, he would accept what fate had in store at the hands of a man purported to run with a renegade. Either way, Faulk prayed he would find an end to his enduring agony.

After the next set of twists and turns, Faulk understood that Dari had hoped to lose Faulk's unwanted escort. He also knew, based on his own attempts to throw the mercenary behind him off his trail, that Drummund would not easily relinquish his task. Faulk signalled this at the next intersection and received a firm nod in response. A final instruction relayed caught Faulk by surprise, but he followed orders regardless.

The street ended at a T-junction. Faulk turned right and took off at a run. He heard a curse behind him when Drummund reached the corner, then the pounding of boots as the mercenary gave chase. Without pause, Faulk aimed for the cellar of an abandoned shop, its door left ajar. He wrenched the door open and leapt down a short flight of stairs, knowing Dari waited below, hoping Drummund would follow.

He whirled at the bottom, drawing his knife in the process, noting the swirl of motion that indicated others lay in wait with Dari. By the flame of a lantern and what light oozed down from the cellar door, Faulk saw a young man who, after a second's inspection proved not a man at all, but Emily in men's clothing, her hair hidden beneath a cap. She held a dagger, her wide eyes watching him without flinching. In front of her, his entire being focused on the door, stood the large bulk of Captain Frederick, sword in hand. Dari flanked him, similarly armed. Faulk nearly wept with relief despite the fierce countenance of his commanding officer, but the other figure he now glimpsed in the shadowed far corner stole his attention.

The hazy image often hovering at the edge of his awareness now solidified into the physical form of a person regarding him without emotion, his own sword held ready. The man stood tall, imposing, piercing blue eyes staring from above a concealing dark blond beard lightly streaked with grey. *This is the man I serve,* Faulk suddenly thought in triumph, right before a black wave of agony slammed into him, dropping him to his knees. Faulk screamed even as he turned his knife to slash across his left biceps, forcing out one pain with another. Breathing heavily, struggling to regain his vision, he only peripherally heard the commotion at the entrance announcing the arrival of Drummund. *I need to help them,* he thought, but mind and body no longer answered his call.

Memory flared, bright and harsh. Fleeing into a dark tunnel with a king, fighting hired soldiers amidst a night of flame and smoke to cut a way to freedom for his liege—*for a renegade*, a foreign insistence screamed in his head. The day he earned the right to serve as King's Guard, that king wearing the face of the man in the corner ... *the face of Whillim* ... drinking to the health of King and country at Swallow's Flight with his comrades—again, that king wearing two faces as true memory and magic collided, each vying for supremacy. Again and again, flashes of his life played out in Faulk's mind, the duality of conflicting memory sucking at his sanity with waves of pain. He no longer saw the room around him, nor the people within, and could only trust that his Captain had things under control, for if Drummund won, Faulk knew he himself would lose more than just his mind.

So he fought the only battle he could, shrieking defiance against a wizard's spell in his head, words he didn't hear falling from his lips. Then he heard a tiny voice at his ear as he knelt helplessly on the ground, a sentence that somehow swept a balming blanket of rightness through him.

"His name is Stefan," whispered the angel.

Faulk finally relaxed, allowing his exhausted brain to slip into blessed darkness as it sought to rest and recover the shattered strands of his sanity.

***

Although Stefan had agreed with, even endorsed, Prichard's plan, he still knew fear. In part for his men and himself, but mostly for his kingdom. If Whillim captured any of his people, Stefan knew they would fight until they didn't know better, their true will broken by Destiny's magic. But if Stefan fell prey to the Destiny Seat, all of Dalasham would suffer under the selfish rule of a petty man more interested in the luxuries kingship afforded him than in the governance of the land to the benefit of all men, not just himself and his favourites. Willi would let the land wither while putting taxes toward such endeavours as hunting and parties and other frivolities that amused him. He had never understood what the privilege and burden of kingship truly entailed.

Even with this knowledge, Stefan had still agreed that their best course of action now put Stefan in precisely this location; a cellar in the middle of Riverbend, waiting for a man who would either lead them to the source of Willi's stolen power, or betray them as a victim of that power. A huge risk, but still the least dangerous of the three roads their little group had taken five days past.

Ambrose rode into a situation that could potentially lead to disaster should even one soldier in Edvard's camp have fallen under Destiny's spell, while Prichard rode at the heart of a diversion devised to draw the attention of a powerful wizard. Stefan, waiting in the darkness of a forgotten basement for the opportunity to infiltrate his own castle through hidden passageways, faced the least danger.

Relatively speaking. After all, he did wait for the arrival of a man known to have fallen under Destiny's control, likely followed by one or more mercenaries whose prey had escaped them for a month.

The cellar door opened, admitting what mid-morning light filtered down between the buildings, and a man in an unadorned tunic and trousers. Dari hurled himself through and down the few stairs, the door left ajar behind him.

"Two," he said on an in-drawn breath, numbering those following the man they wanted. Fred, poised to the left of the stairs with weapon ready gave a curt nod of acknowledgement, while Dari positioned himself to the right. Emily stood behind Fred, stance balanced and dagger steady in her hand as Fred had taught her. Stefan hadn't wanted to put her so close to the danger, but the cellar didn't have a lot of room, and the little librarian had voiced a decent rejoinder with her simple phrase: "Why have me train if I can't use the skill?" Stefan found he didn't have a plausible answer, at least not one she would want to hear.

Stefan himself stood as far to the side as possible. While his skill far outweighed Emily's, Fred had adamantly refused to allow his King close to the entrance, "in the unlikely event that an errant weapon should mar his royal personage." For such a large man with his ferocious reputation, Captain Frederick of the King's Guard did have a way with words sometimes. Stefan would cover Faulk, whatever the man's intentions, while Fred and Dari concentrated on what followed.

Above, the door fell open again and Stefan watched Faulk leap through, whirling as he drew a knife. His light brown hair, usually well kept in a sleek tail, appeared scraggly, untidy, a snarl of lank knots pulled haphazardly behind his head, accenting a thin face grown gaunt. Stefan watched his man take quick stock of those waiting within; the startled acknowledgement of Emily, a strange relief when his eyes lighted on Fred, and then, when he turned to see Stefan—

The scream that dropped Faulk to his knees, his knife turned inward to slice across his own arm to match several other older cuts, startled Stefan. The King had an instant to wonder if Faulk had intended that shout as a diversion away from the other man who had followed him through the door—the mercenary quickly dispatched by Fred—but then recognised that Faulk no longer really saw this room. His eyes blank, expression anguished, Faulk pressed his fists against his temples, knife hilt still clutched tight in his right hand, a vein pulsing like a small snake trying to escape near his eye. He finally squeezed his eyes shut as tears streamed down a ragged face, a tormented moan escaping from a jaw clenched tight. A second mercenary had hesitated in the doorway at Faulk's outburst, and Stefan peripherally saw Dari spring up the stairs to grab the man before he could flee and raise the alarm. Stefan left his guard to it, crouching before Faulk, though careful to keep out of range should this startling display hide a devious purpose.

The moan faded to a whimper as Faulk rocked back and forth, his whole frame trembling. A trickle of blood dribbled down his chin from where he had bitten his lip. The rasping sound Stefan heard resolved itself into Faulk's hoarse and broken whisper, words that sent a shiver through the King.

"Whillim is King, false King. Don't serve. Protect, protect. Can't see. Why can't I see? Face in shadow. Serving false King. Whillim is King. This is the man I serve. I serve him. Who is he?"

Stefan glanced up at an unexpected motion by his side. Across the room, Fred stood over the unmoving bodies of the two mercenaries—unconscious or dead, Stefan didn't know—while Dari secured the doors again, shutting out the daylight, leaving only the lantern to illuminate the cellar. Emily had sheathed her dagger and knelt now next to Faulk. Stefan made to stay her actions, but something in her gentle gaze as she concentrated on his incoherent guard made him hesitate. Without touching Faulk, she leaned close, supporting her weight on her hands as she put her lips next to his ear. Very softly in the quiet of the cellar, the only other sound Faulk's harsh whispers, she spoke.

"His name is Stefan," she said.

To Stefan's shock, Faulk suddenly relaxed, his whispers silenced, his rocking eased. The man smiled, eyes still closed, then slumped to the floor.

Stefan stared down at him, then over to meet Emily's moist gaze.

"What the hell," Fred demanded in a low voice behind them, "just happened?"

"I think Sim was right," Emily said, her gaze sliding back to the prone man. She gently removed the knife from his lax fist and slid it back into its sheath. "He fought the memory, but he didn't know the truth to replace it. He didn't react until he saw the King's face, the 'face in shadow,' he said. Then Destiny's magic tried to force him to recognise something he knew as false in his heart. At a guess, I'd say the spell took Stefan's name and face, but Faulk clung to the belief that something about the Prince didn't fit, and his mind kept trying to reconcile the two things. See his arms and hands? The cuts, old and new?"

"A reminder?" Stefan asked, dismayed at the number of wounds he could see. "To tell him something was wrong?"

"A way to deal with pain," Emily countered. "I've read of cases where a person tries to overcome one kind of pain with another. He seemed fine, ready to fight even, until he saw you. We used to have a librarian who would get intense migraines with the spring storms. Faulk looked like him at his worst, only more so, and his first thought when he felt that pain was to cut himself, as though trying to re-channel the pain so he could think."

"So Destiny's spell uses pain to reinforce itself?" Dari asked.

Emily shrugged.

"For Faulk anyway. At least, that's what it looked like to me. I wonder if he's an anomaly, though. If everyone reacts this way, it seems the Prince and Wizard Destiny would have no time for anything other than reinforcing their lie."

"So how did you end his pain?" Fred wanted to know. "Did you figure out how to break the spell?"

"I just answered his question," she said with a small shake of her head. "Destiny stole the face and name of the King. Seeing Stefan's face triggered the pain; I simply added the name. Faulk's mind did the rest. As to whether it has truly affected Destiny's spell, we can't know until he regains consciousness."

"Which we need to happen sooner rather than later," Stefan said with a sigh, lowering himself to sit now that the danger seemed to have passed. "He looks like he's gone through hell since last we saw him, but we don't have a lot of time here. We need to get to the tunnels, and we need him to tell us where to go from there. Thoughts on how to do that?"

"Easier on his feet than lugging him around," Fred said, staring down at the man from across the cellar. "Draw less attention too. Don't know how long until someone misses these two," he absently nudged one of the mercenaries with a boot, "or even Faulk for that matter."

"Or if anyone spotted our flight," Dari added, crouching next to Stefan. "I kept it quiet up to the last, but if someone saw four men running through the streets—"

"Three soldiers chasing one man," Emily interrupted, gesturing at Faulk's uniform. "Even before the Prince's men roamed the streets instead of the King's, seeing the guard give chase to a commoner wouldn't elicit much comment. People tend to overlook any commotion that might draw similar attention upon themselves."

"True enough," Fred agreed. "But let's not take that chance. How far to the nearest tunnel entrance?"

Emily glanced up. She had drawn a rough sketch of the tunnel system into and through the castle back at Tox's farm, but her memory could locate what they needed faster than the time required for either Fred or Stefan to examine the map. They had brought her with them for that very reason.

"Within the city walls?" she asked. Fred nodded. They stood in enough danger without risking further exposure by retreating back through any gates that led beyond Riverbend. "A stable just outside the Merchant's Quarter, southwestern end of the compound."

"No," a faint voice croaked. Surprised, Stefan's gaze shot down to Faulk. Eyes still squeezed shut, the guard slowly lifted his arm, pushing the back of his palm against his forehead. "She suspects that one."

Stefan traded a puzzled frown with Fred, then Emily.

"Explain," Fred finally said.

"Had to show her where we came out near the forges," Faulk whispered. "She saw the marks. King's room too, and I think the library. Milos sent men-at-arms to find similar marks in the castle. They have some of them watched, though they don't know I know. But she gave those of us on patrol a list of places in the city to watch. Stable's on that list."

Fred swore, a creative string of profanity that Stefan agreed with wholeheartedly.

"How many places on that list?" Emily demanded, her face pale.

"Four," replied Faulk. "Stable, forges, shop next to south Farmer's Market, and a rock in the west Common's Garden."

"The cardinal points on the compass," Emily nodded, chewing her lip. "Nowhere else?"

Faulk shook his head, then grimaced, as though the motion had hurt.

"That leaves us fewer options," she said, meeting Stefan's

gaze. "But still a chance."

He nodded, acknowledging both her words and her caution. Wise not to reveal too much to Faulk. He might have escaped Destiny's magic, but he also might seek to lead them into a trap, or gain information. Impossible to trust him, despite their need of his assistance. Caution served them best, even as an inadequate shield.

"Can you stand?" Stefan asked, his regard upon Faulk once more.

Faulk slitted his eyes to peer up at Stefan. He blanched, shut them tight, and swallowed hard. Then he sat up and pushed to his knees, head hanging low with tendrils of hair floating free of their confines, arms trembling with the effort. With a grunt, he regained his feet and glanced over at Fred. Gave a small nod.

"Pain's less if I don't look at—" A shudder and shake of his head. "If I follow my Captain."

Fred gave Stefan a level stare as the King also stood.

"We can't do this," the Captain said. "Too great a risk he'll stumble, give us away."

"Then tie me up, or better yet, kill me," Faulk said in an oddly flat voice. "Because I can't go on like this, Captain. Serving a petty little tyrant who has no right to sit his arrogant arse on the throne." He gave a slight gasp, then rubbed at the slash he had made in his arm earlier. Using the pain to focus, Emily had surmised, and Stefan judged it probable now. "Use me if you can," he went on as though nothing had interrupted him. "Kill me if you can't. I have no intention of betraying you, but I don't know if I have the luxury of certainty in that intention. She's stolen part of my mind, Captain, though less than others. It's why they watched me. But I can't guarantee her curse won't blind me with pain at the wrong moment. Ask me what you need to know, then kill me. It's the only way to keep," he indicated Stefan without turning to look, "... the man I truly serve ... safe."

Silence as they all stared at Faulk. Stefan could only see his profile—Faulk kept his face averted enough to avoid direct contact with the source of his pain—but the man wore a grim, resigned expression, his jaw set in a hard line. A brave man, fighting a foe he couldn't see, yet ready to lay down his life for someone he could no longer even look at. Pity warred with rage in Stefan's heart. That foul woman would pay for this torment.

"Where is the Destiny Seat?" he demanded, his tone more harsh than he intended.

"In her Sanctum," Faulk answered, visibly checking himself before he could turn to look at Stefan. He stared instead at a spot on the wall about three feet to Stefan's right. "Among the Ambassador suites, directly above the Council Chambers."

"Describe it," Fred said.

"A straight-back chair made of quartz crystal, white with veins of green and pink, sitting ominously in the centre of an otherwise bland room. Once she puts you in it, you can't move until she allows it."

"Do you know how it works?" asked Emily.

"She touches the crown of the chair and it begins to glow, gold to rose to white. After that, people think differently." He stopped, jaw clenched tight and eyes closing on a grimace. His fists shook at his side and he held his breath a moment before it quickened into ragged pants. After a brief time, he mastered himself enough to inhale deeply, his face grey as he struggled to open his eyes and focus again. "And that's something I'm not supposed to think about," he admitted.

"Is her control so poor?" Fred questioned.

Faulk shook his head.

"Sadly not, Captain. Only on me, or at least, I haven't noticed anyone else suffer with their conscience like this."

"Has she used her device on you more than once?" Emily wondered. "You said they watched you because they knew you somehow resisted her spell to a degree. Has she never tried to rectify that?"

His whole body shuddered.

"She planned to, I think, but circumstances arose to delay that. And, I think, King Whillim enjoys my suffering too much."

Stefan let that sit on the air a moment. He would like to think his brother didn't have that level of cruelty—just watching Faulk in this short time, trying to deal with conflicting emotions and memories, made him want to help the man, find a way to ease his malaise—but more and more, Stefan found he couldn't excuse Willi's behaviour.

"What circumstances?" Dari broke the silence.

Faulk closed his eyes again, but not in pain this time. It looked to Stefan more like resignation and defeat. When the

295

soldier parted his lids again, his anguished gaze came to rest on Emily.

"She made me give her your name," he whispered. "I described you as little as possible, but once she had your name, she found others to devise a picture." Watching Emily's face, Stefan saw a shadow of hurt cloud her features as she imagined those others, before compassion erased the thought. "They used my difficulties with Destiny's truth to gauge my reactions, and so, when I saw a man recognise the picture, I tried to hide the fact, which I later realised let them know I had discovered something they wanted to know. That one," he waved contemptuously at one of the motionless mercenaries on the floor, "caught us out and brought us to the wizard. She was not best pleased when I told her Whillim ruled only because of her, and would have put me on the Seat again, but she thought to unbalance me further by learning what the man who saw your picture knew first. After what he said, she lost interest in me."

"What did he say?" Emily asked quietly.

"He described a farm, and a merchant with a sick niece."

"Shit," Fred breathed with agonized emotion.

"Tox," Emily gasped, a hand to her mouth.

"Ambrose," Dari said, eyes wide. "And—"

Stefan held up a hand. Likely useless, but no sense in blurting out what they might not yet have found, unlikely though that seemed.

"What did they find?" he asked, but Faulk shook his head.

"I don't know," his voice pitched tight in frustration. "They didn't trust me before, and less so after that. I've seen nothing but the streets of Riverbend and these two taking turns to make it obvious they've lurked behind me for the last week and a half."

While having the army as backup should he need to call them in would have provided a huge comfort, Stefan had to acknowledge that he couldn't count on it. Which made the goal of this little group of companions all the more urgent.

"We need to concentrate on getting to the castle, then," Stefan said. "On finding a way to either destroy the Destiny Seat, or take Destiny and Willi captive. With luck, Malcolm has diverted Destiny's attention enough that she won't notice us until it's too late." He met Fred's hard stare with firm resolve.

"We end this, one way or another." Fred gave a reluctant nod.

Stefan looked at Emily.

"How close can we get to the Ambassador quarters?"

"Very, Sire, if we can make our way unseen to Kranosohn's Chapel first."

Stefan nodded and turned back to Fred.

"Make it happen, Captain."

"And him?" he asked, staring pointedly at Faulk. Stefan shook his head once, having already resolved to accept responsibility for this burden.

"Bring him." He silenced Faulk's protest with a curt gesture, moving to stand next to the man who couldn't meet his eye. "You serve Dalasham yet soldier. Don't let your King down."

A hesitation, then Faulk drew himself up and dared to bring his gaze as high as Stefan's shoulder. He gave a crisp salute.

"Your man, my Lord, to the utmost of my abilities," he vowed, voice a hoarse rasp.

At a silent command from Fred, Dari moved to flank Faulk. With care, Fred checked the street, then led them from the cellar, Stefan following with Emily, Faulk and Dari trailing. They secured the door as best they could, leaving the mercenaries shut away in the cellar to delay anyone finding the bodies. The leaden sky had birthed a steady drizzle, enabling the companions to hide beneath the hoods of their cloaks without drawing any comment from equally sheltered passersby.

They made their way through the winding streets of Riverbend unmolested to the Chapel of one of the city's earliest rulers. From there, Emily found the hidden entrance near the crypt—the markings hidden within a name—and, with no one in the vicinity to watch their disappearance, the five of them shook off the damp and slipped into darkness, the heavy door to the tunnels grating closed behind them.

Chapter 29

When she first felt the flare of a wizard passing through her ward, Destiny knew a moment of trepidation. She refused to label it fear or even panic, but she thought she knew the flavour of this intruding magic, and its presence unnerved her.

Enough that Whillim had noticed her moment of hesitation as they prepared for a late morning hunt. While Whillim preferred hunting to the rigours of rule, Destiny had hitherto refused such a petty use of her time, but that morning, vexed by the fruitless efforts of nearly a month wasted trying to find an elusive man so she could finally move on to her real goal, she had acquiesced to his suggestion of a morning ride with bow and arrow. Anything to take her mind off her frustration at this point, else she might just kill the next sycophantic courtier to cross her path with their own small agendas in play. Perhaps the clear, crisp air would give her an insight into the mind of an absent King or a cunning librarian, and she could finally leave Whillim to his own games without worrying that he would destroy them all with his mercurial moods.

The presence of another wizard could alter all their plans, so she paid a great deal of attention to that flare in the west.

"What is it?" Whillim asked when she froze, foot to stirrup, gaze far from the commotion of the stable yard.

"A wizard rides a day west of us," she said, slowly lowering her foot to stare out where the sun would set, her heart galloping in her chest even as her horse would not find a matching rhythm this day.

"Is it the one you seek?" he wanted to know, having dismounted and moved to her side so that no others would hear their exchange. His effort to maintain secrecy startled her. Not for the sentiment, but because it demonstrated a level of cunning he rarely bothered to employ. Whillim alone knew her ultimate goal did not lie in helping to subjugate Dalasham to Whillim's rule, that her assistance came as a result of an attempt to perfect a certain spell and not through any desire to change the dynamics on the political world stage. She did not deny that she enjoyed the perks of her position, nor the reputation as a person of importance—she inspired the respect of a few, the fear of many, and both served her for the moment—but neither drove her.

Nathan did, and her desire to see the cruel man who hunted her remember a sister's love instead of a slave's revolt. She needed to make him understand what had forced her hand on a bloody night seven years ago, thereby creating a hated rivalry rather than a united front. She could never know what might have become of the child her mother bore before even weening Destiny had the foul man who sired them not stolen that boy, but she would know what the man he had grown into could accomplish without the blinders of hate and misconception.

She had not thought to face him just yet, though. Concentrating on the swirl of power being hurled at the edge of her ward, Destiny frowned, tasting the malice and intensity of her sire's magic, but it lacked the strength and variety of her brother.

"It's not him," she murmured, heart slowing it's panicked urgency, "but someone who likely trained with him." She remembered those who had followed Nathan in Innosvar, recalled one or two acolytes who studied in the manor alongside him. One of those wizards prowled now inside her ward. Whether they scouted for Nathan, or came of their own accord for another purpose, hardly mattered; she had an errant wizard to deal with.

She had contemplated removing her ward numerous times as a means to widen her search for Emily and Stefan, but had always found an excuse to let it stand. Now she knew a sense of vindication for her procrastination. At least she had warning of the incursion, and time to prepare a course of action.

But even as she devised a plan in her mind, her feet already heading back to the castle, a second stirring, nearly lost in the tumult of the other wizard's casting, intruded on Destiny's awareness. Her head whipped to the north, her hand rising to clutch a gold pendant about her neck as she stumbled to a halt. Whillim, watching from the edge of the stable, moved to her side, his eyes wide and breath quickened as he took in her expression.

Destiny laughed, a surprised sound tinged with admiration.

"Oh, very clever, little girl. Very clever indeed."

"What is it?" Whillim demanded, his voice harsh with excitement. He might not understand the significance of the pendant, but he must have read Destiny's avid attention and guessed the source.

"Emily rides to the north. She's just crossed my ward."

"And Stefan?" the Prince actually shuddered with anticipation. "Does my errant brother ride with her?"

Destiny shook her head.

"I cannot say without time to spy her out, but it seems likely." She glanced in the direction the wizard rode. "Whether they work together with this intruder, or if the two breaches are a coincidence, I have that meddlesome librarian in my sights now, and I will not lose her again."

"It's no coincidence," Whillim stated, echoing Destiny's belief. "They thought to divert us, send us out hunting a wizard while they steal back here." He stared at her, eyes hard and perhaps a little crazed. "Can you deal with him without losing her?"

"I will do better than that," Destiny replied. "Unless the wizard presents himself to the castle, he can fling about as much power as he wants. They won't expect us to ignore this supposed threat, and by the time they figure out that their diversion has failed, neither Stefan nor Emily will have time to escape."

"You're certain?"

"I am," Destiny said with confidence. "Because while they know I can track their wizard, they don't know I can track their librarian."

Whillim's smile might frighten someone of a lesser constitution, but Destiny's grin sent servants hurrying out of the way as the duo returned to the castle, the morning hunt abandoned for larger prey.

Three days later, as the drizzly afternoon stretched toward

evening, Destiny followed the tug of the link she had forged between Emily and her pendant, sensing as the girl wove her way through a warren of tunnels Destiny had yet to penetrate. Her destination, Destiny had determined, lay not far ahead. She wondered where the passage would emerge, so close to her own Sanctum, and where best to place Milos and his mercenaries to snare them the King that had eluded them for so long. She also wondered what they expected to accomplish if they reached the Destiny Seat.

"Soon," she whispered to the eager Prince at her side. "They will likely wait until nightfall."

"Then let us clear their path and await them at their goal," he whispered back. "I will enjoy watching Stefan's face when he realises he has delivered himself into our hands with no means of escape."

***

Although they walked in utter dark, Faulk felt a lightness within he had not known since Milos' men had taken him to Destiny after the riots. Not so long ago, really, and yet an eternity. He still couldn't utter aloud the title of the man he followed as King, nor look directly at him without searing bolts of lightning stabbing across his vision, but in the black of the tunnels, he could convince himself that he had finally found the right path again, the road he had truly chosen to walk six years ago when he had joined the guard. He hadn't freed himself of Destiny's foreign mantra. *Whillim is King* kept intruding at the edges of his awareness, even though he understood the falsity in the statement. But Emily's quiet words, "His name is Stefan," brought an unexpected comfort to overlay the spell corroding his mind, and he held the notion close.

His name is Stefan, he could think with conviction, even as *Whillim is King* maintained his dubious sanity.

They had followed Emily into these dark and dusty corridors, much as they had a month ago, and like on that night of fire, she had only allowed the light of the their lantern from the crypt entrance until they reached a set of narrow stairs leading up, where they paused to share out cold rations. Then she insisted they continue amid the scent of disuse and long neglect without sight.

"If Destiny has found even one of the secret entrances as Faulk suggests, then we must assume she has watchers everywhere," the young woman had said in the confines of the tunnel. "We can't risk alerting anyone to our presence by the betraying glow of a lantern through a watch hole. Once we mount the stairs, we follow my memory alone."

They had prepared for that, Faulk came to understand as Dari had taken a coil of rope from his light pack. Stringing themselves together in a chain, they moved quietly through the enclosed space, Emily now in the lead, followed by Stefan (Faulk could use his name in his head now, just not his title), Dari, Faulk, and finally the Captain, bringing up the rear. They followed her without qualm or question, so absolute their faith in her ability to guide them through this dark place. Faulk remembered his unease the first time she had led them through this maze. He felt only calm resolution now.

He lost track of time, trusting those ahead to navigate the few twists and turns of the tunnels to their destination. They didn't hurry, for they hoped to find night as their ally, and that lay some distance in the future. Finally, though, a hand from Dari halted him, and Faulk reached quickly back to stop the Captain in this prearranged signal.

He knew Emily spoke to the two ahead of him only because he felt the slightest disturbance in the stale air as of a gentle breath of wind, but he heard no words. He could guess, though.

They had reached the Ambassador suites.

From here, Emily would open the door, and Dari would slip out to scout and discover their exact location—though he suspected Emily, at least, knew where they stood—leaving Captain Frederick and Faulk to guard Stefan and Emily. Faulk should have done the scouting as the most expendable among their small ranks, but even he knew they couldn't trust him, not when it concerned magic and the well-being of the man he served. He honestly didn't know why Stefan had allowed Faulk to join them; surely his presence posed far too great a risk. Yet here he stood, loyalty (and sanity) tested as never before. He would rather die than betray that trust, but he also knew that decision might not lie in his own hands. What would happen if Destiny somehow strengthened her spell?

A slight spill of light as Emily unhooded the lantern a shade.

Faulk saw her silhouette as she knelt, head tilted back to examine the walls. She found what she searched for, tracing something Faulk couldn't see, then shuttered the light once more, plunging them back into darkness.

They manoeuvred themselves into position ...

And crouched down to wait. Though pitch black ruled here, the end of day still held sway beyond these sheltered and hidden corridors. The Captain, who had the best sense of time Faulk had ever seen, would let them know when he deemed enough time had passed. In the meanwhile, they waited in silence.

When Frederick shifted beside him some time later, Faulk roused himself from a light doze, instantly awake and aware. He passed along the Captain's signal—a hand squeezed on the shoulder—to Dari, then rose to his feet, working out the kinks from inactivity. The quality of the air changed as Emily activated the mechanism to open the door, allowing access to the castle. Faulk's pulse sped up in anticipation, his eyes and ears straining. He felt his muscles grow tense, ready to move forward or retreat as necessary, the very real possibility of discovery heavy on his mind as Dari crept out into the unlit room beyond. The Captain crossed the door to cover the other side, keeping Stefan and Emily behind him. Faulk, dagger already in hand, pressed his back against the wall next to the entrance, every sense on high alert. Smell alone provided any input, and that the gentle scent of soap from a recently cleaned chamber overlaying the heavy coat of grime that covered them all, ground into cloaks that had dried with time and body heat, mingled with the tang of sweat. He could neither see nor hear anything beyond his own blindness and controlled breathing.

And then a small sound as Dari made his presence known.

"Room's empty," he whispered. "Hall's mostly dark; only one sconce burning across from the room we want. No guards I could see."

Faulk didn't need to repeat what he had told them earlier, that Destiny relied only on a lock to guard her Sanctum because none would dare enter without her consent. She required no one to protect her chamber. He did stress, however, that he had no way of knowing whether magic also safeguarded the Focus, though it seemed likely.

They had replied by producing a ring and a little stick. The ring would detect small wards, Dari had explained, and the stick would unlock any door, courtesy of a magic ally. Faulk didn't ask any questions.

The plan seemed almost too simple to Faulk and yet fraught with intense danger. They would sneak into Destiny's Sanctum and do one of two things: if they could discern some way to damage or destroy the Destiny Seat, they would do so, eliminating the immediate threat. If not, they would wait for Destiny to appear and overpower her, gaining a valuable hostage.

"You have to move fast," Faulk had warned before they had shuttered their light. "She can silence a man or force him to move with but a word. If she has even an instant to speak, she will undo us all."

"We'll provide a distraction, someone to focus her attention," Stefan had said. While this man *would* draw Lady Destiny's gaze, another stood with them whom Faulk believed would draw the wizard even more.

"Begging your pardon, My ... Stefan," Faulk said, pushing past a momentary spasm of pain as he stared over the other man's shoulder. "While King Whillim might pause to gloat should he see you, Lady Destiny will not hesitate to get her hands on you. If she immobilises you, it might not matter if we capture her after. However, though the King wants you above all others, Lady Destiny, I believe, has another obsession." He glanced down at Emily. "Since she learned of you, and how you enabled our escape, Destiny has shown great interest in you."

"Me?" Emily had asked, startled, a hand pressed to her chest. "Why?"

"I think because you're a woman without any real power that she can understand who managed to stand in the way of what she wanted." Faulk had given it some thought, and kept coming to that conclusion. "Any time word came of you, the King would demand to know of your companions, but the Lady only concentrated on you. Seeing Stefan *might* give her pause enough that we can subdue her, but you, Emily, will definitely draw the focus of Lady Destiny. If she walks into her Sanctum and sees only you, she will hesitate."

They hadn't liked the idea, of course—Faulk himself didn't want to put the little librarian at any greater risk than she already faced—but they had eventually agreed with Faulk's reasoning.

So while their little group hovered near the entrance to the hallway, senses stretched as far as possible, Dari hurried back to the Sanctum door, ring and magic key-stick in hand. In short order, he had disengaged the lock, opened Destiny's door, and done a quick sweep of the room beyond with their re-lit lantern. He signalled, and Emily, Stefan, Faulk and Captain Frederick crowded into the suite, closing and locking the door behind them.

The Sanctum looked just as Faulk remembered, though he couldn't see much past the shadows cast by the lantern Dari had placed a few paces in. Sparse furnishing and decoration, the quartz chair dominating all else, drawing the eye even as it sent shivers of dread down the spine, the light from their small flame reflecting off its faceted surface in an almost macabre dance. Or at least, that's how Faulk experienced it.

"This seems too easy," murmured the Captain.

Stefan didn't reply. He moved toward the Destiny Seat, hands reaching to try to topple the chair. Emily put herself in his path.

"We don't know how it works," she said, daring to shove him back a pace, her voice quiet yet intense. "It's attuned to you, Sire. What if you trigger it with a touch?" Then, without awaiting a response, she turned and put her shoulder to the Seat. Faulk could see her muscles straining, but the chair didn't budge. She took a dagger from her belt and scraped it across the crystal face, producing a teeth-clenching screech from the metal, yet she inflicted no damage. Stefan silently handed her his sword. She took it in a grip that surprised Faulk with its adroitness, but even her strong and controlled swing of the weapon elicited no reaction from the Seat save a ringing clang.

"Hsst," Frederick signalled from the door where he, Faulk and Dari had waited. Stefan joined them in two long strides, his back pressed as firmly against the wall as theirs. They all had weapons drawn. Stefan held a long dagger, as his sword still rested in Emily's hands. She stood just to the side of the Destiny Seat, trembling slightly, her breath coming in quick pants now, eyes wide and showing too much white. But she drew herself up tall and faced the door as it swept open, admitting a sphere of magic to further illuminate the room.

Faulk wondered, even as Captain Milos and a dozen of his men swarmed into the room, why they hadn't considered the possibility that Lady Destiny might not come alone. Because Emily did indeed take the wizard's full attention as the tall, black-haired woman set foot in her chamber, her dark eyes fastened on the plain features of the librarian, but the presence of the mercenaries made the fact moot.

"Torn and bloody is fine," said King Whillim as he stepped in beside Lady Destiny, a feverish glint in his eyes when they landed on Stefan. "But I want them alive."

Faulk and those with him felt no such compunction as they battled the mercenaries, but in the end, it didn't matter. Six of Milos' men would not rise again, and the others had not escaped unscathed, but Stefan and his three followers knelt disarmed and struggling in the unrelenting grip of Whillim's hired forces.

Neither Emily nor Destiny had moved, as far as Faulk could tell as he hung shaken and bloodied between two men. The two women faced each other, one tall, regal, composed, the other shorter, unassuming, yet somehow fierce behind her fear. Emily hadn't relinquished her sword; Destiny didn't seem to care. It occurred to Faulk, as he blearily watched them, that not many years separated the pair. Strange, he had never considered Destiny's youth before, far too occupied with unease and dread in the forbidding woman's presence. Faulk didn't know whether Destiny held her immobilised, or if Emily stood motionless for a different reason. It looked to him, strangely, as though Emily guarded the approach to the Destiny Seat, like her presence before the Focus alone could prevent the wizard from using it. He silently applauded her courage even as he knew it for a uselessly defiant gesture. They couldn't prevail against a wizard prepared to meet them.

"So," Destiny drawled into a silence interrupted by the grunts of struggling men. "You're the little librarian who has caused me so much grief."

"No more trouble than you've caused, Girl," Emily retorted in a breathless voice. For some reason Faulk couldn't fathom, Destiny drew back as though struck, though Emily hadn't moved.

"Clever and resourceful," Destiny replied, her tone chill as she regained her poise. "Just as Darien said." And she smiled with a small nod as Emily recoiled this time.

"This is her?" Whillim said, moving to Destiny's side, his tone mingling incredulity and dismay. A perplexed frown had formed on his brow and irritation flashed across his features, a petulant child trying to regain the attention of his playmates. "This common thing had the audacity to try to thwart us?" He studied Emily a moment longer before bursting into laughter. "I'm surprised she hasn't stabbed herself yet," he said, a negligent gesture indicating her sword. "Do you think yourself a soldier, child?"

Emily didn't reply, hadn't even taken her challenging glare from the wizard. King Whillim stood at an angle that allowed Faulk to see his profile, so he had a clear view of the anger that contorted the man's face when he realised that Emily intended to ignore him, a temper many besides Faulk had had the misfortune to witness in recent days.

"Your King asked you a question, girl," he snarled, fists clenched and stance aggressive.

"My King did no such thing," Emily answered boldly, finally deigning to slide her gaze toward Whillim. "I hear only the empty words of an unworthy younger brother who can't even hold power without the assistance of a woman."

Surprisingly, Lady Destiny smiled. Whillim did not. His face darkened to a nearly purple hue as he shook with rage.

"How dare you!" he spat, drawing his hand back to strike. The slap of the back of Whillim's hand across Emily's cheek echoed loudly in the chamber, staggering her. She fell awkwardly to her left side, then wiped blood from a split lip. Startlingly, she still held the sword lightly in her right hand. Faulk remembered many a training lesson that included Captain Frederick's admonishment: "If you lose your sword in battle, you limit your defences." He wondered if Emily had had similar lessons.

Though he had tensed at the violent action, Faulk had known the futility of trying to escape his captors. He noted both Stefan and Dari strained against the men holding them too, spitting out curses, but Whillim's attack against Emily seemed to incense the Captain. With a bellow of rage, Frederick threw off the mercenaries holding him and lunged for Whillim. Milos barely managed to intercept the large man, tackling him to the ground and smashing an elbow across Frederick's jaw. It didn't stop Frederick from cursing Whillim for a coward and spitting a gob of blood at him, even prone beneath the weight of a heavily-breathing Milos, quickly joined by the two the Captain had thrown, but it did stop his advance.

"Interesting," Whillim mused, trying to hide his shaking as he stared down at the growling man. "I had thought my brother might leap to her defence in a misguided attempt at chivalry, but you'll do well enough." And his trembling turned to malice as he stared over at Stefan.

Faulk felt himself pale, knowing Whillim's intention before he signalled to Milos to haul the Captain to his feet. Faulk didn't know whether he himself struggled then, or if the men holding him merely wanted to ensure that he didn't interfere, but the pommel of a sword struck him hard enough to momentarily stun him. When the stars cleared from his vision, magic held Frederick poised helplessly over the Destiny Seat, and Faulk could do nothing but watch.

Destiny had moved behind the chair, kicking a moaning Emily out of her way as the librarian tried to lurch to her feet. With a word, the wizard forced Frederick into the cold embrace of her device. She grinned maliciously at Emily as the other woman again attempted to stand, finally having relinquished her grip on the sword to better balance herself. Then Destiny raised a hand sheathed in her favoured spiked half-glove. That hand rested on the crown of the chair, and the Destiny Seat began to glow.

Faulk screamed as agony tried to drag him into black insensibility.

***

They had stolen their way into Riverbend with the last light of the rainy day, and into Prichard's estate through a hidden tunnel the spymaster had devised years ago. Prichard had kept his appreciation for the irony of so many secret passages in and around Dalasmar to himself when he had learned how Emily had brought the King to safety, but he found no humour tonight.

They would wait an hour past full night, then Marcus would attempt to draw Destiny's attention again. Prichard hoped that, when she discovered the origin of Marcus' attack, she would remember the Councillor who had eluded her. Whillim and Destiny would not know the breadth of Prichard's intelligence operations, but they should understand this open defiance. If luck travelled anywhere near them (which it sadly hadn't yet), Marcus' display would at least distract Destiny from whatever had absorbed her attention this night. He desperately prayed that what held her attention did not include Stefan.

On the cusp of Marcus' attack, Prichard felt his hopes shred when he heard the clatter of a sword falling from numb fingers.

He turned, as did Marcus and Sim, to see Corporal Joseph leaning heavily against the wall, hand to his head. The man looked up, blinked a couple of times, then smiled sheepishly.

"Sorry," he murmured, bending to retrieve his sword. "Too many long nights catching up with me, I guess."

With dread, Prichard met Sim's equally frightened glance.

"Quite all right, lad," Prichard said, forcing levity to his tone. "The King keeps us busy."

Jo nodded.

"Whillim's a good man," he said, then paused with a frown.

Prichard turned quickly to Marcus, his worst fears confirmed. *Stefan rules Dalasham,* he affirmed, wondering how long they had before that changed.

"Now," he said urgently to the wizard. "Everything you've got."

***

Faulk raked his ragged fingernails through fresh and half-healed wounds, seeking solace in a different kind of pain, fighting off an increasingly strong impression of a foreign concept. *Whillim is King,* the world screamed at him as magic stole Captain Frederick's memory, yet in a tiny part of his mind, he heard Emily's soft affirmation: *His name is Stefan.* He stubbornly clung to her voice, ruthlessly shoving aside the more frigid tones of a wizard.

He hadn't even realised he'd fallen to his knees until he pushed himself back to unsteady feet, the men guarding him alert but giving him space. Still sitting on the Destiny Seat, Frederick looked puzzled, then vaguely horrified and self-recriminating as he looked over at Stefan, a man he had helped whom his memories now named a traitor. He pushed to his feet, loathing and bitterness painting a frown across his features. Dari, standing rigid between two mercenaries, had a similar expression, a man waking from an unpleasant dream, realising he had aided a monster.

Emily, however, had tears streaming down her face as she first crouched, arm hugging her ribs, then rose shakily to her full height.

"Oh, Fred, no," she whispered. He turned to look at her, perplexed.

"Emily? What—"

But she pulled her attention away and looked at the smirking wizard.

"How did you make it work?" she demanded, voice steady as she regarded the dark-haired woman with large grey eyes gone intense. Destiny blinked in surprise. "You spoke no words," Emily went on. "So how do you trigger your Focus?"

Destiny regarded the little librarian with curiosity, her head tilting slightly to the side.

"You seek a lesson in magic?" she asked, a slight hitch to her voice.

Emily shrugged, dropping her hands to her side, though Faulk saw her wince, trying to cover discomfort. He wondered if Destiny had bruised Emily's ribs with her kick. He didn't know about her previous injury, mostly healed but still tender, especially when accompanied by a strong leg to the gut.

"I like to learn," Emily replied, drawing an amused sound from Destiny's throat.

"It requires but a thought," Destiny said, her gaze sliding toward Stefan, who alone of the men still stood in the firm grasp of mercenaries. "Shall I demonstrate again?"

"I'd rather you didn't," Emily said.

Destiny laughed and raised her hand to the captive man. Whillim stopped her with a small gesture of his own.

"Let us test the mettle of those returned to our flock instead of using magic," he said, eyes hard and hateful as he gazed down at Stefan despite the calmness of his tone. "Take him if you would, Captain Frederick," he ordered. He glanced at Faulk, then over to Dari. "Help your Captain," he added.

As the King orders, so must one obey. Only, Faulk didn't move. He squeezed his eyes shut on a new wave of pain as conflicting emotions swirled through his mind, his teeth gritted tight, his lips drawn back in a rictus of anguish. He staggered, forcing his eyes wide open as he fought to regain his balance. With his renewed vision, he watched the Captain step forward, taking Stefan from the grip of the mercenaries. Dari moved to his side, grabbing Stefan's other arm.

Stefan met Frederick's glare.

"Don't do this, Fred," he said, a simple phrase, no pleading, just a statement. Frederick didn't balk, nor did he hurry, but he did briefly drop his gaze. Faulk wondered if the Captain fought the same compulsion he did, the need to obey mingling with the knowledge that something didn't sit right. But then Frederick's fingers tightened on Stefan's arm, Dari a firm presence to back up his Captain. Faulk tried to determine what kept his own feet firmly planted against the pull of an order.

Then he watched in astonishment as a slight figure flung herself forward.

Emily launched herself high, scrabbling up Frederick's back and clinging like a spider.

"No, Fred," she screamed, wrapping her arms around as much of the large man as she could, her legs trying to find purchase about his waist. "They'll kill him. You can't!"

Stefan used the startling distraction to throw an elbow into Dari's gut, doubling the younger man over with a gasp. He followed this with a fist smashed into the face of one mercenary, producing a loud crunch and a spray of blood as the man gurgled out his surprise, hands flying to his face to cradle a broken nose. Then a kick to the back of another mercenary's knee, drawing a high-pitched shriek as the paid soldier crumpled to the floor, clutching his twisted leg. Stefan roared with rage and defiance, overlaid with a fine tremor of despair as he spun away from grasping hands. He made it as far as the door before a shadow blocked any escape, resolving itself into another figure Faulk recognised. Pale blue eyes framed by ash blond hair stared out from a rigid face. His hard jaw set in determination, Ambrose threw his shoulder low as he stepped into the room, catching Stefan's breastbone in a charge that took him from his feet.

Even flat on his back with the breath knocked from him, Stefan didn't stop thrashing until Ambrose dropped on top of him, knees pinning his shoulders. Dari threw himself across

Stefan's legs, trying to keep the downed man from bucking. Frederick finally disentangled himself from the eel-like grip of Emily, shoving her away hard. She back-pedalled into Faulk and without thinking, he pulled her tight to his chest, wrapping his arms around her shaking shoulders as they stumbled to a standstill next to the Destiny Seat.

Emily kept screaming, "No, no!" Faulk felt his own tears course down his face to mirror hers.

"Shh," he murmured as Frederick joined his bulk to the trio already on the ground, finally forcing Stefan to stillness. "They'll just hurt you more if you fight."

"They're going to kill the King," she moaned.

The Captain dragged Stefan to his feet, Ambrose and Dari duck-walking the man forward despite his renewed struggles. Frederick glanced over at Emily beside the quartz chair.

"King Whillim is safe now," he said.

"Whillim is no King," Emily shot back, venom in her voice as she strained against Faulk's grip.

"Willi is a coward," Stefan added, blood trickling unheeded from nose and lip. "Hiding behind the strength of others, deluding you with magic from a murderess who killed her own father."

Destiny jerked her head and snarled, dark eyes flashing like obsidian, but Whillim forestalled any rebuttal with a curt gesture toward the Destiny Seat.

"If I'm so impotent, then how do I hold mastery over every man in this room?" Whillim demanded, an ugly sneer crinkling his eyes and tightening his mouth. "I hold a crown in my hands, a royal marriage on the way, an entire kingdom and its wealth at my disposal."

"And none of it through your own efforts," Stefan snapped, somehow regal even suspended among three men dragging him inexorably forward. "Did you truly find life so unappealing as Prince? You don't have the temperament for King, let alone the right, brother. Give up this foolishness."

Whillim turned white; Faulk didn't know whether in fury or fear, for Stefan's words spoke the truth that Destiny's spell tried to rewrite. But looking around, Faulk discovered that he might stand alone with that realisation. Well, he and Emily, the woman utterly rigid in his arms.

"Sit him down," Whillim demanded, a shaking finger pointing

at the quartz chair.

"No," Emily sobbed, pulling against Faulk's grasp, even as Frederick smashed a fist to Stefan's jaw, snapping his head to the side and staggering him just enough that those holding him could sweep him from his feet, landing Stefan on the edge of the Destiny Seat.

That's all it took for the wizard's magic to secure Stefan to the chair. The Captain, Dari and Ambrose stepped back, all three breathing heavily from the effort of overpowering one man.

Whillim's smile stretched wide as he crouched in front of Stefan, one hand on the arm of the chair, the other resting lightly on his knee. Stefan couldn't move more than his head. He took that small victory to spit blood on Whillim's face. The King drew back, startled, and fell on his arse. He scowled and cursed, pulling himself to his feet. Then, with a final silent glare at the man trapped in the Destiny Seat, Whillim met Destiny's dark stare.

"Do it," he said.

Destiny laid her hand on the crown of the chair. She turned her gaze to Emily, standing so close and yet too far away, and smiled.

"But a single thought," she said, and triggered her Focus to Emily's wordless scream.

Faulk set his feet, expecting a renewed shaft of pain as magic flowed. Instead, he felt curiously detached as the Destiny Seat flashed gold, rose, white. Then, only a steady throb behind his eyes as shadows seemed to fill the room in the absence of magic.

Faulk stared without comprehension at the strange man sitting with a blank expression in the quartz chair, his thoughts refusing to make sense. His grip loosened as the woman in his arms sank to the floor, moaning and trembling. With a glance to his King, then to the wizard, Faulk tried to remember why they had all gathered here. *Whillim is King,* he pulled the obvious thought around himself, even as he heard a smaller voice cry, *His name is Stefan.* Neither notion elicited an emotion, and Faulk found that very troubling, for he felt certain something should resonate in his mind.

Destiny shoved at the shoulder of the seated man. He slumped bonelessly forward, sliding from the chair to stare unseeing at the ceiling. King Whillim looked down at him, then up at his wizard as she moved to his side.

"What's happened?" he asked. "What's this?" he waved feebly at the prone man.

Destiny pointed to the knife at the King's belt.

"The renegade must die to seal the spell," she said in an oddly hollow voice. "You insisted upon that much."

King Whillim gazed down again, a frown furrowing his brow.

"You want me to kill him?"

Destiny shook her head sharply, irritation and anger boiling in her eyes.

"It's *your* wish, Majesty, not mine," she insisted, making a mockery of the title. Faulk wondered whether he should find offence in that. "With his death, you seal your reign. Do as you will."

Whillim nodded uncertainly, looking down again. He slowly wrapped his fingers around the haft of his blade and drew the weapon.

Destiny suddenly hissed, her head whipping around to stare at the south wall, though Faulk saw nothing there save bare stone.

"What is it?" the King demanded, hand shaking as it held the knife.

"Another wizard within the city," Destiny snarled. "Nearly within these walls."

Before Faulk, or anyone, could fully comprehend her words, Emily lurched nearly unnoticed to her feet and threw herself into the Destiny Seat. Without knowing why, Faulk took the one step needed to place him behind the chair. He put his hand on the crown and met Emily's desperate stare.

"Trigger it," she cried. Faulk remembered Destiny's words. *A single thought.* He had no idea what Emily hoped to gain by this, but he found he trusted her. She could make his scattered, disconnected thoughts have meaning again. So he put his entire focus into one sentiment and sent the word into the chair. *Work,* he demanded in his mind.

"No!" Destiny screamed, her attention suddenly entirely upon Faulk. Invisible hands lifted him and threw him with jarring force against the wall. He felt pressure and heavy warmth within where none should exist, heard bones snap as he slid down the wall to land in a heap on the floor. Mind-shattering trauma exploded through his body before everything went numb and cold.   Through a narrowing tunnel of grey, he watched as the Destiny Seat flashed around Emily, burning a bright gold that became a rose so dark it flowed nearly scarlet, then pulsed into a white so pure it stole what little vision he had left.

His mind suddenly became clear, regaining a semblance of sanity, and Faulk smiled, finally free of torment, before blessed oblivion gathered him in its warm embrace as life fled from his broken body, and he knew no more.

Chapter 30

He couldn't help himself. Em *knew* that, but it didn't stop her heart from breaking just a little when Fred took Stefan prisoner. Stefan knew that truth also, even as his eyes betrayed his hurt at how his brother had taken his most loyal and fierce defender away, turning him into an enemy. Em had known the futility of trying to stop the large man who had become her mentor, yet she had tried nonetheless, throwing herself on Fred's back and screaming like a terrified feline, hoping to give him pause if nothing else. Anything to prolong the illusion that Stefan might regain his throne.

And then Ambrose had walked in, and Em fully comprehended just how badly they had lost.

Yet the heartache of seeing all turn against their King through the cruel use of magic at the behest of one brother against another felt as nothing next to the heaviness that dragged at her as his own trusted companions forced Stefan into the Destiny Seat.

She screamed her useless defiance as Destiny triggered her Focus, the tall woman's satisfaction at having bested Em evident in the smile she shared, even though Em had not realised they had stood in competition.

The Destiny Seat had flared, cycling through its gem tones of topaz, rose quartz and diamond, and Em sank to the ground, defeated as she stared into the blank gaze of the man held imprisoned in a magical glove. For a moment, she couldn't remember why such a man mattered.

But then, something unexpected happened.

Em recalled the Royal Proofs she had painstakingly copied for the royal personage in front of her, staring without comprehension at the belt knife that Destiny indicated. Documents that detailed the line of succession. And she saw a name that shouldn't exist.

With that name, her own ability that allowed her to remember everything she had ever read pulsed to life, and the truth written in the Royal Proofs burned into her mind.

She spoke the thought to herself. *Stefan, son of Ulrich, son of Detrich, King of Dalasham.* And on the secondary branch, his brother, Prince Whillim. Em blinked, glancing up at that Prince who even now wrapped his fingers around the handle of a blade. Prince, not King. The King lay unmoving before the Destiny Seat, an empty husk waiting for death. Or for someone to fill him with truth again.

Can I do that? Em wondered. Before she could worry about the consequences, she took action. Fate aided her by distracting Destiny—*it seems Wizard Marcus has a use after all,* she thought when Destiny named the proximity of another wizard—and Em leapt to her feet and threw herself into the seat Destiny had forced Stefan to vacate.

Faulk moved behind her, and she feared he meant to stop her, but an eerie light in his eyes gave her hope. She trusted her instinct, and her life, to a man tormented by the Prince who sought to steal a kingdom, and didn't allow any fears for her own sanity to alter that trust.

"Trigger it," she said, not even knowing if he could.

She drew on the mental image of the Royal Proofs, and overlaid it with her absolute certainty of one thing.

"Stefan is King," she murmured, repeating the mantra in her mind with utter conviction.

Destiny screamed her denial and Em felt an absence as Faulk disappeared, she knew not where. A strange sense of peace enveloped Em as lights swirled before her eyes, the same jewel tones elicited when Fred and Stefan sat the Destiny Seat, yet somehow providing comfort and warmth. Molten gold like sunset, darkest rose that felt like the softest flower petals, the shining white of fresh fallen snow bringing the promise of a new start; they all poured around and through Em as Destiny's magic considered her intentions. And then a void of colour as the Destiny Seat shuddered beneath her.

Em squeezed her eyes shut so tight that she saw red and silver lightning streaks arc across the back of her eyelids. She poured her heart into the Focus.

"Stefan is King," she repeated, feeling a power from the Seat beat a counterpoint in time with her words. "Stefan is King, Stefan is King, Stefan is King."

As though from a great distance, she heard grunts and shouts, the scuffling of boots on stone, the smack of fist to flesh, and the screech of swords drawn from scabbards, metal clashing together. And then silence, save for the harsh whisper of her own voice.

"Stefan is King."

A hand on her arm drew a terrified yelp. Her eyes snapped open even as she coiled herself to lash out, but the sight that greeted her froze all movement. Stefan crouched before her, sharp blue eyes clear and aware, though pained, as they met hers.

She quickly swept the room with her gaze. The large mercenary who had taken Fred down lay in a pool of blood, though he still breathed; three of his men, crumpled nearby, did not. Fred crouched over them, wiping the blade of his sword on the big man's cloak with far too much concentration. Dari and Ambrose watched over the remaining mercenaries—the two whom Stefan had injured in his attempt to escape, and a third cradling his arm, left eye swelling shut in a battered face—and an unconscious Prince. Neither man looked away from their charges. Destiny lay insensate at Em's feet, a red welt already forming at her temple, a knife just beyond her outstretched fingers encased in a studded half glove. Someone had shoved a rag in her mouth, in case she regained consciousness too soon.

Em dragged her attention back to the King before her. She read gratitude and a kind of wonder in his face as he regarded her.

"I don't know how you did it," he began, then shook his head, lips pressed together, holding in some deep emotion. He took a ragged breath, then simply said, "Thank you."

Em blinked back at him, barely daring to believe the evidence laid out in front of her. She felt hot tears scald her cheeks.

"Is it over?" she asked, hearing the quaver in her voice.

He glanced over at Whillim, then down at Destiny. With a sigh, he shook his head.

"Not yet, I fear." His eyes flicked down to the chair she sat in, the white quartz somehow shaded to black, as though Em had transformed the crystal as well as the spell. "Not while this exists. Not when a Prince tries to steal a kingdom, and not until a wizard answers for her crimes." He glanced over at his brother. "I don't know what damage Willi has wrought, nor what it will take to undo it, but I will return Dalasham to its rightful place." He met her gaze again. "But this battle, this betrayal, yes. It is over. Thanks to you."

Em felt her face heat even as she began to tremble. A delayed reaction, she knew, but even knowing, she couldn't stop her shaking. And then, to her complete astonishment, Stefan leaned forward and embraced her tightly, drawing her out of the Destiny Seat as he did so. She collapsed against him, sobs wracking her body. He said nothing, just held her while she attempted to regain her composure.

She had nearly done so when she saw something in the shadows against the far wall. Em gasped and pulled herself free of the King, stumbling to the body slumped on the floor. Faulk looked more at peace in death than he had under the influence of Destiny's magic. He even wore a gentle smile, though bloody tears had traced lines down his face, and red ran from ears and mouth.

Em sank to her knees without touching him and wrapped her arms around her middle.

"He triggered the Focus," she said quietly as Stefan joined her. "Without him, you would have died."

Sorrow radiated from the King and she saw him bend his head forward in a nod.

"He fought to the end," Stefan said. "Against a magic no one else could overcome. We won't forget his sacrifice." He reached out to close the dead man's eyes.

Then he pushed himself to his feet, holding out a hand for Em. She hesitated, aware that a King offered his aid to a mere librarian. She didn't know what to think of that, so she pushed it from her mind and accepted his assistance.

When they returned to the others, Fred still wouldn't meet Stefan's regard, nor Em's. Suspecting the reason, Em grabbed his arm, drawing a startled reaction.

"Which do you blame for drawing blood, the sword or the hand that wields that sword?" she demanded.

He just stared at her. She tried again.

"A good soldier will do what with their emotions?"

"Use them before they use him," Ambrose answered from where he stood. He met Em's stare, visibly braced himself, then turned to Stefan and gave him a crisp salute.

Em nodded, looking back up at Fred.

"You could no more disobey your King than that sword could harm without a hand to guide it."

"He wasn't my King," Fred replied, anguish making his voice even deeper.

"He was in your mind," she countered. "Magic changed the face of the King, but not your loyalty to him."

"That hardly matters!" he exploded. "I betrayed—"

"No one," Stefan interjected softly, but his words silenced the Captain. "You did what you had to, Fred, what Willi knew you'd do as Captain of the King's Guard. You did your duty. Accept that and move on."

Fred lowered his eyes, a slight shake to his head, but he didn't refute the King.

"I hurt Emily," he whispered forlornly. "When she came to your aid, I threw her away."

"You pushed me into the arms of the only man who would protect me," she argued, refusing to let him continue to berate himself. "You could have turned me over to one of the mercenaries, or to Destiny or the Prince. Hell, Fred, you could have crushed me if you wanted. But you sent me to Faulk, the one man under your command who managed to fight Destiny's influence. The only one in this room who knew what you faced because he had raged against it far longer. By giving me into his care, you protected me from her."

They all turned to look at Destiny. Em didn't know whether Fred would accept their words—suspected it would take longer for him to convince himself that he should take no blame in actions beyond his control—but he allowed them to shift the topic of conversation.

"What do we do with her, and with the Prince?" he asked, finally meeting Stefan's gaze now.

"Bind them, imprison them, put them on trial." Stefan sighed as he recognised the enormity of what lay ahead. "We'll need

Wizard Marcus to make sure Destiny can't work her magics on us. Beyond that, we need to discern what far-reaching consequences the memory spell had. Did Emily break its hold over everyone when she restored my memory? Do others recall the duplicity of the Prince? Did Willi deplete the treasury to pay his mercenaries, or even just in his notorious excesses? Did he manage to incite enough instability to cause problems? And dare I disburse the army we collected? Did Willi thrust everyone into the Destiny Seat, or will we find prisoners in the dungeons? Not to mention several other problems I'm sure we'll have to deal with that we have yet to discern. And we will need to arrange a funeral for a fallen hero." He said the last with a glance to Faulk's body.

Em felt a moment of gratitude that she might slip back into the comparatively easy work of a librarian, mingled with pity for all that a King must endure.

Stefan sighed again.

"Start by binding them, then we need to find Prichard and Wizard Marcus. One thing at a time, I think."

The King's Guard quickly moved to obey.

Epilogue

As a King worked to regain his throne, as a Prince and his bound wizard awaited the caprices of a trial, as a librarian sought the solitude of her beloved, yet oddly confining, place in the Palace Library, as a master spy hoped to add the gratifying intellect of an oft overlooked woman to his network, and as a Captain struggled to come to terms with a betrayal he couldn't escape, far to the south, a wizard reread a long-awaited missive with a hardened heart and a predatory smile.

Nathan now knew exactly where the Girl who had killed his mentor, Wizard Shelton, the man who had sired him, hid. He knew the absurd name she had taken, and that she used the magic she stole from his father to further her ambitions. In a kingdom with no defence against the likes of a wizard of Nathan's prowess (or any wizard, by all reports he had seen), he believed he would have little difficulty spiriting Girl away to her long-overdue fate. Indeed, who would want to stop him from bringing such wickedness to justice?

His long-time companion, Marcus, would see that those in Dalasham kept Girl imprisoned until Nathan could collect her. And then, oh the torment she would suffer before Nathan stripped her of the power that should have belonged to him.

A nimbus of flames danced around his fist, burning the missive he had memorized, the ashes falling from his hand as he walked away to finalise his plans to sweep into Dalasham and take what he wanted.

Truly, if any sought to stop him, they would rue ever crossing paths with him.

Opposition so often comes in the least expected form ...